classic press, incorporated · san rafael, california

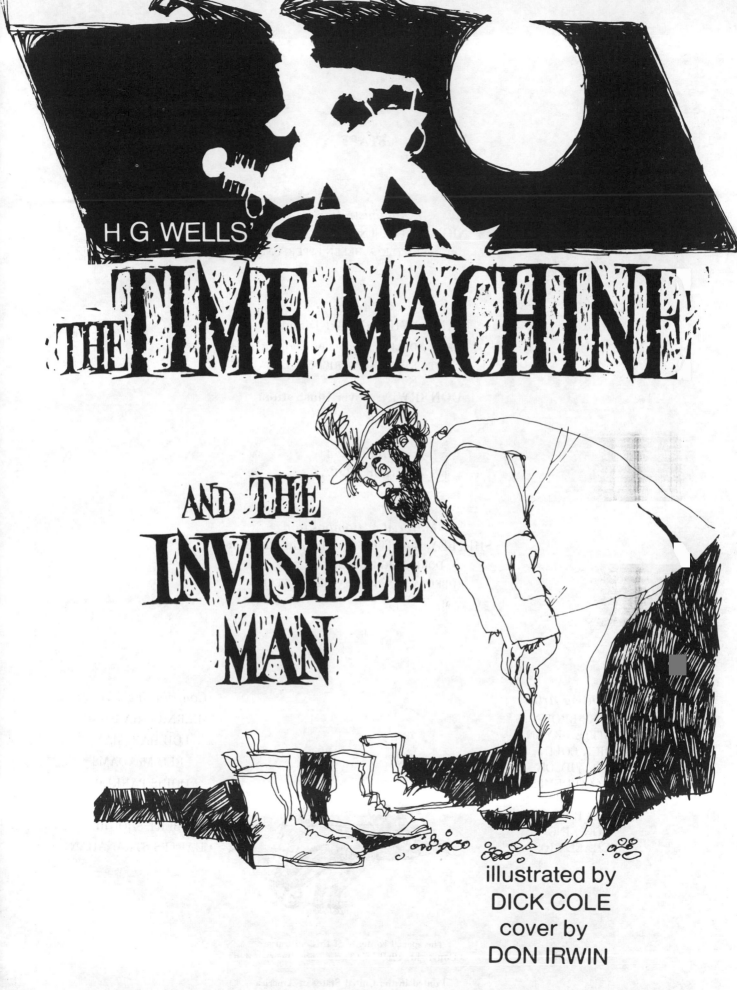

H. G. WELLS'

THE TIME MACHINE

AND THE INVISIBLE MAN

illustrated by
DICK COLE
cover by
DON IRWIN

classic press, incorporated   san rafael, california

STAFF

Administration
NICK ODDO, Executive Director
BETTE CHYLE • HELEN EPPERSON

Art
AL DAVIDSON, Art Director
MARK NOBLES, Production Director
RITA SMITH • PATRICIA WALSH

DON IRWIN, Cover Illustrations

Production
PETER TOPAZ

Editorial & Composition
SHIRLEY BOLTON, Production Director
DORIS PARKER • PEGGY RICE
ROBERTA TUMBIOLO • BETTY WELLS

Contributing Artists
WAYNE BROWN
BRIGITTE BRYAN
DICK COLE
AL DAVIDSON
DUNBRACCO DEMPSTER
DENNIS A. DIERKS
DON IRWIN
RON KING
MICHAEL RIOS

Contributing Writers
BERNICE HARDING
LOU HARTMAN
FRED McADAMS
DORIS PARKER
MARTHA SHOGREN
ROBERT SHOGREN
CHARLES STRANAHAN

Library of Congress Catalog Card Number: 70-79993

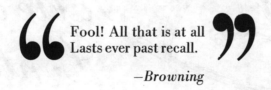

66 Fool! All that is at all
Lasts ever past recall. **99**

—Browning

THE TIME MACHINE

THE INVISIBLE MAN

BACKWORD

As I put on pace, night followed day like the flapping of a black wing

The man who made the Time Machine—the man I shall call the Time Traveler—was well known in scientific circles a few years since, and the fact of his disappearance is also well known. He was a mathematician of peculiar subtlety, and one of our most conspicuous investigators in molecular physics. He did not confine himself to abstract science. Several ingenious, and one or two profitable, patents were his: very profitable they were, these last, as his handsome house at Richmond testified. To those who were his intimates, however, his scientific investigations were as nothing to his gift of speech. In the after-dinner hours he was ever a vivid and variegated talker, and at times his fantastic, often paradoxical, conceptions came so thick and close as to form one continuous discourse. At these times he was as unlike the popular conception of a scientific investigator as a man could be. His cheeks would flush, his eyes grow bright; and the stranger the ideas that sprang and crowded in his brain, the happier and the more animated would be his exposition.

Up to the last there was held at his house a kind of informal gathering, which it was my privilege to attend, and where, at one time or another, I have met most of our distinguished literary and scientific men. There was a plain dinner at seven.

1
THE INVENTOR

molecular physics: A field of natural science pertaining to the investigation and study of molecules. A molecule is the smallest quantity of a substance that can exist and still show all the characteristics of physical matter. It is composed of groups of atoms, or in some cases, of a single atom.

exposition: Detailed explanation.

After that we would adjourn to a room of easy-chairs and little tables, and there, with libations of alcohol and reeking pipes we would invoke the god. At first the conversation was mere fragmentary chatter, with some local *lacunae* of digestive silence; but toward nine or half-past nine, if the god was favorable, some particular topic would triumph by a kind of natural selection, and would become the common interest. So it was, I remember, on the last Thursday but one of all—the Thursday when I first heard of the Time Machine.

I had been jammed in a corner with a gentleman who shall be disguised as Filby. He had been running down Milton—the public neglects poor Filby's little verses shockingly; and as I could think of nothing but the relative status of Filby and the man he criticised, and was much too timid to discuss that, the arrival of that moment of fusion, when our several conversations were suddenly merged into a general discussion, was a great relief to me.

"What's that nonsense?" said a well-known Medical Man, speaking across Filby to the Psychologist.

"He thinks," said the Psychologist, "that Time's only a kind of Space."

"It's not thinking," said the Time Traveler; "it's knowledge."

"Foppish affectation," said Filby, still harping upon his wrongs; but I feigned a great interest in this question of Space and Time.

"Kant—" began the Psychologist.

"Confound Kant!" said the Time Traveler. "I tell you I'm right. I've got experimental proof of it. I'm not a metaphysician." He addressed the Medical Man across the room, and so brought the whole company into his own circle. "It's the most promising departure in experimental work that has ever been made. It will simply revolutionize life. Heaven knows what life will be when I've carried the thing through."

"As long as it's not the water of immortality I don't mind," said the distinguished Medical Man. "What is it?"

"Only a paradox," said the Psychologist.

The Time Traveler said nothing in reply, but smiled and began tapping his pipe upon the fender curb. This was the invariable presage of a dissertation.

"You have to admit that time is a spatial dimension," said the Psychologist, emboldened by immunity and addressing the Medical Man, "and then all sorts of remarkable consequences

lacunae: Latin, meaning gaps.

metaphysician: A person versed in one of the philosophical sciences; often accused of resorting to unreasonable and deceptive explanations to prove his point.

Fender Curb

invariable . . . . dissertation: He always (invariably) began his lengthy talks with a smile and tapping his pipe.

are found inevitable. Among others, that it becomes possible to travel about in time."

The Time Traveler chuckled. "You forget that I'm going to prove it experimentally."

"Let's have your experiment," said the Psychologist.

"I think we'd like the argument first," said Filby.

"It's this," said the Time Traveler. "You must follow me carefully. I shall have to controvert one or two ideas that are almost universally accepted. The geometry, for instance, they taught you at school is founded on a misconception."

"Is not that rather a large thing to expect us to begin upon?" said Filby.

"I do not mean to ask you to accept anything without reasonable ground for it. You will soon admit as much as I want from you. You know, of course, that a mathematical line, a line of thickness *nil*, has no real existence. They taught you that? Neither has a mathematical plane. These things are mere abstractions."

"That is all right," said the Psychologist.

"Nor, having only length, breadth, and thickness, can a cube have a real existence."

"There I object," said Filby.

"Of course a solid body may exist. All real things—"

"So most people think. But wait a moment. Can an instantaneous cube exist?"

"Don't follow you," said Filby.

"Can a cube that does not last for any time at all, have a real existence?"

Filby became pensive.

"Clearly," the Philosophical Inventor proceeded, "any real body must have extension in *four* directions: it must have Length, Breadth, Thickness, and — Duration. But through a natural infirmity of the flesh, which I will explain to you in a moment, we incline to overlook the fact. There are really four dimensions, three which we call the three planes of Space, and a fourth, Time. There is, however, a tendency to draw an unreal distinction between the former three dimensions and the latter, because it happens that our consciousness moves intermittently in one direction along the latter from the beginning to the end of our lives."

"That," said a Very Young Man, making spasmodic efforts to relight his cigar over the lamp: "that—very clear indeed."

THE INVENTOR

controvert: Dispute, change.

nil: Nothing.

abstractions: Separations; considering something separate from anything else. Often, unrealistic ideas.

spasmodic: Quick, sudden movement.

9

"Now, it is very remarkable that this is so extensively overlooked," continued the Philosophical Inventor, with a slight accession of cheerfulness. "Really this is what is meant by the Fourth Dimension, though some people who talk about the Fourth Dimension do not know they mean it. It is only another way of looking at Time. *There is no difference between Time and any of the three dimensions of Space except that our consciousness moves along it.* But some foolish people have got hold of the wrong side of that idea. You have all heard what they have to say about this Fourth Dimension?"

"I have not," said the Provincial Mayor.

"It is simply this, That space, as our mathematicians have it, is spoken of as having three dimensions, which one may call Length, Breadth, and Thickness, and is always definable by reference to these planes, each at right angle to the others. But some philosophical people have been asking why *three* dimensions particularly—why not another direction at right angles to the other three?—and have even tried to construct a Four-Dimensional geometry. Professor Simon Newcomb was expounding this to the New York Mathematical Society only a month or so ago. You know how on a flat surface, which has only two dimensions, we can represent a figure of a Three-Dimensional solid, and similarly they think that by models of three dimensions they could represent one of four—if they could master the perspective of the thing. See?"

"I think so," murmured the Provincial Mayor; and, knitting his brows, he lapsed into an introspective state, his lips moving as one who repeats mystic words. "Yes, I think I see it now," he said after some time, brightening in a quite transitory manner.

"Well, I do not mind telling you I have been at work upon this geometry of Four Dimensions for some time. Some of my results are curious: for instance, here is a portrait of a man at eight years old, another at fifteen, another at seventeen, another at twenty-three, and so on. All these are evidently sections, as it were, Three-Dimensional representations of his Four-Dimensional being, which is a fixed and unalterable thing.

"Scientific people," proceeded the Philosopher, after the pause required for the proper assimilation of this, "know very well that Time is only a kind of Space. Here is a popular scientific diagram, a weather record. This line I trace with my finger shows the movement of the barometer. Yesterday it was so high, yesterday night it fell, then this morning it rose again,

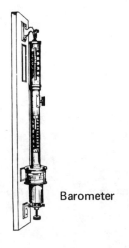

Barometer

and so gently upward to here. Surely the mercury did not trace this line in any of the dimensions of space generally recognized? But certainly it traced such a line, and that line, therefore, we must conclude, was along the Time Dimension."

"But," said the Medical Man, staring hard at a coal in the fire, "if Time is really only a fourth dimension of Space, why is it, and why has it always been, regarded as something different? And why cannot we move about in Time as we move about in the other dimensions of Space?"

The Philosophical Person smiled. "Are you so sure we can move freely in Space? Right and left we can go, backward and forward freely enough, and men always have done so. I admit we move freely in two dimensions. But how about up and down? Gravitation limits us there."

"Not exactly," said the Medical Man. "There are balloons."

"But before the balloons, save for spasmodic jumping and the inequalities of the surface, man had no freedom of vertical movement."

"Still they could move a little up and down," said the Medical Man.

"Easier, far easier, down than up."

"And you cannot move at all in Time. You cannot get away from the present moment."

"My dear sir, that is just where you are wrong. That is just where the whole world has gone wrong. We are always getting away from the present moment. Our mental existences, which are immaterial and have no dimensions, are passing along the Time Dimension with a uniform velocity from the cradle to the grave. Just as we should travel *down* if we began our existence fifty miles above the earth's surface."

"But the great difficulty is this," interrupted the Psychologist: "You *can* move about in all directions of Space, but you cannot move about in Time."

"That is the germ of my great discovery. But you are wrong to say that we cannot move about in Time. For instance, if I am recalling an incident very vividly I go back to the instant of its occurrence; I become absent-minded, as you say. I jump back for a moment. Of course we have no means of staying back for any length of time any more than a savage or an animal has of staying six feet above the ground. But a civilized man is better off than the savage in this respect. He can go up against gravitation in a balloon, and why should we not hope that

**THE
INVENTOR**

Philosophical Person: The Time Traveler had all the qualities of a philosopher; the love and pursuit of knowledge; the calm and sensible attitude necessary to advance and present his own ideas and discoveries.

velocity: Speed.

11

Homer

anachronisms: Things out of their proper historical time.

Homer and Plato: Homer, a poet of ancient Greece (850 B.C.); author of the *Iliad* and the *Odyssey,* whose poems describing the adventures of heroes have greatly influenced the literary tradition of the Western World.

Plato, Greek philosopher, (429–237 B.C.) a follower of Socrates; also Aristotle's teacher.

humbug: A fraud.

ultimately he may be able to stop or accelerate his drift along the Time Dimension; or even to turn about and travel the other way?"

"Oh, *this*," began Filby, "is all—"

"Why not?" said the Philosophical Inventor.

"It's against reason," said Filby.

"What reason?" said the Philosophical Inventor.

"You can show black is white by argument," said Filby, "but you will never convince me."

"Possibly not," said the Philosophical Inventor. "But now you begin to see the object of my investigations into the geometry of Four Dimensions. Long ago I had a vague inkling of a machine—"

"To travel through Time!" said the Very Young Man.

"That shall travel indifferently in any direction of Space and Time, as the driver determines."

Filby contented himself with laughter.

"It would be remarkably convenient," the Psychologist suggested. "One might travel back and witness the battle of Hastings."

"Don't you think you would attract attention?" said the Medical Man. "Our ancestors had no great tolerance for anachronisms."

"One might get one's Greek from the very lips of Homer and Plato," the Very Young Man thought.

"In which case they would certainly plow you for the little-go. The German scholars have improved Greek so much."

"Then, there is the future," said the Very Young Man. "Just think! One might invest all one's money, leave it to accumulate at interest, and hurry on ahead."

"To discover a society," said I, "erected on a strictly communistic basis."

"Of all the wild extravagant theories—" began the Psychologist.

"Yes, so it seemed to me, and so I never talked of it until—"

"Experimental verification!" cried I. "You are going to verify *that!*"

"The experiment!" cried Filby, who was getting brain-weary.

"Let's see your experiment, anyhow," said the Psychologist, "though it's all humbug, you know."

The Time Traveler smiled round at us. Then, still smiling faintly, and with his hands deep in his trousers pockets, he walked slowly out of the room, and we heard his slippers shuffling down the long passage to his laboratory.

The Psychologist looked at us. "I wonder what he's got?"

"Some sleight-of-hand trick or other," said the Medical Man, and Filby tried to tell us about a conjuror he had seen at Burslem, but before he had finished his preface the Time Traveler came back, and Filby's anecdote collapsed.

The thing the Time Traveler held in his hand was a glittering metallic framework, scarcely larger than a small clock, and very delicately made. There was ivory in it, and some transparent crystalline substance. And now I must be explicit, for this that follows—unless his explanation is to be accepted—is an absolutely unaccountable thing. He took one of the small octagonal tables that were scattered about the room, and set it in front of the fire, with two legs on the hearthrug. On this table he placed the mechanism. Then he drew up a chair and sat down. The only other object on the table was a small shaded lamp, the bright light of which fell full upon the model. There were also perhaps a dozen candles about, two in brass candlesticks upon the mantel and several in sconces, so that the room was brilliantly illuminated. I sat in a low armchair nearest the fire, and I drew this forward so as to be almost between the Time Traveler and the fireplace. Filby sat behind him, looking over his shoulder. The Medical Man and the Rector watched him in profile from the right, the Psychologist from the left. We were all on the alert. It appears incredible to me that any kind of trick, however subtly conceived and however adroitly done, could have been played upon us under these conditions.

The Time Traveler looked at us and then at the mechanism.

"Well?" said the Psychologist.

"This little affair," said the Time Traveler, resting his elbows upon the table and pressing his hands together above the apparatus, "is only a model. It is my plan for a machine to travel through Time. You will notice that it looks singularly askew, and that there is an odd twinkling appearance about this bar, as though it was in some way unreal." He pointed to the part with his finger. "Also, here is one little white lever, and here is another."

The Medical Man got up out of his chair and peered into the thing. "It's beautifully made," he said.

"It took two years to make," retorted the Time Traveler. Then, when we had all done as the Medical Man, he said: "Now

conjuror: Magician.

octagonal: Eight-sided.

sconces: Candle-holders which can be fastened to the wall.

quack: Pretender, charlatan. One who pretends to have knowledge or skill he does not really possess.

I want you clearly to understand that this lever, being pressed over, sends the machine gliding into the future, and this other reverses the motion. This saddle represents the seat of a time traveler. Presently I am going to press the lever, and off the machine will go. It will vanish, pass into future time, and disappear. Have a good look at the thing. Look at the table too, and satisfy yourselves there is no trickery. I don't want to waste this model, and then be told I'm a quack."

There was a minute's pause perhaps. The Psychologist seemed about to speak to me, but changed his mind. Then the Time Traveler put forth his finger toward the lever. "No," he said suddenly; "lend me your hand." And turning to the Psychologist, he took that individual's hand in his own and told him to put out his forefinger. So that it was the Psychologist himself who sent forth the model Time Machine on its interminable voyage. We all saw the lever turn. I am absolutely certain there was no trickery. There was a breath of wind, and the lamp flame jumped. One of the candles on the mantel was blown out, and the little machine suddenly swung round, became indistinct, was seen as a ghost for a second perhaps, as an eddy of faintly glittering brass and ivory; and it was gone—vanished! Save for the lamp the table was bare.

Everyone was silent for a minute.

The Psychologist recovered from his stupor, and suddenly looked under the table. At that the Time Traveler laughed cheerfully. "Well?" he said, with a reminiscence of the Psychologist. Then, getting up, he went to the tobacco jar on the mantel, and with his back to us began to fill his pipe.

We stared at each other.

"Look here," said the Medical Man, "are you in earnest about this? Do you seriously believe that that machine has traveled into Time?"

light a spill: Spill here refers to a small piece of wood or strip of paper rolled up and used to light a fire. The Time Traveler lit a spill from the fire to light his pipe.

"Certainly," said the Time Traveler, stooping to light a spill at the fire. Then he turned, lighting his pipe, to look at the Psychologist's face. (The Psychologist, to show that he was not unhinged, helped himself to a cigar and tried to light it uncut.) "What is more, I have a big machine nearly finished in there,"—he indicated the laboratory,—"and when that is put together I mean to have a journey on my own account."

"You mean to say that that machine has traveled into the future?" said Filby.

14

"Into the future or the past—I don't, for certain, know which."

After an interval the Psychologist had an inspiration.

"It must have gone into the past if it has gone anywhere," he said.

"Why?" said the Time Traveler.

"Because I presume that it has not moved in space, and if it traveled into the future it would still be here all this time, since it must have traveled through this time."

"But," said I, "if it traveled into the past it would have been visible when we came first into this room; and last Thursday when we were here; and the Thursday before that; and so forth!"

"Serious objections," remarked the Rector with an air of impartiality, turning toward the Time Traveler.

"Not a bit," said the Time Traveler, and, to the Psychologist: "You think. *You* can explain that. It's presentation below the threshold, you know, diluted presentation."

diluted presentation: Below the threshold or point where the movement can be perceived or seen. The men watching the experiment could not actually see how the model Time Machine traveled; it just seemed to disappear.

"Of course," said the Psychologist, and reassured us. "That's a simple point in psychology. I should have thought of it. It's plain enough, and helps the paradox delightfully. We cannot see it, nor can we appreciate this machine, any more than we can the spoke of a wheel spinning, or a bullet flying through the air. If it is traveling through time fifty times or a hundred times faster than we are, if it gets through a minute while we get through a second, the impression it creates will of course be only one-fiftieth or one-hundredth of what it would make if it were not traveling in time. That's plain enough." He passed his hand through the space in which the machine had been. "You see?" he said laughing.

paradox: A seemingly absurd opinion, different from or conflicting with accepted truth, which can be true in fact.

We sat and stared at the vacant table for a minute or so. Then the Time Traveler asked us what we thought of it all.

"It sounds plausible enough to-night," said the Medical Man; "but wait until to-morrow. Wait for the common sense of the morning."

"Would you like to see the Time Machine itself?" asked the Time Traveler. And therewith, taking the lamp in his hand, he led the way down the long, draughty corridor to his laboratory. I remember vividly the flickering light, his queer, broad head in silhouette, the dance of the shadows, how we all followed him, puzzled but incredulous, and how there in the laboratory we

incredulous: Doubtful.

Quartz: One of the most common minerals. Although it comes in almost every color, it is usually white, and often colorless or transparent (crystalline).

beheld a larger edition of the little mechanism which we had seen vanish from before our eyes. Parts were of nickel, parts of ivory, parts had certainly been filed or sawn out of rock crystal. The thing was generally complete, but the twisted crystalline bars lay unfinished upon the bench beside some sheets of drawings, and I took one up for a better look at it. Quartz it seemed to be.

"Look here," said the Medical Man, "are you perfectly serious? Or is this a trick—like that ghost you showed us last Christmas?"

"Upon that machine," said the Time Traveler, holding the lamp aloft, "I intend to explore Time. Is that plain? I was never more serious in my life."

I don't mind telling you the story,
I can't argue tonight
but I can't argue.

I think that at that time none of us quite believed in the Time Machine. The fact is, the Time Traveler was one of those men who are too clever to be believed; you never felt that you saw all round him; you always suspected some subtle reserve, some ingenuity in ambush, behind his lucid frankness. Had Filby shown the model and explained the matter in the Time Traveler's words, we should have shown *him* far less skepticism. The point is, we should have seen his motives—a pork-butcher could understand Filby. But the Time Traveler had more than a touch of whim among his elements, and we distrusted him.

2
THE TIME TRAVELER RETURNS

skepticism: A feeling of mistrust; disbelief.

whim: Sudden change of mind, apparently not reasonable.

Things that would have made the fame of a clever man seemed tricks in his hands. It is a mistake to do things too easily. The serious people who took him seriously never felt quite sure of his deportment; they were somehow aware that trusting their reputations for judgment with him was like furnishing a nursery with eggshell china. So I don't think any of us said very much about time traveling in the interval between that Thursday and the next, though its odd potentialities ran, no doubt, in most of our minds: its plausibility, that is, its practical incredibleness, the curious possibilities of anachronism and of utter confusion it suggested. For my own part, I was particularly preoccupied with the trick of the model. That I remember discussing with the Medical Man, whom I met on Friday at the Linnaean. He said he had seen a similar thing at Tübingen, and laid considerable stress on the blowing-out of the candle. But how the trick was done he could not explain.

The next Thursday I went again to Richmond—I suppose I was one of the Time Traveler's most constant guests—and, arriving late, found four or five men already assembled in his drawing room. The Medical Man was standing before the fire with a sheet of paper in one hand and his watch in the other. I looked round for the Time Traveler, and—

"It's half-past seven now," said the Medical Man. "I suppose we'd better have dinner?"

"Where's—?" said I, naming our host.

"You've just come? It's rather odd. He's unavoidably detained. He asks me in his note to lead off with dinner at seven if he's not back. Says he'll explain when he comes."

"It seems a pity to let the dinner spoil," said the Editor of a well-known daily paper; and thereupon the Doctor rang the bell.

The Psychologist was the only person besides the Doctor and myself who had attended the previous dinner. The other men were Blank, the Editor afore-mentioned, a certain journalist, and another—a quiet, shy man with a beard—whom I didn't know, and who, as far as my observation went, never opened his mouth all the evening. There was some speculation at the dinner-table about the Time Traveler's absence, and I suggested time traveling, in a half-jocular spirit. The Editor wanted that explained to him, and the Psychologist volunteered a wooden account of the "ingenious paradox and trick" we had witnessed that day week. He was in the midst of his exposition when the door from the corridor opened slowly and without noise. I was facing the door, and saw it first.

"Hallo!" I said. "At last!"

And the door opened wider, and the Time Traveler stood before us. I gave a cry of surprise.

"Good Heavens, man! what's the matter?" cried the Medical Man, who saw him next. And the whole tableful turned toward the door.

He was in an amazing plight. His coat was dusty and dirty, and smeared with green down the sleeves; his hair disordered, and as it seemed to me grayer—either with dust and dirt or because its color had actually faded. His face was ghastly pale; his chin had a brown cut on it—a cut half-healed; his expression was haggard and drawn, as by intense suffering. For a moment he hesitated in the doorway, as if he had been dazzled by the light. Then he came into the room. He walked with just such a limp as I have seen in foot-sore tramps. We stared at him in silence, expecting him to speak.

He said not a word, but came painfully to the table, and made a motion toward the wine. The Editor filled a glass of champagne and pushed it toward him. He drained it, and it seemed to do him good; for he looked round the table, and the ghost of his old smile flickered across his face.

"What on earth have you been up to, man?" said the Doctor.

The Time Traveler did not seem to hear. "Don't let me disturb you," he said, with a certain faltering articulation. "I'm all right." He stopped, held out his glass for more, and took it off at a draught. "That's good," he said. His eyes grew brighter, and a faint color came into his cheeks. His glance flickered over our faces with a certain dull approval, and then went round the warm and comfortable room. Then he spoke again, still, as it were, feeling his way among his words. "I'm going to wash and dress, and then I'll come down and explain things. Save me some of that mutton. I'm starving for a bit of meat."

He looked across at the Editor, who was a rare visitor, and hoped he was all right. The Editor began a question.

"Tell you presently," said the Time Traveler. "I'm—funny! Be all right in a minute."

He put down his glass, and walked toward the staircase door. Again I remarked his lameness and the soft padding sound of his footfall, and standing up in my place I saw his feet as he went out. He had nothing on them but a pair of tattered, blood-

plight: Condition. His haggard, dirty appearance showed he had been through some very difficult experience.

articulation: Speech. His words came slowly, brokenly.

Amateur Cadger: A cadger is a traveling pedler, a hawker, considered a lowly type of work, almost like a tramp. The Journalist was being sarcastic and implying that the Time Traveler was acting this part to the extreme.

Nebuchadnezzar phases: Reference is made to Nebuchadnezzar, King of Babylon from 605 to 562 B.C.; conqueror of Israel. He lavishly rebuilt the temples and walls of Babylon and lived in a state of grandeur. The inference may be that the Time Traveler appeared to go from one extreme to the other—he looked this moment like a poor tramp—did he also go to the other extreme, as did the noted King Nebuchadnezzar?

stained socks. Then the door closed upon him. I had half a mind to follow, till I remembered how he detested any fuss about himself. For a minute, perhaps, my mind was wool gathering. Then, "Remarkable Behavior of an Eminent Scientist," I heard the Editor say, thinking (after his wont) in headlines. And this brought my attention back to the bright dinner table.

"What's the game?" said the Journalist. "Has he been doing the Amateur Cadger? I don't follow."

I met the eye of the Psychologist, and read my own interpretation in his face. I thought of the Time Traveler limping painfully upstairs. I don't think anyone else had noticed his lameness.

The first to recover completely from this surprise was the Medical Man, who rang the bell—the Time Traveler hated to have servants waiting at dinner—for a hot plate. At that the Editor turned to his knife and fork with a grunt, and the Silent Man followed suit. The dinner was resumed. Conversation was exclamatory for a little while, with gaps of wonderment; and then the Editor got fervent in his curiosity.

"Does our friend eke out his modest income with a crossing, or has he his Nebuchadnezzar phases?" he inquired.

"I feel assured it's this business of the Time Machine," I said, and took up the Psychologist's account of our previous meeting.

The new guests were frankly incredulous. The Editor raised objections.

"What *was* this time traveling? A man couldn't cover himself with dust by rolling in a paradox, could he?"

And then, as the idea came home to him, he resorted to caricature. Hadn't they any clothes-brushes in the Future? The Journalist, too, would not believe at any price, and joined the Editor in the easy work of heaping ridicule on the whole thing. They were both the new kind of Journalist—very joyous, irreverent young men. "Our Special Correspondent in the Day After To-Morrow reports," the Journalist was saying—or rather shouting—when the Time Traveler came back. He was dressed in ordinary evening clothes, and nothing save his haggard look remained of the change that had startled me.

"I say," said the Editor hilariously, "these chaps here say you have been traveling into the middle of next week! Tell us all about little Rosebery, will you? What will you take for the lot?"

The Time Traveler came to the place reserved for him without a word. He smiled quietly, in his old way.

"Where's my mutton?" he said. "What a treat it is to stick a fork into meat again!"

"Story!" cried the Editor.

"Story?" said the Time Traveler. "I want something to eat. I won't say a word until I get some peptone into my arteries. Thanks! And the salt."

"One word," said I. "Have you been time traveling?"

"Yes," said the Time Traveler, with his mouth full, nodding his head.

"I'd give a shilling a line for a verbatim note," said the Editor. The Time Traveler pushed his glass toward the Silent Man and rang it with his finger nail; at which the Silent Man, who had been staring at his face, started convulsively, and poured him wine. The rest of the dinner was uncomfortable. For my own part, sudden questions kept on rising to my lips, and I dare say it was the same with the others. The Journalist tried to relieve the tension by telling anecdotes of Hettie Potter. The Time Traveler devoted his attention to his dinner, and displayed the appetite of a tramp. The Medical Man smoked a cigarette, and watched the Time Traveler through his eyelashes. The Silent Man seemed even more clumsy than usual, and drank champagne with regularity and determination out of sheer nervousness. At last the Time Traveler pushed his plate away, and looked round us.

"I suppose I must apologize," he said. "I was simply starving. I've had a most amazing time." He reached out his hand for a cigar, and cut the end. "But come into the smoking room. It's too long a story to tell over greasy plates." And ringing the bell in passing, he led the way into the adjoining room.

"You have told Blank and Dash and Chose about the machine?" he said to me, leaning back in his easy-chair and naming the three new guests.

"But the thing's a mere paradox," said the Editor.

"I can't argue to-night. I don't mind telling you the story, but I can't argue. I will," he went on, "tell you the story of what has happened to me, if you like, but you must refrain from interruptions. I want to tell it. Badly. Most of it will sound like lying. So be it! It's true—every word of it, all the same. I was in my laboratory at four o'clock, and since then— I've lived

peptone: Protein.

verbatim: Word for word; in exactly the same words.

anecdotes: Entertaining stories.

eight days—such days as no human being ever lived before! I'm nearly worn out, but I shan't sleep till I've told this thing over to you. Then I shall go to bed. But no interruptions! Is it agreed?"

"Agreed!" said the Editor, and the rest of us echoed "Agreed!" And with that the Time Traveler began his story as I have set it forth. He sat back in his chair at first, and spoke like a weary man. Afterward he got more animated. In writing it down I feel with only too much keenness the inadequacy of pen and ink—and, above all, my own inadequacy—to express its quality. You read, I will suppose, attentively enough; but you cannot see the speakers white, sincere face in the bright circle of the little lamp, nor hear the intonation of his voice. You cannot know how his expression followed the turns of his story! Most of us hearers were in shadow, for the candles in the smoking room had not been lighted, and only the face of the Journalist and the legs of the Silent Man from the knees downward were illuminated. At first we glanced now and again at each other. After a time we ceased to do that, and looked only at the Time Traveler's face.

animated: Lively and colorful. His speech "came alive" as he talked and warmed to his subject.

intonation: Expression. The rise and fall in the tone of voice.

I gave it a last tap, put one more drop of oil on the quartz rod, and sat myself in the saddle

I told some of you last Thursday of the principles of the Time Machine, and showed you the actual thing itself, incomplete, in the workshop. There it is now, a little travel-worn, truly; and one of the ivory bars is cracked, and a brass rail bent; but the rest of it is sound enough. I expected to finish it on Friday; but on Friday, when the putting together was nearly done, I found that one of the nickel bars was exactly one inch too short, and this I had to get re-made; so that the thing was not complete until this morning. It was at ten o'clock to-day that the first of all Time Machines began its career. I gave it a

3
THE STORY BEGINS

last tap, tried all the screws again, put one more drop of oil on the quartz rod, and sat myself in the saddle. I suppose a suicide who holds a pistol to his skull feels much the same wonder at what will come next as I felt then. I took the starting lever in one hand and the stopping one in the other, pressed the first, and almost immediately the second. I seemed to reel; I felt a nightmare sensation of falling; and, looking round, I saw the laboratory exactly as before. Had anything happened? For a moment I suspected that my intellect had tricked me. Then I noted the clock. A moment before, as it seemed, it had stood at a minute or so past ten; now it was nearly half-past three!

"I drew a breath, set my teeth, gripped the starting lever with both my hands, and went off with a thud. The laboratory got hazy and went dark. Mrs. Watchett came in, and walked, apparently without seeing me, toward the garden door. I suppose it took her a minute or so to traverse the place, but to me she seemed to shoot across the room like a rocket. I pressed the lever over to its extreme position. The night came like the turning out of a lamp, and in another moment came to-morrow. The laboratory grew faint and hazy, then fainter and ever fainter. To-morrow night came black, then day again, night again, day again, faster and faster still. An eddying murmur filled my ears and a strange, dumb confusedness descended on my mind.

"I am afraid I cannot convey the peculiar sensations of time-traveling. They are excessively unpleasant. There is a feeling exactly like that one has upon a switchback—of a helpless headlong motion! I felt the same horrible anticipation, too, of an imminent smash. As I put on pace, day followed night, like the flap, flap, flap of some rotating body. The dim suggestion of the laboratory seemed presently to fall away from me, and I saw the sun hopping swiftly across the sky, leaping it every minute, and every minute marking a day. I supposed the laboratory had been destroyed, and I had come into the open air. I had a dim impression of scaffolding, but I was already going too fast to be conscious of any moving things. The slowest snail that ever crawled dashed by too fast for me. The twinkling succession of darkness and light was excessively painful to the eye. Then in the intermittent darkness, I saw the moon spinning swiftly through her quarters from new to full, and had a faint glimpse of the circling stars. Presently, as I went on, still gaining velocity, the palpitation of night and day

scaffolding: A temporary platform used by workmen during construction. He thought probably the laboratory was being replaced by another building, but had only a fleeting impression of this, due to the speed of his advancement into future time.

palpitation of night and day: Night and day passed each other rapidly, giving the impression of a fast beating or throbbing.

merged into one continuous grayness; the sky took on a wonderful deepness of blue, a splendid luminous color like that of early twilight; the jerking sun became a streak of fire, a brilliant arch in space, the moon a fainter fluctuating band; and I could see nothing of the stars, save now and then a brighter circle flickering in the blue.

"The landscape was misty and vague. I was still on the hillside upon which this house now stands, and the shoulder rose above me gray and dim. I saw trees growing and changing like puffs of vapor, now brown, now green; they grew, spread, fluctuated, and passed away. I saw huge buildings rise up faint and fair, and pass like dreams. The whole surface of the earth seemed changing—melting and flowing under my eyes. The little hands upon the dials that registered my speed raced round faster and faster. Presently I noted that the sun belt swayed up and down, from solstice to solstice, in a minute or less, and that, consequently, my pace was over a year a minute; and minute by minute the white snow flashed across the world and vanished, and was followed by the bright, brief green of spring.

"The unpleasant sensations of the start were less poignant now. They merged at last into a kind of hysterical exhilaration. I remarked, indeed, a clumsy swaying of the machine, for which I was unable to account. But my mind was too confused to attend to it, so with a kind of madness growing upon me I flung myself into futurity. At first I scarce thought of stopping, scarce thought of anything but these new sensations. But presently a fresh series of impressions grew up in my mind,—a certain curiosity, and therewith a certain dread,—until they at last took complete possession of me. What strange developments of humanity, what wonderful advances upon our rudimentary civilization, I thought, might not appear when I came to look nearly into the dim, elusive world that raced and fluctuated before my eyes! I saw great and splendid architectures rising about me, more massive than any buildings of our own time, and yet, as it seemed, built of glimmer and mist. I saw a richer green flow up the hillside, and remain there without any wintry intermission. Even through the veil of my confusion the earth seemed very fair. And so my mind came round to the business of stopping.

"The peculiar risk lay in the possibility of my finding some substance in the space which I, or the machine, occupied. So long as I traveled at a high velocity through time, this scarcely

THE
STORY
BEGINS

fluctuating: Continually changing.

solstice to solstice: The times of the year when the sun is at its farthest point north or south of the equator, normally around June 21st and December 22nd. Speeding through time at the pace of more than a year a minute, summer and winter flashed by the Time Traveler almost as quickly as the wink of an eye.

poignant: Sharply painful.
hysterical exhilaration: He was exhilarated; joyful and excited in a highly emotional way.

rudimentary: Undeveloped.

interstices: Crevices, cracks.

incontinently: Immediately; in an uncontrollable way.

Rhododendron

Winged Sphinx

mattered: I was, so to speak, attenuated—was slipping like a vapor through the interstices of intervening substances! But to come to a stop involved the jamming of myself, molecule by molecule, into whatever lay in my way, meant bringing my atoms into such intimate contact with those of the obstacle that a profound chemical reaction—possibly a far-reaching explosion —would result, and blow myself and my apparatus out of the Rigid Universe—out of all possible dimensions—into the Unknown. This possibility had occurred to me again and again while I was making the machine; but then I had cheerfully accepted it as an unavoidable risk—one of the risks a man has got to take! Now the risk was inevitable, I no longer saw it in the same cheerful light. The fact is that, insensibly, the absolute strangeness of everything, the sickly jarring and swaying of the machine, above all the feeling of prolonged falling, had absolutely upset my nerve. I told myself that I could never stop, and with a gust of petulance I resolved to stop forthwith. Like an impatient fool, I lugged over the lever, and incontinently the thing went reeling over, and I was flung headlong through the air.

"There was the sound of a clap of thunder in my ears. I may have been stunned for a moment. A pitiless hail was hissing round me, and I was sitting on soft turf in front of the overset machine. Everything still seemed gray, but presently I remarked that the confusion in my ears was gone. I looked round me. I was on what seemed to be a little lawn in a garden, surrounded by rhododendron bushes, and I noticed that their mauve and purple blossoms were dropping in a shower under the beating of the hailstones. The rebounding, dancing hail hung in a little cloud over the machine, and drove along the ground like smoke. In a moment I was wet to the skin. 'Fine hospitality,' said I, 'to a man who has traveled innumerable years to see you!'

"Presently I thought what a fool I was to get wet. I stood up and looked round me. A colossal figure, carved apparently in some white stone, loomed indistinctly beyond the rhododendrons through the hazy downpour. But all else of the world was invisible.

"My sensations would be hard to describe. As the columns of hail grew thinner, I saw the white figure more distinctly. It was very large, for a silver birch tree touched its shoulder. It was of white marble, in shape something like a winged sphinx, but the wings, instead of being carried vertically at the sides, were spread so that it seemed to hover. The pedestal, it appeared to me, was of bronze, and was thick with verdigris. It chanced that the face was toward me; the sightless eyes seemed to watch me; there was the faint shadow of a smile on the lips. It was greatly weatherworn, and that imparted an unpleasant suggestion of disease. I stood looking at it for a little space—half a minute, perhaps, or half an hour. It seemed to advance and to recede as the hail drove before it denser or thinner. At last I tore my eyes from it for a moment, and saw that the hail curtain had worn threadbare, and that the sky was lightening with the promise of the sun.

"I looked up again at the crouching white shape, and the full temerity of my voyage came suddenly upon me. What might appear when that hazy curtain was altogether withdrawn? What might not have happened to men? What if cruelty had grown into a common passion? What if in this interval the race had lost its manliness, and had developed into something inhuman, unsympathetic, and overwhelmingly powerful? I might seem some old-world savage animal, only the more dreadful and disgusting for our common likeness—a foul creature to be incontinently slain.

"Already I saw other vast shapes—huge buildings with intricate parapets and tall columns, with a wooded hillside dimly creeping in upon me through the lessening storm. I was seized with a panic fear. I turned frantically to the Time Machine, and strove hard to readjust it. As I did so the shafts of the sun smote through the thunderstorm. The gray downpour was swept aside and vanished like the trailing garments of a ghost. Above me, in the intense blue of the summer sky, some faint brown shreds of clouds whirled into nothingness. The great buildings about me stood out clear and distinct, shining with the wet of the thunderstorm, and picked out in white by the unmelted hailstones piled along their courses. I felt naked in a strange world. I felt as perhaps a bird may feel in the clear air, knowing the hawk wings above and will swoop. My fear grew to frenzy. I took a breathing space, set my teeth, and again grappled fiercely, wrist and knee, with the machine. It gave under my desperate onset and turned over. It struck my chin violently. One hand on the saddle, the other on the lever, I stood panting heavily in attitude to mount again.

THE STORY BEGINS

verdigris: A green coating that forms like rust on certain metals.

temerity: Foolhardiness.

parapets: Low walls or protective railings.

buskins: High, thick-soled, laced boots or half-boots.

consumptive: A person afflicted with consumption, a disease of the lungs, more commonly known as tuberculosis. This disease often causes a pale, fragile look which at one time was considered a type of beauty.

"But with this recovery of a prompt retreat my courage recovered. I looked more curiously and less fearfully at this world of the remote future. In a circular opening, high up in the wall of the nearer house, I saw a group of figures clad in rich soft robes. They had seen me, and their faces were directed toward me.

"Then I heard voices approaching me. Coming through the bushes by the white sphinx were the heads and shoulders of men running. One of these emerged in a pathway leading straight to the little lawn upon which I stood with my machine. He was a slight creature—perhaps four feet high—clad in a purple tunic, girdled at the waist with a leather belt. Sandals or buskins—I could not clearly distinguish which—were on his feet; his legs were bare to the knees, and his head was bare. Noticing that, I noticed for the first time how warm the air was.

"He struck me as being a very beautiful and graceful creature, but indescribably frail. His flushed face reminded me of the more beautiful kind of consumptive—that hectic beauty of which we used to hear so much. At the sight of him I suddenly regained confidence. I took my hands from the machine.

Then came one laughing toward me, carrying a chain of beautiful flowers.

In another moment we were standing face to face, I and this fragile thing out of futurity. He came straight up to me and laughed into my eyes. The absence of any sign of fear from his bearing struck me at once. Then he turned to the two others who were following him and spoke to them in a strange and very sweet and liquid tongue.

"There were others coming, and presently a little group of perhaps eight or ten of these exquisite creatures were about me.

4
THE
GOLDEN AGE

29

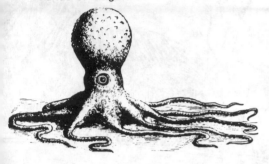

tentacles: Long feelers such as those of an octopus. Here, tentacles refer to the Future Peoples' hands or fingers.

One of them addressed me. It came into my head, oddly enough, that my voice was too harsh and deep for them. So I shook my head, and pointing to my ears, shook it again. He came a step forward, hesitated, and then touched my hand. Then I felt other soft little tentacles upon my back and shoulders. They wanted to make sure I was real. There was nothing in this at all alarming. Indeed, there was something in these pretty little people that inspired confidence—a graceful gentleness, a certain childlike ease. And besides, they looked so frail that I could fancy myself flinging the whole dozen of them about like ninepins. But I made a sudden motion to warn them when I saw their little pink hands feeling at the Time Machine. Happily then, when it was not too late, I thought of a danger I had hitherto forgotten, and reaching over the bars of the machine I unscrewed the little levers that would set it in motion, and put these in my pocket. Then I turned again to see what I could do in the way of communication.

"And then, looking more nearly into their features, I saw some further peculiarities in their Dresden china type of prettiness. Their hair, which was uniformly curly, came to a sharp end at the neck and cheek; there was not the faintest suggestion of it on the face, and their ears were singularly minute. The mouths were small, with bright red, rather thin lips, and the little chins ran to a point. The eyes were large and mild; and—this may seem egotism on my part—I fancied even then that there was a certain lack of the interest I might have expected in them.

"As they made no effort to communicate with me, but simply stood round me smiling and speaking in soft cooing notes to each other, I began the conversation. I pointed to the Time Machine and to myself. Then, hesitating for a moment how to express Time, I pointed to the sun. At once a quaintly pretty little figure in checkered purple and white, followed my gesture, and then astonished me by imitating the sound of thunder.

"For the moment I was staggered, though the import of his gesture was plain enough. The question had come into my mind abruptly: Were these creatures fools? You may hardly understand how it took me. You see I had always anticipated that the people of the year Thirty-two Thousand odd would be incredibly in front of us in knowledge, art, everything. Then one of them suddenly asked me a question that showed him to be on the intellectual level of one of our five-year-old children—asked me, in fact, if I had come from the sun in a thunderstorm! It let loose the judgment I had suspended upon their clothes, their frail, light limbs, and fragile features. A flow of disappointment rushed across my mind. For a moment I felt that I had built the Time Machine in vain.

"I nodded, pointed to the sun, and gave them such a vivid rendering of a thunderclap as startled them. They all withdrew a pace or so and bowed. Then came one laughing toward me, carrying a chain of beautiful flowers, altogether new to me, and put it about my neck. The idea was received with melodious applause; and presently they were all running to and fro for flowers, and laughingly flinging them upon me until I was almost smothered with blossom. You who have never seen the like can scarcely imagine what delicate and wonderful flowers countless years of culture had created. Then someone suggested that their plaything should be exhibited in the nearest building, and so I was led past the sphinx of white marble, which had seemed to watch me all the while with a smile at my astonishment, toward a vast gray edifice of fretted stone. As I went with them the memory of my confident anticipations of a profoundly grave and intellectual posterity came, with irresistible merriment, to my mind.

"The building had a large entry and was altogether of colossal dimensions. I was naturally most occupied with the growing crowd of little people, and with the big open portals that yawned before me shadowy and mysterious. My general impression of the world I saw over their heads was of a tangled waste of beautiful bushes and flowers, a long neglected and yet weedless garden. I saw a number of tall spikes of strange white flowers, measuring a foot perhaps across the spread of the waxen petals. They grew scattered, as if wild, among the variegated shrubs, but, as I say, I did not examine them closely at this time. The Time Machine was left deserted on the turf among the rhododendrons.

"The arch of the doorway was richly carved, but naturally I did not observe the carving very narrowly, though I fancied I saw suggestions of old Phoenician decorations as I passed through, and it struck me that they were very badly broken and weather-worn. Several more brightly clad people met me in the doorway, and so we entered, I, dressed in dingy nineteenth century garments, looking grotesque enough, garlanded with

Fretted Stone

intellectual posterity: Mentally superior descendants. These childlike people were far from intellectual and were a great disappointment to the Time Traveler.

portals: Large doorways or gates.

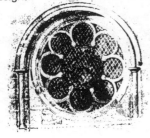

flowers, and surrounded by an eddying mass of bright, soft-colored robes and shining white limbs, in a melodious whirl of laughter and laughing speech.

"The big doorway opened into a proportionately great hall hung with brown. The roof was in shadow, and the windows, partially glazed with colored glass, and partially unglazed, admitted a tempered light. The floor was made up of huge blocks of some very hard white metal, not plates nor slabs—blocks, and it was so much worn, as I judged by the going to and fro of past generations, as to be deeply channeled along the more frequented ways. Transverse to the length were innumerable tables made of slabs of polished stone, raised, perhaps, a foot from the floor, and upon these were heaps of fruits. Some I recognized as a kind of hypertrophied raspberry and orange, but for the most part they were strange.

"Between the tables were scattered a great number of cushions. Upon these my conductors seated themselves, signing for me to do likewise. With a pretty absence of ceremony they began to eat the fruit with their hands, flinging peel, and stalks, and so forth, into the round openings in the sides of the tables. I was not loth to follow their example, for I felt thirsty and hungry. As I did so I surveyed the hall at my leisure.

"And perhaps the thing that struck me most was its dilapidated look. The stained-glass windows, which displayed only a geometrical pattern, were broken in many places, and the curtains that hung across the lower end were thick with dust. And it caught my eye that the corner of the marble table near me was fractured. Nevertheless, the general effect was extremely rich and picturesque. There were, perhaps, a couple of hundred people dining in the hall, and most of them, seated as near to me as they could come, were watching me with interest, their little eyes shining over the fruit they were eating. All were clad in the same soft, and yet strong, silky material.

"Fruit, by the bye, was all their diet. These people of the remote future were strict vegetarians, and while I was with them, in spite of some carnal cravings, I had to be frugivorous also. Indeed, I found afterward that horses, cattle, sheep, dogs, had followed the ichthyosaurus into extinction. But the fruits were very delightful; one, in particular, that seemed to be in season all the time I was there,—a floury thing in a three-sided husk,—was especially good, and I made it my staple. At first I was puzzled by all these strange fruits, and by the strange flowers I saw, but later I began to perceive their import.

"However, I am telling you of my fruit dinner in the distant future now. So soon as my appetite was a little checked, I determined to make a resolute attempt to learn the speech of these new men of mine. Clearly that was the next thing to do. The fruits seemed a convenient thing to begin upon, and holding one of these up I began a series of interrogative sounds and gestures. I had some considerable difficulty in conveying my meaning. At first my efforts met with a stare of surprise or inextinguishable laughter, but presently a fair-haired little creature seemed to grasp my intention and repeated a name. They had to chatter and explain their business at great length to each other, and my first attempts to make their exquisite little sounds of the language caused an immense amount of genuine, if uncivil amusement. However, I felt like a schoolmaster amid children, and persisted, and presently I had a score of noun substantives at least, at my command; and then I got to demonstrative pronouns, and even the verb 'to eat.' But it was slow work, and the little people soon tired and wanted to get away from my interrogations, so I determined, rather of necessity, to let them give their lessons in little doses when they felt inclined. And very little doses I found they were before long, for I never met people more indolent or more easily fatigued.

THE GOLDEN AGE

interrogative . . . . gestures: Questioning tones of voice and movements of hands and face. We might say a kind of sign language.

indolent: Idle, lazy.

Here and there among the greenery were palace-like buildings, but the house and cottage which form such characteristic features of our landscape were gone

5
SUNSET

A queer thing I soon discovered about my little hosts, and that was their lack of interest. They would come to me with eager cries of astonishment, like children, but, like children, they would soon stop examining me, and wander away after some other toy. The dinner and my conversational beginnings ended, I noted for the first time that almost all those who had surrounded me at first were gone. It is odd, too, how speedily I came to disregard these little people. I went out through the portal into the sunlit world again as soon as my hunger was satisfied. I was continually meeting more of these men of the future, who would follow me a little distance, chatter and laugh about me, and, having smiled and gesticulated in a friendly way, leave me again to my own devises.

"The calm of evening was upon the world as I emerged from the great hall, and the scene was lit by the warm glow of the setting sun. At first things were very confusing. Everything was so entirely different from the world I had known—even the flowers. The big building I had left was situated on the slope of a broad river valley, but the Thames had shifted, perhaps a mile from its present position. I resolved to mount to the summit of a crest, possibly a mile and a half away, from which I could get a wider view of this our planet in the year 802,701, A. D. For that, I should explain, was the date the little dials of my machine recorded.

"As I walked I was watchful of every impression that could possibly help to explain the condition of ruinous splendor in which I found the world—for ruinous it was. A little way up the hill, for instance, was a great heap of granite, bound together by masses of aluminum, a vast labyrinth of precipitous walls and crumbled heaps, amid which were thick heaps of very beautiful pagoda-like plants—nettles possibly, but wonderfully tinted with brown about the leaves, and incapable of stinging. It was evidently the derelict remains of some vast structure, built to what end I could not determine. It was here that I was destined, at a later date, to have a very strange experience—the first intimation of a still stranger discovery—but of that I will speak in its proper place.

"Looking round, with a sudden thought, from a terrace on which I had rested for a while, I realized that there were no small houses to be seen. Apparently the single house, and possibly even the household, had vanished. Here and there among the greenery were palace-like buildings, but the house and the cottage, which form such characteristic features of our own English landscape, had disappeared.

" 'Communism,' said I to myself.

"And on the heels of that came another thought. I looked at the half dozen little figures that were following me. Then, in a flash, I perceived that all had the same form of costume, the same soft hairless visage, and the same girlish rotundity of limb. It may seem strange, perhaps, that I had not noticed this before. But everything was so strange. Now, I saw the fact plainly enough. In costume, and in all the differences of texture and

labyrinth of precipitous walls: Numerous passages, complicated and puzzling in arrangement, formed of high and cliff-like walls.

nettles: Plants covered with fine stinging hairs.

rotundity: Roundness, plumpness.

bearing that now mark off the sex from each other, these people of the future were alike. And the children seemed to my eyes to be but the miniatures of their parents. I judged then that children of that time were extremely precocious, physically at least, and I found afterward abundant verification of my opinion.

"Seeing the ease and security in which these people were living, I felt that this close resemblance of the sexes was, after all, what one would expect; for the strength of a man and the softness of a woman, the institution of the family, and the differentiation of occupations are mere militant necessities of an age of physical force. Where population is balanced and abundant, much child-bearing becomes an evil rather than a blessing to the State; where violence comes but rarely and offspring are secure, there is less necessity—indeed there is no necessity—of an efficient family, and the specialization of the sexes with reference to their children's needs disappears. We see some beginnings of this even in our own time, and in this future age it was complete. This, I must remind you, was my speculation at the time. Later, I was to appreciate how far it fell short of the reality.

"While I was musing upon these things, my attention was attracted by a pretty little structure, like a well under a cupola. I thought in a transitory way of the oddness of wells still existing, and then resumed the thread of my speculations. There were no large buildings toward the top of the hill, and as my walking powers were evidently miraculous, I was presently left alone for the first time. With a strange sense of freedom and adventure I pushed up to the crest.

"There I found a seat of some yellow metal that I did not recognize, corroded in places with a kind of pinkish rust and half smothered in soft moss, the arm rests cast and filed into the resemblance of griffins' heads. I sat down on it, and I surveyed the broad view of our old world under the sunset of that long day. It was as sweet and fair a view as I have ever seen. The sun had already gone below the horizon and the west was flaming gold, touched with some horizontal bars of purple and crimson. Below was the valley of the Thames, in which the river lay like a band of burnished steel. I have ready spoken of the great palaces dotted about among the variegated greenery, some in ruins and some still occupied. Here and there rose a white or

cupola: A rounded roof or dome.

transitory: Temporary; a passing thought.

Griffin

silvery figure in the waste garden of the earth, here and there came the sharp vertical line of some cupola or obelisk. There were no hedges, no signs of proprietary rights, no evidences of agriculture; the whole earth had become a garden.

"So watching, I began to put my interpretation upon the things I had seen, and as it shaped itself to me that evening, my interpretation was something in this way (afterward I found I had got only a half truth, or only a glimpse of one facet of the truth):

"It seemed to me that I had happened upon humanity upon the wane. The ruddy sunset set me thinking of the sunset of mankind. For the first time I began to realize an odd consequence of the social effort in which we are at present engaged. And yet, come to think, it is a logical consequence enough. Strength is the outcome of need; security sets a premium on feebleness. The work of ameliorating the conditions of life—the true civilizing process that makes life more and more secure—had gone steadily on to a climax. One triumph of a united humanity over Nature had followed another. Things that are now mere dreams had become projects deliberately put in hand and carried forward. And the harvest was what I saw!

"After all, the sanitation and the agriculture of to-day are still in the rudimentary stage. The science of our time has attacked but a little department of the field of human disease, but, even so, it spreads its operations very steadily and persistently. Our agriculture and horticulture destroy just here and there a weed and cultivate perhaps a score or so of wholesome plants, leaving the greater number to fight out a balance as they can. We improve our favorite plants and animals—and how few they are—gradually by selective breeding; now a new and better peach, now a seedless grape, now a sweeter and larger flower, now a more convenient breed of cattle. We improve them gradually, because our ideals are vague and tentative, and our knowledge is very limited; because Nature, too, is shy and slow in our clumsy hands. Some day all this will be better organized, and still better. That is the drift of the current in spite of the eddies. The whole world will be intelligent, educated, and co-operating; things will move faster and faster toward the subjugation of Nature. In the end, wisely and carefully we shall readjust the balance of animal and vegetable life to suit our human needs.

SUNSET

obelisk: A tall, four-sided stone pillar, often carved all over with ancient writings called hieroglyphics.

ameliorating: Bettering, improving.

Gnat

connubial jealousy: Jealousy of one's husband or wife.

"This adjustment, I say, must have been done, and done well: done indeed for all time, in the space of Time across which my machine had leaped. The air was free from gnats, the earth from weeds or fungi; everywhere were fruits and sweet and delightful flowers; brilliant butterflies flew hither and thither. The ideal of preventive medicine was attained. Diseases had been stamped out. I saw no evidence of any contagious diseases during all my stay. And I shall have to tell you later that even the processes of putrefaction and decay had been profoundly affected by these changes.

"Social triumphs, too, had been effected. I saw mankind housed in splendid shelters, gloriously clothed, and as yet I had found them engaged in no toil. There were no signs of struggle, neither social nor economical struggle. The shop, the advertisement, traffic, all that commerce which constitutes the body of our world, was gone. It was natural on that golden evening that I should jump at the idea of a social paradise.

"The difficulty of increasing population had been met, I guessed, and population had ceased to increase.

"But with this change in condition comes inevitably adaptations to the change. What, unless biological science is a mass of errors, is the cause of human intelligence and vigor? Hardship and freedom: conditions under which the active, strong, and subtle survive and the weaker go to the wall; conditions that put a premium upon the loyal alliance of capable men, upon self-restraint, patience, and decision. And the institution of the family, and the emotions that arise therein, the fierce jealousy, the tenderness for offspring, parental self-devotion, all found their justification and support in the imminent dangers of the young. *Now*, where are those imminent dangers? There is a sentiment arising, and it will grow, against connubial jealousy, against fierce maternity, against passion of all sorts; unnecessary things now, and things that make us uncomfortable, savage survivals, discords in a refined and pleasant life.

"I thought of the physical slightness of the people, their lack of intelligence, and those big abundant ruins, and it strengthened my belief in a perfect conquest of Nature. For after the battle comes Quiet. Humanity had been strong, energetic, and intelligent, and had used all its abundant vitality to alter the conditions under which it lived. And now came the reaction of the altered conditions.

"Under the new conditions of perfect comfort and security, that restless energy, that with us is strength, would become weakness. Even in our own time certain tendencies and desires, once necessary to survival, are a constant source of failure. Physical courage and the love of battle, for instance, are no great help—may even be hindrances—to a civilized man. And in a state of physical balance and security, power, intellectual as well as physical, would be out of place. For countless years I judged there had been no danger of war or solitary violence, no danger from wild beasts, no wasting disease to require strength of constitution, no need of toil. For such a life, what we should call the weak are as well equipped as the strong, are, indeed, no longer weak. Better equipped indeed they are, for the strong would be fretted by an energy for which there was no outlet. No doubt the exquisite beauty of the buildings I saw was the outcome of the last surgings of the now purposeless energy of mankind before it settled down into perfect harmony with the conditions under which it lived—the flourish of that triumph which began the last great peace. This has ever been the fate of energy in security; it takes to art and to eroticism, and then come languor and decay.

"Even this artistic impetus would at last die away—had almost died in the Time I saw. To adorn themselves with flowers, to dance, to sing in the sunlight; so much was left of the artistic spirit, and no more. Even that would fade in the end into a contented inactivity. We are kept keen on the grindstone of pain and necessity, and it seemed to me that here was that hateful grindstone broken at last!

"As I stood there in the gathering dark I thought that in this simple explanation I had mastered the problem of the world—mastered the whole secret of these delicious people. Possibly the checks they had devised for the increase of population had succeeded too well, and their numbers had rather diminished than kept stationary. That would account for the abandoned ruins. Very simple was my explanation, and plausible enough—as most wrong theories are.

"As I stood there musing over this too perfect triumph of man, the full moon, yellow and gibbous, came up out of an overflow of silver light in the northeast. The bright little figure ceased to move about below, a noiseless owl flitted by, and I shivered with the chill of the night. I determined to descend and find where I could sleep.

"I looked for the building I knew. Then my eye traveled along to the figure of the white sphinx upon the pedestal of

fretted: Constantly disturbed and worried. Strong and exceedingly energetic people would be very discontented and frustrated if they had no outlet or work to burn up their energy.

gibbous: Rounded and bulging, referring to the shape of the moon when it is between its half and full phases.

bronze, growing distinct as the light of the rising moon grew brighter. I could see the silver birch against it. There was the tangle of rhododendron bushes, black in the pale light, and there was the little lawn. I looked at the lawn again. A queer doubt chilled my complacency. 'No,' said I stoutly to myself, 'that was not the lawn.'

"But it *was* the lawn. For the white leprous face of the sphinx was toward it. Can you imagine what I felt as this conviction came home to me? But you cannot. The Time Machine was gone!

"At once, like a lash across the face, came the possibility of losing my own age, of being left helpless in this strange new world. The bare thought of it was an actual physical sensation. I could feel it grip me at the throat and stop my breathing.

leprous: Covered with white scales, as one suffering from the disease of leprosy.

Above me towered the sphinx upon the bronze pedestal, white, shining, leprous in the light of the rising moon.

In another moment I was in a passion of fear, and running with great, leaping strides down the slope. Once I fell headlong and cut my face. I lost no time in stanching the blood, but jumped up and ran on, with a warm trickle down my cheek and chin. All the time I ran I was saying to myself: 'They have moved it a little—pushed it under the bushes out of the way.' Nevertheless, I ran with all my might. All the time, with the certainty that sometimes comes with excessive dread, I knew that such assurance was folly, knew instinctively that the machine was removed out of my reach.

6
THE MACHINE IS LOST

intellectual inadequacy: Insufficient intelligence.

intervention: Intrusion; an interference.

malachite: A very hard mineral of various shades of green, often with a marble-like appearance, which can be highly polished.

"My breath came with pain. I suppose I covered the whole distance, from the hill crest to the little lawn, two miles perhaps, in ten minutes. And I am not a young man. I cursed aloud as I ran at my confident folly in leaving the machine, wasting good breath thereby. I cried aloud, and none answered. Not a creature seemed to be stirring in that moonlit world.

"When I reached the lawn my worst fears were realized. Not a trace of the thing was to be seen. I felt faint and cold when I faced the empty space among the black tangle of bushes. I ran round it furiously, as if the thing might be hidden in a corner, and then stopped abruptly with my hands clutching my hair. Above me towered the sphinx upon the bronze pedestal, white, shining, leprous in the light of the rising moon. It seemed to smile in mockery of my dismay.

"I might have consoled myself by imagining the little people had put the mechanism in some shelter for me, had not I felt assured of their physical and intellectual inadequacy. That is what dismayed me: the sense of some hitherto unsuspected power through whose intervention my invention had vanished. Yet of one thing I felt assured: unless some other age had produced its exact duplicate, the machine could not have moved in Time. The attachment of the levers—I will show you the method later—prevented anyone from tampering with it in that way when they were removed. It had been moved, and was hid, only in Space. But, then, where could it be?

"I think I must have had a kind of frenzy. I remember running violently in and out among the moonlit bushes all round the sphinx, and startling some white animal that in the dim light I took for a small deer. I remember, too, late that night, beating the bushes with my clenched fists until my knuckles were gashed and bleeding from the broken twigs.

"Then, sobbing and raving in my anguish of mind, I went down to the great building of stone. The big hall was dark, silent, and deserted. I slipped on the uneven floor and fell over one of the malachite tables, almost breaking my shin. I lit a match and went on past the dusty curtains of which I have told you.

"There I found a second great hall covered with cushions, upon which perhaps a score or so of the little people were sleeping. I have no doubt they found my second appearance strange enough, coming suddenly out of the quiet darkness with inarticulate noises and the splutter and flare of a match. For they had forgotten about matches. 'Where is my Time Machine?' I began, bawling like an angry child, laying hands upon them and shaking them up together. It must have been very queer to them. Some laughed, most of them looked sorely frightened. When I saw them standing round me, it came into my head that I was doing as foolish a thing as it was possible for me to do under the circumstances, in trying to revive the sensation of fear. For reasoning from the daylight behavior I thought that fear must be forgotten.

"Abruptly I dashed down the match, and knocking one of the people over in my course, went blundering across the big dining hall again out under the moonlight. I heard cries of terror and their little feet running and stumbling this way and that. I do not remember all I did as the moon crept up the sky. I suppose it was the unexpected nature of my loss that maddened me. I felt hopelessly cut off from my own kind, a strange animal in an unknown world. I must have raved to and fro, screaming and crying upon God and Fate. I have a memory of horrible fatigue, as the long night of despair wore away, of looking in this impossible place and that, of groping among moonlit ruins and touching strange creatures in the black shadows; at last, of lying on the ground near the sphinx and weeping with absolute wretchedness, even anger at the folly of leaving the machine. I had nothing left but misery.

"Then I slept, and when I woke again it was full day, and a couple of sparrows were hopping around me upon the turf within reach of my arm.

"I sat up in the freshness of the morning trying to remember how I had got there, and why I had such a profound sense of desertion and despair. Then things came clear in my mind. With the plain, reasonable daylight I could look my circumstances fairly in the face. I saw the wild folly of my frenzy overnight, and I could reason with myself.

" 'Suppose the worst,' said I, 'suppose the machine altogether lost—perhaps destroyed. It behooves me to be calm and patient, to learn the way of the people, to get a clear idea of the method of my loss and the means of getting materials and tools; so that in the end, perhaps, I may make another. That would be my only hope, a poor hope, perhaps, but better than despair. And, after all, it was a beautiful and curious world.

" 'But probably the machine had only been taken away. Still, I must be calm and patient, find its hiding place, and recover it

Sparrow

stolid: Dull, slow to react.

sloth: A slow-moving, tree-dwelling animal.

by force or cunning.' And with that I scrambled to my feet and looked about me, wondering where I could bathe. I felt weary, stiff, and travel-soiled. The freshness of the morning made me desire an equal freshness. I had exhausted my emotion. Indeed, as I went about my business, I found myself wondering at my intense excitement overnight.

"That morning I made a careful examination of the ground about the little lawn. I wasted some time in futile questionings conveyed as well as I was able to such of the little people as came by. They all failed to understand my gestures—some were simply stolid; some thought it was a jest, and laughed at me. I had the hardest task in the world to keep my hands off their pretty, laughing faces. It was a foolish impulse, but the devil begotten of fear and blind anger was ill curbed, and still eager to take advantage of my perplexity. The turf gave better counsel. I found a groove ripped in it, about midway between the pedestal of the sphinx and the marks of my feet where, on arrival, I had struggled with the overturned machine. There were other signs of the removal of a heavy body about, of queer, narrow footprints like those I could imagine made by a sloth. This directed my closer attention to the pedestal. It was, as I think I have said, of bronze. It was not a mere block, but highly decorated with deep-framed panels on either side. I went and rapped at these. The pedestal was hollow. Examining the panels with care, I found them discontinuous with the frames. There were no handles nor keyholes, but possibly the panels, if they were doors, as I supposed, opened from within. One thing was clear enough to my mind. It took no very great mental effort to infer that my Time Machine was inside that pedestal. But how it got there was a different problem.

"I saw the heads of two orange-clad people coming through the bushes and under some blossom-covered apple trees toward me. I turned, smiling, to them, and beckoned them to me. They came, and then, pointing to the bronze pedestal, I tried to intimate my wish to open it. But at my first gesture toward this, they behaved very oddly. I don't know how to convey their expression to you. Suppose you were to use a grossly improper gesture to a delicate-minded woman—it is how she would look. They went off as if they had received the last possible insult.

"However, I wanted access to the Time Machine; so I tried a sweet-looking little chap in white next, with exactly the same result. Somehow, his manner made me ashamed of myself. But, as I say, I wanted the Time Machine. I tried one more. As he turned off like the others, my temper got the better of me. In three strides I was after him, had him by the loose part of his robe round the neck, and began dragging him toward the sphinx. Then I saw the horror and repugnance of his face, and all of a sudden I let him go.

"But I was not beaten yet. I banged with my fist at the bronze panels. I thought I heard something stir inside—to be explicit, I thought I heard a sound like a chuckle—but I must have been mistaken. Then I got a big pebble from the river, and came and hammered till I had flattened a coil in the decorations, and the verdigris came off in powdery flakes. The delicate little people must have heard me hammering in gusty outbreaks a mile away on either hand, but nothing came of it. I saw a crowd of them upon the slopes, looking furtively at me. At last, hot and tired, I sat down to watch the place. But I was too restless to watch long, and, besides, I am too Occidental for a long vigil. I could work at a problem for years, but to wait inactive for twenty-four hours—that is another matter.

"I got up after a time, and began walking aimlessly through the bushes toward the hill again.

"'Patience,' said I to myself. 'If you want your machine again, you must leave that sphinx alone. If they mean to take your machine away, it's little good your wrecking their bronze panels, and if they don't, you will get it back so soon as you can ask for it. To sit among all those unknown things before a puzzle like that is hopeless. That way lies monomania. Face this world. Learn its ways; watch it; be careful of too hasty guesses at its meaning. In the end you will find clews to it all.'

"Then suddenly the humor of the situation came into my mind: the thought of the years I had spent in study and toil to get into the future age, and now my passion of anxiety to get out of it. I had made myself the most complicated and the most hopeless trap that ever a man devised. Although it was at my own expense, I could not help myself. I laughed aloud.

"Going through the big palace it seemed to me that the little people avoided me. It may have been my fancy, or it may have had something to do with my hammering at the gates of bronze. Yet I felt tolerably sure of the avoidance. I was careful, however, to show no concern, and to abstain from any pursuit of them, and in the course of a day or two things got back to the old footing.

THE MACHINE IS LOST

repugnance: Loathing; a feeling of disgust and fear.

Occidental: Of the Western World; energetic, restless and not passively patient, as people of the Oriental World.

monomania: Extreme anxiety concerning one thing, bordering on insanity.

clews: Also, clues. Evidence that leads to a solution.

Suddenly I halted spell-bound, a pair of eyes, luminous by the reflection of the daylight without, was watching me

I made what progress I could in the language, and in addition I pushed my explorations here and there. Either I missed some subtle point or their language was excessively simple, almost exclusively composed of concrete substantives and verbs. There seemed to be few, if any, abstract terms, or little use of figurative language. Their sentences were usually simple and of two words, and I failed to convey or understand any but the simplest propositions. I determined to put the thought of my Time Machine, and the mystery of the bronze doors under the sphinx, as much as possible in a corner of my memory until my growing knowledge would lead me back to them in a natural way. Yet a certain feeling you may understand tethered me in a circle of a few miles round the point of my arrival.

"So far as I could see, all the world displayed the same exuberant richness as the Thames valley. From every hill I climbed I saw the same abundance of splendid buildings, endlessly varied in material and style, the same clustering thickets of evergreens, the same blossom-laden trees and tree ferns. Here and there water shone like silver, and beyond, the land rose into blue undulating hills and so faded into the serenity of the sky.

7

THE STRANGE ANIMAL

Tree-fern

undulating: Rolling.

47

"A peculiar feature that presently attracted my attention was certain circular wells that appeared to sink to a profound depth. One lay by the path up the hill which I had followed during my first walk. These wells were rimmed with bronze, curiously wrought, and often protected by small cupolas from the rain. Sitting by the side of these, and peering down, I failed to see any gleam of water, and could catch no reflection from a lighted match. I heard a peculiar dull sound; thud, thud, thud, like the beating of some big engine, and I discovered from the flaring of the match that a steady current of air set down the shaft.

"Moreover, I carelessly threw a scrap of paper into the throat of the well, and instead of fluttering slowly down, it was at once sucked swiftly out of sight. After a time, too, I came to connect with these wells certain tall towers that stood here and there upon the hill slopes. Above these there was often apparent a peculiar flicker of the air, much as one sees it on a hot day above a sun-scorched beach.

"Putting these things together there certainly seemed to me a strong suggestion of an extensive system of subterraneous ventilation, though its true import was difficult to imagine. I was at first inclined to associate it with the sanitary apparatus of these people. It was the obvious suggestion of these things, but it was absolutely wrong.

"And here I must admit that I learned very little of drains, and bells, and modes of conveyance and the like conveniences during my time in this real future. In some of the fictitious visions of Utopias and coming times I have read, there is a vast amount of detail about building construction and social arrangements and so forth. But while such details are easy enough to obtain when the whole world lies in one's imagination, they are altogether inaccessible to a real traveler amid such realities as surrounded me. Conceive what tale of London a negro from Central Africa would take back to his tribe. What would he know of railway companies, of social movements, of telephone and telegraph wires, of the parcels delivery company, and postal orders? And yet we at least would be willing enough to explain these things. And even of what he knew, how much could he make his untraveled friend believe? Then think how little is the gap between a negro and a man of our times, and how wide the interval between myself and the Golden Age people. I was sensible of much that was unseen, and which contributed to my

subterraneous: Under the surface of the earth.

Utopias: Imaginary, ideal places, perfect in every way.

comfort, but save for a general impression of automatic organization, I fear I can convey very little of the difference to your minds.

"In the matter of sepulcher, for instance, I could see no traces of crematoria or anything suggestive of tombs. But it occurred to me that possibly cemeteries or crematoria existed at some spot beyond the range of my explorations. This again was a question I deliberately put to myself, and upon which my curiosity was a first entirely defeated. Neither were there any old or infirm among them.

"I must confess that my satisfaction with my first theories at an automatic civilization and a decadent humanity did not endure. Yet I could think of none other. Let me put my difficulties. The several big palaces I had explored were mere living places, great dining halls and sleeping apartments. I could find no machinery, no appliances of any kind. Yet these people were clothed in pleasant fabrics that must at times need renewal, their sandals though without ornament were fairly complex specimens of metal work. Somehow such things must be made. And the little people displayed no vestige of the creative tendencies of our time. There were no shops, no workshops, no indications of importations from any other part of the earth. They spent all their time in playing gently, in bathing in the river, in making love in a half-playful fashion, in eating fruit, and sleeping. I could not see how things were kept going.

"Then again about the Time Machine. Something, I knew not what, had taken it into the hollow pedestal of the sphinx. Why? For the life of me I could not imagine.

"Then there were those wells without water, those flickering pillars. I felt I missed a clew somewhere. I felt—how shall I say it? Suppose you found an inscription with sentences here and there in excellent plain English, and interpolated therewith others made up of words, even of letters, absolutely unknown to you. That was how the world of 802,701 presented itself to me on the third day of my stay.

"On that day, too, I made a friend—of a sort. It happened that as I was watching some of the little people bathing in a shallow of the river, one of them was seized with cramp and began drifting down the stream. The main current of the stream ran rather swiftly there, but not too swiftly for even a moderate swimmer. It will give you an idea, therefore, of the strange want

THE STRANGE ANIMAL

sepulcher: Tomb, grave.
crematoria: Furnaces used for the cremation (burning to ashes) of corpses. Cremation was first practiced by the ancient pagans. The custom was outlawed by the early Christians, but has become increasingly common within the last 50 years.

vestige: Trace, mark. The pretty little people showed absolutely no creative leanings or ambitions.

interpolated: Inserted or put in. The Time Traveler was able to reason out many changes he saw in the world of 802,701, but some things seemed unexplainable and broke his chain of deduction.

of ideas of these people, when I tell you that none made the slightest attempt to rescue the weakly crying little creature who was drowning before their eyes.

"When I realized this I hurriedly slipped off my garments, and wading in from a point lower down, caught the poor little soul and brought her to land.

"A little rubbing of the limbs soon brought her round, and I had the satisfaction of seeing that she was all right before I left her. I had got to such a low estimate of these little folks that I did not expect gratitude. In that, however, I was wrong.

"The incident happened in the morning. In the afternoon I met my little woman, as I believe it was, when I was returning toward my center from one of my explorations, and she received me with cries of delight and presented me with a big garland of flowers—evidently prepared for me.

Garland of Flowers

"The action took my imagination. Very possibly I had been feeling desolate. At any rate I did my best to display my appreciation of the gift.

"We were soon seated together in a little stone arbor, engaged in a conversation that was chiefly smiles.

"The little creature's friendliness affected me exactly as a child's might. We passed each other flowers and she kissed my hands. I did the same to hers. Then I tried conversation and found out her name was Weena, which, though I don't know what it meant, somehow seemed appropriate enough. That was the beginning of a queer friendship that lasted altogether a week and ended—as I will tell you.

"She was exactly like a child. She wanted to be with me always. She tried to follow me everywhere, and it went to my heart to tire her out upon my next exploration and leave her behind at last exhausted, and calling after me rather plaintively. But the problems of the world had to be mastered. I had not, I said to myself, come into the future to carry on a miniature flirtation. Yet her distress when I left her was very great, her expostulations at the parting sometimes frantic, and I think altogether I had as much trouble as comfort from her affection. And yet she was, somehow, a very great comfort.

expostulations: Objections. Weena begged him not to leave her.

"I thought it was mere childish affection that made her cling to me. Until it was too late, I did not clearly know what I had inflicted upon her when I left her. Nor, until it was too late, did I clearly understand what she was to me. For the little doll of a creature, by merely seeming fond of me and showing in her weak futile way that she cared for me, presently gave my return to the neighborhood of the white sphinx, almost the feeling of coming home. I would watch for her little figure of white and gold so soon as I came over the hill.

"It was from her, too, that I learned that fear had not altogether left the world. She was fearless enough in the daylight, and she had the oddest confidence in me—for once in a foolish moment I made threatening grimaces at her, and she simply laughed at them. But she dreaded the dark, dreaded shadows, dreaded black things. Darkness to her was the one fearful thing. It was a singularly passionate dread, and it set me thinking and observing. I discovered then, among other things, that these little people gathered into the great houses after dark, and slept a number together. To enter upon them without a light was to put them into a tumult of apprehension. I never found one out of doors or one sleeping alone within doors after dark.

"Yet I was still such a blockhead that I missed the lesson of that fear, and in spite of Weena's evident distress insisted upon sleeping away from these slumbering heaps of humanity. It troubled her greatly, but usually her odd affection for me triumphed, and for five of the nights of our acquaintance, including the last night of all, she slept with her head pillowed beside mine. But my story slips away from me as I speak of her.

"It must have been on the night before I rescued Weena that I woke up about dawn. I had been restless, dreaming most disagreeably that I was drowned and that sea anemones were feeling over my face with their soft palps. I awoke with a start, and with an odd fancy that some grayish animal had just rushed out of the chamber in which I slept.

"I tried to get to sleep again, but I felt restless and uncomfortable. It was that dim gray hour when things are just creeping out of the darkness, when everything is colorless and clear cut and yet unreal. I got up and went down into the great hall and out upon the flagstones in front of the palace. I thought I would make a virtue of necessity and see the sunrise.

"The moon was setting, and the dying moonlight and first pallor of dawn mingled together in a ghastly half-light. The bushes were inky black, the ground a somber gray, the sky colorless and cheerless. And up the hill slope I thought I saw

51

ghosts. Several times as I scanned the slope I saw white figures. Twice I fancied I saw a solitary white ape-like creature running rather quickly up the hill, and once near the ruins I saw a group of two carrying some dark body. They moved hastily. I did not see what became of them. It seemed that they vanished among the bushes.

"The dawn was still indistinct, you must understand. I was feeling that chill, uncertain, early morning feeling you may have experienced. I doubted my eyes. As the eastern sky grew brighter, and the light of the day increased, and vivid coloring came back to the world once more, I scanned the view keenly, but I saw no confirmation of my white figures. They were mere creatures of the half light.

" 'They must have been ghosts,' said I; 'I wonder whence they dated.'

"For a queer notion of Grant Allen's came into my head and amused me. If each generation dies and leaves ghosts, he argues, the world at last will get overcrowded with them. On that theory they would have become very thick in eight hundred thousand years from now, and it was no great wonder to see four all at once. But the jest was unsatisfactory, and I was thinking of these figures all the morning until the rescue of Weena drove the subject out of my head. I associated them in some indefinite way with the white animal I had startled in my first passionate search for the Time Machine. But Weena was a pleasant substitute for such a topic.

"These ghostly shapes were soon destined to take possession of my mind in a far more vivid fashion. I think I have said how much hotter than our own was the weather of this future age. I cannot account for it. It may be the sun was hotter, or else the earth was nearer the sun. It is usual to assume that the sun will go on cooling steadily in the future, but people unfamiliar with such speculations as those of the younger Darwin, forget that the planets must ultimately, one by one, fall back into the parent body. As these catastrophies occur the sun will blaze out again with renewed energy. It may be that some inner planet had suffered this fate. Whatever the reason, the fact remains that the sun was very much hotter than it is now.

"It was one very hot morning, my fourth morning, I think, as I was seeking a refuge from the heat and glare in a colossal ruin near the great house where I sheltered, that this remarkable incident occurred. Clambering among these heaps of masonry, I

younger Darwin: Sir George Howard Darwin, well-known astronomer, son of Charles Robert Darwin.

found a long narrow gallery, the end and side windows of which were blocked by fallen masses of masonry and which by contrast with the brilliance outside seemed at first impenetrably dark to me.

"I entered it groping, for the change from light to blackness made spots of color swim before me. Suddenly I halted spell-bound. A pair of eyes, luminous by reflection against the daylight without, was watching me out of the obscurity!

"The old instinctive dread of wild animals came upon me. I clenched my hands and steadfastly looked into the glaring eyeballs. I feared to turn. Then the thought of the absolute security in which humanity appeared to be living came to my mind. Then I remembered that strange dread of the dark.

"Overcoming my fear to some extent, I advanced a step, and spoke. I will admit that my voice was hoarse and ill controlled. I put out my hand, and touched something soft.

"At once the eyes darted sideways, and something white ran past me. I turned, with my heart in my mouth, and saw a queer little ape-like figure, with the head held down in a peculiar manner, running across the sunlit space behind me. It blundered against a block of granite, staggered aside, and in a moment was hidden in a black shadow beneath another pile of ruined masonry.

"My impression of it was of course very imperfect. It was of a dull white color, and had strange, large, grayish-red eyes. There was some flaxen hair on its head and down its back. But, as I say, it went too fast for me to see distinctly. I cannot even say whether it ran on all fours, or only with its fore arms held very low.

"After a momentary hesitation I followed the creature into the second heap of ruins. I could not find it there at first, but after a time, in the profound obscurity I came upon one of those round, well-like openings, of which I have told you, half closed by a fallen pillar. A sudden thought came to me. Could the thing have vanished down the shaft? I lit a match, and, looking down, saw a small white moving figure, with large bright eyes, that regarded me steadfastly as it retreated.

"The thing made me shudder. It was so like a human spider. It was clambering down the wall of the shaft, and now I noticed for the first time a number of metal projections for foot and hand, forming a kind of ladder down.

"Suddenly the light burned my fingers and fell out of my

portentous: Ominous.

nocturnal: Active at night.

apertures: Openings, holes.

hand, going out as it dropped; and when I had lit another, the little monster had disappeared.

"I do not know how long I sat peering down the portentous well. Very slowly could I persuade myself that the thing I had seen was a man. But gradually the real truth dawned upon me; that man had not remained one species, but had differentiated into two distinct animals; that my graceful children of the upperworld were not the only descendants of the men of my generation, but that this bleached, nocturnal thing that had flashed before me, was also heir to our age.

"I thought of the flickering pillars, and of my theory of an underground ventilation. I began to suspect their true import.

"But what was this creature doing in my scheme of a perfectly balanced organization? How was it related to the indolent serenity of the beautiful overworld people? And what was hidden down below there? I sat upon the edge of the well, telling myself I had nothing to fear in descending, and that there I must go for the solution of my difficulties, and withal I was absolutely afraid to go down.

"As I hesitated, two of the beautiful upperworld people came running in their amorous sport, across the daylight into the shadow. One pursued the other, flinging flowers at her as he ran. They seemed disappointed when they found me with my arm against the overturned pillar, peering down the well. Apparently, it was considered bad form to notice these apertures, for when I pointed to it, and tried to frame a question about it in their tongue, they seemed distressed, and turned away. They were, however, interested by my matches, and I struck several to amuse them.

"However, all my attempts to woo them toward the subject I wanted failed; and presently I left them. I resolved to go back to Weena, and see what I could get from her.

"But my mind was already in revolution, my guesses and impressions slipping and sliding to a new adjustment. I had now the clew to these wells, to the ventilating towers, to the problem of the ghosts, and a hint, indeed, of the meaning of the bronze gates and the fate of the Time Machine. Vaguely indeed, there came a suggestion toward the economic problem that had puzzled me.

"Here was the new view: Evidently this second species of man was subterranean. There were three circumstances in

54

particular that made me think its rare emergence upon the surface was the outcome of long subterraneous habit. In the first place, the bleached appearance, common in most animals that live largely in the dark—the white fish of the Kentucky caves, for instance. Then the large eyes and their capacity for reflecting the light—a common feature of nocturnal eyes, witness the owl and the cat. And finally the evident confusion in the sunlight, the hasty flight toward dark shadow, and the carriage of the head while in the light, re-enforced the idea of an extremely sensitive retina.

"Beneath my feet, then, the earth must be tunneled out to an enormous extent, and in these caverns the new race lived. The presence of ventilating shafts and wells all along the hill slopes—everywhere, in fact, except along the river valley— showed how universally the ramifications of the underworld extended.

"And it was natural to assume that it was in the underworld that the necessary work of the overworld was performed. This was so plausible that I accepted it unhesitatingly. From that I went on to assume how the splitting of the human species came about. I dare say you will anticipate what shape my theory took, though I soon felt it was still short of the truth of the case.

"But at first, starting from the problems of our own age, it seemed as clear as daylight to me that the gradual widening of the present merely temporary and social difference of the capitalist from the laborer was the key to the explanation. No doubt it will seem grotesque enough to you and wildly incredible, and yet even now there are circumstances that point in the way things have gone. There is a tendency plainly enough to utilize underground space for the less ornamental purposes of civilization; there is the Metropolitan Railway in London, for instance, and all these new electric railways; there are subways, and underground workrooms, restaurants, and so forth. Evidently, I thought, this tendency had increased until industry had gradually lost sight of the day, going into larger and larger underground factories, in which the workers would spend an increasing amount of their time. Even now, an East End worker lives in such artificial conditions as practically to be cut off from the natural surface of the earth and the clear sky altogether.

ramifications: Offshoots. The underworld caverns seemed to spread everywhere.

social stratification: Arrangement of social classes.

etiolated: Bleached from lack of sun.

Cicerone: A guide, usually one who shows the antiquities or curiosities of a place to strangers.

"Then again, the exclusive tendency of richer people, due, no doubt, to the increasing refinement of their education and the widening gulf between them and the rude violence of the poor, is already leading to the closing of considerable portions of the surface of the country against these latter. About London, for instance, perhaps half the prettier country is shut up from such intrusion. And the same widening gulf, due to the length and expense of the higher educational process and the increased facilities for, and temptation toward, forming refined habits among the rich, will make that frequent exchange between class and class, that promotion and intermarriage which at present retards the splitting of our species along the lines of social stratification, less and less frequent.

"So, in the end, you would have above ground the Haves, pursuing health, comfort, and beauty, and below ground the Have-nots, the workers, getting continually adapted to their labor. No doubt, once they were below ground, considerable rents would be charged for the ventilation of their caverns. Workers who struck work would starve or be suffocated for arrears of ventilator rent; workers who were so constituted as to be miserable and rebellious would die. In the end, if the balance was held permanent, the survivors would become as well adapted to the conditions of their subterranean life as the overworld people were to theirs, and as happy in their way. It seemed to me that the refined beauty of the overworld, and the etiolated pallor of the lower, followed naturally enough.

"The great triumph of humanity I had dreamed of now took a different shape in my mind. It had been no triumph of universal education and general co-operation, such as I had imagined at the first. Instead, I saw a real aristocracy, armed with a perfected science and working out to a logical conclusion the industrial system of to-day. The triumph of the overworld humanity had not been simply a triumph over nature, but a triumph over nature and their fellowmen.

"I must warn you this was my theory at the time. I had no convenient Cicerone on the pattern of the Utopian books. My explanation may be absolutely wrong. I still think it the most plausible one. But even on this supposition the balanced civilization that was at last attained must have long since passed its zenith, and was now far gone in decay. The too perfect security of the overworld had led these to a slow movement of degeneration at last—to a general dwindling of size, strength, and intelligence. That I already saw clearly enough, but what had happened to the lower world I did not yet suspect. Yet from what I had seen of the Morlocks,—that, by the by, was the name by which these creatures were called,—I could imagine the modification of the human type was far more profound in the underworld than among the Eloi, the beautiful race that I already knew.

"Then came some troublesome doubts. Why had the Morlocks taken my Time Machine? For I felt sure these under-people had taken it. Why, too, if the Eloi were masters, could they not restore the thing to me? And why were the Eloi so afraid of the dark?

"I determined, as I have said, to question Weena about this underworld, but here again I was disappointed. At first she would not understand my questions, and then she refused to answer. She shivered as though the topic was unendurable. And when I pressed her, perhaps a little harshly, she burst into tears.

"They were the only tears I ever saw in that future age, except my own. When I saw them I ceased abruptly to trouble about the Morlocks, and was only concerned in driving these signs of her human inheritance out of her eyes again. And presently she was smiling and clapping her hands while I solemnly burnt a match.

I snatched at my matches and hastily striking one saw three grotesque white creatures....

8

THE MORLOCKS

spirit: Alcohol.

It may seem odd to you, but it was two days before I could follow up the clew of these Morlocks in what was manifestly the proper way, and descend into the well. I felt a peculiar shrinking from their pallid bodies. They were just the half-bleached color of the worms and things one sees preserved in spirit in a zoological museum. And they were cold to the touch. Probably my shrinking was largely due to the sympathetic influence of the Eloi, whose disgust of the Morlocks I now began to appreciate.

"The next night I did not sleep very well. Possibly my health was a little disordered. I was oppressed with doubt and perplexity. Once or twice I had a feeling of intense fear for which I could perceive no definite reason. I remember creeping noiselessly into the great hall where the little people were sleeping in the moonlight—that night it was that Weena was among them—and feeling reassured by their presence. It occurred to me even then that when in the course of a few days the moon passed through its last quarter and the nights became dark, the appearance of these unpleasant creatures from below, these whitened Lemurs, these new vermin that had replaced the old, might be more abundant.

"On both these days I had the restless feeling of one who shirks an inevitable duty. I felt assured that the Time Machine was only to be recovered by boldly penetrating these subterranean mysteries. Yet I could not face it. If I had only had a companion it would have been different. But I was so horribly alone, and even to clamber down into the darkness of the well appalled me.

"I don't know if you will understand my feeling, but I never felt quite safe at my back.

"It was this restless feeling, perhaps, that drove me further than I had hitherto gone in my exploring expeditions. Going to the southwestward toward the rising country that is now called Combe Wood, I observed far off, in the direction of nineteenth century Banstead, a vast green pile, of a different character from any I had hitherto seen. It was larger than even the largest of the palaces or ruins I knew, and the facade appeared to me Oriental in its character. The face of it had the luster as well as the pale green tint, a kind of bluish green, of a certain type of Chinese porcelain. The difference in appearance in the building suggested a difference in its use. I was minded to push on and explore it. But the day was growing late and I had come upon the sight of the place after a long and tiring circuit. I resolved to postpone this examination for the following day, and returned to the welcome and caresses of little Weena.

"But the next morning I was in a mood of remorse for my hesitation in descending the well and facing the Morlocks in their caverns. I perceived my curiosity regarding this great pile of Green Porcelain was a mere self-deception to shirk the experience I dreaded by another day. I resolved I would make

Lemurs: Furry, nocturnal animals resembling monkeys, but with longer, sharper noses.

facade: The face or front of a building.

the descent without further waste of time, and started out in the early morning toward a well near the ruins of granite and aluminum.

"Little Weena ran by my side. She followed me to the well dancing, but when she saw me lean over the mouth and look downward, she seemed strangely disconcerted.

" 'Good-by, little Weena,' said I, kissing her, and then putting her down I began to feel over the parapet for the climbing hooks—rather hastily, for I feared my courage might leak away.

"At first Weena watched me in amazement, and then she gave a most piteous cry, and running to me began to pull at me with her little hands. I think her opposition nerved me rather to proceed. I shook her off, perhaps a little roughly, and in another moment I was in the throat of the well.

"I saw her agonized face over the parapet, and smiled to reassure her. Then I had to look down at the unstable hooks by which I hung.

"I had to clamber down a shaft of perhaps two hundred yards. The descent was effected by means of metallic bars projecting from the sides of the well, and since they were adapted to the needs of a creature much smaller and lighter than myself, I was speedily cramped and fatigued by the descent. And not simply fatigued. My weight suddenly bent one of the hooks and almost swung me off it down into the blackness beneath.

"For a moment I hung by one hand, and after that experience I did not dare to rest again, and though my arms and back were presently acutely painful, I continued to clamber with as quick a motion as possible down the sheer descent. Glancing upward I saw the aperture, a mere small blue disk above me, in which a star was visible, and little Weena's head appeared as a round black projection. The thudding sound of some machine below me grew louder and more oppressive. Everything save that minute circle above was profoundly dark. When I looked up again Weena had disappeared.

"I was in an agony of discomfort. I had some thought of trying to go up the shaft again, and leave the underworld alone. But while I turned this over in my mind I continued to descend.

"It was with intense relief that I saw dimly coming up a foot to the right of me, a slender loophole in the wall of the shaft, and swinging myself in, found it was the aperture of a narrow horizontal tunnel in which I could lie down and rest.

"It was not too soon. My arms ached, my back was cramped, and I was trembling with the prolonged fear of falling. Besides this, the unbroken darkness had had a distressing effect upon my eyes. The air was full of the throbbing and hum of the machinery that pumped the air down the shaft.

"I do not know how long I lay in that tunnel. I was roused by a soft hand touching my face. Starting up in the darkness, I snatched at my matches and hastily striking one saw three grotesque, white creatures, similar to the one I had seen above ground in the ruin, hastily retreating before the light. Living as they did in what appeared to me impenetrable darkness, their eyes were abnormally large and sensitive, just as are the eyes of the abyssmal fishes or of any purely nocturnal creatures, and they reflected the light in the same way. I have no doubt they could see me in that rayless obscurity, and they did not seem to have any fear of me apart from the light. But so soon as I struck a match in order to see them, they fled incontinently, vanishing up dark gutters and tunnels from which their eyes glared at me in the strangest fashion.

abyssmal: (abyssal) Of the ocean depths; of the bottom of the sea.

"I tried to call to them, but what language they had was apparently a different one from that of the overworld people. So that I was needs left to my own unaided exploration. The thought of flight rather than exploration was even at that time in my mind.

needs: Here, necessarily.

" 'You are in for it now,' said I to myself, and went on.

"Feeling my way along this tunnel of mine, the confused noise of machinery grew louder, and presently the walls fell away from me and I came to a large open space, and striking another match saw I had entered a vast arched cavern extending into darkness, at last, beyond the range of my light.

"The view I had of this cavern was as much as one could see in the burning of a match. Necessarily my memory of it is very vague. Great shapes like big machines rose out of the dim and threw grotesque black shadows, in which the spectral Morlocks sheltered from the glare. The place, by the by, was very stuffy and oppressive, and the faint *halitus* of freshly shed blood was in the air. Some way down the central vista was a little table of white metal upon which a meal seemed to be spread. The Morlocks at any rate were carnivorous. Even at the time I remember thinking what large animal could have survived to furnish the red joint I saw. It was all very indistinct, the heavy

spectral: Ghostly.

halitus: A Latin word meaning breath; here, odor or smell.

61

smell, the big unmeaning shapes, the white figures lurking in the shadows, and only waiting for the darkness to come at me again. Then the match burned down and stung my fingers and fell, a wriggling red spot in the black.

"I have thought since how particularly ill equipped I was. When I had started with the Time Machine I had started with the absurd assumption that the men of the future would certainly be infinitely in front of us in all their appliances. I had come without arms, without medicine, without anything to smoke,—at times I missed tobacco frightfully,—even without enough matches. If I had only thought of a kodak! I could have flashed that glimpse of the underworld in a second and examined it at leisure. But as it was, I stood there with only the weapons and powers that Nature had endowed me with—hands, feet, and teeth—except four safety matches that still remained to me.

"I was afraid to push my way in among all this machinery in the dark, and it was only with my last glimpse of light I discovered that my store of matches had run low. It had never occurred to me until that moment that there was any need to economize them, and I had wasted almost half of the box in astonishing the aboveground people, to whom fire was a novelty. As I say, I had four left.

"Then while I stood in the dark a hand touched mine; then some lank fingers came feeling over my face. I was sensible of a dull, unpleasant odor. I fancy I detected the breathing of a number of those little beings about me. I felt the box of matches in my hand being gently disengaged, and other hands behind me plucking at my clothing.

"The sense of these unseen creatures examining me was indescribably unpleasant. The sudden realization of my ignorance of their ways of thinking and possible actions came home to me very vividly in the darkness. I shouted at them as loudly as I could. They started away from me, and then I could feel them approaching me again. They clutched at me more boldly, whispering odd sounds to each other. I shivered violently and shouted again, rather discordantly. This time they were not so seriously alarmed and made a queer laughing noise as they came toward me again.

"I will confess I was horribly frightened. I determined to strike another match and escape under its glare. Eking it out with a scrap of paper from my pocket, I made good my retreat

discordantly: Harshly.

Eking: Increasing. Actually, he prolonged the life of the light from the match by lighting a scrap of paper.

to the narrow tunnel. But hardly had I entered this when my light was blown out, and I could hear them in the blackness rustling like wind among leaves and pattering like the rain, as they hurried after me.

"In a moment I was clutched by several hands again, and there was no mistake now that they were trying to draw me back. I struck another light and waved it in their dazzled faces. You can scarcely imagine how nauseatingly inhuman those pale, chinless faces and great lidless, pinkish-gray eyes seemed, as they stared stupidly, evidently blinded by the light.

"So I gained time and retreated again, and when my second match had ended struck my third. That had almost burned through as I reached the opening of the tunnel upon the well. I lay down on the edge, for the throbbing whirl of the air-pumping machine below made me giddy, and felt sideways for the projecting hooks. As I did so my feet were grasped from behind and I was violently tugged backward. I lit my last match—and it incontinently went out. But I had my hand on the climbing bars now, and kicking violently disengaged myself from the clutches of the Morlocks, and was speedily clambering up the shaft again.

"They remained peering and blinking up the shaft, except one little wretch who followed me for some way, and indeed well-nigh captured my boot as a trophy.

"That upward climb seemed unending. While I still had the last twenty or thirty feet of it above me, a deadly nausea came upon me. I had the greatest difficulty in keeping my hold. The last few yards was a frightful struggle against this faintness. Several times my head swam and I felt all the sensations of falling.

"At last I got over the well mouth somehow and staggered out of the ruin into the blinding sunlight. I fell upon my face. Even the soil seemed sweet and clean.

"Then I remember Weena kissing my hands and ears, and the voices of others of the Eloi. Then probably I was insensible for a time.

Then the tall pinnacles of the Palace of Green Porcelain, and the polished gleam of it's walls, came back to my memory, and in the evening, taking Weena like a child on my shoulders...

9
WHEN THE NIGHT CAME

malign: Evil, wicked.

Now, indeed, I seemed to be in a worse case than before. Hitherto, except during my night's anguish at the loss of the Time Machine, I had felt a sustaining hope of ultimate escape, but my hope was staggered by these new discoveries. Hitherto, I had merely thought myself impeded by the childish simplicity of the little people and by some unknown forces which I had only to understand in order to overcome. But there was an altogether new element in the sickening quality of the Morlocks, something inhuman and malign. Instinctively I loathed them. Before, I had felt as a man might feel who had fallen into a pit; my concern was with the pit and how to get out again. But now I felt like a beast in a trap, whose enemy would presently come.

"The enemy I dreaded may surprise you. It was the darkness of the new moon. Weena had put this into my head by some, at first, incomprehensible remarks about the Dark Nights. It was not now such a very difficult problem to guess what the coming Dark Nights might mean. The moon was on the wane; each night there was a longer interval of darkness. And I now understood, to some slight degree, at least, the reason of the fear of the little upperworld people for the dark. I wondered vaguely what foul villany it might be that the Morlocks did under the darkness of the new moon.

"Whatever the origin of the existing conditions, I felt pretty sure now that my second hypothesis was all wrong. The upperworld people might once have been the favored aristocracy of the world, and the Morlocks their mechanical servants, but that state of affairs had passed away long since. The two species that had resulted from the evolution of man were sliding down toward, or had already arrived at, an altogether new relationship. The Eloi, like the Carlovingian kings, had decayed to a mere beautiful futility. They still possessed the earth on sufferance, since the Morlocks, subterranean for innumerable generations, had come at last to find the daylit surface unendurable. And the Morlocks made their garments, I inferred, and maintained them in their habitual need, perhaps through the survival of an old habit of service. They did it, as a standing horse paws with his foot, or as a man enjoys killing animals in sport—because ancient and departed necessities had impressed it on the organism. But clearly the old order was already in part reversed. The Nemesis of the delicate ones was creeping on apace. Ages ago, thousands of generations ago, man had thrust his brother man out of the ease and sunlight of life. And now that brother was coming back—changed. Already the Eloi had begun to learn one old lesson anew. They were becoming acquainted again with Fear.

"Then suddenly came into my head the memory of the meat I had seen in the underworld. It seemed odd how this memory floated into my mind, not stirred up, as it were, by the current of my meditations, but coming in almost like a question from outside. I tried to recall the form of it. I had a vague sense of something familiar, but at that time I could not tell what it was.

"Still, however helpless the little people might be in the presence of their mysterious Fear, I was differently constituted. I came out of this age of ours, this ripe prime of the human

hypothesis: Supposition. What he had supposed concerning the Morlocks and the Eloi could not be true.

inferred: Deduced, reasoned.

Nemesis: Just punishment.

race, when fear does not paralyze and mystery has lost its terrors. I at least would defend myself. Without further delay I determined to make myself arms and a fastness where I might sleep with some security. From that refuge as a base I could face the strange world with some confidence again, a confidence I had lost now that I realized to what uncanny creatures I nightly lay exposed. I felt I could never sleep again until my bed was secure from them. I shuddered with horror to think how they must already have examined me during my sleep.

"I wandered during the afternoon along the valley of the Thames, but found nothing that commended itself to my mind as a sufficiently inaccessible retiring place. All the buildings and trees seemed easily practicable to such dexterous climbers as the Morlocks—to judge by their wells—must be. Then the tall pinnacles of the Palace of Green Porcelain, and the polished gleam of its walls, came back to my memory, and in the evening, taking Weena like a child upon my shoulder, I went up the hills toward the southwest.

"Now the distance I had reckoned was seven or eight miles, but it must have been nearer eighteen. I had first seen the Palace on a moist afternoon when distances are deceptively diminished. In addition, the heel of one of my shoes was loose, and a nail was working through the sole,—they were comfortable old shoes I wear about indoors,—so that I was lame. It was already long past sunset before I came in sight of the Palace, standing out in black silhouette against the pale yellow of the sky.

"Weena had been hugely delighted when first I carried her, but after a time she desired me to let her down and ran along by the side of me, occasionally darting off on either hand to pick flowers to stick in my pockets. My pockets had always puzzled Weena, but at the last she had concluded they were an eccentric kind of vase for floral decoration. At least she utilized them for that purpose.

"And that reminds me! As I changed my jacket I found—"

(The Time Traveler paused, put his hand into his pocket, and silently placed two withered flowers, not unlike very large white mallows, upon the little table. Then he resumed his narrative.)

"As the hush of evening crept over the world and we proceeded over the hill-crest toward Wimbledon, Weena became tired and wanted to return to the house of gray stone. But I pointed out the distant pinnacles of the Palace of Green

inaccessible: Hard to reach or enter.
dexterous: Nimble, agile; quick and light movement of the limbs and body.

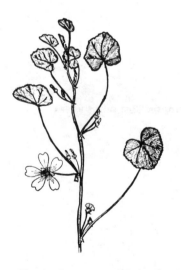

mallows: Common wild plants with hairy stems and large flowers.

66

Porcelain to her, and contrived to make her understand that we were seeking a refuge there from her Fear.

"You know that great pause that comes upon things before the dusk. Even the breeze stops in the trees. There is to me always an air of expectation about that evening stillness. The sky was clear, remote, and empty, save for a few horizontal bars far down in the sunset.

"That night the expectation took the color of my fears. In the darkling calm my senses seemed preternaturally sharpened. I fancied I could even feel the hollowness of the ground beneath my feet, could indeed almost see through it, the Morlocks in their ant-hill going hither and thither and waiting for the dark. In this excited state I fancied that they would take my invasion of their burrows as a declaration of war. And why had they taken my Time Machine?

"So we went on in the quiet, and the twilight deepened into night. The clear blue of the distance faded and one star after another came out. The ground grew dim and the trees black. Weena's fears and her fatigue grew upon her. I took her in my arms and talked to her and caressed her. Then as the darkness grew profounder she put her arms round my neck, and closing her eyes tightly pressed her face against my shoulder.

"We went down a long slope into a valley, and there in the dimness I almost walked into a little river. This I waded, and went up the opposite side of the valley, past a number of sleeping houses, and by a statue that appeared to me in the indistinct light to represent a faun, or some such figure, minus the head. Here, too, were acacias. So far, I had seen nothing of the Morlocks, but it was yet early in the night, and the darker hours before the old moon rose were still to come.

"From the brow of the next hill I saw a thick wood spreading wide and black before me. At this I hesitated. I could see no end to it either to the right or to the left. Feeling tired,—my feet, in particular, were very sore,—I carefully lowered Weena from my shoulder as I halted, and sat down upon the turf. I could no longer see the Palace of Green Porcelain, and I was in doubt of my direction.

"I looked into the thickness of the wood, and thought of what it might hide. Under that dense tangle of branches one would be out of sight of the stars. Even were there no other lurking danger there,—a danger I did not care to let my

preternaturally: More than naturally; out of the ordinary.

Branch of Acacia Tree

Constellations Ursa Major and Ursa Minor. See if you can find the Big Dipper and Little Dipper.

Milky Way: A great belt or galaxy, containing about 100,000 million stars, of which our sun is one.

Sirius: From the Greek word, Seirios, meaning "the scorcher." Serius is the brightest star in the heavens.

terrestrial: Earthly.

precessional cycle: The axis of the Earth is very gradually changing position; in fact, it is moving in a circular "wobble" which takes approximately 26,000 years to complete. This movement is called precession and affects the equinoxes—the times when the sun's center crosses the equator, making day and night of equal length and occurring twice a year. Eventually, the seasons will be reversed due to the precessional cycle.

imagination loose upon,—there would still be all the roots to stumble over, and the tree boles to strike myself against. I was very tired, too, after the excitements of the day, and I decided that I would not face it, but would pass the night upon the open hill.

"Weena, I was glad to discover, was fast asleep. I carefully wrapped her in my jacket, and sat down beside her to wait for the moonrise. The hillside upon which I sat was quiet and deserted, but from the black of the wood there came now and then a stir of living things.

"Above me shone the stars, for the night was clear. I felt a certain sense of friendly comfort in their twinkling. All the old constellations had gone from the sky, however, for that slow movement that is imperceptible in a dozen human lifetimes, had long ago rearranged them in unfamiliar groupings. But the Milky Way, it seemed to me, was still the same tattered streamer of star dust as of yore. Southward—as I judged it—was a very bright red star that was new to me. It was even more splendid than our own green Sirius. Amid all these scintillating points of light, one planet shone kindly and steadily like the face of an old friend.

"Looking at these stars suddenly dwarfed my own troubles and all the gravities of terrestrial life. I thought of their unfathomable distance, and the slow, inevitable drift of their movements out of the unknown past into the unknown future. I thought of the great precessional cycle that the pole of the earth describes in the heavens. Only forty times had that silent revolution occurred during all the years I had traversed. And during those few revolutions, all the activity, all the traditions, the carefully planned organizations, the nations, languages, literature, aspirations, even the mere memory of man as I knew man, had been swept out of existence. Instead were these frail creatures who had forgotten their high ancestry, and the white animals of which I went in fear. Then I thought of the great fear there was between these two species, and for the first time, with a sudden shiver, came the clear knowledge of what the meat I had seen might be. Yet it was too horrible! I looked at little Weena sleeping beside me, her face white and starlike under the stars, and forthwith dismissed the thought from my mind.

"Through that long night I kept my mind off the Morlocks as well as I could, and whiled away the time by trying to fancy I could find traces of the old constellations among the new confusion. The sky kept very clear, except a hazy cloud or so. No doubt I dozed at times. Then, as my vigil wore on, came a faintness in the eastward sky like the reflection of some colorless fire, and the old moon rose thin and peaked and white. And close behind and overtaking it and overflowing it the dawn came, pale at first and then growing pink and warm.

"No Morlocks had approached us. Indeed, I had seen none upon the hill that night. And in the confidence of renewed day it almost seemed to me that my fear had been unreasonable. I stood up, and found my foot with the loose heel swollen at the ankle and painful under the heel. I sat down again, took off my shoes, and flung them away.

"I awakened Weena, and forthwith we went down into the wood, now green and pleasant, instead of black and forbidding. And there we found some fruit wherewith to break our fast. We soon met others of the dainty ones, laughing and dancing in the sunlight, as though there was no such thing in nature as the night.

"Then I thought once more of the meat that I had seen. I felt assured now of what it was, and, from the bottom of my heart, I pitied this last feeble rill from the great flood of humanity. Clearly, somewhere in the long ages of human decay, the food of the Morlocks had run short. Possibly they had lived on rats and suchlike vermin. Even now, man is far less discriminating and exclusive in his food than he was, far less than any monkey. His prejudice against human flesh is no deep-seated instinct. And so these inhuman sons of men—

rill: Trickle; small stream or brook.

"I tried to look at the thing in a scientific spirit. After all, these were scarcely to be counted human beings; less human they were and more remote than our cannibal ancestors of three or four thousand years ago. And the minds that would have made this state torment were gone. Why should I trouble? The Eloi were mere fatted cattle, which the antlike Morlocks preserved and preyed upon, probably saw to the breeding of. And there was Weena dancing by my side!

"Then I tried to preserve myself from the horror that was coming upon me by regarding it as a rigorous punishment of human selfishness; man had been content to live in ease and delight upon the labors of his fellow-men; had taken Necessity as his watchword and excuse, and in fullness of time Necessity had come home to him. I tried even a Carlyle-like scorn of these wretched aristocrats in decline.

Carlyle-like scorn: Thomas Carlyle, 19th century Scottish essayist and historian, had a fanatic zeal for work and only scorn for the indolent and lazy which he forcefully presented in his essay, *Sartor Resartus* (The Tailor Re-tailored).

69

Battering-ram

"But this attitude of mind was impossible. However great their intellectual degradation, the Eloi had kept too much of the human form not to claim my sympathy, and to make me perforce a participant in their degradation and their Fear.

"I had at this time very vague ideas of what course I should pursue. My first idea was to secure some safe place of refuge for Weena and myself, and to make myself such arms of metal or stone as I could contrive. That necessity was immediate. In the next place, I hoped to procure some means of fire, so that I should have the weapon of a torch at hand, for nothing, I knew, would be more efficient against these Morlocks. Then I wanted to arrange some contrivance to break open the doors of bronze under the white sphinx. I had in mind a battering ram. I had a persuasion that if I could enter these doors and carry a blaze of light before me, I should discover the Time Machine and escape. I could not imagine the Morlocks were powerful enough to remove it far. Weena I had resolved to bring with me to our own Time.

"Turning such schemes over in my mind, I pursued our way toward the building which my fancy had chosen as our dwelling-place.

Then I perceived, standing strange and gaunt in the center of the hall what was clearly the skeleton of some huge animal.

his Palace of Green Porcelain, when we approached it about noon, was, I found, deserted and falling into ruin. Only ragged vestiges of glass remained in its windows, and great sheets of the green facing had fallen away in places from the corroded metallic framework. It lay very high upon a turfy down, and, looking northeastward before I entered it, I was surprised to see a large estuary, or an arm of the sea, where I judged Wandsworth and Battersea must once have been. I thought then—though I never followed the thought up—of what might have happened, or might be happening, to the living things in the sea.

10
THE PALACE OF GREEN PORCELAIN

Wandsworth and Battersea: Suburbs of London.

megatherium: A species of extinct giant animals, resembling the sloth.

Brontosaurus

Sea-urchin

"The material of the Palace proved, on examination, to be indeed porcelain, and above the face of it I saw an inscription in some unknown characters. I thought, rather foolishly, that Weena might help me to interpret this, but I only learned that the bare idea of writing had never entered her head. She always seemed to me, I fancy, more human than she was, perhaps because her affection was so human.

"Within the big valves of the door—which were open and broken—we found, instead of the customary hall, a long gallery lit by many side windows. Even at the first glance I was reminded of a museum. The tiled floor was thick with dust, and a remarkable array of miscellaneous objects were shrouded in the same gray covering. Clearly, the place had been derelict for a very considerable time.

"Then I perceived, standing strange and gaunt in the center of the hall, what was clearly the lower part of the skeleton of some huge animal. As I approached this I recognized by the oblique feet that it was some extinct creature after the fashion of the *megatherium*. The skull and the upper bones lay beside it in the thick dust, and in one place where rain water had dripped through some leak in the roof, the skeleton had decayed away. Further along the gallery was the huge skeleton barrel of a *brontosaurus*. My museum hypothesis was confirmed. Going toward the side of the gallery I found what appeared to be sloping shelves, and clearing away the thick dust, I found the old familiar glass cases of our own time. But these must have been air-tight to judge from the fair preservation of some of their contents.

"Clearly we stood among the ruins of some latter day South Kensington. Here apparently was the Palaeontological Section, and a very splendid array of fossils it must have been; though the inevitable process of decay that had been warded off for a time, and had, through the extinction of bacteria and fungi, lost ninety-nine-hundreths of its force, was nevertheless, with extreme sureness, if with extreme slowness, at work again upon all its treasures. Here and there I found traces of the little people in the shape of rare fossils broken to pieces or threaded in strings upon reeds. And the cases had in some instances been bodily removed—by the Morlocks, as I judged.

"The place was very silent. The thick dust deadened our footsteps. Weena, who had been rolling a sea urchin down the sloping glass of a case, presently came, as I stared about me, and very quietly took my hand and stood beside me.

"At first I was so much surprised by this ancient monument of an intellectual age that I gave no thought to the possibilities it presented me. Even my preoccupation about the Time Machine and the Morlocks receded a little from my mind. The curiosity concerning human destiny that had led to my time traveling was removed. Now, judging from the size of the place, this Palace of Green Porcelain had a great deal more in it than a gallery of palaeontology; possibly historical galleries, it might be even a library. To me, at least in my present circumstances, these would be vastly more interesting than this spectacle of old-time geology in decay.

"Exploring, I found another short gallery running transversely to the first. This appeared to be devoted to minerals, and the sight of a block of sulphur set my mind running on gunpowder. But I could find no saltpeter; indeed no nitrates of any kind. Doubtless they had deliquesced ages ago. Yet the sulphur hung in my mind and set up a train of thinking. As for the rest of the contents of that place, though on the whole they were the best preserved of all I saw—I had little interest. I am no specialist in mineralogy, and I soon went on down a very ruinous aisle running parallel to the first hall I had entered.

"Apparently this section had been devoted to Natural History, but here everything had long since passed out of recognition. A few shriveled vestiges of what had once been stuffed animals, dried-up mummies in jars that had once held spirit, a brown dust of departed plants, that was all. I was sorry for this, because I should have been glad to trace the patient readjustments by which the conquest of animated nature had been attained.

"From this we come to a gallery of simply colossal proportions, but singularly ill lit, and with its floor running downward at a slight angle from the end at which I entered it. At intervals there hung white globes from the ceiling,—many of them cracked and smashed,—which suggested that originally the place had been artificially lit. Here I was more in my element, for I found rising on either side of me the huge bulks of big machines, all greatly corroded, and many broken down, but some still fairly complete in all their parts. You know I have a certain weakness for mechanism, and I was inclined to linger

deliquesced: Melted away or disappeared due to decay.

mineralogy: The scientific study of minerals.

73

among these, the more so since for the most part they had the interest of puzzles, and I could make only the vaguest guesses of what they were for. I fancied if I could solve these puzzles I should find myself in the possession of powers that might be of use against the Morlocks.

"Suddenly Weena came very close to my side, so suddenly that she startled me.

"Had it not been for her I do not think I should have noticed that the floor of the gallery sloped at all. The end I had entered was quite above ground, and was lit by rare slit-like windows. As one went down the length of the place, the ground came up against these windows, until there was at last a pit like the 'area' of a London house, before each, and only a narrow line of daylight at the top. I went slowly along, puzzling about the machines, and had been too intent upon them to notice the gradual diminution of the light, until Weena's increasing apprehension attracted my attention.

"Then I saw that the gallery ran down at last into a thick darkness. I hesitated about proceeding, and then as I looked around me, I saw that the dust was here less abundant and its surface less even. Further away toward the dim, it appeared to be broken by a number of small narrow footprints. At that my sense of the immediate presence of the Morlocks revived. I felt that I was wasting my time in my academic examination of this machinery. I called to mind that it was already far advanced in the afternoon, and that I had still no weapon, no refuge, and no means of making a fire. And then, down in the remote black of the gallery, I heard a peculiar pattering and those same odd noises I had heard down the well.

"I took Weena's hand. Then struck with a sudden idea, I left her, and turned to a machine from which projected a lever not unlike those in a signal box. Clambering upon the stand of the machine and grasping this lever in my hands, I put all my weight upon it sideways. Weena, deserted in the central aisle, began suddenly to whimper. I had judged the strength of the lever pretty correctly, for it snapped after a minute's strain, and I rejoined Weena with a mace in my hand more than sufficient, I judged, for any Morlock skull I might encounter.

"And I longed very much to kill a Morlock or so. Very inhuman, you may think, to want to go killing one's own descendants, but it was impossible somehow to feel any humanity in the things. Only my disinclination to leave Weena, and a

academic: Detailed, as a scholar might examine an object in his field of study.

mace: A heavy club with a metal head, often spiked, used extensively during the Middle Ages.

persuasion that if I began to slake my thirst for murder my Time Machine might suffer, restrained me from going straight down the gallery and killing the brutes I heard there.

"Mace in one hand and Weena in the other we went out of that gallery and into another still larger, which at the first glance reminded me of a military chapel hung with tattered flags. The brown and charred rags that hung from the sides of it, I presently recognized as the decaying vestiges of books. They had long since dropped to pieces and every semblance of print had left them. But here and there were warped and cracked boards and metallic clasps that told the tale well enough.

"Had I been a literary man I might perhaps have moralized upon the futility of all ambition, but as it was, the thought that struck me with keenest force, was the enormous waste of labor rather than of hope, to which this somber gallery of rotting paper testified. At the time I will confess, though it seems a petty trait now, that I thought chiefly of the Philosophical Transactions, and my own seventeen papers upon physical optics.

"Then going up a broad staircase we came to what may once have been a gallery of technical chemistry. And here I had not a little hope of discovering something to help me. Except at one end where the roof had collapsed, this gallery was well preserved. I went eagerly to every unbroken case. And at last, in one of the really air-tight cases, I found a box of matches. Very eagerly I tried them. They were perfectly good. They were not even damp.

"At that discovery I suddenly turned to Weena. 'Dance!' I cried to her in her own tongue. For now I had a weapon indeed against the horrible creatures we feared. And so in that derelict museum, upon the thick soft coating of dust, to Weena's huge delight, I solemnly performed a sort of composite dance, whistling 'The Land of the Leal' as cheerfully as I could. In part it was a modest cancan, in part a step dance, in part a skirt dance,—so far as my tail coat permitted,—and in part original. For naturally I am inventive, as you know.

"Now, I still think that for this box of matches to have escaped the wear of time for immemorial years was a strange, and for me, a most fortunate thing. Yet oddly enough I found here a far more unlikely substance, and that was camphor. I found it in a sealed jar, that, by chance, I supposed had been really hermetically sealed. I fancied at first the stuff was

THE PALACE OF GREEN PORCELAIN

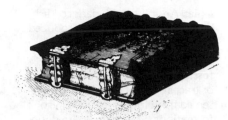

Metallic Clasps

Philosophical Transactions: Scientific writings or records. The Time Traveler could see his own work in the same state of deterioration—a discouraging thought.

hermetically: Sealed so as to be air-tight; possibly, vacuum sealed.

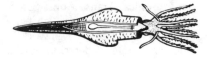
paraffin wax, and smashed the jar accordingly. But the odor of camphor was unmistakable. It struck me as singularly odd, that among the universal decay, this volatile substance had chanced to survive, perhaps through many thousand years. It reminded me of a sepia painting I had once seen done from the ink of a fossil Belemnite that must have perished and become fossilized millions of years ago. I was about to throw this camphor on one side, and then remembering that it was inflammable and burnt with a good bright flame, I put it into my pocket.

"I found no explosives, however, or any means of breaking down the bronze doors. As yet my iron crowbar was the most hopeful thing I had chanced upon. Nevertheless I left that gallery greatly elated by my discoveries.

"I cannot tell you the whole story of my exploration through that long afternoon. It would require a great effort of memory to recall it at all in the proper order. I remember a long gallery containing the rusting stands of arms of all ages, and that I hesitated between my crowbar and a hatchet or a sword. I could not carry both, however, and my bar of iron, after all, promised best against the bronze gates. There were rusty guns, pistols, and rifles here; most of them were masses of rust, but many of aluminum, and still fairly sound. But any cartridges or powder there may have been had rotted into dust. One corner I saw was charred and shattered; perhaps, I thought, by an explosion among the specimens there. In another place was a vast array of idols—Polynesian, Mexican, Grecian, Phoenician, every country on earth, I should think. And here, yielding to an irresistible impulse, I wrote my name upon the nose of a steatite monster from South America that particularly took my fancy.

"As the evening drew on my interest waned. I went through gallery after gallery, dusty, silent, often ruinous, the exhibits sometimes mere heaps of rust and lignite, sometimes fresher. In one place I suddenly found myself near a model of a tin mine, and then by the merest accident I discovered in an air-tight case two dynamite cartridges; I shouted 'Eureka!' and smashed the case joyfully. Then came a doubt. I hesitated, and then selecting a little side gallery I made my essay. I never felt such a bitter disappointment as I did then, waiting five, ten, fifteen minutes for the explosion that never came. Of course the things were dummies, as I might have guessed from their presence there. I really believe had they not been so, I should have rushed off incontinently there and then, and blown sphinx, bronze doors, and, as it proved, my chances of finding the Time Machine all together into non-existence.

"It was after that, I think, that we came to a little open court within the palace, turfed and with three fruit trees. There it was we rested and refreshed ourselves.

"Toward sunset I began to consider our position. Night was now creeping upon us and my inaccessible hiding-place was still to be found. But that troubled me very little now. I had in my possession a thing that was perhaps the best of all defenses against the Morlocks. I had matches again. I also had the camphor in my pocket if a blaze were required. It seemed to me that the best thing we could do would be to pass the night in the open again, protected by a fire.

"In the morning there was the Time Machine to obtain. Toward that as yet I had only my iron mace. But now with my growing knowledge I felt very differently toward the bronze doors than I had done hitherto. Up to this I had refrained from forcing them, largely because of the mystery on the other side. They had never impressed me as being very strong, and I hoped to find my bar of iron not altogether inadequate for the work.

THE PALACE
OF GREEN
PORCELAIN

Now, upon the scrubby hill upon the edge of this, Weena would have stopped, fearing the darkness before us.

11
IN THE DARKNESS OF THE FOREST

We emerged from the Palace of Green Porcelain while the sun was still in part above the horizon. I was determined to reach the white sphinx early the next morning, and I proposed before the dusk came to push through the woods that had stopped me on the previous journey. My plan was to go as far as possible that night, and then, building a fire about us, to sleep under the protection of its glare. Accordingly as we went along I gathered any sticks or dried grass I saw, and presently had my arms full of such litter. So loaded, our progress was slower than I had anticipated, and besides, Weena was tired. I, too, began to suffer from sleepiness, and it was fully night before we reached the wood.

"Now, upon the shrubby hill upon the edge of this, Weena would have stopped, fearing the darkness before us. But a singular sense of impending calamity, that should indeed have served me as a warning, drove me onward. I had been without sleep for the length of a night and two days, and I was feverish and irritable. I felt sleep coming upon me, and with it the Morlocks.

"While we hesitated I saw among the bushes up the slope behind us, and dim against the sky, three crouching figures. There was scrub and long grass all about us, and I did not feel safe from their insidious approach. The forest, I calculated, was rather less than a mile in breadth. If we could get through it, the hillside beyond was bare, and to me it seemed an altogether safer resting-place. I thought that with my matches and the camphor I could contrive to keep my path illuminated through the woods. Yet it was evident that if I was to flourish matches with my hands I should have to abandon my firewood. So rather reluctantly I put this down.

"Then it came into my head that I would amaze our friends behind by lighting it. Ultimately I was to discover the atrocious folly of this proceeding, but just then it came to my mind as an ingenious move for covering our retreat.

"I don't know if you have ever thought what a rare thing in the absence of man and in a temperate climate, flames must be. The sun's heat is rarely strong enough to burn even when focussed by dewdrops, as is sometimes the case in more tropical districts. Lightning may blast and blacken, but it rarely gives rise to widespread fire. Decaying vegetation may occasionally smoulder with the heat of its fermentation, but this again rarely results in flames. Now, in this decadent age the art of fire-making had been altogether forgotten on the earth. The red tongues that went licking up my heap of wood were an altogether new and strange thing to Weena.

"She wanted to run to it and play with it. I believe she would have cast herself into it had I not restrained her. But I caught her up and in spite of her struggles plunged boldly before me into the wood. For a little way the glare of my fire lit the path. Looking back presently I could see, through the crowded tree stems, that from my heap of sticks the blaze had spread to some bushes adjacent, and a curved line of fire was creeping up the grass of the hill. I laughed at that.

impending calamity: Threatening disaster.

insidious: Sly, treacherous. The Morlocks sneaked up on their prey, waiting in bushes and always in the dark of night.

79

convulsively: Without deliberation. Weena clung to the Time Traveler in spasms of fear.

"Then I turned toward the dark trees before me again. It was very black and Weena clung to me convulsively, but there was still, as my eyes grew accustomed to the darkness, sufficient light for me to avoid blundering against the stems. Overhead it was simply black, except when here and there a gap of remote blue sky shone down upon me. I lit none of my matches because I had no hand free. Upon my left arm I carried my little one, in my right hand I had the iron bar I had wrenched from the machine.

"For some way I heard nothing but the crackling twigs under my feet, the faint rustle of the breeze above, and my breathing and the throb of the blood vessels in my ears. Then I seemed to hear a pattering about me.

"I pushed on grimly. The pattering became more distinct, and then I heard the same queer sounds and voices I had heard before in the underworld. There were evidently several of the Morlocks, and they were closing in upon me.

"In another minute I felt a tug at my coat, then something at my arm. Weena shivered violently and became quite still.

"It was time for a match. But to get at that I must put her down. I did so, and immediately as I fumbled with my pocket a struggle began in the darkness about my knees, perfectly silent on her part and with the same peculiar cooing sounds on the part of the Morlocks. Soft little hands, too, were creeping over my coat and back, touching even my neck.

"The match scratched and fizzed. I held it flaring, and immediately the white backs of the Morlocks became visible as they fled amid the trees. I hastily took a lump of camphor from my pocket and prepared to light it as soon as the match waned.

"Then I looked at Weena. She was lying clutching my feet and quite motionless, with her face to the ground. With a sudden fright I stooped to her. She seemed scarcely to breathe. I lit the block of camphor and flung it to the ground, and as it spit and flared up and drove back the Morlocks and the shadows, I knelt down and lifted up Weena. The wood behind seemed full of the stir and murmur of a great company of creatures.

"Apparently she had fainted. I put her carefully upon my shoulder and rose to push on, and then came a horrible realization.

"While maneuvering with my matches and Weena, I had turned myself about several times, and now I had not the faintest idea in what direction my path lay. For all I knew I might be facing back toward the Palace of Green Porcelain.

"I found myself in a cold perspiration. I had to think rapidly what to do. I determined to build a fire and encamp where we were. I put the motionless Weena down upon a turfy bole. Very hastily, as my first lump of camphor waned, I began collecting sticks and leaves.

"Here and there out of the darkness round me the eyes of the Morlocks shone like carbuncles.

"Presently the camphor flickered and went out. I lit a match, and as I did so saw two white forms that had been approaching Weena dash hastily back. One was so blinded by the light that he came straight for me, and I felt his bones grind under the blow of my fist. He gave a whoop of dismay, staggered a little way, and fell down.

"I lit another piece of camphor and went on gathering my bonfire. Presently I noticed how dry was some of the foliage above me, for since I had arrived on the Time Machine, a matter of a week, no rain had fallen. So instead of casting about among the trees for fallen twigs I began leaping up and dragging down branches. Very soon I had a choking smoky fire of green wood and dry sticks, and could save my other lumps of camphor.

"Then I turned to where Weena lay beside my iron mace. I tried what I could to revive her, but she lay like one dead. I could not even satisfy myself whether or not she breathed.

"Now the smoke of the fire beat over toward me, and it must have made me suddenly heavy. Moreover the vapor of camphor was in the air. My fire would not want replenishing for an hour or so. I felt very weary after my exertion and sat down. The wood, too, was full of a slumberous murmur that I did not understand.

"I seemed merely to nod and open my eyes. Then it was all dark around me, and the Morlocks had their hands upon me. Flinging off their clinging fingers I hastily felt in my pocket for the match-box, and—it had gone! Then they gripped and closed with me again.

"In a moment I knew what had happened. I had slept, and my fire had gone out, and the bitterness of death came over my soul. The forest seemed full of the smell of burning wood. I was caught by the neck, by the hair, by the arms, and pulled down. It was indescribably horrible in the darkness to feel all these

IN THE DARKNESS OF THE FOREST

turfy bole: A tree stump or log overgrown with grass and moss-like plants.

carbuncles: Precious stones of a deep fiery-red color.

exultation: Filled with vigor and joy. The Time Traveler had held back from attacking these repulsive, evil creatures, but now he felt a sort of joy to fly into battle and fight for his and Weena's life—at least for the moment.

agape: In wondering expectation.

soft creatures heaped upon me. I felt as if I was in a monstrous spider's web. I was overpowered. Down I went.

"I felt some little teeth nipping at my neck. Abruptly I rolled over, and as I did so, my hand came against my iron lever. Somehow this gave me strength for another effort. I struggled up, shaking off these human rats from me, and then holding the bar short, I thrust where I judged their faces might be. I could feel the succulent giving of flesh and bone under my blows, and for a moment I was free.

"The strange exultation that so often seems to accompany fighting came upon me. I knew that both I and Weena were lost, but I determined to make the Morlocks pay for their meat. I stood with my back to a tree swinging the iron bar before me. The whole wood was full of the stir and cries of them.

"A minute passed. Their voices seemed to rise to a higher pitch of excitement and their movements became faster. Yet none came within reach of me. I stood glaring at the blackness. Then suddenly came hope.

"What if the Morlocks had no courage?

"And close on the heels of that came a strange thing. The darkness seemed to grow luminous. Very dimly I began to see the Morlocks about me,—three, battered at my feet,—and then I perceived with incredulous surprise that the others were running, in an incessant stream, as it seemed to me, from behind me, and away through the wood in front of me. And their backs seemed no longer white, but reddish.

"Then as I stood agape I saw, across a gap of starlight between the branches, a little red spark go drifting and vanish. And at that I understood the smell of burning wood, the slumberous murmur that was growing now into a gusty roaring, the red glow, and the flight of the Morlocks.

"Stepping out from behind my tree and looking back, I saw through the back pillars of the nearer trees the flames of the burning forest. No doubt it was my first fire coming after me. With that I hastily looked round for Weena, but she was gone. The hissing and crackling behind me, the explosive thud as each fresh tree burst into flame, left little time for reflection. With my iron bar still in hand I followed in the path of the Morlocks.

"It was a close race. Once the flames crept forward so swiftly on my right as I ran, that I was outflanked and had to strike off to the left. But at last I emerged upon a small open place, and as

I did so, a Morlock came blundering toward me and passed me, and went on straight into the fire.

"And now I was to see the most weird and horrible scene, I think, of all that I beheld in that future age.

"This whole space was as bright as day with the reflection of the fire. In the center was a small hillock or tumulus surmounted by a scorched hawthorn. Beyond this hill was another arm of the burning forest from which yellow tongues were already writhing, and completely encircling the space with a fence of fire. Upon the hillside were perhaps thirty or forty Morlocks, dazzled by the light and heat of the fire, which was now very bright and hot, blundering hither and thither against each other in their bewilderment. At first I did not realize their blindness, and struck furiously at them with my bar in a frenzy of fear as they approached me, killing one and crippling several others. But when I had watched the gestures of one of them groping under the hawthorn against the red sky, and heard the moans to which they all gave vent, I was assured of their absolute helplessness and refrained from striking any of them again. Yet every now and then one would come straight toward me, setting loose a quivering horror, that made me quick to elude him. At one time the flames died down somewhat, and I feared these foul creatures would presently be able to see me, and I was even thinking of beginning the fight by killing some of them before this should happen, but the fire burst out again brightly and I stayed my hand. I walked about the hill among them and avoiding them, looking for some trace of Weena, but I found nothing.

"At last I sat down upon the summit of the hillock and watched this strange incredible company of the blind, groping to and fro and making uncanny noises to one another, as the glare of the fire beat upon them. The coiling uprush of smoke streamed across the sky, and through the rare tatters of that red canopy, remote as though they belonged to another universe, shone the little stars. Two or three Morlocks came blundering into me and I drove them off, trembling myself as I did so, with blows of my fists. For the most of that night I was persuaded it was a nightmare. I bit myself and screamed aloud in a passionate desire to awake. I beat on the ground with my hands, and got up, and sat down again, and wandered here and there, and again sat down on the crest of the hill. Then I would fall to rubbing my eyes and calling upon God to let me awake. Thrice I

IN THE DARKNESS OF THE FOREST

hillock: A little hill.
tumulus: A little hill, possibly an ancient grave.

Branches of Hawthorne with Fruit and Flowers

saw Morlocks put their heads down in a kind of agony and rush into the flames. But at last, above the subsiding red of the fire, above the streaming masses of black smoke and the whitening and blackening tree stumps, and the diminishing number of these dim creatures, came the white light of the day.

"I searched again over the open space for some traces of Weena, but could find none. I had half feared to discover her mangled remains, but clearly they had left her poor little body in the forest. I cannot describe how it relieved me to think that it had escaped the awful fate to which it seemed destined. As I thought of that I was almost moved to begin a massacre of the defenseless abominations about me, but I contained myself. This hillock, as I have said, was a kind of island in the forest. From its summit I could now make out, through a haze of smoke, the Palace of Green Porcelain, and from that I could get my bearings for the white sphinx. And so leaving the remnant of these damned souls going hither and thither and moaning, as the day grew clearer, I tied some grass about my feet and limped on across smoking ashes and among black stems that still pulsated internally with fire, toward the hiding place of the Time Machine.

"I walked slowly, for I was almost exhausted as well as lame, and I felt the most intense wretchedness on account of the horrible death of little Weena, which then seemed an overwhelming calamity. Yet even now, as I tell you of it in this old familiar room, it seems more like the sorrow of a dream than an actual loss. But it left me absolutely lonely again that morning— terribly alone. I began to think of this house of mine, of this fireside, of some of you, and with such thoughts came a longing that was pain.

"As I walked over the smoking ashes under the bright morning sky I made a discovery. In my trouser pocket were still some loose matches. The box must have leaked before it was lost!

Within was a small apartment, and on a raised place in the corner of this was the Time Machine

12

THE TRAP OF THE WHITE SPHINX

So about eight or nine in the morning I came to the same seat of yellow metal from which I had viewed the world upon the evening of my arrival. I thought of my hasty conclusions upon that evening and could not refrain from laughing bitterly at my confidence. Here was the same beautiful scene, the same abundant foliage, the same splendid palaces and magnificent ruins, the same silver river running between its fertile banks. The gay robes of the beautiful people moved hither and thither among the trees. Some were bathing in exactly the place where I had saved Weena, and that suddenly gave me a keen stab of pain. And like blots upon the landscape rose the cupolas above the ways to the underworld. I understood now what all the beauty of the overworld people covered. Very pleasant was their day, as pleasant as the day of the cattle in the field. Like the cattle they knew of no enemies, and provided against no needs. And their end was the same.

"I grieved to think how brief the dream of the human intellect had been. It had committed suicide. It had set itself steadfastly toward comfort and ease, a balanced society with

85

intellectual versatility: The ability of intelligent creatures to change and apply their thinking to different circumstances when necessary.

initiative: The wit and energy to begin any necessary project and to apply oneself with originality and ambition.

theorizing: Meditating. He was thinking how and why various changes had overtaken mankind and trying to form mental pictures that could develop an idea or theory.

security and permanence as its watchwords, it had attained its hopes—to come to this at last. Once, life and property must have reached almost absolute safety. The rich had been assured of his wealth and comfort, the toiler assured of his life and work. No doubt in that perfect world there had been no unemployed problem, no social question left unsolved. And a great quiet had followed.

"It is a law of nature we overlook, that intellectual versatility is the compensation for change, danger, and trouble. An animal perfectly in harmony with its environment is a perfect mechanism. Nature never appeals to intelligence until habit and instinct are useless. There is no intelligence where there is no change and no need of change. Only those animals partake of intelligence that have to meet a huge variety of needs and dangers.

"So, as I see it, the upperworld man had drifted toward his feeble prettiness, and the underworld to mere mechanical industry. But that perfect state had lacked one thing even of mechanical perfection—absolute permanency. Apparently as time went on the feeding of the underworld, however it was effected, had become disjointed. Mother Necessity, who had been staved off for a few thousand years, came back again, and she began below. The underworld, being in contact with machinery which, however perfect, still needs some little thought outside of habit, had probably retained, perforce, rather more initiative, if less of every other human character, than the upper. And when other meat failed them, they turned to what old habit had hitherto forbidden. So I say I saw it in my last view of the world of 802,701. It may be as wrong an explanation as mortal wit could invent. It is how the thing shaped itself to me, and as that I give it to you.

"After the fatigues, excitements, and terrors of the past days, and in spite of my grief, this seat and the tranquil view and the warm sunlight were very pleasant. I was very tired and sleepy, and soon my theorizing passed into dozing. Catching myself at that I took my own hint, and spreading myself out upon the turf, I had a long and refreshing sleep.

"I awoke a little before sunsetting. I now felt safe against being caught napping by the Morlocks, and stretching myself I came on down the hill toward the white sphinx. I had my crowbar in one hand, and the other played with the matches in my pocket.

"And now came a most unexpected thing. As I approached the pedestal of the sphinx I found the bronze panels were open. They had slid down into grooves.

"At that I stopped short before them, hesitating to enter.

"Within was a small apartment, and on a raised place in the corner of this was the Time Machine. I had the small levers in my pocket. So here, after all my elaborate preparations for the siege of the white sphinx, was a meek surrender. I threw my iron bar away, almost sorry not to use it.

"A sudden thought came into my head as I stooped toward the portal. For once at least I grasped the mental operations of the Morlocks. Suppressing a strong inclination to laugh, I stepped through the bronze frame and up to the Time Machine. I was surprised to find it had been carefully oiled and cleaned. I have suspected since that the Morlocks had even partially taken it to pieces while trying in their dim way to grasp its purpose.

portal: Doorway.

"Now, as I stood and examined it, finding a pleasure in the mere touch of the contrivance, the thing I had expected happened. The bronze panels suddenly slid up and struck the frame with a clang. I was in the dark—trapped. So the Morlocks thought. At that I chuckled gleefully.

"I could already hear their murmuring laughter as they came toward me. Very calmly I tried to strike the match. I had only to fix on the levers and depart then like a ghost. But I had overlooked one little thing. The matches were of that abominable kind that light only on the box.

"You may imagine how all my calm vanished. The little brutes were close upon me. One touched me. I made a sweeping blow in the dark at them with the lever, and began to scramble into the saddle of the Machine. Then came one hand upon me and then another.

"Then I had simply to fight against their persistent fingers for my levers, and at the same time feel for the studs over which these fitted. One, indeed, they almost got away from me. As it slipped from my hand I had to butt in the dark with my head—I could hear the Morlock's skull ring—to recover it. It was a nearer thing than the fight in the forest, I think, this last scramble.

"But at last the lever was fixed and pulled over. The clinging hands slipped from me. The darkness presently fell from my eyes. I found myself in the same gray light and tumult I have already described.

Looking around me I saw that quite near to me, what I had taken to be a reddish mass of rock was moving slowly toward me

13
THE
FURTHER
VISION

I have already told you of the sickness and confusion that comes with time traveling. And this time I was not seated properly in the saddle, but sideways and in an unstable fashion. For an indefinite time I clung to the machine as it swayed and vibrated, quite unheeding how I went, and when I brought myself to look at the dials again I was amazed to find where I had arrived. One dial records days, another thousands of days, another millions of days, and another thousands of millions. Now instead of reversing the levers I had pulled them over so as to go forward with them, and when I came to look at these indicators I found that the thousands hand was sweeping round as fast as the seconds hand of a watch, into futurity.

"Very cautiously, for I remembered my former headlong fall, I began to reverse my motion. Slower and slower went the circling hands, until the thousands one seemed motionless and the daily one was no longer a mere mist upon its scale. Still slower, until the gray haze around me became distincter, and dim outlines of a low hill and a sea became visible.

"But as my motion became slower there was, I found, no blinking change of day and night. A steady twilight brooded over the earth. And the band of light that had indicated the sun had, I now noticed, become fainter, had faded indeed to invisibility in the east, and in the west was increasingly broader and redder. The circling of the stars growing slower and slower had given place to creeping points of light. At last, some time before I stopped, the sun, red and very large, halted motionless upon the horizon, a vast dome glowing with a dull heat. The work of the tidal drag was accomplished. The earth had come to rest with one face to the sun even as in our own time the moon faces the earth.

"I stopped very gently and sat upon the Time Machine looking round me.

"The sky was no longer blue. Northeastward it was inky black, and out of the blackness shone brightly and steadily the pale white stars. Overhead it was a deep Indian red, and starless, and southeastward it grew brighter to where, cut by the horizon, lay the motionless hull of the huge red sun.

"The rocks about me were of a harsh reddish color, and all the trace of life that I could see at first was the intensely green vegetation that covered every projecting point on its southeastern side. It was the same rich green that one sees on forest moss or on the lichen in caves, plants which, like these, grow in a perpetual twilight.

"The Machine was standing on a sloping beach. The sea stretched away to the southwest to rise into a sharp bright horizon against the wan sky. There were no breakers and no waves, for not a breath of wind was stirring. Only a slight oily swell rose and fell like a gentle breathing, and showed that the eternal sea was still moving and living. And along the margin where the water sometimes broke was a thick incrustation of salt—pink under the lurid sky.

"There was a sense of oppression in my head and I noticed that I was breathing very fast. The sensations remind me of my

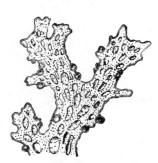

lichen: Lichens are plants made up of algae cells growing inside a fungus. They look like crusty grey mosses, growing on rocks.

lurid: Red, glowing, as fire seen through a haze.

89

only experience of mountaineering, and from that I judged the air was more rarified than it is now.

"Far away up the desolate slope I heard a harsh scream, and saw a thing like a huge white butterfly go slanting and fluttering up into the sky and, circling, disappear over some low hillocks beyond.

"The sound of its voice was so dismal that I shivered, and seated myself more firmly upon the Machine.

"Looking round me I saw that, quite near to me, what I had taken to be a reddish mass of rock was moving slowly toward me. Then I saw the thing was really a monstrous crab-like creature. Can you imagine a crab as large as yonder table, with its numerous legs moving slowly and uncertainly, its big claws swaying, its long antennae like carters' whips, waving and feeling, and its stalked eyes gleaming at you on either side of its metallic front? Its back was corrugated and ornamented with ungainly bosses, and a greenish incrustation blotched it here and there. I could see the numerous palps of its complicated mouth flickering and feeling as it approached.

corrugated: Wrinkled or ridged.

ungainly bosses: Large, ugly, bulging knobs; warty-looking, like a huge toad's outer skin.

"As I stared at this sinister apparition crawling toward me, I felt a tickling on my cheeks as though a fly had alighted there.

"I tried to brush it away with my hand, but in a moment it returned, and almost immediately after another came near my ear. I struck at this and caught something threadlike. It was drawn swiftly out of my hand. With a frightful qualm I turned and saw I had grasped the antennae of another monster crab that stood immediately behind me. Its evil eyes were wriggling on their stalks, its mouth was all alive with appetite, and its vast ungainly claws, smeared with green slime, were descending upon me.

"In a moment my hand was on the lever of the Time Machine, and I had placed a month between myself and these monsters. But I found I was still on the same beach and I saw them distinctly now as soon as I stopped. Dozens of them seemed to be crawling here and there in the somber light among the foliated sheets of intense green.

abominable desolation: Horribly wasted and barren, filling one with an unknown fear and dread.

"I cannot convey the sense of abominable desolation that hung over the world. The red eastern sky, the northward blackness, the salt Dead sea, the stony beach crawling with these foul, slow-stirring monsters, the uniform, poisonous-looking green of the lichenous plants, the thin air that hurt one's lungs; all contributed to an appalling effect.

"I moved on a hundred years, and there was the same red sun, the same dying sea, the same chill air, and the same crowd of earthly crustacea creeping in and out among the green weed and the red rocks.

"So I traveled, stopping ever and again, in great strides of a thousand years or more, drawn on by the mystery of the earth's fate, tracing with a strange fascination how the sun was growing larger and duller in the westward sky, and the life of the old earth ebbing out. At last, more than thirty million years hence, the huge red-hot dome of the sun had come to obscure nearly a sixth part of the darkling heavens. Then it was I stopped, for the crawling multitude of crabs had disappeared, and the red beach, save for its livid green liverworts and lichens, seemed lifeless again.

"As soon as I stopped a bitter cold assailed me. The air felt keenly cold, and rare white flakes ever and again came eddying down. To the northeastward the glare of snow lay under the starlight of the sable sky, and I could see an undulating crest of pinkish white hillocks. There were fringes of ice along the sea margin, drifting masses further out, but the main expanse of that salt ocean, all bloody under the eternal sunset, was still unfrozen.

"I looked about me to see if any traces of animals remained. A certain indefinable apprehension still kept me in the saddle of the Machine. I saw nothing moving, on earth or sky or sea. The green slime on the rocks alone testified that life was not extinct. A shallow sandbank had appeared in the sea and the water had receded from the beach. I fancied I saw some black object flopping about upon this bank, but it became motionless as I looked at it, and I judged my eye had been deceived and that the object was merely a rock. The stars in the sky were intensely bright and seemed to me to twinkle very little.

"Suddenly I noticed that the circular outline, westward, of the sun had changed, that a concavity, a bay, had appeared in the curve. I saw this grow larger. For a minute, perhaps, I stared aghast at this blackness that was creeping over the day, and then I realized that an eclipse was beginning. No doubt, now that the moon was creeping ever nearer to the earth, and the earth to the sun, eclipses were of frequent occurrence.

"The darkness grew apace, a cold wind began to blow in freshening gusts from the east, and then the white flakes that were falling out of the air increased. The tide was creeping in

THE FURTHER VISION

crustacea: Shellfish.

liverworts: Plants which resemble the liver in shape and color, and grow in damp ground and on rocks.

concavity: Here, an inward curving shadow appeared.

91

weltering: Rolling, tossing.

decadent humanity: The condition reached by mankind through deterioration; a gradual decline into a lower level of culture.

with a ripple and a whisper. Beyond these lifeless sounds the world was silent—silent! It would be hard to convey to you the stillness of it. All the sounds of man, the bleating of sheep, the cries of birds, the hum of insects, the stir that makes the background of our lives, were over. As the darkness thickened the eddying flakes became more abundant, dancing before my eyes; and the cold of the air more intense. At last, swiftly, one after the other, the white peaks of the distant hills vanished into blackness. The breeze grew to a moaning wind. I saw the black central shadow of the eclipse sweeping toward me. In another moment the pale stars alone were visible. All else was rayless obscurity. The sky was absolutely black.

"A horror of this great darkness came upon me. The cold that smote to my marrow, and the pain I felt in breathing, overcame me. I shivered and a deadly nausea seized me. Then like a red-hot bow in the sky appeared the edge of the sun.

"I got off the Machine to recover myself. I felt giddy and incapable of facing the return journey. As I stood sick and confused I saw again the moving thing upon the shoal—there was no mistake now that it was a moving thing—against the red water of the sea. It was a round thing, of the size of a football perhaps, or bigger; it seemed black against the weltering blood-red water, and it was hopping fitfully about. Then I felt I was fainting. A terrible dread of lying helpless in that remote twilight sustained me while I clambered upon the saddle.

"So I came home. For a long time I must have been insensible upon the Machine. The blinking succession of the days and nights was resumed, the sun grew golden again, the sky blue. I breathed with greater freedom. The fluctuating contours of the land ebbed and flowed. The hands spun backward upon the dials. At last I saw again the dim shadows of homes, the evidences of decadent humanity. These, too, changed and passed, and others came. Presently when the millions dial was at zero I slackened speed, and began to recognize our own pretty and familiar architecture. The thousands hand ran back to the starting point, the night and day flapped slower and slower. Then the old walls of the laboratory came round me. Very gently now I diminished the pace of the mechanism.

"I saw one little thing that seemed odd to me. I think I have told you that when I set out, before my velocity became very high, Mrs. Watchett had walked across the room, traveling, as it seemed to me, like a rocket. As I returned I passed again across that minute when she traversed the laboratory. But now every motion appeared to be the exact inversion of her previous one. The door at the lower end opened and she glided quietly up the laboratory, back foremost, and disappeared behind the door by which she had previously entered.

"Then I stopped the Machine, and saw about me again the old familiar laboratory, my tools, my appliances, just as I had left them. I got off the thing very shakily and sat down upon my bench. For several minutes I trembled violently. Then I became calmer. Around me was my old workshop again, exactly as it had been. I might have slept there and the whole thing have been a dream.

"And yet not exactly. The thing had started from the southeast corner of the laboratory. It had come to rest again in the northwest, against the wall, where you will find it. That gives you the exact distance from my little lawn to the pedestal of the white sphinx.

"For a time my brain became stagnant. Presently I got up and came through the passage here, limping, because my heel was still painful, and feeling sorely begrimed. I saw the *Pall Mall Gazette* on the table by the door. I found the date was indeed to-day, and looking at the time-piece, saw the hour was almost eight o'clock. I heard your voices and the clatter of plates. I hesitated—I felt so sick and weak. Then I sniffed good wholesome meat, and opened the door. You know the rest. I washed and dined, and now I am telling you the story.

"I know," he said after a while, "that all this will be absolutely incredible to you, but to me the one incredible thing is that I am here to-night in this old familiar room, looking into your wholesome faces, and telling you all these strange adventures."

He looked at the Medical Man.

"No; I cannot expect you to believe it. Take it as a lie, or a prophecy. Say I dreamed it in the workshop. Consider I have been speculating upon the destinies of our race, until I have hatched this fiction. Treat my assertion of its truth as a mere stroke of art to enhance its interest. And taking it as a story, what do you think of it?"

He took up his pipe and began in his old accustomed manner to tap upon the bars of the grate.

THE FURTHER VISION

inversion: Reversal. Just the opposite.

begrimed: Dirty.

hatched: Invented; brought into existence.

The Time Machine had gone. Save for a subsiding stir of dust, the central space of the laboratory was empty. A pane of the skylight had apparently blown in.

14
AFTER THE TIME TRAVELER'S STORY

There was a momentary stillness. Then chairs began to creak and shoes to scrape upon the carpet. I took my eyes off the Time Traveler's face and looked round at his audience. They were in the dark and little spots of color swam before them. The Medical Man seemed absorbed in the contemplation of our host. The Editor was looking hard at the end of his cigar—the sixth. The Journalist fumbled for his watch. The others as far as I remember were motionless.

The Editor stood up with a sigh.

"What a pity it is you're not a writer of stories!" he said, putting his hand on the Time Traveler's shoulder.

"You don't believe it?"

"Well—"

"I thought not." The Time Traveler turned round to us. "Where are the matches?" he said. He lit one and spoke over his pipe, puffing, "To tell you all the truth—I hardly believe it myself—and yet—"

His eyes fell with a mute inquiry upon the withered white flowers upon the little table. Then he turned over the hand holding his pipe, and I saw he was looking at some half healed scars on his knuckles.

The Medical Man rose, came to the lamp, and examined the flowers. "The gynoecium's odd," he said.

The Psychologist leaned forward to see, holding out his hand for a specimen.

"I'm hanged if it isn't a quarter to one," said the Journalist. "How shall we get home?"

"Plenty of cabs at the station," said the Psychologist.

"It's a curious thing," said the Medical Man; "but I certainly don't know the natural order of these flowers. May I have them?"

The Time Traveler hesitated. Then suddenly, "Certainly not."

"Where did you really get them?" said the Medical Man.

The Time Traveler put his hand to his head. He spoke like one who was trying to keep hold of an idea that eluded him. "They were put into my pocket by Weena—when I traveled into Time." He stared round the room. "I'm d—d if it isn't all going. This room and you and the atmosphere of everyday is too much for my memory. Did I ever make a Time Machine, or a model of a Time Machine, or is it all only a dream? They say life is a dream, a precious poor dream at times—but I can't stand another that won't fit. It's madness. And where did the dream come from? I must look at that Machine. If there *is* one."

He caught up the lamp swiftly and carried it flaring redly through the door into the corridor.

We followed him.

There in the flickering light of the lamp was the Machine, sure enough, squat, ugly, and askew, a thing of brass, ebony, ivory, and translucent, glimmering quartz. Solid to the touch— for I put out my hand and felt the rail of it—and with brown spots and smears upon the ivory, and bits of grass and moss upon the lower parts, and one rail bent awry.

gynoecium: Pistils; part of the center of a flower that has to do with reproduction.

eluded: Escaped.

The Time Traveler put the lamp down on the bench, and ran his hand along the broken rail.

"It's all right now," he said. "The story I told you was true. I'm sorry to have brought you out here—in the cold."

He took up the lamp, and in an absolute silence we returned to the smoking room.

The Time Traveler came into the hall with us and helped the Editor on with his coat. The Medical Man looked into our host's face and, with a certain hesitation, told him he was suffering from overwork, at which he laughed hugely. I remember him standing in the open doorway bawling good-night.

I shared a cab with the Editor. He thought the tale a "gaudy lie." For my own part I was unable to come to any conclusion about the matter. The story was so fantastic and incredible, the telling so credible and sober. I lay awake most of the night thinking about it. I determined to go next day and see the Time Traveler again.

I was told he was in the laboratory, and being on easy terms in the house I went up to him. The laboratory, however, was empty. I stared for a minute at the Time Machine and put out my hand and touched a lever. At that the squat, substantial-looking mass swayed like a bough shaken by the wind. Its instability startled me extremely, and I had a queer reminiscence of childish days when I used to be forbidden to meddle. I came back through the corridor. The Time Traveler met me in the smoking room. He was coming from the house. He had a small camera under one arm and a knapsack under the other. He laughed when he saw me and gave me an elbow to shake.

"I'm frightfully busy," he said; "with that thing in there."

"But is it not some hoax?" said I. "Do you really travel through Time?"

"Really and truly I do." And he looked frankly into my eyes.

He hesitated. His eye wandered round the room. "I only want half an hour," he said. "I know why you came, and it's awfully good of you. There's some magazines here. If you'll stop to lunch I'll prove this time traveling to you up to the hilt. Specimens and all. If you'll forgive my leaving you now?"

I consented, hardly comprehending then the full import of his words, and he nodded and went on down the corridor. I heard the door of the laboratory slam, seated myself in a chair, and took up the *New Review*. What was he going to do before lunch time? Then suddenly I was reminded by an advertisement

credible: Believable.
sober: Serious, earnest.

hoax: A joke, a trick.

96

that I had promised to meet Richardson the publisher at two. I looked at my watch, and saw I could barely save that engagement. I got up and went down the passage to tell the Time Traveler.

As I took hold of the handle of the door I heard an exclamation oddly truncated at the end, and a click and a thud. A gust of air whirled round me as I opened the door, and from within came the sound of broken glass falling on the floor. The Time Traveler was not there. I seemed to see a ghostly indistinct figure sitting in a whirling mass of black and brass for a moment, a figure so transparent that the bench behind with its sheets of drawings was absolutely distinct; but this phantasm I immediately perceived was illusory. The Time Machine had gone. Save for a subsiding stir of dust the central space of the laboratory was empty. A pane of the skylight had apparently just been blown in.

I felt an unreasonable amazement. I knew that something strange had happened, and for a moment could not distinguish what the strange thing might be. As I stood staring, the door into the garden opened, and the man-servant appeared.

We looked at each other. Then ideas began to come.

"Has Mr. — gone out that way?" said I.

"No, sir. No one has come out this way. I was expecting to find him here."

At that I understood. At the risk of disappointing Richardson I remained waiting for the Time Traveler, waiting for the second, perhaps still stranger, story, and the specimens and photographs he would bring with him.

But I am beginning to fear now that I must wait a lifetime for that. The Time Traveler vanished three years ago. Up to the present he has not returned, and when he does return he will find his home in the hands of strangers and his little gathering of auditors broken up forever. Filby has exchanged poetry for playwriting, and is a rich man—as literary men go—and extremely unpopular. The Medical Man is dead, the Journalist is in India, and the Psychologist has succumbed to paralysis. Some of the other men I used to meet there have dropped as completely out of existence as if they, too, had traveled off upon some similar anachronisms. And so, ending in a kind of dead wall, the story of the Time Machine must remain for the present at least.

AFTER THE TIME TRAVELER'S STORY

truncated: Cut short.

phantasm: A mental image.

"Being but dark earth though made diaphanall"

His gloved hands were clasped behind him, and he seemed to be lost in thought

The stranger came early in February, one wintry day, through a biting wind and a driving snow, the last snowfall of the year, over the down, walking as it seemed from Bramblehurst railway station, and carrying a little black portmanteau in his thickly gloved hand. He was wrapped up from head to foot, and the brim of his soft felt hat hid every inch of his face but the shiny tip of his nose; the snow had piled itself against his shoulders and chest, and added a white crest to the burden he carried. He staggered into the Coach and Horses, more dead than alive as it seemed, and flung his portmanteau down. "A fire," he cried, "in the name of human charity! A room and a fire!" He stamped and shook the snow from off himself in the bar, and followed Mrs. Hall into her guest parlour to strike his bargain. And with that much introduction, that and a ready acquiescence to terms and a couple of sovereigns flung upon the table, he took up his quarters in the inn.

Mrs. Hall lit the fire and left him there while she went to prepare him a meal with her own hands. A guest to stop at Iping in the winter-time was an unheard-of piece of luck, let alone a guest who was no "haggler," and she was resolved to show herself worthy of her good fortune. As soon as the bacon was well under way, and Millie, her lymphatic aid, had been brisked up a bit by a few deftly chosen expressions of contempt, she carried the cloth, plates, and glasses into the parlour and began to lay them with the utmost *éclat*. Although the fire was burning up briskly, she was surprised to see that her visitor still wore his hat and coat, standing with his back to her and staring out of the window at the falling snow in the yard. His gloved hands were clasped behind him, and he seemed to be lost in

1
THE STRANGE MAN'S ARRIVAL

portmanteau: A suitcase or trunk which opens into two halves, very much like two suitcases in one.

lymphatic: Slow, lackadaisical.

éclat: Noise, clatter.

103

side-lights: Curved extensions of the lens which increase the range of vision.

in a quick staccato: In a quick succession of light blows or taps.

stateliness: Dignity.

thought. She noticed that the melted snow that still sprinkled his shoulders dropped upon her carpet. "Can I take your hat and coat, sir," she said, "and give them a good dry in the kitchen?"

"No," he said without turning.

She was not sure she had heard him, and was about to repeat her question.

He turned his head and looked at her over his shoulder. "I prefer to keep them on," he said with emphasis, and she noticed that he wore big blue spectacles with side-lights, and had a bushy side-whisker over his coat-collar that completely hid his cheeks and face.

"Very well, sir," she said. "*As* you like. In a bit the room will be warmer."

He made no answer, and had turned his face away from her again, and Mrs. Hall, feeling that her conversational advances were ill-timed, laid the rest of the table things in a quick staccato and whisked out of the room. When she returned he was still standing there, like a man of stone, his back hunched, his collar turned up, his dripping hat-brim turned down, hiding his face and ears completely. She put down the eggs and bacon with considerable emphasis, and called rather than said to him, "Your lunch is served, sir."

"Thank you," he said at the same time, and did not stir until she was closing the door. Then he swung round and approached the table with a certain eager quickness.

As she went behind the bar to the kitchen she heard a sound repeated at regular intervals. Chirk, chirk, chirk, it went, the sound of a spoon being rapidly whisked round a basin. "That girl!" she said. "There! I clean forgot it. It's her being so long!" And while she herself finished mixing the mustard, she gave Millie a few verbal stabs for her excessive slowness. She had cooked the ham and eggs, laid the table, and done everything, while Millie (help indeed!) had only succeeded in delaying the mustard. And him a new guest and wanting to stay! Then she filled the mustard pot, and, putting it with a certain stateliness upon a gold and black tea-tray, carried it into the parlour.

She rapped and entered promptly. As she did so her visitor moved quickly, so that she got but a glimpse of a white object disappearing behind the table. It would seem he was picking something from the floor. She rapped down the mustard pot on the table, and then she noticed the overcoat and hat had been

104

taken off and put over a chair in front of the fire, and a pair of wet boots threatened rust to her steel fender. She went to these things resolutely. "I suppose I may have them to dry now," she said in a voice that brooked no denial.

"Leave the hat," said her visitor, in a muffled voice, and turning she saw he had raised his head and was sitting and looking at her.

For a moment she stood gaping at him, too surprised to speak.

He held a white cloth—it was a *serviette* he had brought with him—over the lower part of his face, so that his mouth and jaws were completely hidden, and that was the reason of his muffled voice. But it was not that which startled Mrs. Hall. It was the fact that all his forehead above his blue glasses was covered by a white bandage, and that another covered his ears, leaving not a scrap of his face exposed excepting only his pink, peaked nose. It was bright, pink, and shiny just as it had been at first. He wore a dark-brown velvet jacket with a high, black, linen-lined collar turned up about his neck. The thick black hair, escaping as it could below and between the cross bandages, projected in curious tails and horns, giving him the strangest appearance conceivable. This muffled and bandaged head was so unlike what she had anticipated, that for a moment she was rigid.

He did not remove the *serviette*, but remained holding it, as she saw now, with a brown gloved hand, and regarding her with his inscrutable blue glasses. "Leave the hat," he said, speaking very distinctly through the white cloth.

Her nerves began to recover from the shock they had received. She placed the hat on the chair again by the fire. "I didn't know, sir," she began, "that—" and she stopped embarrassed.

"Thank you," he said drily, glancing from her to the door and then at her again.

"I'll have them nicely dried, sir, at once," she said, and carried his clothes out of the room. She glanced at his white-swathed head and blue goggles again as she was going out of the door; but his napkin was still in front of his face. She shivered a little as she closed the door behind her, and her face was eloquent of her surprise and perplexity. "I *never*," she whispered. "There!" She went quite softly to the kitchen, and was too preoccupied to ask Millie what she was messing about with *now*, when she got there.

brooked: Permitted, allowed.

serviette: A large napkin.

inscrutable: Mysterious.

eloquent: Expressive, revealing.

clothes-horse: A frame on which to hang clothes to dry or to prevent wrinkling.

going off at a tangent: Changing the subject abruptly.

animation: Liveliness.

nothing loath: Not reluctant; willing.

The visitor sat and listened to her retreating feet. He glanced inquiringly at the window before he removed his *serviette*, and resumed his meal. He took a mouthful, glanced suspiciously at the window, took another mouthful, then rose and, taking the *serviette* in his hand, walked across the room and pulled the blind down to the top of the white muslin that obscured the lower panes. This left the room in a twilight. This done, he returned with an easier air to the table and his meal.

"The poor soul's had an accident or an operation or something," said Mrs. Hall. "What a turn them bandages did give me, to be sure!"

She put on some more coal, unfolded the clothes-horse, and extended the traveller's coat upon this. "And they goggles! Why, he looked more like a divin' helmet than a human man!" She hung his muffler on a corner of the horse. "And holding that handkercher over his mouth all the time. Talkin' through it! . . . Perhaps his mouth was hurt too—maybe."

She turned round, as one who suddenly remembers. "Bless my soul alive!" she said, going off at a tangent; "ain't you done them taters *yet*, Millie?"

When Mrs. Hall went to clear away the stranger's lunch, her idea that his mouth must also have been cut or disfigured in the accident she supposed him to have suffered, was confirmed, for he was smoking a pipe, and all the time that she was in the room he never loosened the silk muffler he had wrapped round the lower part of his face to put the mouthpiece to his lips. Yet it was not forgetfulness, for she saw he glanced at it as it smouldered out. He sat in the corner with his back to the window-blind and spoke now, having eaten and drunk and being comfortably warmed through, with less aggressive brevity than before. The reflection of the fire lent a kind of red animation to his big spectacles they had lacked hitherto.

"I have some luggage," he said, "at Bramblehurst station," and he asked her how he could have it sent. He bowed his bandaged head quite politely in acknowledgment of her explanation. "To-morrow!" he said. "There is no speedier delivery?" and seemed quite disappointed when she answered, "No." Was she quite sure? No man with a trap who would go over?

Mrs. Hall, nothing loath, answered his questions and developed a conversation. "It's a steep road by the down, sir," she said in answer to the question about a trap; and then, snatching at an opening, said, "It was there a carriage was upsettled, a

106

year ago and more. A gentleman killed, besides his coachman. Accidents, sir, happen in a moment, don't they?"

But the visitor was not to be drawn so easily. "They do," he said through his muffler, eyeing her quietly through his impenetrable glasses.

"But they take long enough to get well, sir, don't they? . . . There was my sister's son, Tom, jest cut his arm with a scythe, tumbled on it in the 'ayfield, and, bless me! he was three months tied up, sir. You'd hardly believe it. It's regular given me a dread of a scythe, sir."

"I can quite understand that," said the visitor.

"He was afraid, one time, that he'd have to have an opration—he was that bad, sir."

The visitor laughed abruptly, a bark of a laugh that he seemed to bite and kill in his mouth. "*Was* he?" he said.

"He was, sir. And no laughing matter to them as had the doing for him, as I had—my sister being took up with her little ones so much. There was bandages to do, sir, and bandages to undo. So that if I may make so bold as to say it, sir—"

"Will you get me some matches?" said the visitor, quite abruptly. "My pipe is out."

Mrs. Hall was pulled up suddenly. It was certainly rude of him, after telling him all she had done. She gasped at him for a moment, and remembered the two sovereigns. She went for the matches.

"Thanks," he said concisely, as she put them down, and turned his shoulder upon her and stared out of the window again. It was altogether too discouraging. Evidently he was sensitive on the topic of operations and bandages. She did not "make so bold as to say," however, after all. But his snubbing way had irritated her, and Millie had a hot time of it that afternoon.

The visitor remained in the parlour until four o'clock, without giving the ghost of an excuse for an intrusion. For the most part he was quite still during that time; it would seem he sat in the growing darkness smoking in the firelight, perhaps dozing.

Once or twice a curious listener might have heard him at the coals, and for the space of five minutes he was audible pacing the room. He seemed to be talking to himself. Then the armchair creaked as he sat down again.

THE STRANGE MAN'S ARRIVAL

drawn: Brought into conversation.

Scythe

Sovereign

concisely: Briefly, shortly.

Her visitor,
she saw as she opened
the door,
was seated in the
armchair before the fire,
dozing it would seem,
with his bandaged head
drooping on one side.

2

MR. TEDDY HENFREY'S FIRST IMPRESSIONS

clock-jobber: A clock repairman who is hired as jobs need to be done. Today, such a man would probably own his business, sell clocks and, perhaps, jewelry in addition to doing repairs.

At four o'clock, when it was fairly dark and Mrs. Hall was screwing up her courage to go in and ask her visitor if he would take some tea, Teddy Henfrey, the clock-jobber, came into the bar. "My sakes! Mrs. Hall," said he, "but this is terrible weather for thin boots!" The snow outside was falling faster.

Mrs. Hall agreed with him, and then noticed he had his bag, and hit upon a brilliant idea. "Now you're here, Mr. Teddy," said she, "I'd be glad if you'd give th' old clock in the parlour a bit of a look. 'T is going, and it strikes well and hearty; but the hour-hand won't do nuthin' but point at six."

And leading the way, she went across to the parlour door and rapped and entered.

Her visitor, she saw as she opened the door, was seated in the armchair before the fire, dozing it would seem, with his bandaged head drooping on one side. The only light in the room was the red glow from the fire—which lit his eyes like adverse railway signals, but left his downcast face in darkness—and the scanty vestiges of the day that came in through the open door. Everything was ruddy, shadowy, and indistinct to her, the more so since she had just been lighting the bar lamp, and her eyes were dazzled. But for a second it seemed to her that the man she looked at had an enormous mouth wide open,—a vast and incredible mouth that swallowed the whole of the lower portion of his face. It was the sensation of a moment: the white-bound head, the monstrous goggle eyes, and this huge yawn below it. Then he stirred, started up in his chair, put up his hand. She opened the door wide, so that the room was lighter, and she saw him more clearly, with the muffler held to his face just as she had seen him hold the *serviette* before. The shadows, she fancied, had tricked her.

"Would you mind, sir, this man a-coming to look at the clock, sir?" she said, recovering from her momentary shock.

"Look at the clock?" he said, staring round in a drowsy manner, and speaking over his hand, and then, getting more fully awake, "certainly."

Mrs. Hall went away to get a lamp, and he rose and stretched himself. Then came the light, and Mr. Teddy Henfrey, entering, was confronted by this bandaged person. He was, he says, "taken aback."

"Good-afternoon," said the stranger, regarding him, as Mr. Henfrey says, with a vivid sense of the dark spectacles, "like a lobster."

"I hope," said Mr. Henfrey, "that it's no intrusion."

"None whatever," said the stranger. "Though, I understand," he said, turning to Mrs. Hall, "that this room is really to be mine for my own private use."

"I thought, sir," said Mrs. Hall, "you'd prefer the clock—" She was going to say "mended."

"Certainly," said the stranger, "certainly—but, as a rule, I like to be alone and undisturbed.

"But I'm really glad to have the clock seen to," he said, seeing a certain hesitation in Mr. Henfrey's manner. "Very glad." Mr. Henfrey had intended to apologise and withdraw, but

adverse railway signals: Stop signs at railway crossings, which are flashing red lights.

this anticipation reassured him. The stranger stood round with his back to the fireplace and put his hands behind his back. "And presently," he said, "when the clock-mending is over, I think I should like to have some tea. But not till the clock-mending is over."

Mrs. Hall was about to leave the room,—she made no conversational advances this time, because she did not want to be snubbed in front of Mr. Henfrey,—when her visitor asked her if she had made any arrangements about his boxes at Bramble-hurst. She told him she had mentioned the matter to the postman, and that the carrier could bring them over on the morrow. "You are certain that is the earliest?" he said.

She was certain, with a marked coldness.

"I should explain," he added, "what I was really too cold and fatigued to do before, that I am an experimental investigator."

"Indeed, sir," said Mrs. Hall, much impressed.

"And my baggage contains apparatus and appliances."

"Very useful things, indeed, they are, sir," said Mrs. Hall.

"And I'm naturally anxious to get on with my inquiries."

"Of course, sir."

"My reason for coming to Iping," he proceeded, with a certain deliberation of manner, "was—a desire for solitude. I do not wish to be disturbed in my work. In addition to my work, an accident—"

"I thought as much," said Mrs. Hall to herself.

"—necessitates a certain retirement. My eyes—are sometimes so weak and painful that I have to shut myself up in the dark for hours together. Lock myself up. Sometimes—now and then. Not at present, certainly. At such times the slightest distur-bance, the entry of a stranger into the room, is a source of excruciating annoyance to me—it is well these things should be understood."

"Certainly, sir," said Mrs. Hall. "And if I might make so bold as to ask—"

"That, I think, is all," said the stranger, with that quietly irresistible air of finality he could assume at will. Mrs. Hall reserved her question and sympathy for a better occasion.

After Mrs. Hall had left the room, he remained standing in front of the fire, glaring, so Mr. Henfrey puts it, at the clock-mending. Mr. Henfrey not only took off the hands of the clock, and the face, but extracted the works; and he tried to work in as slow and quiet and unassuming a manner as possible.

excrutiating: Very painful and dis-tressing.

110

He worked with the lamp close to him, and the green shade threw a brilliant light upon his hands, and upon the frame and wheels, and left the rest of the room shadowy. When he looked up, coloured patches swam in his eyes. Being constitutionally of a curious nature, he had removed the works—a quite unnecessary proceeding—with the idea of delaying his departure and perhaps falling into conversation with the stranger. But the stranger stood there, perfectly silent and still. So still, it got on Henfrey's nerves. He felt alone in the room and looked up, and there, grey and dim, was the bandaged head and huge blue lenses staring fixedly, with a mist of green spots drifting in front of them. It was so uncanny-looking to Henfrey that for a minute they remained staring blankly at one another. Then Henfrey looked down again. Very uncomfortable position! One would like to say something. Should he remark that the weather was very cold for the time of year?

He looked up as if to take aim with that introductory shot. "The weather"—he began.

"Why don't you finish and go?" said the rigid figure, evidently in a state of painfully suppressed rage. "All you've got to do is to fix the hour-hand on its axle. You're simply humbugging—"

"Certainly, sir—one minute more, sir. I overlooked—" And Mr. Henfrey finished and went.

But he went off feeling excessively annoyed. "Damn it!" said Mr. Henfrey to himself, trudging down the village through the thawing snow; "a man must do a clock at times, sure lie."

And again: "Can't a man look at you?—Ugly!"

And yet again: "Seemingly not. If the police was wanting you you couldn't be more wrooped and bandaged."

At Gleeson's corner he saw Hall, who had recently married the stranger's hostess at the Coach and Horses, and who now drove the Iping conveyance, when occasional people required it, to Sidderbridge Junction, coming towards him on his return from that place. Hall had evidently been "stopping a bit" at Sidderbridge, to judge by his driving. " 'Ow do, Teddy?" he said, passing.

"You got a rum un up home!" said Teddy.

Hall very sociably pulled up. "What's that?" he asked.

"Rum-looking customer stopping at the Coach and Horses," said Teddy. "My sakes!"

And he proceeded to give Hall a vivid description of his

MR. TEDDY HENFREY'S FIRST IMPRESSIONS

constitutionally: Naturally, or by temperamental makeup.

humbugging: Faking; pretending that the job is more involved than it really is.

rum un: (Rum one) Queer or odd one.

sluggish apprehension: Slow to understand.

rated: Berated, scolded.

scrutinised: Examined.

interminable: So long that they seemed endless.

grotesque guest. "Looks a bit like a disguise, don't it? I'd like to see a man's face if I had him stopping in *my* place," said Henfrey. "But women are that trustful,—where strangers are concerned. He's took your rooms and he ain't even given a name, Hall."

"You don't say so!" said Hall, who was a man of sluggish apprehension.

"Yes," said Teddy. "By the week. Whatever he is, you can't get rid of him under the week. And he's got a lot of luggage coming to-morrow, so he says. Let's hope it won't be stones in boxes, Hall."

He told Hall how his aunt at Hastings had been swindled by a stranger with empty portmanteaux. Altogether he left Hall vaguely suspicious. "Get up, old girl," said Hall. "I s'pose I must see 'bout this."

Teddy trudged on his way with his mind considerably relieved.

Instead of "seeing 'bout it," however, Hall on his return was severely rated by his wife on the length of time he had spent in Sidderbridge, and his mild inquiries were answered snappishly and in a manner not to the point. But the seed of suspicion Teddy had sown germinated in the mind of Mr. Hall in spite of these discouragements. "You wim' don't know everything," said Mr. Hall, resolved to ascertain more about the personality of his guest at the earliest possible opportunity. And after the stranger had gone to bed, which he did about half-past nine, Mr. Hall went very aggressively into the parlour and looked very hard at his wife's furniture, just to show that the stranger wasn't master there, and scrutinised closely and a little contemptuously a sheet of mathematical computation the stranger had left. When retiring for the night he instructed Mrs. Hall to look very closely at the stranger's luggage when it came next day.

"You mind your own business, Hall," said Mrs. Hall, "and I'll mind mine."

She was all the more inclined to snap at Hall because the stranger was undoubtedly an unusually strange sort of stranger, and she was by no means assured about him in her own mind. In the middle of the night she woke up dreaming of huge white heads like turnips, that came trailing after her, at the end of interminable necks, and with vast black eyes. But being a sensible woman, she subdued her terrors and turned over and went to sleep again.

They saw the dog's teeth had slipped
the hand, heard a kick
saw the dog execute a flanking jump and get home
on the strangers leg.

So it was that on the twenty-ninth day of February, at the beginning of the thaw, this singular person fell out of infinity into Iping Village. Next day his luggage arrived through the slush. And very remarkable luggage it was. There were a couple of trunks indeed, such as a rational man might need, but in addition there were a box of books,—big, fat books, of which some were just in an incomprehensible handwriting,—and a dozen or more crates, boxes, and cases, containing objects packed in straw, as it seemed to Hall, tugging with a casual curiosity at the straw—glass bottles. The stranger, muffled in hat, coat, gloves, and wrapper, came out impatiently to meet

3
THE
THOUSAND AND
ONE BOTTLES

infinity: Usually eternity or boundless space, but here it means out of nowhere.

in a dilettante spirit: In a casual, possibly even haughty, manner. A dilettante is a person who dabbles in the arts. A dilettante spirit, therefore, is not deep or dedicated. It can even be purely snobbish.

slipped: Here, escaped.
flanking: Sidewise.

singular: Peculiar, unusual.
indeterminate: Not precisely defined; vaguely outlined.

concussion: A violent shock.

Fearenside's cart, while Hall was having a word or so of gossip preparatory to helping bring them in. Out he came, not noticing Fearenside's dog, who was sniffing in a *dilettante* spirit at Hall's legs. "Come along with those boxes," he said. "I've been waiting long enough."

And he came down the steps towards the tail of the cart as if to lay hands on the smaller crate.

No sooner had Fearenside's dog caught sight of him, however, than it began to bristle and growl savagely, and when he rushed down the steps it gave an undecided hop, and then sprang straight at his hand. "Whup!" cried Hall, jumping back, for he was no hero with dogs, and Fearenside howled, "Lie down!" and snatched his whip.

They saw the dog's teeth had slipped the hand, heard a kick, saw the dog execute a flanking jump and get home on the stranger's leg, and heard the rip of his trousering. Then the finer end of Fearenside's whip reached his property, and the dog, yelping with dismay, retreated under the wheels of the waggon. It was all the business of a swift half-minute. No one spoke, every one shouted. The stranger glanced swiftly at his torn glove and at his leg, made as if he would stoop to the latter, then turned and rushed swiftly up the steps into the inn. They heard him go headlong across the passage and up the uncarpeted stairs to his bedroom.

"You brute, you!" said Fearenside, climbing off the waggon with his whip in his hand, while the dog watched him through the wheel. "Come here!" said Fearenside—"You'd better."

Hall had stood gaping. "He wuz bit," said Hall. "I'd better go and see to en," and he trotted after the stranger. He met Mrs. Hall in the passage. "Carrier's darg," he said, "bit en."

He went straight upstairs, and the stranger's door being ajar, he pushed it open and was entering without any ceremony, being of a naturally sympathetic turn of mind.

The blind was down and the room dim. He caught a glimpse of a most singular thing, what seemed a handless arm waving towards him, and a face of three huge indeterminate spots on white, very like the face of a pale pansy. Then he was struck violently in the chest, hurled back, and the door slammed in his face and locked. It was so rapid that it gave him no time to observe. A waving of indecipherable shapes, a blow, and a concussion. There he stood on the dark little landing, wondering what it might be that he had seen.

A couple of minutes after, he rejoined the little group that had formed outside the Coach and Horses. There was Fearenside telling about it all over again for the second time; there was Mrs. Hall saying his dog didn't have no business to bite her guests; there was Huxter, the general dealer from over the road, interrogative; and Sandy Wadgers from the forge, judicial; besides women and children,—all of them saying fatuities: "Wouldn't let en bite *me*, I knows;" " 'Tasn't right *have* such dargs;" "Whad *'e* bite *'n* for then?" and so forth.

Mr. Hall, staring at them from the steps and listening, found it incredible that he had seen anything so very remarkable happen upstairs. Besides, his vocabulary was altogether too limited to express his impressions.

"He don't want no help, he says," he said in answer to his wife's inquiry. "We'd better be a-takin' of his luggage in."

"He ought to have it cauterised at once," said Mr. Huxter; "especially if it's at all inflamed."

"I'd shoot en, that's what I'd do," said a lady in the group.

Suddenly the dog began growling again.

"Come along," cried an angry voice in the doorway, and there stood the muffled stranger, with his collar turned up, and his hat-brim bent down. "The sooner you get those things in the better I'll be pleased." It is stated by an anonymous bystander that his trousers and gloves had been changed.

"Was you hurt, sir?" said Fearenside. "I'm rare sorry the darg—"

"Not a bit," said the stranger. "Never broke the skin. Hurry up with those things."

He then swore to himself, so Mr. Hall asserts.

Directly the first crate was, in accordance with his directions, carried into the parlour, the stranger flung himself upon it with extraordinary eagerness, and began to unpack it, scattering the straw with an utter disregard of Mrs. Hall's carpet. And from it he began to produce bottles,—little fat bottles containing powders, small and slender bottles containing coloured and white fluids, fluted blue bottles labelled *Poison*, bottles with round bodies and slender necks, large green-glass bottles, large white-glass bottles, bottles with glass stoppers and frosted labels, bottles with fine corks, bottles with bungs, bottles with wooden caps, wine bottles, salad-oil bottles,—putting them in rows on the chiffonnier, on the mantel, on the table under the window, round the floor, on the book-shelf,—everywhere. The

THE THOUSAND AND ONE BOTTLES

fatuities: Foolish remarks.

cauterised: Seared closed by a doctor using a hot surgical iron.

fluted: Decorated with grooves.

chiffonier: A high, narrow chest of drawers.

115

chemist's shop in Bramblehurst could not boast half so many. Quite a sight it was. Crate after crate yielded bottles, until all six were empty and the table high with straw; the only things that came out of these crates besides the bottles were a number of test-tubes and a carefully packed balance.

And directly the crates were unpacked, the stranger went to the window and set to work, not troubling in the least about the litter of straw, the fire which had gone out, the box of books outside, nor for the trunks and other luggage that had gone upstairs.

When Mrs. Hall took his dinner in to him, he was already so absorbed in his work, pouring little drops out of the bottles into test-tubes, that he did not hear her until she had swept away the bulk of the straw and put the tray on the table, with some little emphasis perhaps, seeing the state that the floor was in. Then he half turned his head and immediately turned it away again. But she saw he had removed his glasses; they were beside him on the table, and it seemed to her that his eye sockets were extraordinarily hollow. He put on his spectacles again, and then turned and faced her. She was about to complain of the straw on the floor when he anticipated her.

"I wish you wouldn't come in without knocking," he said in the tone of abnormal exasperation that seemed so characteristic of him.

"I knocked, but seemingly—"

"Perhaps you did. But in my investigations—my really very urgent and necessary investigations—the slightest disturbance, the jar of a door— I must ask you—"

"Certainly, sir. You can turn the lock if you're like that, you know,—any time."

"A very good idea," said the stranger.

"This stror, sir, if I might make so bold as to remark—"

"Don't. If the straw makes trouble put it down in the bill." And he mumbled at her—words suspiciously like curses.

He was so odd, standing there, so aggressive and explosive, bottle in one hand and test-tube in the other, that Mrs. Hall was quite alarmed. But she was a resolute woman. "In which case, I should like to know, sir, what you consider—"

"A shilling. Put down a shilling. Surely a shilling's enough?"

"So be it," said Mrs. Hall, taking up the table-cloth and beginning to spread it over the table. "If you're satisfied, of course—"

He turned and sat down, with his coat-collar towards her.

All the afternoon he worked with the door locked and, as Mrs. Hall testifies, for the most part in silence. But once there was a concussion and a sound of bottles ringing together as though the table had been hit, and the smash of a bottle flung violently down, and then a rapid pacing athwart the room. Fearing "something was the matter," she went to the door and listened, not caring to knock.

"I can't go on," he was raving. "I *can't* go on. Three hundred thousand, four hundred thousand! The huge multitude! Cheated! All my life it may take me! Patience! Patience indeed! Fool and liar!"

There was a noise of hobnails on the bricks in the bar, and Mrs. Hall had very reluctantly to leave the rest of his soliloquy. When she returned the room was silent again, save for the faint crepitation of his chair and the occasional clink of a bottle. It was all over. The stranger had resumed work.

When she took in his tea she saw broken glass in the corner of the room under the concave mirror, and a golden stain that had been carelessly wiped. She called attention to it.

"Put it down in the bill," snapped her visitor. "For God's sake don't worry me. If there's damage done, put it down in the bill;" and he went on ticking a list in the exercise book before him.

"I'll tell you something," said Fearenside, mysteriously. It was late in the afternoon, and they were in the little beer-shop of Iping Hanger.

"Well?" said Teddy Henfrey.

"This chap you're speaking of, what my dog bit. Well—he's black. Leastways, his legs are. I seed through the tear of his trousers and the tear of his glove. You'd have expected a sort of pinky to show, wouldn't you? Well—there wasn't none. Just blackness. I tell you, he's as black as my hat."

"My sakes!" said Henfrey. "It's a rummy case altogether. Why, his nose is as pink as paint!"

"That's true," said Fearenside. "I knows that. And I tell ee what I'm thinking. That marn's a piebald, Teddy. Black here and white there—in patches. And he's ashamed of it. He's a kind of half-breed, and the colour's come off patchy instead of mixing. I've heard of such things before. And it's the common way with horses, as any one can see."

THE THOUSAND AND ONE BOTTLES

athwart: Across.

soliloquy: A speech addressed to one's self.

crepitation: Creaking.

concave mirror: A mirror with the glass rounded inward.

Concave

117

He rarely went abroad by daylight, but at twilight he would go out muffled up invisibly...

4

MR. CUSS INTERVIEWS THE STRANGER

cursorily: Hastily, without going into detail.

penury: Want, poverty.

I have told the circumstances of the stranger's arrival in Iping with a certain fulness of detail, in order that the curious impression he created may be understood by the reader. But excepting two odd incidents, the circumstances of his stay until the extraordinary day of the Club Festival may be passed over very cursorily. There were a number of skirmishes with Mrs. Hall on matters of domestic discipline, but in every case until late in April, when the first signs of penury began, he over-rode her by the easy expedient of an extra payment. Hall did not like him, and whenever he dared he talked of the advisability of getting rid of him; but he showed his dislike chiefly by concealing it ostentatiously, and avoiding his visitor as much as possible. "Wait till the summer," said Mrs. Hall, sagely, "when the artisks are beginning to come. Then we'll see. He may be a bit overbearing, but bills settled punctual is bills settled punctual, whatever you like to say."

The stranger did not go to church, and indeed made no difference between Sunday and the irreligious days, even in costume. He worked, as Mrs. Hall thought, very fitfully. Some days he would come down early and be continuously busy. On others he would rise late, pace his room, fretting audibly for hours together, smoke, sleep in the armchair by the fire. Communication with the world beyond the village he had none. His temper continued very uncertain; for the most part his manner was that of a man suffering under almost unendurable provocation, and once or twice things were snapped, torn, crushed, or broken in spasmodic gusts of violence. He seemed under a chronic irritation of the greatest intensity. His habit of talking to himself in a low voice grew steadily upon him, but though Mrs. Hall listened conscientiously she could make neither head nor tail of what she heard.

He rarely went abroad by daylight, but at twilight he would go out muffled up invisibly, whether the weather were cold or not, and he chose the loneliest paths and those most overshadowed by trees and banks. His goggling spectacles and ghastly bandaged face under the penthouse of his hat, came with a disagreeable suddenness out of the darkness upon one or two home-going labourers, and Teddy Henfrey, tumbling out of the Scarlet Coat one night, at half-past nine, was scared shamefully by the stranger's skull-like head (he was walking hat in hand) lit by the sudden light of the opened inn door. Such children as saw him at nightfall dreamt of bogies, and it seemed doubtful whether he disliked boys more than they disliked him, or the reverse,—but there was certainly a vivid dislike enough on either side.

It was inevitable that a person of so remarkable an appearance and bearing should form a frequent topic in such a village as Iping. Opinion was greatly divided about his occupation. Mrs. Hall was sensitive on the point. When questioned, she explained very carefully that he was an "experimental investigator," going gingerly over the syllables as one who dreads pitfalls. When asked what an experimental investigator was, she would say

ostentatiously: In a showy manner. He made a big production of trying to conceal his dislike.

penthouse: Here, the sloping top.

bogies: Imaginary figures—terrifying persons or things.

with a touch of superiority that most educated people knew such things as that, and would thus explain that he "discovered things." Her visitor had had an accident, she said, which temporarily discoloured his face and hands, and being of a sensitive disposition, he was averse to any public notice of the fact.

Out of her hearing there was a view largely entertained that he was a criminal trying to escape from justice by wrapping himself up so as to conceal himself altogether from the eye of the police. This idea sprang from the brain of Mr. Teddy Henfrey. No crime of any magnitude dating from the middle or end of February was known to have occurred. Elaborated in the imagination of Mr. Gould, the probationary assistant in the National School, this theory took the form that the stranger was an Anarchist in disguise, preparing explosives, and he resolved to undertake such detective operations as his time permitted. These consisted for the most part in looking very hard at the stranger whenever they met, or in asking people who had never seen the stranger, leading questions about him. But he detected nothing.

Another school of opinion followed Mr. Fearenside, and either accepted the piebald view or some modification of it; as, for instance, Silas Durgan, who was heard to assert that "if he choses to show enself at fairs he'd make his fortune in no time," and being a bit of a theologian, compared the stranger to the man with the one talent. Yet another view explained the entire matter by regarding the stranger as a harmless lunatic. That had the advantage of accounting for everything straight away.

Between these main groups there were waverers and compromisers. Sussex folk have few superstitions, and it was only after the events of early April that the thought of the supernatural was first whispered in the village. Even then it was only credited among the women folks.

But whatever they thought of him, people in Iping, on the whole, agreed in disliking him. His irritability, though it might have been comprehensible to an urban brain-worker, was an amazing thing to these quiet Sussex villagers. The frantic gesticulations they surprised now and then, the headlong pace after nightfall that swept him upon them round quiet corners, the inhuman bludgeoning of all the tentative advances of curiosity, the taste for twilight that led to the closing of doors, the pulling down of blinds, the extinction of candles and lamps,—who could agree with such goings on? They drew aside as he passed down the village, and when he had gone by, young humourists would up with coat-collars and down with hat-brims, and go pacing nervously after him in imitation of his occult bearing. There was a song popular at that time called the "Bogey Man"; Miss Statchell sang it at the schoolroom concert (in aid of the church lamps), and thereafter whenever one or two of the villagers were gathered together and the stranger appeared, a bar or so of this tune, more or less sharp or flat, was whistled in the midst of them. Also belated little children would call "Bogey Man!" after him, and make off tremulously elated.

Cuss, the general practitioner, was devoured by curiosity. The bandages excited his professional interest, the report of the thousand and one bottles aroused his jealous regard. All through April and May he coveted an opportunity of talking to the stranger, and at last towards Whitsuntide, he could stand it no longer, but hit upon the subscription-list for a village nurse as an excuse. He was surprised to find that Mr. Hall did not know his guest's name. "He give a name," said Mrs. Hall,—an assertion which was quite unfounded,—"but I didn't rightly hear it." She thought it seemed so silly not to know the man's name.

Cuss rapped at the parlour door and entered. There was a fairly audible imprecation from within. "Pardon my intrusion," said Cuss, and then the door closed and cut Mrs. Hall off from the rest of the conversation.

She could hear the murmur of voices for the next ten minutes, then a cry of surprise, a stirring of feet, a chair flung aside, a bark of laughter, quick steps to the door, and Cuss appeared, his face white, his eyes staring over his shoulder. He left the door open behind him, and without looking at her strode across the hall and went down the steps, and she heard his feet hurrying along the road. He carried his hat in his hand. She stood behind the door, looking at the open door of the parlour. Then she heard the stranger laughing quietly, and then his footsteps came across the room. She could not see his face where she stood. The parlour door slammed, and the place was silent again.

Cuss went straight up the village to Bunting the vicar. "Am I mad?" Cuss began abruptly, as he entered the shabby little study. "Do I look like an insane person?"

occult: Mysterious, hidden.

tremulously elated: Shaking with joy.

coveted: Longed for.

imprecation: Curse.

ammonite: A spiral-shaped fossil shell used here as a paperweight.

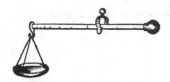

Balance

Evening Primrose

"What's happened?" said the vicar, putting the ammonite on the loose sheets of his forthcoming sermon.

"That chap at the inn—"

"Well?"

"Give me something to drink," said Cuss, and he sat down.

When his nerves had been steadied by a glass of cheap sherry,—the only drink the good vicar had available,—he told him of the interview he had just had. "Went in," he gasped, "and began to demand a subscription for that Nurse Fund. He'd stuck his hands in his pockets as I came in, and he sat down lumpily in his chair. Sniffed. I told him I'd heard he took an interest in scientific things. He said yes. Sniffed again. Kept on sniffing all the time; evidently recently caught an infernal cold. No wonder, wrapped up like that! I developed the nurse idea, and all the while kept my eyes open. Bottles—chemicals—everywhere. Balance, test-tubes in stands, and a smell of—evening primrose. Would he subscribe? Said he'd consider it. Asked him, point-blank, was he researching. Said he was. A long research. Got quite cross. 'A damnable long research,' said he, blowing the cork out, so to speak. 'Oh,' said I. And out came the grievance. The man was just on the boil, and my questions boiled him over. He had been given a prescription, most valuable prescription—what for he wouldn't say. Was it medical? 'Damn you! What are you fishing after?' I apologised. Dignified sniff and cough. He resumed. He'd read it. Five ingredients. Put it down; turned his head. Draught of air from window lifted the paper. Swish, rustle. He was working in a room with an open fireplace, he said. Saw a flicker, and there was the prescription burning and lifting chimneyward. Rushed towards it just as it whisked up chimney. So! Just at that point, to illustrate his story, out came his arm."

"Well?"

"No hand,—just an empty sleeve. Lord! I thought, *that's* a deformity! Got a cork arm, I suppose, and has taken it off. Then, I thought, there's something odd in that. What the devil keeps that sleeve up and open, if there's nothing in it? There was nothing in it, I tell you. Nothing down it, right down to the joint. I could see right down it to the elbow, and there was a glimmer of light shining through a tear of the cloth. 'Good God!' I said. Then he stopped. Stared at me with those black goggles of his, and then at his sleeve."

"Well?"

122

"That's all. He never said a word; just glared, and put his sleeve back in his pocket quickly. 'I was saying,' said he, 'that there was the prescription burning, wasn't I?' Interrogative cough. 'How the devil,' said I, 'can you move an empty sleeve like that?' 'Empty sleeve?' 'Yes,' said I, 'an empty sleeve.'

" 'It's an empty sleeve, is it? You saw it was an empty sleeve?' He stood up right away. I stood up too. He came towards me in three very slow steps, and stood quite close. Sniffed venomously. I didn't flinch, though I'm hanged if that bandaged knob of his, and those blinkers, aren't enough to unnerve any one, coming quietly up to you.

" 'You said it was an empty sleeve?' he said. 'Certainly,' I said. Then very quietly he pulled his sleeve out of his pocket again, and raised his arm towards me as though he would show it to me again. He did it very, very slowly. I looked at it. Seemed an age. 'Well?' said I, clearing my throat, 'there's nothing in it.' Had to say something. I was beginning to feel frightened. I could see right down it. He extended it straight towards me, slowly, slowly,—just like that,—until the cuff was six inches from my face. Queer thing to see an empty sleeve come at you like that! And then—"

"Well?"

"Something—exactly like a finger and thumb it felt—nipped my nose."

Bunting began to laugh.

"There wasn't anything there!" said Cuss, his voice running up into a shriek at the "there." "It's all very well for you to laugh, but I tell you I was so startled, I hit his cuff hard, and turned round, and cut out of the room—I left him—"

Cuss stopped. There was no mistaking the sincerity of his panic. He turned round in a helpless way and took a second glass of the excellent vicar's very inferior sherry. "When I hit his cuff," said Cuss, "I tell you, it felt exactly like hitting an arm. And there wasn't an arm! There wasn't the ghost of an arm!"

Mr. Bunting thought it over. He looked suspiciously at Cuss. "It's a most remarkable story," he said. He looked very wise and grave indeed. "It's really," said Mr. Bunting with judicial emphasis, "a most remarkable story."

venomously: Poisonously; in a hateful way.

judicial: Like a judge passing judgment on a case.

At that he returned to his bedroom, armed himself with the most obvious weapon, the poker, and descended the staircase as noiselessly as possible.

5
THE BURGLARY AT THE VICARAGE

Whit-Monday: The day after Whit-Sunday, the seventh Sunday after Easter, observed in commemoration of the descent of the Holy Spirit on the day of Pentecost.

The facts of the burglary at the vicarage came to us chiefly through the medium of the vicar and his wife. It occurred in the small hours of Whit-Monday,—the day devoted in Iping to the Club festivities. Mrs. Bunting, it seems, woke up suddenly in the stillness that comes before the dawn, with the strong impression that the door of their bedroom had opened and closed. She did not arouse her husband at first, but sat up in bed listening. She then distinctly heard the pad, pad, pad of bare feet coming out of the adjoining dressing-room and walking along the passage

124

towards the staircase. As soon as she felt assured of this, she aroused the Rev. Mr. Bunting as quietly as possible. He did not strike a light, but putting on his spectacles, her dressing-gown, and his bath slippers, he went out on the landing to listen. He heard quite distinctly a fumbling going on at his study desk downstairs, and then a violent sneeze.

At that he returned to his bedroom, armed himself with the most obvious weapon, the poker, and descended the staircase as noiselessly as possible. Mrs. Bunting came out on the landing.

The hour was about four, and the ultimate darkness of the night was past. There was a faint shimmer of light in the hall, but the study doorway yawned impenetrably black. Everything was still except the faint creaking of the stairs under Mr. Bunting's tread, and the slight movements in the study. Then something snapped, the drawer was opened, and there was a rustle of papers. Then came an imprecation, and a match was struck and the study was flooded with yellow light. Mr. Bunting was now in the hall, and through the crack of the door he could see the desk and the open drawer and a candle burning on the desk. But the robber he could not see. He stood there in the hall undecided what to do, and Mrs. Bunting, her face white and intent, crept slowly downstairs after him. One thing kept up Mr. Bunting's courage: the persuasion that this burglar was a resident in the village.

They heard the chink of money, and realised that the robber had found the housekeeping reserve of gold,—two pounds ten in half-sovereigns altogether. At that sound Mr. Bunting was nerved to abrupt action. Gripping the poker firmly, he rushed into the room, closely followed by Mrs. Bunting. "Surrender!" cried Mr. Bunting, fiercely, and then stopped amazed. Apparently the room was perfectly empty.

Yet their conviction that they had, that very moment, heard somebody moving in the room had amounted to a certainty. For half a minute, perhaps, they stood gaping, then Mrs. Bunting went across the room and looked behind the screen, while Mr. Bunting, by a kindred impulse, peered under the desk. Then Mrs. Bunting turned back the window-curtains, and Mr. Bunting looked up the chimney and probed it with the poker. Then Mrs. Bunting scrutinised the waste-paper basket and Mr. Bunting opened the lid of the coal-scuttle. Then they came to a stop and stood with eyes interrogating each other.

"I could have sworn—" said Mr. Bunting.

landing: The level part of a staircase, at the end of a flight of stairs.

two pounds ten: Two pounds, ten shillings. One pound sterling is worth 20 shillings or $2.35 in American money. A shilling is worth about 12 cents. Therefore, two pounds ten would be equal to about $5.90 in our currency, to-day.

kindred: Similar, related.

Coal-scuttle

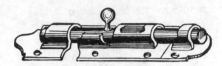

bolts . . . shot: The bolts were being pushed out of their fastenings; unlocked.

scullery: A place where kitchen utensils are cleaned and kept, or where coarse kitchen work is done.

guttering: Flaming; flaring up with a sudden unsteady light.

"The candle!" said Mr. Bunting. "Who lit the candle?"

"The drawer!" said Mrs. Bunting. "And the money's gone!" She went hastily to the doorway.

"Of all the extraordinary occurrences—"

There was a violent sneeze in the passage. They rushed out, and as they did so the kitchen door slammed. "Bring the candle," said Mr. Bunting, and led the way. They both heard a sound of bolts being hastily shot back.

As he opened the kitchen door he saw through the scullery that the back door was just opening, and the faint light of early dawn displayed the dark masses of the garden beyond. He is certain that nothing went out of the door. It opened, stood open for a moment, and then closed with a slam. As it did so, the candle Mrs. Bunting was carrying from the study flickered and flared. It was minute or more before they entered the kitchen.

The place was empty. They refastened the back door, examined the kitchen, pantry, and scullery thoroughly, and at last went down into the cellar. There was not a soul to be found in the house, search as they would.

Daylight found the vicar and his wife, a quaintly-costumed little couple, still marvelling about on their own ground floor by the unnecessary light of a guttering candle.

126

she screamed and turned, and then the chair legs came gently but firmly against her back and impelled her and Hall out of the room.

N ow it happened that in the early hours of Whit-Monday, before Millie was hunted out for the day, Mr. Hall and Mrs. Hall both rose and went noiselessly down into the cellar. Their business there was of a private nature, and had something to do with the specific gravity of their beer. They had hardly entered the cellar when Mrs. Hall found she had forgotten to bring down a bottle of sarsaparilla from their joint-room. As she was the expert and principal operator in this affair, Hall very properly went upstairs for it.

sarsaparilla: (say SASS pa rilla) A carbonated beverage with a root beer-like flavor.

127

On the landing he was surprised to see that the stranger's door was ajar. He went on into his own room and found the bottle as he had been directed.

But returning with the bottle, he noticed that the bolts of the front door had been shot back, that the door was in fact simply on the latch. And with a flash of inspiration he connected this with the stranger's room upstairs and the suggestions of Mr. Teddy Henfrey. He distinctly remembered holding the candle while Mrs. Hall shot these bolts overnight. At the sight he stopped, gaping, then with the bottle still in his hand went upstairs again. He rapped at the stranger's door. There was no answer. He rapped again; then pushed the door wide open and entered.

It was as he expected. The bed, the room also, was empty. And what was stranger, even to his heavy intelligence, on the bedroom chair and along the rail of the bed were scattered the garments, the only garments so far as he knew, and the bandages of their guest. His big slouch hat even was cocked jauntily over the bed-post.

As Hall stood there he heard his wife's voice coming out of the depth of the cellar, with that rapid telescoping of the syllables and interrogative cocking up of the final words to a high note, by which the West Sussex villager is wont to indicate a brisk impatience. "Gearge! You gart what a wand?"

At that he turned and hurried down to her. "Janny," he said, over the rail of the cellar steps, " 'tas the truth what Henfrey sez. 'E's not in uz room, 'e ent. And the front door's unbolted."

At first Mrs. Hall did not understand, and as soon as she did she resolved to see the empty room for herself. Hall, still holding the bottle, went first. "If'e ent there," he said, "his close are. And what's 'e doin' without his close, then? 'Tas a most curious basness."

As they came up the cellar steps, they both, it was afterwards ascertained, fancied they heard the front door open and shut, but seeing it closed and nothing there, neither said a word to the other about it at the time. Mrs. Hall passed her husband in the passage and ran on first upstairs. Some one sneezed on the staircase. Hall, following six steps behind, thought that he heard her sneeze. She, going on first, was under the impression that Hall was sneezing. She flung open the door and stood regarding the room. "Of all the curious!" she said.

wont: Accustomed; in the habit of.

128

She heard a sniff close behind her head as it seemed, and, turning, was surprised to see Hall a dozen feet off on the topmost stair. But in another moment he was beside her. She bent forward and put her hand on the pillow and then under the clothes.

"Cold," she said. "He's been up this hour or more."

As she did so, a most extraordinary thing happened,—the bedclothes gathered themselves together, leapt up suddenly into a sort of peak, and then jumped headlong over the bottom rail. It was exactly as if a hand had clutched them in the centre and flung them aside. Immediately after, the stranger's hat hopped off the bed-post, described a whirling flight in the air through the better part of a circle, and then dashed straight at Mrs. Hall's face. Then as swiftly came the sponge from the washstand; and then the chair, flinging the stranger's coat and trousers carelessly aside, and laughing drily in a voice singularly like the stranger's, turned itself up with its four legs at Mrs. Hall, seemed to take aim at her for a moment, and charged at her. She screamed and turned, and then the chair legs came gently but firmly against her back and impelled her and Hall out of the room. The door slammed violently and was locked. The chair and bed seemed to be executing a dance of triumph for a moment, and then abruptly everything was still.

Mrs. Hall was left almost in a fainting condition in Mr. Hall's arms on the landing. It was with the greatest difficulty that Mr. Hall and Millie, who had been roused by her scream of alarm, succeeded in getting her downstairs, and applying the restoratives customary in these cases.

" 'Tas sperits," said Mrs. Hall. "I know 'tas sperits. I've read in papers of en. Tables and chairs leaping and dancing!—"

"Take a drop more, Janny," said Hall. " 'T will steady ye."

"Lock him out," said Mrs. Hall. "Don't let him come in again. I half guessed— I might ha' known. With them goggling eyes and bandaged head, and never going to church of a Sunday. And all they bottles—more 'n it's right for any one to have. He's put the sperits into the furniture.—My good old furniture! 'T was in that very chair my poor dear mother used to sit when I was a little girl. To think it should rise up against me now!"

"Just a drop more, Janny," said Hall. "Your nerves is all upset."

described: Traced the outline of.

restoratives: Something that restores a person to consciousness, probably smelling salts: an aromatic preparation of carbonate of ammonium and some scent.

They sent Millie across the street through the golden five o'clock sunshine to rouse up Mr. Sandy Wadgers, the blacksmith. Mr. Hall's compliments and the furniture upstairs was behaving most extraordinary. Would Mr. Wadgers come round? He was a knowing man, was Mr. Wadgers, and very resourceful. He took quite a grave view of the case. "Arm darmed ef thet ent witchcraft," was the view of Mr. Sandy Wadgers. "You warnt horseshoes for such gentry as he."

He came round greatly concerned. They wanted him to lead the way upstairs to the room, but he didn't seem to be in any hurry. He preferred to talk in the passage. Over the way Huxter's apprentice came out and began taking down the shutters of the tobacco window. He was called over to join the discussion. Mr. Huxter naturally followed over in the course of a few minutes. The Anglo-Saxon genius for parliamentary government asserted itself; there was a great deal of talk and no decisive action. "Let's have the facts first," insisted Mr. Sandy Wadgers. "Let's be sure we'd be acting perfectly right in bustin' that there door open. A door onbust is always open to bustin', but ye can't onbust a door once you've busted en."

And suddenly and most wonderfully the door of the room upstairs opened of its own accord, and as they looked up in amazement, they saw descending the stairs the muffled figure of the stranger staring more blackly and blankly than ever with those unreasonably large blue glass eyes of his. He came down stiffly and slowly, staring all the time; he walked across the passage staring, then stopped.

"Look there!" he said, and their eyes followed the direction of his gloved finger and saw a bottle of sarsaparilla hard by the cellar door. Then he entered the parlour, and suddenly, swiftly, viciously, slammed the door in their faces.

Not a word was spoken until the last echoes of the slam had died away. They stared at one another. "Well, if that don't lick everything!" said Mr. Wadgers, and left the alternative unsaid.

"I'd go in and ask'n 'bout it," said Wadgers, to Mr. Hall. "I'd d'mand an explanation."

It took some time to bring the landlady's husband up to that pitch. At last he rapped, opened the door, and got as far as, "Excuse me—"

"Go to the devil!" said the stranger in a tremendous voice, and "Shut that door after you." So that brief interview terminated.

He took off his hat, and with a violent gesture tore at his whiskers and bandages.

The stranger went into the little parlour of the Coach and Horses about half-past five in the morning, and there he remained until near midday, the blinds down, the door shut, and none, after Hall's repulse, venturing near him.

All that time he must have fasted. Thrice he rang his bell, the third time furiously and continuously, but no one answered him. "Him and his 'go to the devil' indeed!" said Mrs. Hall. Presently came an imperfect rumour of the burglary at the vicarage, and two and two were put together. Hall, assisted by Wadgers, went off to find Mr. Shuckleforth, the magistrate, and

7
THE
UNVEILING
OF THE STRANGER

imperfect rumour: Incomplete and inaccurate, as rumors generally are.

piqué: (Say P K) Patterned.

cocoanut shy: A stand where people try to knock down cocoanuts by tossing balls at them. Prizes are given to those who succeed.

Union Jack (British Flag)

pungent twang: A sharp, biting smell.

take his advice. No one ventured upstairs. How the stranger occupied himself is unknown. Now and then he would stride violently up and down, and twice came an outburst of curses, a tearing of paper, and a violent smashing of bottles.

The little group of scared but curious people increased. Mrs. Huxter came over; some gay young fellows resplendent in black ready-made jackets and *piqué* paper ties, for it was Whit-Monday, joined the group with confused interrogations. Young Archie Harker distinguished himself by going up the yard and trying to peep under the window-blinds. He could see nothing, but gave reason for supposing that he did, and others of the Iping youth presently joined him.

It was the finest of all possible Whit-Mondays, and down the village street stood a row of nearly a dozen booths, a shooting gallery, and on the grass by the forge were three yellow and chocolate waggons and some picturesque strangers of both sexes putting up a cocoanut shy. The gentlemen wore blue jerseys, the ladies white aprons and quite fashionable hats with heavy plumes. Wodger, of the Purple Fawn, and Mr. Jaggers, the cobbler, who also sold second-hand ordinary bicycles, were stretching a string of union-jacks and royal ensigns (which had originally celebrated the Jubilee) across the road. . . .

And inside, in the artificial darkness of the parlour, into which only one thin jet of sunlight penetrated, the stranger, hungry we must suppose, and fearful, hidden in his uncomfortable hot wrappings, pored through his dark glasses upon his paper or chinked his dirty little bottles, and occasionally swore savagely at the boys, audible if invisible, outside the windows. In the corner by the fireplace lay the fragments of half a dozen smashed bottles, and a pungent twang of chlorine tainted the air. So much we know from what was heard at the time and from what was subsequently seen in the room.

About noon he suddenly opened his parlour door and stood glaring fixedly at the three or four people in the bar. "Mrs. Hall," he said. Somebody went sheepishly and called for Mrs. Hall.

Mrs. Hall appeared after an interval, a little short of breath, but all the fiercer for that. Hall was still out. She had deliberated over this scene, and she came holding a little tray with an unsettled bill upon it. "Is it your bill you're wanting, sir?" she said.

"Why wasn't my breakfast laid? Why haven't you prepared my meals and answered my bell? Do you think I live without eating?"

"Why isn't my bill paid?" said Mrs. Hall. "That's what I want to know."

"I told you three days ago I was awaiting a remittance—"

"I told you two days ago I wasn't going to await no remittances. You can't grumble if your breakfast waits a bit, if my bill's been waiting these five days, can you?"

The stranger swore briefly but vividly.

"Nar, nar!" from the bar.

"And I'd thank you kindly, sir, if you'd keep your swearing to yourself, sir," said Mrs. Hall.

The stranger stood looking more like an angry diving-helmet than ever. It was universally felt in the bar that Mrs. Hall had the better of him. His next words showed as much.

"Look here, my good woman—" he began.

"Don't good woman *me*," said Mrs. Hall.

"I've told you my remittance hasn't come—"

"Remittance indeed!" said Mrs. Hall.

"Still, I daresay in my pocket—"

"You told me two days ago that you hadn't anything but a sovereign's worth of silver upon you—"

"Well, I've found some more—"

" 'Ul-*lo!*" from the bar.

"I wonder where you found it?" said Mrs. Hall.

That seemed to annoy the stranger very much. He stamped his foot. "What do you mean?" he said.

"That I wonder where you found it," said Mrs. Hall. "And before I take any bills or get any breakfasts, or do any such things whatsoever, you got to tell me one or two things I don't understand, and what nobody don't understand, and what everybody is very anxious to understand. I want know what you been doing t' my chair upstairs, and I want know how 't is your room was empty, and how you got in again. Them as stops in this house comes in by the doors,—that's the rule of the house, and that you *didn't* do, and what I want know is how you *did* come in. And I want know—"

Suddenly the stranger raised his gloved hands clenched, stamped his foot, and said, "Stop!" with such extraordinary violence that he silenced her instantly.

"You don't understand," he said, "who I am or what I am.

remittance: A payment.

metamorphosed: Strikingly or drastically changed; transformed.

I'll show you. By Heaven! I'll show you." Then he put his open palm over his face and withdrew it. The centre of his face became a black cavity. "Here," he said. He stepped forward and handed Mrs. Hall something which she, staring at his metamorphosed face, accepted automatically. Then, when she saw what it was, she screamed loudly, dropped it, and staggered back. The nose—it was the stranger's nose! pink and shining—rolled on the floor.

Then he removed his spectacles, and every one in the bar gasped. He took off his hat, and with a violent gesture tore at his whiskers and bandages. For a moment they resisted him. A flash of horrible anticipation passed through the bar. "Oh, my Gard!" said some one. Then off they came.

It was worse than anything. Mrs. Hall, standing open-mouthed and horror-struck, shrieked at what she saw, and made for the door of the house. Every one began to move. They were prepared for scars, disfigurements, tangible horrors, but *nothing!* The bandages and false hair flew across the passage into the bar, making a hobbledehoy jump to avoid them. Every one tumbled on every one else down the steps. For the man who stood there shouting some incoherent explanation, was a solid gesticulating figure up to the coat-collar of him, and then—nothingness, no visible thing at all!

People down the village heard shouts and shrieks, and looking up the street saw the Coach and Horses violently firing out its humanity. They saw Mrs. Hall fall down and Mr. Teddy Henfrey jump to avoid tumbling over her, and then they heard the frightful screams of Millie, who, emerging suddenly from the kitchen at the noise of the tumult, had come upon the headless stranger from behind. These ceased suddenly.

hobbledehoy: Awkward, clumsy.

tumult: An uproar; a violent outburst.

Forthwith every one all down the street, the sweetstuff seller, cocoanut shy proprietor and his assistant, the swing man, little boys and girls, rustic dandies, smart wenches, smocked elders and aproned gipsies, began running towards the inn, and in a miraculously short space of time a crowd of perhaps forty people, and rapidly increasing, swayed and hooted and inquired and exclaimed and suggested, in front of Mrs. Hall's establishment. Every one seemed eager to talk at once, and the result was babel. A small group supported Mrs. Hall, who was picked up in a state of collapse. There was a conference, and the incredible evidence of a vociferous eye-witness. "O Bogey!"

babel: A confusion of voices.

vociferous: Loud and noisy.

134

"What's he been doin,' then?" Ain't hurt the girl, 'as 'e?" "Run at en with a knife, I believe." "No 'ed, I tell ye. I don't mean no manner of speaking, I mean *marn 'ithout a 'ed!*" "Narnsense! 'tas some conjuring trick." "Fetched off 'is wrappin's, 'e did—"

In its struggles to see in through the open door, the crowd formed itself into a straggling wedge, with the more adventurous apex nearest the inn. "He stood for a moment, I heerd the gal scream, and he turned. I saw her skirts whisk, and he went after her. Didn't take ten seconds. Back he comes with a knife in uz hand and a loaf; stood just as if he was staring. Not a moment ago. Went in that there door. I tell 'e, 'e ain't gart no 'ed 't all. You just missed en—"

There was a disturbance behind, and the speaker stopped to step aside for a little procession that was marching very resolutely towards the house,—first Mr. Hall, very red and determined, then Mr. Bobby Jaffers, the village constable, and then the wary Mr. Wadgers. They had come now armed with a warrant.

People shouted conflicting information of the recent circumstances. " 'Ed or no 'ed," said Jaffers, "I got to 'rest en, and 'rest en I *will.*"

Mr. Hall marched up the steps, marched straight to the door of the parlour and flung it open. "Constable," he said, "do your duty."

Jaffers marched in, Hall next, Wadgers last. They saw in the dim light the headless figure facing them, with a gnawed crust of bread in one gloved hand and a chunk of cheese in the other.

"That's him!" said Hall.

"What the devil's this?" came in a tone of angry expostulation from above the collar of the figure.

"You're a damned rum customer, mister," said Mr. Jaffers. "But 'ed or no 'ed, the warrant says 'body,' and duty's duty—"

"Keep off!" said the figure, starting back.

Abruptly he whipped down the bread and cheese, and Mr. Hall just grasped the knife on the table in time to save it. Off came the stranger's left glove and was slapped in Jaffers' face. In another moment Jaffers, cutting short some statement concerning a warrant, had gripped him by the handless wrist and caught his invisible throat. He got a sounding kick on the shin that made him shout, but he kept his grip. Hall sent the knife sliding along the table to Wadgers, who acted as goal-keeper for the

THE UNVEILING OF THE STRANGER

conjuring: Magic.

apex: Usually top; here, the people at the very front of the wedge-shaped crowd.

warrant: A legal document that authorizes an action; here, it authorizes the Invisible Man's arrest.

expostulation: Protest.

offensive, so to speak, and then stepped forward as Jaffers and the stranger swayed and staggered towards him, clutching and hitting in. A chair stood in the way, and went aside with a crash as they came down together.

"Get the feet," said Jaffers between his teeth.

Mr. Hall, endeavouring to act on instructions, received a sounding kick in the ribs that disposed of him for a moment, and Mr. Wadgers, seeing the decapitated stranger had rolled over and got the upper side of Jaffers, retreated towards the door, knife in hand, and so collided with Mr. Huxter and the Siddermorton carter coming to the rescue of law and order. At the same moment down came three or four bottles from the chiffonnier and shot a web of pungency into the air of the room.

"I'll surrender," cried the stranger, though he had Jaffers down, and in another moment he stood up panting, a strange figure, headless and handless,—for he had pulled off his right glove now as well as his left. "It's no good," he said, as if sobbing for breath.

It was the strangest thing in the world to hear that voice coming as if out of empty space, but the Sussex peasants are perhaps the most matter-of-fact people under the sun. Jaffers got up also and produced a pair of handcuffs. Then he started.

"I say!" said Jaffers, brought up short by a dim realisation of the incongruity of the whole business, "Darm it! Can't use 'em as I can see."

The stranger ran his arm down his waistcoat, and as if by a miracle the buttons to which his empty sleeve pointed became undone. Then he said something about his shin, and stooped down. He seemed to be fumbling with his shoes and socks.

"Why!" said Huxter, suddenly, "that's not a man at all. It's just empty clothes. Look! You can see down his collar and the linings of his clothes. I could put my arm—"

He extended his hand; it seemed to meet something in mid-air, and he drew it back with a sharp exclamation. "I wish you'd keep your fingers out of my eye," said the aerial voice, in a tone of savage expostulation. "The fact is, I'm all here: head, hands, legs, and all the rest of it, but it happens I'm invisible. It's a confounded nuisance, but I am. That's no reason why I should be poked to pieces by every stupid bumpkin in Iping, is it?"

carter: A cart driver.

incongruity: Inconsistency.

bumpkin: An awkward country fellow.

136

The suit of clothes, now all unbuttoned and hanging loosely upon its unseen supports, stood up, arms akimbo.

Several other of the men folks had now entered the room, so that it was closely crowded. "Invisible, eigh?" said Huxter, ignoring the stranger's abuse. "Who ever heard the likes of that?"

"It's strange, perhaps, but it's not a crime. Why am I assaulted by a policeman in this fashion?"

"Ah! that's a different matter," said Jaffers. "No doubt you are a bit difficult to see in this light, but I got a warrant and it's all correct. What I'm after ain't no invisibility,—it's burglary. There's a house been broken into and money took."

"Well?"

"And circumstances certainly point—"

"Stuff and nonsense!" said the Invisible Man.

"I hope so, sir; but I've got my instructions."

"Well," said the stranger, "I'll come. I'll *come*. But no handcuffs."

"It's the regular thing," said Jaffers.

"No handcuffs," stipulated the stranger.

"Pardon me," said Jaffers.

Abruptly the figure sat down, and before any one could realise what was being done, the slippers, socks, and trousers had been kicked off under the table. Then he sprang up again and flung off his coat.

"Here, stop that," said Jaffers, suddenly realising what was happening. He gripped the waistcoat; it struggled, and the shirt slipped out of it and left it limp and empty in his hand. "Hold him!" said Jaffers, loudly. "Once he gets they things off—!"

"Hold him!" cried every one, and there was a rush at the fluttering white shirt which was now all that was visible of the stranger.

The shirt-sleeve planted a shrewd blow in Hall's face that stopped his open-armed advance, and sent him backward into old Toothsome the sexton, and in another moment the garment was lifted up and became convulsed and vacantly flapping about the arms, even as a shirt that is being thrust over a man's head. Jaffers clutched at it, and only helped to pull it off; he was struck in the mouth out of the air, and incontinently drew his truncheon and smote Teddy Henfrey savagely upon the crown of his head.

**THE
UNVEILING
OF THE STRANGER**

akimbo: Resting on the hips with the elbows turned outward.

sexton: A church officer in charge of caring for the property, ringing the bells, and digging graves.

incontinently: Without restraint.

rout: A mob; an unruly crowd.

mêleé: A confused brawl.

prostrate: Lying flat on the ground.

transit: Passage.

"Look out!" said everybody, fencing at random and hitting at nothing. "Hold him! Shut the door! Don't let him loose! I got something! Here he is!" A perfect babel of noises they made. Everybody, it seemed, was being hit all at once, and Sandy Wadgers, knowing as ever and his wits sharpened by a frightful blow in the nose, reopened the door and led the rout. The others, following incontinently, were jammed for a moment in the corner by the doorway. The hitting continued. Phipps, the Unitarian, had a front tooth broken, and Henfrey was injured in the cartilage of his ear. Jaffers was struck under the jaw, and, turning, caught at something that intervened between him and Huxter in the *mêleé*, and prevented their coming together. He felt a muscular chest, and in another moment the whole mass of struggling, excited men shot out into the crowded hall.

"I got him!" shouted Jaffers, choking and reeling through them all, and wrestling with purple face and swelling veins against his unseen enemy.

Men staggered right and left as the extraordinary conflict swayed swiftly towards the house door, and went spinning down the half-dozen steps of the inn. Jaffers cried in a strangled voice,—holding tight, nevertheless, and making play with his knee,—spun round, and fell heavily undermost with his head on the gravel. Only then did his fingers relax.

There were excited cries of "Hold him!" "Invisible!" and so forth, and a young fellow, a stranger in the place whose name did not come to light, rushed in at once, caught something, missed his hold, and fell over the constable's prostrate body. Half-way across the road a woman screamed as something pushed by her; a dog, kicked apparently, yelped and ran howling into Huxter's yard, and with that the transit of the Invisible Man was accomplished. For a space people stood amazed and gesticulating, and then came Panic, and scattered them abroad through the village as a gust scatters dead leaves.

But Jaffers lay quite still, face upward and knees bent.

He heard close to him the sound as of a man coughing, sneezing...

he eighth chapter is exceedingly brief, and relates that Gibbins, the amateur naturalist of the district, while lying out on the spacious open downs without a soul within a couple of miles of him, as he thought, and almost dozing, heard close to him the sound as of a man coughing, sneezing, and then swearing savagely to himself; and looking, beheld nothing. Yet the voice was indisputable. It continued to swear with that breadth and variety that distinguishes the swearing of a culti-vated man. It grew to a climax, diminished again, and died away in the distance, going as it seemed to him in the direction of Adderdean. It lifted to a spasmodic sneeze and ended. Gibbins had heard nothing of the morning's occurrences, but the phenomenon was so striking and disturbing that his philosophi-cal tranquillity vanished; he got up hastily, and hurried down the steepness of the hill towards the village, as fast as he could go.

8

IN
TRANSIT

In a leisurely manner—
he did everything in a leisurely
manner— he was contemplating
trying on a pair of boots.

9

MR. THOMAS MARVEL

embonpoint: Stoutness.

You must picture Mr. Thomas Marvel as a person of copious, flexible visage, a nose of cylindrical protrusion, a liquorish, ample, fluctuating mouth, and a beard of bristling eccentricity. His figure inclined to embonpoint; his short limbs accentuated this inclination. He wore a furry silk hat, and the frequent substitution of twine and shoe-laces for buttons, apparent at critical points of his costume, marked a man essentially bachelor.

Mr. Thomas Marvel was sitting with his feet in a ditch by the roadside over the down towards Adderdean, about a mile and a half out of Iping. His feet, save for socks of irregular open-work, were bare, his big toes were broad, and pricked like the ears of a watchful dog. In a leisurely manner—he did everything in a leisurely manner—he was contemplating trying on a pair of boots. They were the soundest boots he had come across for a long time, but too large for him; whereas the ones he had were, in dry weather, a very comfortable fit, but too thin-soled for damp. Mr. Thomas Marvel hated roomy shoes, but then he hated damp. He had never properly thought out which he hated most, and it was a pleasant day, and there was nothing better to do. So he put the four shoes in a graceful group on the turf and looked at them. And seeing them there among the grass and springing agrimony, it suddenly occurred to him that both pairs were exceedingly ugly to see. He was not at all startled by a voice behind him.

"They're boots, anyhow," said the voice.

"They are—charity boots," said Mr. Thomas Marvel, with his head on one side regarding them distastefully; "and which is the ugliest pair in the whole blessed universe, I'm darned if I know!"

"H'm," said the voice.

"I've worn worse,—in fact, I've worn none. But none so owdacious ugly,—if you'll allow the expression. I've been cadging boots—in particular—for days. Because I was sick of *them.* They're sound enough, of course. But a gentleman on tramp sees such a thundering lot of his boots. And if you'll believe me, I've raised nothing in the whole blessed county, try as I would, but THEM. Look at 'em! And a good county for boots, too, in a general way. But it's just my promiscuous luck. I've got my boots in this county ten years or more. And then they treat you like this."

"It's a beast of a county," said the voice. "And pigs for people."

"Ain't it?" said Mr. Thomas Marvel. "Lord! But them boots! It beats it."

He turned his head over his shoulder to the right, to look at the boots of his interlocutor with a view to comparisons, and lo! where the boots of his interlocutor should have been were neither legs nor boots. He turned his head over his shoulder to the left, and there also were neither legs nor boots. He was

agrimony: A yellow-flowered herb of the rose family, having toothed leaves and bur-like fruits.

cadging: Begging.

promiscuous: Mixed and irregular; first good, then bad.

interlocutor: A person with whom one speaks.

irradiated: Intellectually enlightened. We would probably say 'it finally dawned on him.'

ventriloquising: 'Throwing' one's voice so that it seems to come from another source.

peewit: A small European black-headed gull; the Lapwing.

off . . . chump: Losing one's mind.

irradiated by the dawn of a great amazement. "Where *are* yer?" said Mr. Thomas Marvel over his shoulder and coming on all fours. He saw a stretch of empty downs with the wind swaying the remote green-pointed furze bushes.

"Am I drunk?" said Mr. Marvel. "Have I had visions? Was I talking to myself? What the—"

"Don't be alarmed," said a voice.

"None of your ventriloquising *me*," said Mr. Thomas Marvel, rising sharply to his feet. "Where are yer? Alarmed, indeed!"

"Don't be alarmed," repeated the voice.

"*You'll* be alarmed in a minute, you silly fool," said Mr. Thomas Marvel. "Where *are* yer? Lemme get my mark on yer—

"Are you *buried?*" said Mr. Thomas Marvel, after an interval.

There was no answer. Mr. Thomas Marvel stood bootless and amazed, his jacket nearly thrown off.

"Peewit," said a peewit, very remote.

"Peewit, indeed!" said Mr. Thomas Marvel. "This ain't no time for foolery." The down was desolate, east and west, north and south; the road, with its shallow ditches and white bordering stakes, ran smooth and empty north and south, and, save for that peewit, the blue sky was empty too. "So help me," said Mr. Thomas Marvel, shuffling his coat on to his shoulders again. "It's the drink! I might ha' known."

"It's not the drink," said the voice. "You keep your nerves steady."

"Ow!" said Mr. Marvel, and his face grew white amidst its patches. "It's the drink," his lips repeated noiselessly. He remained staring about him, rotating slowly backwards. "I could have *swore* I heard a voice," he whispered.

"Of course you did."

"It's there again," said Mr. Marvel, closing his eyes and clasping his hand on his brow with a tragic gesture. He was suddenly taken by the collar and shaken violently, and left more dazed than ever. "Don't be a fool," said the voice.

"I'm—off—my—blooming—chump," said Mr. Marvel. "It's no good. It's fretting about them blarsted boots. I'm off my blessed blooming chump. Or it's spirits."

"Neither one thing nor the other," said the voice. "Listen!"

"Chump," said Mr. Marvel.

"One minute," said the voice, penetratingly,—tremulous with self-control.

"Well?" said Mr. Thomas Marvel, with a strange feeling of having been dug in the chest by a finger.

"You think I'm just imagination? Just imagination?"

"What else *can* you be?" said Mr. Thomas Marvel, rubbing the back of his neck.

"Very well," said the voice, in a tone of relief. "Then I'm going to throw flints at you till you think differently."

"But where *are* yer?"

The voice made no answer. Whizz came a flint, apparently out of the air, and missed Mr. Marvel's shoulder by a hair's-breadth. Mr. Marvel, turning, saw a flint jerk up into the air, trace a complicated path, hang for a moment, and then fling at his feet with almost invisible rapidity. He was too amazed to dodge. Whizz it came, and ricochetted from a bare toe into the ditch. Mr. Thomas Marvel jumped a foot and howled aloud. Then he started to run, tripped over an unseen obstacle, and came head over heels into a sitting position.

"*Now*," said the voice, as a third stone curved upward and hung in the air above the tramp. "Am I imagination?"

Mr. Marvel by way of reply struggled to his feet, and was immediately rolled over again. He lay quiet for a moment. "If you struggle any more," said the voice, "I shall throw the flint at your head."

"It's a fair do," said Mr. Thomas Marvel, sitting up, taking his wounded toe in hand and fixing his eye on the third missile. "I don't understand it. Stones flinging themselves. Stones talking. Put yourself down. Rot away. I'm done."

The third flint fell.

"It's very simple," said the voice. "I'm an invisible man."

"Tell us something I don't know," said Mr. Marvel, gasping with pain. "Where you've hid—how you do it—I *don't* know. I'm beat."

"That's all," said the voice. "I'm invisible. That's what I want you to understand."

"Any one could see that. There is no need for you to be so confounded impatient, mister. *Now* then. Give us a notion. How are you hid?"

"I'm invisible. That's the great point. And what I want you to understand is this—"

"But whereabouts?" interrupted Mr. Marvel.

"Here! Six yards in front of you."

flints: Very hard, somewhat shiny stones often used to start fires.

ricochetted: Bounced crazily.

fair do: A pretty good trick.

"Oh, *come!* I ain't blind. You'll be telling me next you're just thin air. I'm not one of your ignorant tramps—"

"Yes, I am—thin air. You're looking through me."

"What! Ain't there any stuff to you? *Vox et*—what is it?—jabber. Is it that?"

"I am just a human being—solid, needing food and drink, needing covering too— But I'm invisible. You see? Invisible. Simple idea. Invisible."

"What, real like?"

"Yes, real."

"Let's have a hand of you," said Marvel, "if you *are* real. It won't be so darn out-of-the-way like, then— *Lord!*" he said, "how you made me jump!—gripping me like that!"

He felt the hand that had closed round his wrist with his disengaged fingers, and his fingers went timorously up the arm, patted a muscular chest, and explored a bearded face. Marvel's face was astonishment.

"I'm dashed!" he said. "If this don't beat cock-fighting! Most remarkable!— And there I can see a rabbit clean through you, 'arf a mile away! Not a bit of you visible—except—"

He scrutinised the apparently empty space keenly. "You 'aven't been eatin' bread and cheese?" he asked, holding the invisible arm.

"You're quite right, and it's not quite assimilated into the system."

"Ah!" said Mr. Marvel. "Sort of ghostly, though."

"Of course, all this isn't half so wonderful as you think."

"It's quite wonderful enough for *my* modest wants," said Mr. Thomas Marvel. "Howjer manage it! How the dooce is it done?"

"It's too long a story. And besides—"

"I tell you, the whole business fair beats me," said Mr. Marvel.

"What I want to say at present is this: I need help. I have come to that—I came upon you suddenly. I was wandering, mad with rage, naked, impotent. I could have murdered. And I saw you—"

"*Lord!*" said Mr. Marvel.

"I came up behind you—hesitated—went on—"

Mr. Marvel's expression was eloquent.

"—then stopped. 'Here,' I said, 'is an out-cast like myself. This is the man for me.' So I turned back and came to you—you. And—"

144

"*Lord!*" said Mr. Marvel. "But I'm all in a dizzy. May I ask—How is it? And what you may be requiring in the way of help?—Invisible!"

"I want you to help me get clothes—and shelter—and then, with other things. I've left them long enough. If you won't—well! But you *will—must.*"

"Look here," said Mr. Marvel. "I'm too flabbergasted. Don't knock me about any more. And leave me go. I must get steady a bit. And you've pretty near broken my toe. It's all so unreasonable. Empty downs, empty sky. Nothing visible for miles except the bosom of Nature. And then comes a voice. A voice out of heaven! And stones! And a fist—Lord!"

"Pull yourself together," said the voice, "for you have to do the job I've chosen for you."

Mr. Marvel blew out his cheeks, and his eyes were round.

"I've chosen you," said the voice. "You are the only man except some of those fools down there, who knows there is such a thing as an invisible man. You have to be my helper. Help me—and I will do great things for you. An invisible man is a man of power." He stopped for a moment to sneeze violently.

"But if you betray me," he said, "if you fail to do as I direct you—"

He paused and tapped Mr. Marvel's shoulder smartly. Mr. Marvel gave a yelp of terror at the touch. "*I* don't want to betray you," said Mr. Marvel, edging away from the direction of the fingers. "Don't you go a-thinking that, whatever you do. All I want to do is to help you—just tell me what I got to do. (Lord!) Whatever you want done, that I'm most willing to do."

flabbergasted: Amazed.

He turned the corner by the church, and directed his way to the Coach and Horses

10

MR. MARVEL'S VISIT TO IPING

impregnably: Completely safe from all attack.

After the first gusty panic had spent itself Iping became argumentative. Scepticism suddenly reared its head,—rather nervous scepticism, not at all assured of its back, but scepticism nevertheless. It is so much easier not to believe in an invisible man; and those who had actually seen him dissolve into air, or felt the strength of his arm, could be counted on the fingers of two hands. And of these witnesses Mr. Wadgers was presently missing, having retired impregnably behind the bolts and bars of his own house, and Jaffers was lying stunned in the parlour of the Coach and Horses. Great and strange ideas transcending experience often have less effect upon men and women than smaller, more tangible considerations. Iping was gay with bunting, and everybody was in gala dress. Whit-Monday had been looked forward to for a month or more. By the afternoon even those who believed in the Unseen were beginning to resume their little amusements in a tentative fashion, on the supposition that he had quite gone away, and with the sceptics he was already a jest. But people, sceptics and believers alike, were remarkably sociable all that day.

Haysman's meadow was gay with a tent, in which Mrs. Bunting and other ladies were preparing tea, while, without, the Sunday-school children ran races and played games under the noisy guidance of the curate and the Misses Cuss and Sackbut. No doubt there was a slight uneasiness in the air, but people for the most part had the sense to conceal whatever imaginative qualms they experienced. On the village green an inclined string, down which, clinging the while to a pulley-swung handle, one could be hurled violently against a sack at the other end, came in for considerable favour among the adolescent, as also did the swings and the cocoanut shies. There was also promenading, and the steam organ attached to the swings filled the air with a pungent flavour of oil and with equally pungent music. Members of the Club, who had attended church in the morning, were splendid in badges of pink and green, and some of the gayer-minded had also adorned their bowler hats with brilliant-coloured favours of ribbon. Old Fletcher, whose conceptions of holiday-making were severe, was visible through the jasmine about his window or through the open door (whichever way you chose to look), poised delicately on a plank supported on two chairs, and whitewashing the ceiling of his front room.

About four o'clock a stranger entered the village from the direction of the downs. He was a short, stout person in an extraordinarily shabby top hat, and he appeared to be very much out of breath. His cheeks were alternately limp and tightly puffed. His mottled face was apprehensive, and he moved with a sort of reluctant alacrity. He turned the corner by the church, and directed his way to the Coach and Horses. Among others old Fletcher remembers seeing him, and indeed the old gentleman was so struck by his peculiar agitation that he inadvertently allowed a quantity of whitewash to run down the brush into the sleeve of his coat while regarding him.

This stranger, to the perceptions of the proprietor of the cocoanut shy, appeared to be talking to himself, and Mr. Huxter

bunting: A thin wool or cotton used for flags or patriotic decorations.

curate: An assistant to the vicar or rector.

promenading: Walking for pleasure in a public place.

Jasmine

alacrity: Briskness.

remarked the same thing. He stopped at the foot of the Coach and Horses steps, and, according to Mr. Huxter, appeared to undergo a severe internal struggle before he could induce himself to enter the house. Finally he marched up the steps, and was seen by Mr. Huxter to turn to the left and open the door of the parlour. Mr. Huxter heard voices from within the room and from the bar apprising the man of his error. "That room's private!" said Hall, and the stranger shut the door clumsily and went into the bar.

In the course of a few minutes he reappeared, wiping his lips with the back of his hand with an air of quiet satisfaction that somehow impressed Mr. Huxter as assumed. He stood looking about him for some moments, and then Mr. Huxter saw him walk in an oddly furtive manner towards the gates of the yard, upon which the parlour window opened. The stranger, after some hesitation, leant against one of the gate-posts, produced a short clay pipe, and prepared to fill it. His fingers trembled while doing so. He lit it clumsily, and folding his arms began to smoke in a languid attitude, an attitude which his occasional quick glances up the yard altogether belied.

All this Mr. Huxter saw over the canisters of the tobacco window, and the singularity of the man's behaviour prompted him to maintain his observation.

Presently the stranger stood up abruptly and put his pipe in his pocket. Then he vanished into the yard. Forthwith Mr. Huxter, conceiving he was witness of some petty larceny, leapt round his counter and ran out into the road to intercept the thief. As he did so, Mr. Marvel reappeared, his hat askew, a big bundle in a blue table-cloth in one hand, and three books tied together—as it proved afterwards with the Vicar's braces—in the other. Directly he saw Huxter he gave a sort of gasp, and turning sharply to the left, began to run. "Stop thief!" cried Huxter, and set off after him. Mr. Huxter's sensations were vivid but brief. He saw the man just before him and spurting briskly for the church corner and the hill road. He saw the village flags and festivities beyond, and a face or so turned towards him. He bawled, "Stop!" again. He had hardly gone ten strides before his shin was caught in some mysterious fashion, and he was no longer running, but flying with inconceivable rapidity through the air. He saw the ground suddenly close to his face. The world seemed to splash into a million whirling specks of light, and subsequent proceedings interested him no more.

induce: Persuade.

furtive: Sly, stealthy.

languid: Very slow and relaxed.

askew: To one side; crooked.

Cuss turned the pages over with a face suddenly disappointed.

Now in order clearly to understand what had happened in the inn, it is necessary to go back to the moment when Mr. Marvel first came into view of Mr. Huxter's window. At that precise moment Mr. Cuss and Mr. Bunting were in the parlour. They were seriously investigating the strange occurrences of the morning, and were, with Mr. Hall's permission, making a thorough examination of the Invisible Man's belongings. Jaffers had partially recovered from his fall and had gone home in the charge of his sympathetic friends. The stranger's scattered

11

IN THE COACH AND HORSES

garments had been removed by Mrs. Hall and the room tidied up. And on the table under the window where the stranger had been wont to work, Cuss had hit almost at once on three big books in manuscript labelled "Diary."

"Diary!" said Cuss, putting the three books on the table. "Now, at any rate, we shall learn something." The Vicar stood with his hands on the table.

"Diary," repeated Cuss, sitting down, putting two volumes to support the third, and opening it. "H'm—no name on the fly-leaf. Bother!—cypher. And figures."

The Vicar came round to look over his shoulder.

Cuss turned the pages over with a face suddenly disappointed. "I'm—dear me! It's all cypher, Bunting."

"There are no diagrams?" asked Mr. Bunting. "No illustrations throwing light—"

"See for yourself," said Mr. Cuss. "Some of it's mathematical and some of it's Russian or some such language (to judge by the letters), and some of it's Greek. Now the Greek I thought *you*—"

"Of course," said Mr. Bunting, taking out and wiping his spectacles and feeling suddenly very uncomfortable,—for he had no Greek left in his mind worth talking about; "yes—the Greek, of course, may furnish a clue."

"I'll find you a place."

"I'd rather glance through the volumes first," said Mr. Bunting, still wiping. "A general impression first, Cuss, and *then*, you know, we can go looking for clues."

He coughed, put on his glasses, arranged them fastidiously, coughed again, and wished something would happen to avert the seemingly inevitable exposure. Then he took the volume Cuss handed him in a leisurely manner. And then something did happen.

The door opened suddenly.

Both gentlemen started violently, looked round, and were relieved to see a sporadically rosy face beneath a furry silk hat. "Tap?" asked the face, and stood staring.

"No," said both gentlemen at once.

"Over the other side, my man," said Mr. Bunting. And "Please shut that door," said Mr. Cuss, irritably.

"All right," said the intruder, as it seemed, in a low voice curiously different from the huskiness of its first inquiry.

150

"Right you are," said the intruder in the former voice. "Stand clear!" and he vanished and closed the door.

"A sailor, I should judge," said Mr. Bunting. "Amusing fellows, they are. Stand clear! indeed. A nautical term, referring to his getting back out of the room, I suppose."

"I daresay so," said Cuss. "My nerves are all loose to-day. It quite made me jump—the door opening like that."

Mr. Bunting smiled as if he had not jumped. "And now," he said with a sigh, "these books."

"One minute," said Cuss, and went and locked the door. "Now I think we are safe from interruption."

Some one sniffed as he did so.

"One thing is indisputable," said Bunting, drawing up a chair next to that of Cuss. "There certainly have been very strange things happen in Iping during the last few days—very strange. I cannot of course believe in this absurd invisibility story—"

"It's incredible," said Cuss, "—incredible. But the fact remains that I saw—I certainly saw right down his sleeve—"

"But did you—are you sure? Suppose a mirror, for instance, —hallucinations are so easily produced. I don't know if you have ever seen a really good conjuror—"

"I won't argue again," said Cuss. "We've thrashed that out, Bunting. And just now there's these books— Ah! here's some of what I take to be Greek! Greek letters certainly."

He pointed to the middle of the page. Mr. Bunting flushed slightly and brought his face nearer, apparently finding some difficulty with his glasses. Suddenly he became aware of a strange feeling at the nape of his neck. He tried to raise his head, and encountered an immovable resistance. The feeling was a curious pressure, the grip of a heavy, firm hand, and it bore his chin irresistibly to the table. "*Don't move, little men,*" whispered a voice, "*or I'll brain you both!*" He looked into the face of Cuss, close to his own, and each saw a horrified reflection of his own sickly astonishment.

"I'm sorry to handle you roughly," said the Voice, "but it's unavoidable.

"Since when did you learn to pry into an investigator's private memoranda," said the Voice; and two chins struck the table simultaneously, and two sets of teeth rattled.

"Since when did you learn to invade the private rooms of a man in misfortune?" and the concussion was repeated.

hallucinations: Apparent perceptions; seeing objects that aren't there.

nape: The back of the neck at the hairline.

"Where have they put my clothes?

"Listen," said the Voice. "The windows are fastened and I've taken the key out of the door. I am a fairly strong man, and I have the poker handy—besides being invisible. There's not the slightest doubt that I could kill you both and get away quite easily if I wanted to—do you understand? Very well. If I let you go will you promise not to try any nonsense and do what I tell you?"

The Vicar and the Doctor looked at one another, and the Doctor pulled a face. "Yes," said Mr. Bunting, and the Doctor repeated it. Then the pressure on the necks relaxed, and the Doctor and the Vicar sat up, both very red in the face and wriggling their heads.

"Please keep sitting where you are," said the Invisible Man. "Here's the poker, you see.

"When I came into this room" continued the Invisible Man, after presenting the poker to the tip of the nose of each of his visitors, "I did not expect to find it occupied, and I expected to find, in addition to my books of memoranda, an outfit of clothing. Where is it? No,—don't rise. I can see it's gone. Now, just at present, though the days are quite warm enough for an invisible man to run about stark, the evenings are chilly. I want clothing—and other accommodation; and I must also have those three books."

pulled a face: Made a face; grimaced.

But Hall had hardly run a dozen yards before he gave a loud shout of astonishment and went flying headlong sideways...

t is unavoidable that at this point the narrative should break off again, for a certain very painful reason that will presently be apparent. And while these things were going on in the parlour, and while Mr. Huxter was watching Mr. Marvel smoking his pipe against the gate, not a dozen yards away were Mr. Hall and Teddy Henfrey discussing in a state of cloudy puzzlement the one Iping topic.

Suddenly there came a violent thud against the door of the parlour, a sharp cry, and then—silence.

"*Hul*—lo!" said Teddy Henfrey.

"Hul—*lo!*" from the Tap.

Mr. Hall took things in slowly but surely. "That ain't right," he said, and came round from behind the bar towards the parlour door.

12

THE INVISIBLE MAN LOSES HIS TEMPER

subdued: Quiet; in low volume.

sotto voce: An Italian phrase meaning 'in an undertone.'

obdurate: Stubbornly hard.

He and Teddy approached the door together, with intent faces. Their eyes considered. "Summat wrong," said Hall, and Henfrey nodded agreement. Whiffs of an unpleasant chemical odour met them, and there was a muffled sound of conversation, very rapid and subdued.

"You all raight thur?" asked Hall, rapping.

The muttered conversation ceased abruptly, for a moment silence, then the conversation was resumed, in hissing whispers, then a sharp cry of "No! no, you don't!" There came a sudden motion and the oversetting of a chair, a brief struggle. Silence again.

"What the dooce?" exclaimed Henfrey, *sotto voce*.

"You—all—raight—thur?" asked Mr. Hall, sharply, again.

The Vicar's voice answered with a curious jerking intonation: "Quite ri—ight. Please don't—interrupt."

"Odd!" said Mr. Henfrey.

"Odd!" said Mr. Hall.

"Says, 'Don't interrupt,'" said Henfrey.

"I heerd 'n," said Hall.

"And a sniff," said Henfrey.

They remained listening. The conversation was rapid and subdued. "I *can't*," said Mr. Bunting, his voice rising; "I tell you, sir, I *will* not."

"What was that?" asked Henfrey.

"Says he wi' nart," said Hall. "Warn't speakin' to us, wuz he?"

"Disgraceful!" said Mr. Bunting, within.

"'Disgraceful,'" said Mr. Henfrey. "I heard it—*distinct*."

"Who's that speaking now?" asked Henfrey.

"Mr. Cuss, I s'pose," said Hall. "Can you hear—anything?"

Silence. The sounds within indistinct and perplexing.

"Sounds like throwing the table-cloth about," said Hall.

Mrs. Hall appeared behind the bar. Hall made gestures of silence and invitation. This roused Mrs. Hall's wifely opposition. "What yer listenin' there for, Hall?" she asked. "Ain't you nothin' better to do—busy day like this?"

Hall tried to convey everything by grimaces and dumb show, but Mrs. Hall was obdurate. She raised her voice. So Hall and Henfrey, rather crestfallen, tiptoed back to the bar, gesticulating to explain to her.

At first she refused to see anything in what they had heard at all. Then she insisted on Hall keeping silence, while Henfrey told her his story. She was inclined to think the whole business nonsense—perhaps they were just moving the furniture about. "I heerd'n say 'disgraceful'; *that* I did," said Hall.

"*I* heerd that, Mis' Hall," said Henfrey.

"Like as not—" began Mrs. Hall.

"Hsh!" said Mr. Teddy Henfrey. "Didn't I hear the window?"

"What window?" asked Mrs. Hall.

"Parlour window," said Henfrey.

Everyone stood listening intently. Mrs. Hall's eyes, directed straight before her, saw without seeing the brilliant oblong of the inn door, the road white and vivid, and Huxter's shop-front blistering in the June sun. Abruptly Huxter's door opened and Huxter appeared, eyes staring with excitement, arms gesticulating. "*Yap!*" cried Huxter. "Stop thief!" and he ran obliquely across the oblong towards the yard gates, and vanished.

Simultaneously came a tumult from the parlour, and a sound of windows being closed.

Hall, Henfrey, and the human contents of the Tap rushed out at once pell-mell into the street. They saw some one whisk round the corner towards the down road, and Mr. Huxter executing a complicated leap in the air that ended on his face and shoulder. Down the street people were standing astonished or running towards them.

Mr. Huxter was stunned. Henfrey stopped to discover this, but Hall and the two labourers from the Tap rushed at once to the corner, shouting incoherent things, and saw Mr. Marvel vanishing by the corner of the church wall. They appear to have jumped to the impossible conclusion that this was the Invisible Man suddenly become visible, and set off at once along the lane in pursuit. But Hall had hardly run a dozen yards before he gave a loud shout of astonishment and went flying headlong sideways, clutching one of the labourers and bringing him to the ground. He had been charged just as one charges a man at football. The second labourer came round in a circle, stared, and conceiving that Hall had tumbled over of his own accord, turned to resume the pursuit, only to be tripped by the ankle just as Huxter had been. Then, as the first labourer struggled to his feet, he was kicked sideways by a blow that might have felled an ox.

As he went down, the rush from the direction of the village green came round the corner. The first to appear was the

pell-mell: In furious haste.

incoherent: Unconnected, inconsistent.

proprietor of the cocoanut shy, a burly man in a blue jersey. He was astonished to see the lane empty save for three men sprawling absurdly on the ground. And then something happened to his rear-most foot, and he went headlong and rolled sideways just in time to graze the feet of his brother and partner, following headlong. The two were then kicked, knelt on, fallen over, and cursed by quite a number of over-hasty people.

Now when Hall and Henfrey and the labourers ran out of the house, Mrs. Hall, who had been disciplined by years of experience, remained in the bar next the till. And suddenly the parlour door was opened, and Mr. Cuss appeared, and without glancing at her rushed at once down the steps towards the corner. "Hold him!" he cried. "Don't let him drop that parcel! You can see him so long as he holds the parcel." He knew nothing of the existence of Marvel. For the Invisible Man had handed over the books and bundle in the yard. The face of Mr. Cuss was angry and resolute, but his costume was defective, a sort of limp white kilt that could only have passed muster in Greece. "Hold him!" he bawled. "He's got my trousers! And every stitch of the Vicar's clothes!

" 'Tend to him in a minute!" he cried to Henfrey as he passed the prostrate Huxter, and coming round the corner to join the tumult, was promptly knocked off his feet into an indecorous sprawl. Somebody in full flight trod heavily on his finger. He yelled, struggled to regain his feet, was knocked against and thrown on all fours again, and became aware that he was involved not in a capture, but a rout. Everyone was running back to the village. He rose again and was hit severely behind the ear. He staggered and set off back to the Coach and Horses forthwith, leaping over the deserted Huxter, who was now sitting up, on his way.

Behind him as he was halfway up the inn steps he heard a sudden yell of rage, rising sharply out of the confusion of cries, and a sounding smack in someone's face. He recognised the voice as that of the Invisible Man, and the note was that of a man suddenly infuriated by a painful blow.

In another moment Mr. Cuss was back in the parlour. "He's coming back, Bunting!" he said, rushing in. "Save yourself! He's gone mad!"

Mr. Bunting was standing in the window engaged in an attempt to clothe himself in the hearth-rug and a West Surrey

Gazette. "Who's coming?" he said, so startled that his costume narrowly escaped disintegration.

"Invisible Man," said Cuss, and rushed to the window. "We'd better clear out from here! He's fighting mad! Mad!"

In another moment he was out in the yard.

"Good heavens!" said Mr. Bunting, hesitating between two horrible alternatives. He heard a frightful struggle in the passage of the inn, and his decision was made. He clambered out of the window, adjusted his costume hastily, and fled up the village as fast as his fat little legs would carry him.

From the moment when the Invisible Man screamed with rage and Mr. Bunting made his memorable flight up the village, it became impossible to give a consecutive account of affairs in Iping. Possibly the Invisible Man's original intention was simply to cover Marvel's retreat with the clothes and books. But his temper, at no time very good, seems to have gone completely at some chance blow, and forthwith he set to smiting and overthrowing, for the mere satisfaction of hurting.

You must figure the street full of running figures, of doors slamming and fights for hiding-places. You must figure the tumult suddenly striking on the unstable equilibrium of old Fletcher's planks and two chairs,—with cataclysmal results. You must figure an appalled couple caught dismally in a swing. And then the whole tumultuous rush has passed and the Iping street with its gauds and flags is deserted save for the still raging Unseen, and littered with cocoanuts, overthrown canvas screens, and the scattered stock in trade of a sweetstuff stall. Everywhere there is a sound of closing shutters and shoving bolts, and the only visible humanity is an occasional flitting eye under a raised eyebrow in the corner of a window pane.

The Invisible Man amused himself for a little while by breaking all the windows in the Coach and Horses, and then he thrust a street lamp through the parlour window of Mrs. Gribble. He it must have been who cut the telegraph wire to Adderdean just beyond Higgins' cottage on the Adderdean road. And after that, as his peculiar qualities allowed, he passed out of human perceptions altogether, and he was neither heard, seen, nor felt in Iping any more. He vanished absolutely.

But it was the best part of two hours before any human being ventured out again into the desolation of Iping street.

clambered: Climbed with difficulty.

equilibrium: Balance.

gauds: Displays.

157

He was accompanied by a voice other than his own, and ever and again he winced under the touch of unseen hands.

13
MR. MARVEL DISCUSSES HIS RESIGNATION

ligature: Banding.
rubicund: Ruddy, reddish.

When the dusk was gathering and Iping was just beginning to peep timorously forth again upon the shattered wreckage of its Bank Holiday, a short, thickset man in a shabby silk hat was marching painfully through the twilight behind the beechwoods on the road to Bramblehurst. He carried three books bound together by some sort of ornamental elastic ligature, and a bundle wrapped in a blue table-cloth. His rubicund face expressed consternation and fatigue; he appeared to be in a spasmodic sort of hurry. He was accompanied by a Voice other than his own, and ever and again he winced under the touch of unseen hands.

"If you give me the slip again," said the Voice; "if you attempt to give me the slip again—"

"Lord!" said Mr. Marvel. "That shoulder's a mass of bruises as it is."

"—on my honour," said the Voice, "I will kill you."

"I didn't try to give you the slip," said Marvel, in a voice that was not far remote from tears. "I swear I didn't. I didn't know the blessed turning, that was all! How the devil was I to know the blessed turning? As it is, I've been knocked about—"

"You'll get knocked about a great deal more if you don't mind," said the Voice, and Mr. Marvel abruptly became silent. He blew out his cheeks, and his eyes were eloquent of despair.

"It's bad enough to let these floundering yokels explode my little secret, without *your* cutting off with my books. It's lucky for some of them they cut and ran when they did! Here am I— No one knew I was invisible! And now what am I to do?"

"What am *I* to do?" asked Marvel, *sotto voce.*

"It's all about. It will be in the papers! Everybody will be looking for me; everyone on their guard—" The Voice broke off into vivid curses and ceased.

The despair of Mr. Marvel's face deepened, and his pace slacked.

"Go on!" said the Voice.

Mr. Marvel's face assumed a greyish tint between the ruddier patches.

"Don't drop those books, stupid," said the Voice, sharply— overtaking him.

"The fact is," said the Voice, "I shall have but to make use of you. You're a poor tool, I must."

"I'm a *miserable* tool," said Marvel.

"You are," said the Voice.

"I'm the worst possible tool you could have," said Marvel.

"I'm not strong," he said after a discouraging silence.

"I'm not over strong," he repeated.

"No?"

"And my heart's weak. That little business—I pulled it through, of course—but bless you! I could have dropped."

"Well?"

"I haven't the nerve and strength for the sort of thing you want."

"*I'll* stimulate you."

floundering: Clumsy.

assumed: Took on.

159

funk: Here, panic.

"I wish you wouldn't. I wouldn't like to mess up your plans, you know. But I might,—out of sheer funk and misery."

"You'd better not," said the Voice, with quiet emphasis.

"I wish I was dead," said Marvel.

"It ain't justice," he said; "you must admit— It seems to me I've a perfect right—"

"*Get* on!" said the Voice.

Mr. Marvel mended his pace, and for a time they went in silence again.

"It's devilish hard," said Mr. Marvel.

This was quite ineffectual. He tried another tack.

"What do I make by it?" he began again in a tone of unendurable wrong.

"Oh! *shut up!*" said the Voice, with sudden amazing vigour. "I'll see to you all right. You do what you're told. You'll do it all right. You're a fool and all that, but you'll do—"

"I tell you, sir, I'm not the man for it. Respectfully—but it is so—"

"If you don't shut up I shall twist your wrist again," said the Invisible Man. "I want to think."

Presently two oblongs of yellow light appeared through the trees, and the square tower of a church loomed through the gloaming. "I shall keep my hand on your shoulder," said the Voice, "all through the village. Go straight through and try no foolery. It will be the worse for you if you do."

"I know that," sighed Mr. Marvel, "I know all that."

obsolete: Out of date and fashion.

The unhappy-looking figure in the obsolete silk hat passed up the street of the little village with his burdens, and vanished into the gathering darkness beyond the lights of the windows.

"Pleasant day" said the mariner. Mr Marvel glanced about him with something very like terror.

Ten o'clock the next morning found Mr. Marvel, unshaven, dirty, and travel-stained, sitting with the books beside him and his hands deep in his pockets, looking very weary, nervous, and uncomfortable, and inflating his cheeks at frequent intervals, on the bench outside a little inn on the outskirts of Port Stowe. Beside him were the books, but now they were tied with string. The bundle had been abandoned in the pinewoods beyond Bramblehurst, in accordance with a change in the plans of the Invisible Man. Mr. Marvel sat on the bench, and although no one took the slightest notice of him, his agitation remained at fever heat. His hands would go ever and again to his various pockets with a curious nervous fumbling.

14
AT
PORT
STOWE

When he had been sitting for the best part of an hour, however, an elderly mariner, carrying a newspaper, came out of the inn and sat down beside him. "Pleasant day," said the mariner.

Mr. Marvel glanced about him with something very like terror. "Very," he said.

"Just seasonable weather for the time of year," said the mariner, taking no denial.

"Quite," said Mr. Marvel.

The mariner produced a toothpick, and (saving his regard) was engrossed thereby for some minutes. His eyes meanwhile were at liberty to examine Mr. Marvel's dusty figure, and the books beside him. As he had approached Mr. Marvel he had heard a sound like the dropping of coins into a pocket. He was struck by the contrast of Mr. Marvel's appearance with this suggestion of opulence. Thence his mind wandered back again to a topic that had taken a curiously firm hold of his imagination.

"Books?" he said suddenly, noisily finishing with the toothpick.

Mr. Marvel started and looked at them. "Oh, yes," he said. "Yes, they're books."

"There's some ex-traordinary things in books," said the mariner.

"I believe you," said Mr. Marvel.

"And some extra-ordinary things out of 'em," said the mariner.

"True likewise," said Mr. Marvel. He eyed his interlocutor, and then glanced about him.

"There's some extraordinary things in newspapers, for example," said the mariner.

"There are."

"In *this* newspaper," said the mariner.

"Ah!" said Mr. Marvel.

"There's a story," said the mariner, fixing Mr. Marvel with an eye that was firm and deliberate; "there's a story about an Invisible Man, for instance."

Mr. Marvel pulled his mouth askew and scratched his cheek and felt his ears glowing. "What will they be writing next?" he asked faintly. "Ostria, or America?"

"Neither," said the mariner. "*Here!*"

"Lord!" said Mr. Marvel, starting.

engrossed: Absorbed, fully occupied.

opulence: Wealth.

162

"When I say *here*," said the mariner, to Mr. Marvel's intense relief, "I don't of course mean here in this place, I mean hereabouts."

"An Invisible Man!" said Mr. Marvel. "And what's *he* been up to?"

"Everything," said the mariner, controlling Marvel with his eye, and then amplifying: "Every Blessed Thing."

"I ain't seen a paper these four days," said Marvel.

"Iping's the place he started at," said the mariner.

"In-*deed!*" said Mr. Marvel.

"He started there. And where he came from, nobody don't seem to know. Here it is: Pe Culiar Story from Iping. And it says in this paper that the evidence is extraordinary strong—extra-ordinary."

"Lord!" said Mr. Marvel.

"But then, it's a extra-ordinary story. There is a clergyman and a medical gent witnesses,—saw 'im all right and proper—or leastways, didn't see 'im. He was staying, it says, at the Coach an' Horses, and no one don't seem to have been aware of his misfortune, it says, aware of his misfortune, until in an Alteration in the inn, it says, his bandages on his head was torn off. It was then ob-served that his head was invisible. Attempts were At Once made to secure him, but casting off his garments, it says, he succeeded in escaping, but not until after a desperate struggle, In Which he had inflicted serious injuries, it says, on our worthy and able constable, Mr. J.A. Jaffers. Pretty straight story, eigh? Names and everything."

"Lord!" said Mr. Marvel, looking nervously about him, trying to count the money in his pockets by his unaided sense of touch, and full of a strange and novel idea. "It sounds most astonishing."

"Don't it? Extra-ordinary, *I* call it. Never heard tell of Invisible Men before, I haven't, but nowadays one hears such a lot of extra-ordinary things—that—"

"That all he did?" asked Marvel, trying to seem at his ease.

"It's enough, ain't it?" said the Mariner.

"Didn't go Back by any chance?" asked Marvel. "Just escaped and that's all, eh?"

"All!" said the Mariner. "Why!—ain't it enough?"

"Quite enough," said Marvel.

"I should think it was enough," said the Mariner. "I should think it was enough."

"He didn't have any pals—it don't say he had any pals, does it?" asked Mr. Marvel, anxious.

"Ain't one of a sort enough for you?" asked the Mariner. "No, thank Heaven, as one might say, he didn't."

He nodded his head slowly. "It makes me regular uncomfortable, the bare thought of that chap running about the country! He is at present At Large, and from certain evidence it is supposed that he has—taken—*took*, I suppose they mean—the road to Port Stowe. You see we're right *in* it! None of your American wonders, this time. And just think of the things he might do! Where'd you be, if he took a drop over and above, and had a fancy to go for you? Suppose he wants to rob—who can prevent him? He can trespass, he can burgle, he could walk through a cordon of policemen as easy as me or you could give the slip to a blind man! Easier! For these here blind chaps hear uncommon sharp, I'm told. And where-ever there was liquor he fancied—"

"He's got a tremenjous advantage, certainly," said Mr. Marvel. "And—well."

"You're right," said the Mariner. "He *has*."

All this time Mr. Marvel had been glancing about him intently, listening for faint footfalls, trying to detect imperceptible movements. He seemed on the point of some great resolution. He coughed behind his hand.

He looked about him again, listened, bent towards the Mariner, and lowered his voice: "The fact of it is—I happen—to know just a thing or two about this Invisible Man. From private sources."

"Oh!" said the Mariner, interested. "*You?*"

"Yes," said Mr. Marvel. "Me."

"Indeed!" said the Mariner. "And may I ask—"

"You'll be astonished," said Mr. Marvel behind his hand. "It's tremenjous."

"Indeed!" said the Mariner.

"The fact is," began Mr. Marvel eagerly in a confidential undertone. Suddenly his expression changed marvellously. "Ow!" he said. He rose stiffly in his seat. His face was eloquent of physical suffering. "Wow!" he said.

"What's up?" said the Mariner, concerned.

"Toothache," said Mr. Marvel, and put his hand to his ear. He caught hold of his books. "I must be getting on, I think," he said. He edged in a curious way along the seat away from his

cordon: A line in the form of a ring around an area.

164

interlocutor. "But you was just agoing to tell me about this here Invisible Man!" protested the Mariner. Mr. Marvel seemed to consult with himself. "Hoax," said a voice. "It's a hoax," said Mr. Marvel.

"But it's in the paper," said the Mariner.

"Hoax all the same," said Marvel. "I know the chap that started the lie. There ain't no Invisible Man whatsoever— Blimey."

"But how 'bout this paper? D'you mean to say—?"

"Not a word of it," said Marvel, stoutly.

The Mariner stared, paper in hand. Mr. Marvel jerkily faced about. "Wait a bit," said the Mariner, rising and speaking slowly. "D'you mean to say—?"

"I do," said Mr. Marvel.

"Then why did you let me go on and tell you all this blarsted stuff, then? What d'yer mean by letting a man make a fool of himself like that for? Eigh?"

Mr. Marvel blew out his cheeks. The Mariner was suddenly very red indeed; he clenched his hands. "I been talking here this ten minutes," he said; "and you, you little pot-bellied, leathery-faced son of an old boot, couldn't have the elementary manners—"

"Don't you come bandying words with *me*," said Mr. Marvel.

"Bandying words! I'm a jolly good mind—"

"Come up," said a voice, and Mr. Marvel was suddenly whirled about and started marching off in a curious spasmodic manner. "You'd better move on," said the Mariner. "*Who's moving on?*" said Mr. Marvel. He was receding obliquely with a curious hurrying gait, with occasional violent jerks forward. Some way along the road he began a muttered monologue, protests and recriminations.

"Silly devil!" said the Mariner, legs wide apart, elbows akimbo, watching the receding figure. "I'll show you, you silly ass,—hoaxing *me!* It's here—on the paper!"

Mr. Marvel retorted incoherently and, receding, was hidden by a bend in the road, but the Mariner still stood magnificent in the midst of the way, until the approach of a butcher's cart dislodged him. Then he turned himself towards Port Stowe. "Full of extra-ordinary asses," he said softly to himself. "Just to take me down a bit—that was his silly game— It's on the paper!"

And there was another extraordinary thing he was presently

to hear, that had happened quite close to him. And that was a vision of a "fist full of money" (no less) travelling without visible agency, along by the wall at the corner of St. Michael's Lane. A brother mariner had seen this wonderful sight that very morning. He had snatched at the money forthwith and had been knocked headlong, and when he had got to his feet the butterfly money had vanished. Our mariner was in the mood to believe anything, he declared, but that was a bit *too* stiff. Afterwards, however, he began to think things over.

The story of the flying money was true. And all about that neighbourhood, even from the august London and Country Banking Company, from the tills of shops and inns—doors standing that sunny weather entirely open—money had been quietly and dexterously making off that day in handfuls and rouleaux, floating quietly along by walls and shady places, dodging quickly from the approaching eyes of men. And it had, though no man had traced it, invariably ended its mysterious flight in the pocket of that agitated gentleman in the obsolete silk hat, sitting outside the little inn on the outskirts of Port Stowe.

august: Awe-inspiring.

rouleaux: Little rolls.

... and then his attention was attracted by the little figure of a man, inky black, running over the hill brow toward him.

In the early evening time Doctor Kemp was sitting in his study in the belvedere on the hill overlooking Burdock. It was a pleasant little room, with three windows, north, west, and south, and bookshelves covered with books and scientific publications, and a broad writing-table, and, under the north window, a microscope, glass slips, minute instruments, some cultures, and scattered bottles of reagents. Doctor Kemp's solar lamp was lit, albeit the sky was still bright with the sunset light, and his blinds were up because there was no offence of peering

15
THE MAN
WHO WAS
RUNNING

reagents: Any substances which are used in detecting, examining, or measuring other substances.

outsiders to require them pulled down. Doctor Kemp was a tall and slender young man, with flaxen hair and a moustache almost white, and the work he was upon would earn him, he hoped, the fellowship of the Royal Society, so highly did he think of it.

And his eye presently wandering from his work caught the sunset blazing at the back of the hill that is over against his own. For a minute perhaps he sat, pen in mouth, admiring the rich golden colour above the crest, and then his attention was attracted by the little figure of a man, inky black, running over the hill-brow towards him. He was a shortish little man, and he wore a high hat, and he was running so fast that his legs verily twinkled.

"Another of those fools," said Doctor Kemp. "Like that ass who ran into me this morning round a corner, with his ' 'Visible Man a-coming, sir!' I can't imagine what possesses people. One might think we were in the thirteenth century."

He got up, went to the window, and stared at the dusky hillside, and the dark little figure tearing down it. "He seems in a confounded hurry," said Doctor Kemp, "but he doesn't seem to be getting on. If his pockets were full of lead, he couldn't run heavier.

"Spurted, sir," said Doctor Kemp.

In another moment the higher of the villas that had clambered up the hill from Burdock, had occulted the running figure. He was visible again for a moment, and again, and then again, three times between the three detached houses that came next, and the terrace hid him.

"Asses!" said Doctor Kemp, swinging round on his heel and walking back to his writing-table.

But those who saw the fugitive nearer, and perceived the abject terror on his perspiring face, being themselves in the open roadway, did not share in the doctor's contempt. By the man pounded, and as he ran he chinked like a well-filled purse that is tossed to and fro. He looked neither to the right nor the left, but his dilated eyes stared straight downhill to where the lamps were being lit, and the people were crowded in the street. And his ill-shaped mouth fell apart, and a glairy foam lay on his lips, and his breath came hoarse and noisy. All he passed stopped and began staring up the road and down, and interrogating one another with an inkling of discomfort for the reason of his haste.

168

And then presently, far up the hill, a dog playing in the road yelped and ran under a gate, and as they still wondered something,—a wind—a pad, pad, pad,—a sound like a panting breathing,—rushed by.

People screamed. People sprang off the pavement. It passed in shouts, it passed by instinct down the hill. They were shouting in the street before Marvel was halfway there. They were bolting into houses and slamming the doors behind them, with the news. He heard it and made one last desperate spurt. Fear came striding by, rushed ahead of him, and in a moment had seized the town.

"The Invisible Man is coming! *The Invisible Man!*"

The Jolly Cricketers is just at the bottom of the hill, where the tram-lines begin. The barman leant his fat red arms on the counter and talked of horses with an anaemic cabman, while a black-bearded man in grey snapped up biscuit and cheese, drank Burton, and conversed in American with a policeman off duty.

"What's the shouting about!" said the anaemic cabman, going off at a tangent, trying to see up the hill over the dirty yellow blind in the low window of the inn. Somebody ran by outside. "Fire, perhaps," said the barman.

Footsteps approached, running heavily, the door was pushed open violently, and Marvel, weeping and dishevelled, his hat gone, the neck of his coat torn open, rushed in, made a convulsive turn, and attempted to shut the door. It was held half open by a strap.

"Coming!" he bawled, his voice shrieking with terror. "He's coming. The 'Visible Man! After me! For Gawd's sake! Elp! Elp! Elp!"

"Shut the doors," said the policeman. "Who's coming? What's the row?" He went to the door, released the strap, and it slammed. The American closed the other door.

anaemic: Pale because the blood lacks red cells.

"Lemme go inside," said Marvel, staggering and weeping, but still clutching the books. "Lemme go inside. Lock me in—somewhere. I tell you he's after me. I give him the slip. He said he'd kill me and he will."

"*You're* safe," said the man with the black beard. "The door's shut. What's it all about?"

"Lemme go inside," said Marvel, and shrieked aloud as a blow suddenly made the fastened door shiver and was followed by a hurried rapping and a shouting outside. "Hullo," cried the policeman, "who's there?" Mr. Marvel began to make frantic dives at panels that looked like doors. "He'll kill me—he's got a knife or something. For Gawd's sake!"

"Here you are," said the barman. "Come in here." And he held up the flap of the bar.

Mr. Marvel rushed behind the bar as the summons outside was repeated. "Don't open the door," he screamed. "*Please* don't open the door. *Where* shall I hide?"

"This, this Invisible Man, then?" asked the man with the black beard, with one hand behind him. "I guess it's about time we saw him."

The window of the inn was suddenly smashed in, and there was a screaming and running to and fro in the street. The policeman had been standing on the settee staring out, craning to see who was at the door. He got down with raised eyebrows. "It's that," he said. The barman stood in front of the bar-parlour door which was now locked on Mr. Marvel, stared at the smashed window, and came round to the two other men.

Everything was suddenly quiet. "I wish I had my truncheon," said the policeman, going irresolutely to the door. "Once we open, in he comes. There's no stopping him."

"Don't you be in too much hurry about that door," said the anaemic cabman, anxiously.

"Draw the bolts," said the man with the black beard, "and if he comes—" He showed a revolver in his hand.

"That won't do," said the policeman; "that's murder."

"I know what country I'm in," said the man with the beard. "I'm going to let off at his legs. Draw the bolts."

"Not with that thing going off behind me," said the barman, craning over the blind.

"Very well," said the man with the black beard, and stooping down, revolver ready, drew them himself. Barman, cabman, and policeman faced about.

settee: A seat with a back, usually for two or three people.

irresolutely: With hesitation.

Draw: Pull back, unlock.

172

"Come in," said the bearded man in an undertone, standing back and facing the unbolted doors with his pistol behind him. No one came in, the door remained closed. Five minutes afterwards when a second cabman pushed his head in cautiously, they were still waiting, and an anxious face peered out of the bar-parlour and supplied information. "Are all the doors of the house shut?" asked Marvel. "He's going round—prowling round. He's as artful as the devil."

artful: Crafty, cunning, sly.

"Good Lord!" said the burly barman. "There's the back! Just watch them doors! I say!—" He looked about him helplessly. The bar-parlour door slammed and they heard the key turn. "There's the yard door and the private door. The yard door—"

He rushed out of the bar.

In a minute he reappeared with a carving-knife in his hand. "The yard door was open!" he said, and his fat underlip dropped. "He may be in the house now!" said the first cabman.

"He's not in the kitchen," said the barman. "There's two women there, and I've stabbed every inch of it with this little beef slicer. And they don't think he's come in. They haven't noticed—"

"Have you fastened it?" asked the first cabman.

"I'm out of frocks," said the barman.

The man with the beard replaced his revolver. And even as he did so the flap of the bar was shut down and the bolt clicked, and then with a tremendous thud the catch of the door snapped and the bar-parlour door burst open. They heard Marvel squeal like a caught leveret, and forthwith they were clambering over the bar to his rescue. The bearded man's revolver cracked and the looking-glass at the back of the parlour started and came smashing and tinkling down.

leveret: A hare in its first year.

As the barman entered the room he saw Marvel, curiously crumpled up and struggling against the door that led to the yard and kitchen. The door flew open while the barman hesitated, and Marvel was dragged into the kitchen. There was a scream and a clatter of pans. Marvel, head down, and lugging back obstinately, was forced to the kitchen door, and the bolts were drawn.

obstinately: Stubbornly.

Then the policeman, who had been trying to pass the barman, rushed in, followed by one of the cabmen, gripped the wrist of the invisible hand that collared Marvel, was hit in the face and went reeling back. The door opened, and Marvel made a frantic effort to obtain a lodgment behind it. Then the cabman collared something. "I got him," said the cabman. The barman's red hands came clawing at the unseen. "Here he is!" said the barman.

Mr. Marvel, released, suddenly dropped to the ground and made an attempt to crawl behind the legs of the fighting men. The struggle blundered round the edge of the door. The voice of the Invisible Man was heard for the first time, yelling out sharply, as the policeman trod on his foot. Then he cried out passionately and his fists flew round like flails. The cabman suddenly whooped and doubled up, kicked under the diaphragm. The door into the bar-parlour from the kitchen slammed and covered Mr. Marvel's retreat. The men in the kitchen found themselves clutching at and struggling with empty air.

"Where's he gone?" cried the man with the beard. "Out?"

"This way," said the policeman, stepping into the yard and stopping.

A piece of tile whizzed by his head and smashed among the crockery on the kitchen table.

"I'll show him," shouted the man with the black beard, and suddenly a steel barrel shone over the policeman's shoulder, and five bullets had followed one another into the twilight whence the missile had come. As he fired, the man with the beard moved his hand in a horizontal curve, so that his shots radiated out into the narrow yard like spokes from a wheel.

A silence followed. "Five cartridges," said the man with the black beard. "That's the best of all. Four aces and the joker. Get a lantern, someone, and come and feel about for his body."

...he perceived a coiled and bloodstained bandage of linen rag hanging in mid-air between him and the wash-hand stand.

octor Kemp had continued writing in his study until the shots aroused him. Crack, crack, crack, they came one after the other.

"Hullo!" said Doctor Kemp, putting his pen into his mouth again and listening. "Who's letting off revolvers in Burdock? What are the asses at now?"

He went to the south window, threw it up, and leaning out stared down on the network of windows, beaded gas-lamps and shops, with its black interstices of roofs that made up the town

17
DOCTOR KEMP'S VISITOR

beaded: Decorated with glass beads.

faceted: Many sided.

slackly: Slowly; not busily.

balustrade: A stair rail; bannister.

syphon: A bottle for holding aerated (gas-charged) water. The water is driven out by the gas through a bent tube in the neck of the bottle.

at night. "Looks like a crowd down the hill," he said. "by the Cricketers," and remained watching. Thence his eyes wandered over the town to far away where the ships' lights shone, and the pier glowed, a little illuminated faceted pavilion like a gem of yellow light. The moon in its first quarter hung over the western hill, and the stars were clear and almost tropically bright.

After five minutes, during which his mind had travelled into a remote speculation of social conditions of the future, and lost itself at last over the time dimension, Doctor Kemp roused himself with a sigh, pulled down the window again, and returned to his writing-desk.

It must have been about an hour after this that the front-door bell rang. He had been writing slackly, and with intervals of abstraction, since the shots. He sat listening. He heard the servant answer the door, and waited for her feet on the staircase, but she did not come. "Wonder what that was," said Doctor Kemp.

He tried to resume his work, failed, got up, went downstairs from his study to the landing, rang, and called over the balustrade to the housemaid as she appeared in the hall below. "Was that a letter?" he asked.

"Only a runaway ring, sir," she answered.

"I'm restless to-night," he said to himself. He went back to his study, and this time attacked his work resolutely. In a little while he was hard at work again, and the only sounds in the room were the ticking of the clock and the subdued shrillness of his quill, hurrying in the very centre of the circle of light his lampshade threw on his table.

It was two o'clock before Doctor Kemp had finished his work for the night. He rose, yawned, and went downstairs to bed. He had already removed his coat and vest, when he noticed that he was thirsty. He took a candle and went down to the dining-room in search of a syphon and whiskey.

Doctor Kemp's scientific pursuits have made him a very observant man, and as he recrossed the hall, he noticed a dark spot on the linoleum near the mat at the foot of the stairs. He went on upstairs, and then it suddenly occurred to him to ask himself what the spot on the linoleum might be. Apparently some subconscious element was at work. At any rate, he turned with his burden, went back to the hall, put down the syphon and whiskey, and bending down, touched the spot. Without any great surprise he found it had the stickiness and colour of drying blood.

He took up his burden again, and returned upstairs, looking about him and trying to account for the blood-spot. On the landing he saw something and stopped astonished. The door-handle of his own room was blood-stained.

He looked at his own hand. It was quite clean, and then he remembered that the door of his room had been open when he came down from his study, and that consequently he had not touched the handle at all. He went straight into his room, his face quite calm—perhaps a trifle more resolute than usual. His glance, wandering inquisitively, fell on the bed. On the counter-pane was a mess of blood, and the sheet had been torn. He had not noticed this before because he had walked straight to the dressing-table. On the further side the bed-clothes were depressed as if someone had been recently sitting there.

Then he had an odd impression that he had heard a loud voice say, "Good Heavens!—*Kemp!*" But Doctor Kemp was no believer in Voices.

He stood staring at the tumbled sheets. Was that really a voice? He looked about again, but noticed nothing further than the disordered and blood-stained bed. Then he distinctly heard a movement across the room, near the wash-hand stand. All men, however highly educated, retain some superstitious ink-lings. The feeling that is called "eerie" came upon him. He closed the door of the room, came forward to the dressing-table, and put down his burdens. Suddenly, with a start, he perccived a coiled and blood-stained bandage of linen rag hanging in mid-air, between him and the wash-hand stand.

He stared at this in amazement. It was an empty bandage, a bandage properly tied but quite empty. He would have advanced to grasp it, but a touch arrested him, and a voice speaking quite close to him.

"Kemp!" said the Voice.

"Eigh?" said Kemp, with his mouth open.

"Keep your nerve," said the Voice. "I'm an Invisible Man."

Kemp made no answer for a space, simply stared at the bandage. "Invisible Man," he said.

"I'm an Invisible Man," repeated the Voice.

The story he had been active to ridicule only that morning rushed through Kemp's brain. He does not appear to have been

DOCTOR KEMP'S VISITOR

counterpane: A bedspread.

superstitious inklings: Irrational beliefs regarding the unknown.

ridicule: Call ridiculous; make fun of.

either very much frightened or very greatly surprised at the moment. Realisation came later.

"I thought it was all a lie," he said. The thought uppermost in his mind was the reiterated arguments of the morning. "Have you a bandage on?" he asked.

"Yes," said the Invisible Man.

"Oh!" said Kemp, and then roused himself. "I say!" he said. "But this is nonsense. It's some trick." He stepped forward suddenly, and his hand, extended towards the bandage, met invisible fingers.

He recoiled at the touch and his colour changed.

"Keep steady, Kemp, for God's sake! I want help badly. Stop!"

The hand gripped his arm. He struck at it.

"Kemp!" cried the Voice. "Kemp! Keep steady!" and the grip tightened.

A frantic desire to free himself took possession of Kemp. The hand of the bandaged arm gripped his shoulder, and he was suddenly tripped and flung backwards upon the bed. He opened his mouth to shout, and the corner of the sheet was thrust between his teeth. The Invisible Man had him down grimly, but his arms were free and he struck and tried to kick savagely.

"Listen to reason, will you?" said the Invisible Man, sticking to him in spite of a pounding in the ribs. "By Heaven! you'll madden me in a minute!

"Lie still, you fool!" bawled the Invisible Man in Kemp's ear.

Kemp struggled for another moment and then lay still.

"If you shout I'll smash your face," said the Invisible Man, relieving his mouth.

"I'm an Invisible Man. It's no foolishness, and no magic. I really am an Invisible Man. And I want your help. I don't want to hurt you, but if you behave like a frantic rustic, I must. Don't you remember me, Kemp? Griffin, of University College?"

"Let me get up," said Kemp. "I'll stop where I am. And let me sit quiet for a minute."

He sat up and felt his neck.

"I am Griffin, of University College, and I have made myself invisible. I am just an ordinary man—a man you have known— made invisible."

"Griffin?" said Kemp.

"Griffin," answered the Voice,—"a younger student, almost an albino, six feet high, and broad, with a pink and white face and red eyes,—who won the medal for chemistry."

"I am confused," said Kemp. "My brain is rioting. What has this to do with Griffin?"

"I *am* Griffin."

Kemp thought. "It's horrible," he said. "But what devilry must happen to make a man invisible?"

"It's no devilry. It's a process, sane and intelligible enough—"

"It's horrible!" said Kemp. "How on earth—?"

"It's horrible enough. But I'm wounded and in pain, and tired— Great God! Kemp, you are a man. Take it steady. Give me some food and drink, and let me sit down here."

Kemp stared at the bandage as it moved across the room, then saw a basket chair dragged across the floor and come to rest near the bed. It creaked, and the seat was depressed the quarter of an inch or so. He rubbed his eyes and felt his neck again. "This beats ghosts," he said, and laughed stupidly.

"That's better. Thank Heaven, you're getting sensible!"

"Or silly," said Kemp, and knuckled his eyes.

"Give me some whiskey. I'm near dead."

"It didn't feel so. Where are you? If I get up shall I run into you? *There!* all right. Whiskey? Here. Where shall I give it you?"

The chair creaked and Kemp felt the glass drawn away from him. He let go by an effort; his instinct was all against. it. It came to rest poised twenty inches above the front edge of the seat of the chair. He stared at it in infinite perplexity. "This is—this *must* be—hypnotism. You must have suggested you are invisible."

"Nonsense," said the Voice.

"It's frantic."

"Listen to me."

"I demonstrated conclusively this morning," began Kemp, "that invisibility—"

"Never mind what you've demonstrated!—I'm starving," said the Voice, "and the night is—chilly to a man without clothes."

"Food!" said Kemp.

The tumbler of whiskey tilted itself. "Yes," said the Invisible Man rapping it down. "Have you got a dressing-gown?"

Kemp made some exclamation in an undertone. He walked to a wardrobe and produced a robe of dingy scarlet. "This do?" he

DOCTOR KEMP'S VISITOR

albino: A person born with a pigment deficiency resulting in very light hair and skin color, and, in this case, red eyes.

Basket Chair

hypnotism: A state of mind induced in one person by another.

dressing-gown: A loose robe worn while dressing or lounging.

179

asked. It was taken from him. It hung limp for a moment in mid-air, fluttered weirdly, stood full and decorous buttoning itself, and sat down in his chair. "Drawers, socks, slippers would be a comfort," said the Unseen, curtly. "And food."

"Anything. But this is the insanest thing I ever was in, in my life!"

He turned out his drawers for the articles, and then went downstairs to ransack his larder. He came back with some cold cutlets and bread, pulled up a light table, and placed them before his guest. "Never mind knives," said his visitor, and a cutlet hung in mid-air, with a sound of gnawing.

"Invisible!" said Kemp, and sat down on a bedroom chair.

"I always like to get something about me before I eat," said the Invisible Man, with a full mouth, eating greedily. "Queer fancy!"

"I suppose that wrist is all right," said Kemp.

"Trust me," said the Invisible Man.

"Of *all* the strange and wonderful—"

"Exactly. But it's odd I should blunder into *your* house to get my bandaging. My first stroke of luck! Anyhow I meant to sleep in this house to-night. You must stand that! It's a filthy nuisance, my blood showing, isn't it? Quite a clot over there. Gets visible as it coagulates, I see. I've been in the house three hours."

"But how's it done?" began Kemp, in a tone of exasperation. "Confound it! The whole business—it's unreasonable from beginning to end."

"Quite reasonable," said the Invisible Man. "Perfectly reasonable."

He reached over and secured the whiskey bottle. Kemp stared at the devouring dressing gown. A ray of candle-light penetrating a torn patch in the right shoulder, made a triangle of light under the left ribs. "What were the shots?" he asked. "How did the shooting begin?"

"There was a fool of a man—a sort of confederate of mine—curse him!—who tried to steal my money. *Has* done so."

"Is *he* invisible too?"

"No."

"Well?"

"Can't I have some more to eat before I tell you all that? I'm hungry—in pain. And you want me to tell stories!"

Kemp got up. "*You* didn't do any shooting?" he asked.

"Not me," said his visitor. "Some fool I'd never seen fired at random. A lot of them got scared. They all got scared at me. Curse them!— I say—I want more to eat than this, Kemp."

"I'll see what there is more to eat downstairs," said Kemp. "Not much, I'm afraid."

After he had done eating, and he made a heavy meal, the Invisible Man demanded a cigar. He bit the end savagely before Kemp could find a knife, and cursed when the outer leaf loosened. It was strange to see him smoking; his mouth, and throat, pharynx and nares, became visible as a sort of whirling smoke cast.

"This blessed gift of smoking!" he said, and puffed vigorously. "I'm lucky to have fallen upon you, Kemp. You must help me. Fancy tumbling on you just now! I'm in a devilish scrape. I've been mad, I think. The things I have been through! But we will do things yet. Let me tell you—"

He helped himself to more whiskey and soda. Kemp got up, looked about him, and fetched himself a glass from his spare room. "It's wild—but I suppose I may drink."

"You haven't changed much, Kemp, these dozen years. You fair men don't. Cool and methodical—after the first collapse. I must tell you. We will work together!"

"But how was it all done?" said Kemp, "and how did you get like this?"

"For God's sake, let me smoke in peace for a little while! And then I will begin to tell you."

But the story was not told that night. The Invisible Man's wrist was growing painful, he was feverish, exhausted, and his mind came round to brood upon his chase down the hill and the struggle about the inn. He spoke in fragments of Marvel, he smoked faster, his voice grew angry. Kemp tried to gather what he could.

"He was afraid of me, I could see he was afraid of me," said the Invisible Man many times over. "He meant to give me the slip—he was always casting about! What a fool I was!

"The cur!

"I should have killed him—"

"Where did you get the money?" asked Kemp, abruptly.

The Invisible Man was silent for a space. "I can't tell you to-night," he said.

DOCTOR KEMP'S VISITOR

pharynx: The cavity behind the nose, mouth, and larynx.
nares: Nostrils.

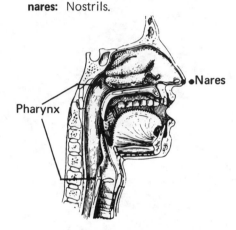

brood: To think moodily.

181

dozes: Naps, brief periods of light sleep.

He groaned suddenly and leant forward, supporting his invisible head on invisible hands. "Kemp," he said, "I've had no sleep for near three days,—except a couple of dozes of an hour or so. I must sleep soon."

"Well, have my room—have this room."

"But how can I sleep? If I sleep—he will get away. Ugh! What does it matter?"

"What's the shot-wound?" asked Kemp abruptly.

"Nothing—scratch and blood. Oh, God! How I want sleep!"

"Why not?"

The Invisible Man appeared to be regarding Kemp. "Because I've a particular objection to being caught by my fellow-men," he said slowly.

Kemp started.

"Fool that I am!" said the Invisible Man, striking the table smartly. "I've put the idea into your head."

smartly: Sharply, violently.

Kemp stood in the middle of the room staring at the headless garment.

Exhausted and wounded as the Invisible Man was, he refused to accept Kemp's word that his freedom should be respected. He examined the two windows of the bedroom, drew up the blinds, and opened the sashes, to confirm Kemp's statement that a retreat by them would be possible. Outside the night was very quiet and still, and the new moon was setting over the down. Then he examined the keys of the bedroom and the two dressing-room doors, to satisfy himself that these also could be made an assurance of freedom. Finally he expressed himself

18
THE INVISIBLE MAN SLEEPS

sashes: Sliding window frames in which glass panes are set.

183

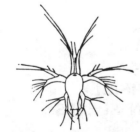

satisfied. He stood on the hearth rug and Kemp heard the sound of a yawn.

"I'm sorry," said the Invisible Man, "if I cannot tell you all that I have done to-night. But I am worn out. It's grotesque, no doubt. It's horrible! But believe me, Kemp, in spite of your arguments of this morning, it is quite a possible thing. I have made a discovery. I meant to keep it to myself. I can't. I must have a partner. And you— We can do such things— But to-morrow. Now, Kemp, I feel as though I must sleep or perish."

Kemp stood in the middle of the room staring at the headless garment. "I suppose I must leave you," he said. "It's— incredible. Three things happening like this, overturning all my preconceptions, would make me insane. But it's real! Is there anything more that I can get you?"

"Only bid me good-night," said Griffin.

"Good-night," said Kemp, and shook an invisible hand. He walked sideways to the door. Suddenly the dressing-gown walked quickly towards him. "Understand me!" said the dressing-gown. "No attempts to hamper me, or capture me! Or—"

Kemp's face changed a little. "I thought I gave you my word," he said.

Kemp closed the door softly behind him, and the key was turned upon him forthwith. Then, as he stood with an expression of passive amazement on his face, the rapid feet came to the door of the dressing-room and that too was locked. Kemp slapped his brow with his hand. "Am I dreaming? Has the world gone mad—or have I?"

He laughed, and put his hand to the locked door. "Barred out of my own bedroom, by a flagrant absurdity!" he said.

He walked to the head of the staircase, turned, and stared at the locked doors. "It's fact," he said. He put his fingers to his slightly bruised neck. "Undeniable fact!

"But—"

He shook his head hopelessly, turned, and went downstairs.

He lit the dining-room lamp, got out a cigar, and began pacing the room, ejaculating. Now and then he would argue with himself.

"Invisible!" he said.

"Is there such a thing as an invisible animal? In the sea, yes. Thousands! millions! All the larvae, all the little nauplii and tornarias, all the microscopic things, the jelly-fish. In the sea

184

there are more things invisible than visible! I never thought of that before. And in the ponds too! All those little pond-life things,—specks of colourless translucent jelly! But in air? No!

"It can't be.

"But after all—why not?

"If a man was made of glass he would still be visible."

His meditation became profound. The bulk of three cigars had passed into the invisible or diffused as a white ash over the carpet before he spoke again. Then it was merely an exclamation. He turned aside, walked out of the room, and went into his little consulting-room and lit the gas there. It was a little room, because Dr. Kemp did not live by practice, and in it were the day's newspapers. The morning's paper lay carelessly opened and thrown aside. He caught it up, turned it over, and read the account of a "Strange Story from Iping" that the mariner at Port Stowe had spelt over so painfully to Mr. Marvel. Kemp read it swiftly.

"Wrapped up!" said Kemp. "Disguised! Hiding it! 'No one seems to have been aware of his misfortune.' What the devil *is* his game?"

He dropped the paper, and his eye went seeking. "Ah!" he said, and caught up the "St. James' Gazette," lying folded up as it arrived. "Now we shall get at the truth," said Dr. Kemp. He rent the paper open; a couple of columns confronted him. "An Entire Village in Sussex goes Mad" was the heading.

"Good Heavens!" said Kemp, reading eagerly an incredulous account of the events in Iping, of the previous afternoon, that have already been described. Over the leaf the report in the morning paper had been reprinted.

He re-read it. "Ran through the streets striking right and left. Jaffers insensible. Mr. Huxter in great pain—still unable to describe what he saw. Painful humiliation—vicar. Woman ill with terror! Windows smashed. This extraordinary story probably a fabrication. Too good not to print—*cum grano!*"

He dropped the paper and stared blankly in front of him. "Probably a fabrication!"

He caught up the paper again, and re-read the whole business. "But when does the Tramp come in? Why the deuce was he chasing a Tramp?"

He sat down abruptly on the surgical couch. "He's not only invisible," he said, "but he's mad! Homicidal!"

THE INVISIBLE MAN SLEEPS

translucent: Partially transparent; light passes through, but details are obscured, as with frosted glass.

incredulous: Unbelievable, fantastic.

cum grano: Latin, meaning "with a grain."

explicit: Clear and detailed.

baldly: Direct; bare of ornament and grace.

shoal: Crowd, throng.

When dawn came to mingle its pallor with the lamp-light and cigar smoke of the dining-room, Kemp was still pacing up and down, trying to grasp the incredible.

He was altogether too excited to sleep. His servants, descending sleepily, discovered him, and were inclined to think that over-study had worked this ill on him. He gave them extraordinary but quite explicit instructions to lay breakfast for two in the belvedere study—and then to confine themselves to the basement and ground-floor. Then he continued to pace the dining-room until the morning's paper came. That had much to say and little to tell, beyond the confirmation of the evening before, and a very baldly written account of another remarkable tale from Port Burdock. This gave Kemp the essence of the happenings at the Jolly Cricketers, and the name of Marvel. "He has made me keep with him twenty-four hours," Marvel testified. Certain minor facts were added to the Iping story, notably the cutting of the village telegraph-wire. But there was nothing to throw light on the connexion between the Invisible Man and the Tramp; for Mr. Marvel had supplied no information about the three books, or the money with which he was lined. The incredulous tone had vanished and a shoal of reporters and inquirers were already at work elaborating the matter.

Kemp read every scrap of the report and sent his housemaid out to get every one of the morning papers she could. These also he devoured.

"He is invisible!" he said. "And it reads like rage growing to mania! The things he may do! The things he may do! And he's upstairs free as the air. What on earth ought I to do?

"For instance, would it be a breach of faith if—? No."

He went to a little untidy desk in the corner, and began a note. He tore this up half written, and wrote another. He read it over and considered it. Then he took an envelope and addressed it to "Colonel Adye, Port Burdock."

The Invisible Man awoke even as Kemp was doing this. He awoke in an evil temper, and Kemp, alert for every sound, heard his pattering feet rush suddenly across the bedroom overhead. Then a chair was flung over and the wash-hand stand tumbler smashed. Kemp hurried upstairs and rapped eagerly.

...he looked across to where Griffin sat at the breakfast table— a headless, handless dressing gown.

W hat's the matter?" asked Kemp, when the Invisible Man admitted him.

"Nothing," was the answer.

"But, confound it! The smash?"

"Fit of temper," said the Invisible Man. "Forgot this arm; and it's sore."

"You're rather liable to that sort of thing."

"I am."

Kemp walked across the room and picked up the fragments of broken glass. "All the facts are out about you," said Kemp, standing up with the glass in his hand; "all that happened in Iping, and down the hill. The world has become aware of its invisible citizen. But no one knows you are here."

The Invisible Man swore.

"The secret's out. I gather it was a secret. I don't know what your plans are, but of course I'm anxious to help you."

The Invisible Man sat down on the bed.

19
CERTAIN
FIRST
PRINCIPLES

"There's breakfast upstairs," said Kemp, speaking as easily as possible, and he was delighted to find his strange guest rose willingly. Kemp led the way up the narrow staircase to the belvedere.

"Before we can do anything else," said Kemp, "I must understand a little more about this invisibility of yours." He had sat down, after one nervous glance out of the window, with the air of a man who has talking to do. His doubts of the sanity of the entire business flashed and vanished again as he looked across to where Griffin sat at the breakfast-table,—a headless, handless dressing-gown, wiping unseen lips on a miraculously held serviette.

"It's simple enough—and credible enough," said Griffin, putting the serviette aside and leaning the invisible head on an invisible hand.

"No doubt, to you, but—" Kemp laughed.

"Well, yes; to me it seemed wonderful at first, no doubt. But now, great God!— But we will do great things yet! I came on the stuff first at Chesilstowe."

"Chesilstowe?"

"I went there after I left London. You know I dropped medicine and took up physics? *No!*—well, I did. *Light*—fascinated me."

"Ah!"

"Optical density! The whole subject is a network of riddles— a network with solutions glimmering elusively through. And being but two and twenty and full of enthusiasm, I said, 'I will devote my life to this. This is worth while.' You know what fools we are at two and twenty?"

"Fools then or fools now," said Kemp.

"As though Knowing could be any satisfaction to a man!

"But I went to work. And I had hardly worked and thought about the matter six months before light came through one of the meshes suddenly—blindingly! I found a general principle of pigments and refraction,—a formula, a geometrical expression involving four dimensions. Fools, common men, even common mathematicians, do not know anything of what some general expression may mean to the student of molecular physics. In the books—the books that Tramp has hidden—there are marvels, miracles! But this was not a method, it was an idea, that might lead to a method by which it would be possible, without changing any other property of matter,—except, in some instances, colours,—to lower the refractive index of a substance,

pigments: Organic coloring substances in men and plants.
refraction: Deflection or turning aside from a straight course.

solid or liquid, to that of air—so far as all practical purposes are concerned."

"Phew!" said Kemp. "That's odd! But still I don't see quite— I can understand that thereby you could spoil a valuable stone, but personal invisibility is a far cry."

"Precisely," said Griffin. "But consider: Visibility depends on the action of the visible bodies on light. Either a body absorbs light, or it reflects or refracts it, or does all these things. If it neither reflects nor refracts nor absorbs light, it cannot of itself be visible. You see an opaque red box, for instance, because the colour absorbs some of the light and reflects the rest, all the red part of the light, to you. If it did not absorb any particular part of the light, but reflected it all, then it would be a shining white box. Silver! A diamond box would neither absorb much of the light nor reflect much from the general surface, but just here and there where the surfaces were favourable the light would be reflected and refracted, so that you would get a brilliant appearance of flashing reflections and translucencies,—a sort of skeleton of light. A glass box would not be so brilliant, not so clearly visible, as a diamond box, because there would be less refraction and reflection. See that? From certain points of view you would see quite clearly through it. Some kinds of glass would be more visible than others, a box of flint glass would be brighter than a box of ordinary window glass. A box of very thin common glass would be hard to see in a bad light, because it would absorb hardly any light and refract and reflect very little. And if you put a sheet of common white glass in water, still more if you put it in some denser liquid than water, it would vanish almost altogether, because light passing from water to glass is only slightly refracted or reflected or indeed affected in any way. It is almost as invisible as a jet of coal gas or hydrogen is in air. And for precisely the same reason!"

"Yes," said Kemp, "that is pretty plain sailing."

"And here is another fact you will know to be true. If a sheet of glass is smashed, Kemp, and beaten into a powder, it becomes much more visible while it is in the air; it becomes at last an opaque white powder. This is because the powdering multiplies the surfaces of the glass at which refraction and reflection occur. In the sheet of glass there are only two surfaces; in the powder the light is reflected or refracted by each grain it passes through, and very little gets right through the powder. But if the white powdered glass is put into water, it

opaque: Impervious to light rays; not reflecting or giving out light.

forthwith vanishes. The powdered glass and water have much the same refractive index; that is, the light undergoes very little refraction or reflection in passing from one to the other.

"You make the glass invisible by putting it into a liquid of nearly the same refractive index; a transparent thing becomes invisible if it is put in any medium of almost the same refractive index. And if you will consider only a second, you will see also that the powder of glass might be made to vanish in air, if its refractive index could be made the same as that of air; for then there would be no refraction or reflection as the light passed from glass to air."

"Yes, yes," said Kemp. "But a man's not powdered glass!"

"No," said Griffin. "*He's more transparent!*"

"Nonsense!"

"That from a doctor! How one forgets! Have you already forgotten your physics, in ten years? Just think of all the things that are transparent and seem not to be so. Paper, for instance, is made up of transparent fibres, and it is white and opaque only for the same reason that a powder of glass is white and opaque. Oil white paper, fill up the interstices between the particles with oil so that there is no longer refraction or reflection except at the surfaces, and it becomes as transparent as glass. And not only paper, but cotton fibre, linen fibre, wool fibre, woody fibre, and *bone*, Kemp, *flesh*, Kemp, *hair*, Kemp, *nails* and *nerves*, Kemp, in fact the whole fabric of a man except the red of his blood and the black pigment of hair, are all made up of transparent, colourless tissue. So little suffices to make us visible one to the other. For the most part the fibres of a living creature are no more opaque than water."

"Great Heavens!" cried Kemp. "Of course, of course! I was thinking only last night of the sea larvae and all jelly-fish!"

"*Now* you have me! And all that I knew and had in mind a year after I left London—six years ago. But I kept it to myself. I had to do my work under frightful disadvantages. Oliver, my professor, was a scientific bounder, a journalist by instinct, a thief of ideas,—he was always prying! And you know the knavish system of the scientific world. I simply would not publish, and let him share my credit. I went on working, I got nearer and nearer making my formula into an experiment, a reality. I told no living soul, because I meant to flash my work upon the world with crushing effect,—to become famous at a blow. I took up the question of pigments to fill up certain gaps.

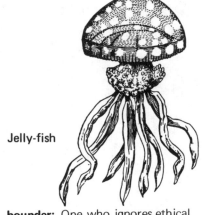

Jelly-fish

bounder: One who ignores ethical bounds.

knavish: Fraudulent, phony,

And suddenly, not by design but by accident, I made a discovery in physiology."

"Yes?"

"You know the red colouring matter of blood; it can be made white—colourless—and remain with all the functions it has now!"

Kemp gave a cry of incredulous amazement.

The Invisible Man rose and began pacing the little study. "You may well exclaim. I remember that night. It was late at night,—in the daytime one was bothered with the gaping, silly students,—and I worked then sometimes till dawn. It came suddenly, splendid and complete into my mind. I was alone; the laboratory was still, with the tall lights burning brightly and silently. In all my great moments I have been alone. 'One could make an animal—a tissue—transparent! One could make it invisible! All except the pigments—I could be invisible!' I said, suddenly realizing what it meant to be an albino with such knowledge. It was overwhelming. I left the filtering I was doing, and went and stared out of the great window at the stars. 'I could be invisible!' I repeated.

"To do such a thing would be to transcend magic. And I beheld, unclouded by doubt, a magnificent vision of all that invisibility might mean to a man,—the mystery, the power, the freedom. Drawbacks I saw none. You have only to think! And I, a shabby, poverty-struck, hemmed-in demonstrator, teaching fools in a provincial college, might suddenly become—this. I ask you, Kemp, if *you*— Anyone, I tell you, would have flung himself upon that research. And I worked three years, and every mountain of difficulty I toiled over showed another from its summit. The infinite details! And the exasperation,—a professor, a provincial professor, always prying. 'When are you going to publish this work of yours?' was his everlasting question. And the students, the cramped means! Three years I had of it—

"And after three years of secrecy and exasperation, I found that to complete it was impossible,—impossible."

"How?" asked Kemp.

"Money," said the Invisible Man, and went again to stare out of the window.

He turned round abruptly. "I robbed the old man—robbed my father.

"The money was not his, and he shot himself."

gaping: Staring with open mouths.

transcend: Go beyond.

provincial: In the provinces; remote from large cities, consequently, narrow and limited in knowledge and interests.

I remember the funeral, the cheap hearse, the scant ceremony, the windy frost-bitten hillside, and the old college friend who read the service over him...

20
AT THE HOUSE IN GREAT PORTLAND STREET

For a moment Kemp sat in silence, staring at the back of the headless figure at the window. Then he started, struck by a thought, rose, took the Invisible Man's arm, and turned him away from the outlook.

"You are tired," he said, "and while I sit, you walk about. Have my chair."

He placed himself between Griffin and the nearest window.

For a space Griffin sat silent, and then he resumed abruptly:—

"I had left the Chesilstowe cottage already," he said, "when that happened. It was last December. I had taken a room in London, a large unfurnished room in a big ill-managed lodging-house in a slum near Great Portland Street. The room was soon full of the appliances I had bought with his money; the work was going on steadily, successfully, drawing near an end. I was like a man emerging from a thicket, and suddenly coming on some unmeaning tragedy. I went to bury him. My mind was still on this research, and I did not lift a finger to save his character. I remember the funeral, the cheap hearse, the scant ceremony, the windy frost-bitten hillside, and the old college friend of his who read the service over him,—a shabby, black, bent old man with a snivelling cold.

"I remember walking back to the empty home, through the place that had once been a village and was now patched and tinkered by the jerry builders into the ugly likeness of a town. Every way the roads ran out at last into the desecrated fields and ended in rubble heaps and rank wet weeds. I remember myself as a gaunt black figure, going along the slippery, shiny pavement, and the strange sense of detachment I felt from the squalid respectability, the sordid commercialism of the place.

"I did not feel a bit sorry for my father. He seemed to me to be the victim of his own foolish sentimentality. The current cant required my attendance at his funeral, but it was really not my affair.

"But going along the High Street, my old life came back to me for a space, for I met the girl I had known ten years since. Our eyes met.

"Something moved me to turn back and talk to her. She was a very ordinary person.

"It was all like a dream, that visit to the old places. I did not feel then that I was lonely, that I had come out from the world into a desolate place. I appreciated my loss of sympathy, but I put it down to the general inanity of things. Re-entering my room seemed like the recovery of reality. There were the things I knew and loved. There stood the apparatus, the experiments arranged and waiting. And now there was scarcely a difficulty left, beyond the planning of details.

"I will tell you, Kemp, sooner or later, all the complicated processes. We need not go into that now. For the most part, saving certain gaps I chose to remember, they are written in cypher in those books that tramp has hidden. We must hunt

scant: Brief; scarcely sufficient.

jerry builders: Builders who construct cheaply and insubstantially.

squalid: Morally repulsive and degraded.

cant: Conventions; behavior which is dictated and expected by society. Cant usually refers to a particular use of language by a social group.

inanity: Pointlessness; lack of significance.

193

Dynamo

him down. We must get those books again. But the essential phase was to place the transparent object whose refractive index was to be lowered between two radiating centres of a sort of ethereal vibration, of which I will tell you more fully later. No, not these Roentgen vibrations—I don't know that these others of mine have been described. Yet they are obvious enough. I needed two little dynamos, and these I worked with a cheap gas engine. My first experiment was with a bit of white wool fabric. It was the strangest thing in the world to see it in the flicker of the flashes soft and white, and then to watch it fade like a wreath of smoke and vanish.

"I could scarcely believe I had done it. I put my hand into the emptiness, and there was the thing as solid as ever. I felt it awkwardly, and threw it on the floor. I had a little trouble finding it again.

"And then came a curious experience. I heard a miaow behind me, and turning, saw a lean white cat, very dirty, on the cistern cover outside the window. A thought came into my head. 'Everything ready for you,' I said, and went to the window, opened it, and called softly. She came in, purring,—the poor beast was starving,—and I gave her some milk. All my food was in a cupboard in the corner of the room. After that she went smelling round the room,—evidently with the idea of making herself at home. The invisible rag upset her a bit; you should have seen her spit at it! But I made her comfortable on the pillow of my truckle-bed. And I gave her butter to get her to wash."

"And you processed her?"

"I processed her. But giving drugs to a cat is no joke, Kemp! And the process failed."

"Failed!"

"In two particulars. These were the claws and the pigment stuff—what is it?—at the back of the eye in a cat. You know?"

"*Tapetum.*"

"Yes, the *tapetum*. It didn't go. After I'd given the stuff to bleach the blood and done certain other things to her, I gave the beast opium, and put her and the pillow she was sleeping on, on the apparatus. And after all the rest had faded and vanished, there remained two little ghosts of her eyes."

"Odd!"

"I can't explain it. She was bandaged and clamped, of course,—so I had her safe; but she woke while she was still misty, and miaowled dismally, and someone came knocking. It was an old woman from downstairs, who suspected me of vivisecting,—a drink-sodden old creature, with only a white cat to care for in all the world. I whipped out some chloroform, applied it, and answered the door. 'Did I hear a cat?' she asked. 'My cat?' 'Not here,' said I, very politely. She was a little doubtful and tried to peer past me into the room; strange enough to her no doubt,—bare walls, uncurtained windows, truckle-bed, with the gas engine vibrating, and the seethe of the radiant points, and that faint ghastly stinging of chloroform in the air. She had to be satisfied at last and went away again."

"How long did it take?" asked Kemp.

"Three or four hours—the cat. The bones and sinews and the fat were the last to go, and the tips of the coloured hairs. And, as I say, the back part of the eye, tough iridescent stuff it is, wouldn't go at all.

"It was night outside long before the business was over, and nothing was to be seen but the dim eyes and the claws. I stopped the gas engine, felt for and stroked the beast, which was still insensible, and then, being tired, left it sleeping on the invisible pillow and went to bed. I found it hard to sleep. I lay awake thinking weak aimless stuff, going over the experiment over and over again, or dreaming feverishly of things growing misty and vanishing about me, until everything, the ground I stood on, vanished, and so I came to that sickly falling nightmare one gets. About two, the cat began miaowling about the room. I tried to hush it by talking to it, and then I decided to turn it out. I remember the shock I had when striking a light—there were just the round eyes shining green—and nothing round them. I would have given it milk, but I hadn't any. It wouldn't be quiet, it just sat down and miaowled at the door. I tried to catch it, with an idea of putting it out of the window, but it wouldn't be caught, it vanished. Then it began miaowling in different parts of the room. At last I opened the window and made a bustle. I suppose it went out at last. I never saw any more of it.

"Then—Heaven knows why—I fell thinking of my father's funeral again, and the dismal windy hillside, until the day had come. I found sleeping was hopeless, and, locking my door after me, wandered out into the morning streets."

"You don't mean to say there's an invisible cat at large!" said Kemp.

AT THE HOUSE IN GREAT PORTLAND STREET

vivisecting: Operating on living animals for experimental purposes.

chloroform: An anesthetic with a heavy, sweet smell.

seethe: Throb.

iridescent: Shiny, glowing.

195

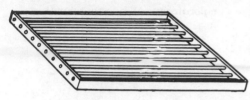

grating: A covering of parallel bars.

apathetic: Indifferent, uncaring.

compass: Move past; go through.

transient: Temporary, passing.

strychnine: A stimulant for the central nervous system that is highly poisonous in pure form.

palaeolithic: Of the Stone Age. Here, reaching back in time, past all refinement of civilization, to an age of unleashed terror and ferocity.

"If it hasn't been killed," said the Invisible Man. "Why not?"

"Why not?" said Kemp. "I didn't mean to interrupt."

"It's very probably been killed," said the Invisible Man. "It was alive four days after, I know, and down a grating in Great Tichfield Street; because I saw a crowd round the place, trying to see whence the miaowing came."

He was silent for the best part of a minute. Then he resumed abruptly:—

"I remember that morning before the change very vividly. I must have gone up Great Portland Street. I remember the barracks in Albany Street, and the horse soldiers coming out, and at last I found myself sitting in the sunshine and feeling very ill and strange, on the summit of Primrose Hill. It was a sunny day in January,—one of those sunny, frosty days that came before the snow this year. My weary brain tried to formulate the position, to plot out a plan of action.

"I was surprised to find, now that my prize was within my grasp, how inconclusive its attainment seemed. As a matter of fact I was worked out; the intense stress of nearly four years' continuous work left me incapable of any strength of feeling. I was apathetic, and I tried in vain to recover the enthusiasm of my first inquiries, the passion of discovery that had enabled me to compass even the downfall of my father's grey hairs. Nothing seemed to matter. I saw pretty clearly this was a transient mood, due to overwork and want of sleep, and that either by drugs or rest it would be possible to recover my energies.

"All I could think clearly was that the thing had to be carried through; the fixed idea still ruled me. And soon, for the money I had was almost exhausted. I looked about me at the hillside, with children playing and girls watching them, and tried to think of all the fantastic advantages an invisible man would have in the world. After a time I crawled home, took some food and a strong dose of strychnine, and went to sleep in my clothes on my unmade bed. Strychnine is a grand tonic, Kemp, to take the flabbiness out of a man."

"It's the devil," said Kemp. "It's the palaeolithic in a bottle."

"I awoke vastly invigorated and rather irritable. You know?"

"I know the stuff."

"And there was someone rapping at the door. It was my landlord with threats and inquiries, an old Polish Jew in a long grey coat and greasy slippers. I had been tormenting a cat in the night, he was sure,—the old woman's tongue had been busy. He insisted on knowing all about it. The laws of this country against vivisection were very severe,—he might be liable. I denied the cat. Then the vibration of the little gas engine could be felt all over the house, he said. That was true, certainly. He edged round me into the room, peering about over his German-silver spectacles, and a sudden dread came into my mind that he might carry away something of my secret. I tried to keep between him and the concentrating apparatus I had arranged, and that only made him more curious. What was I doing? Why was I always alone and secretive? Was it legal? Was it dangerous? I paid nothing but the usual rent. His had always been a most respectable house—in a disreputable neighbourhood. Suddenly my temper gave way. I told him to get out. He began to protest, to jabber of his right of entry. In a moment I had him by the collar; something ripped, and he went spinning out into his own passage. I slammed and locked the door and sat down quivering.

"He made a fuss outside, which I disregarded, and after a time he went away.

"But this brought matters to a crisis. I did not know what he would do, nor even what he had power to do. To move to fresh apartments would have meant delay; all together I had barely twenty pounds left in the world,—for the most part in a bank,—and I could not afford that. Vanish! It was irresistible. Then there would be an inquiry, the sacking of my room—

"At the thought of the possibility of my work being exposed or interrupted at its very climax, I became angry and active. I hurried out with my three books of notes, my cheque-book,— the tramp has them now,—and directed them from the nearest Post Office to a house of call for letters and parcels in Great Portland Street. I tried to go out noiselessly. Coming in, I found my landlord going quietly upstairs; he had heard the door close, I suppose. You would have laughed to see him jump aside on the landing as I came tearing after him. He glared at me as I went by him, and I made the house quiver with the slamming of my door. I heard him come shuffling up to my floor, hesitate, and go down. I set to work upon my preparations forthwith.

"It was all done that evening and night. While I was still sitting under the sickly, drowsy influence of the drugs that decolourise blood, there came a repeated knocking at the door. It ceased, footsteps went away and returned, and the knocking

AT THE HOUSE IN GREAT PORTLAND STREET

concentrating apparatus: The instruments for concentrating or focusing rays, bringing the rays to a central point.

disreputable: Not respectable or desirable.

sacking: Ransacking; searching out and carrying away of valuables.

was resumed. There was an attempt to push something under the door—a blue paper. Then in a fit of irritation I rose and went and flung the door wide open. 'Now then?' said I.

"It was my landlord, with a notice of ejectment or something. He held it out to me, saw something odd about my hands, I expect, and lifted his eyes to my face.

"For a moment he gaped. Then he gave a sort of inarticulate cry, dropped candle and writ together, and went blundering down the dark passage to the stairs. I shut the door, locked it, and went to the looking-glass. Then I understood his terror. My face was white—like white stone.

"But it was all horrible. I had not expected the suffering. A night of racking anguish, sickness and fainting. I set my teeth, though my skin was presently afire, all my body afire; but I lay there like grim death. I understood now how it was the cat had howled until I chloroformed it. Lucky it was I lived alone and untended in my room. There were times when I sobbed and groaned and talked. But I stuck to it. I became insensible and woke languid in the darkness.

"The pain had passed. I thought I was killing myself and I did not care. I shall never forget that dawn, and the strange horror of seeing that my hands had become as clouded glass, and watching them grow clearer and thinner as the day went by, until at last I could see the sickly disorder of my room through them, though I closed my transparent eyelids. My limbs became glassy, the bones and arteries faded, vanished, and the little white nerves went last. I gritted my teeth and stayed there to the end. At last only the dead tips of the fingernails remained, pallid and white, and the brown stain of some acid upon my fingers.

"I struggled up. At first I was as incapable as a swathed infant,—stepping with limbs I could not see. I was weak and very hungry. I went and stared at nothing in my shaving-glass, at nothing save where an attenuated pigment still remained behind the retina of my eyes, fainter than mist. I had to hang on to the table and press my forehead to the glass.

"It was only by a frantic effort of will that I dragged myself back to the apparatus and completed the process.

"I slept during the forenoon, pulling the sheet over my eyes to shut out the light, and about midday I was awakened again by a knocking. My strength had returned. I sat up and listened and heard a whispering. I sprang to my feet and as noiselessly as possible began to detach the connections of my apparatus, and to distribute it about the room, so as to destroy the suggestions of its arrangement. Presently the knocking was renewed and voices called, first my landlord's, and then two others. To gain time I answered them. The invisible rag and pillow came to hand and I opened the window and pitched them out on to the cistern cover. As the window opened, a heavy crash came at the door. Someone had charged it with the idea of smashing the lock. But the stout bolts I had screwed up some days before stopped him. That startled me, made me angry. I began to tremble and do things hurriedly.

"I tossed together some loose paper, straw, packing paper and so forth, in the middle of the room, and turned on the gas. Heavy blows began to rain upon the door. I could not find the matches. I beat my hands on the wall with rage. I turned down the gas again, stepped out of the window on the cistern cover, very softly lowered the sash, and sat down, secure and invisible, but quivering with anger, to watch events. They split a panel, I saw, and in another moment they had broken away the staples of the bolts and stood in the open doorway. It was the landlord and his two step-sons, sturdy young men of three or four and twenty. Behind them fluttered the old hag of a woman from downstairs.

"You may imagine their astonishment to find the room empty. One of the younger men rushed to the window at once, flung it up and stared out. His staring eyes and thick-lipped bearded face came a foot from my face. I was half minded to hit his silly countenance, but I arrested my doubled fist. He stared right through me. So did the others as they joined him. The old man went and peered under the bed, and then they all made a rush for the cupboard. They had to argue about it at length in Yiddish and Cockney English. They concluded I had not answered them, that their imagination had deceived them. A feeling of extraordinary elation took the place of my anger as I sat outside the window and watched these four people—for the old lady came in, glancing suspiciously about her like a cat, trying to understand the riddle of my behaviour.

"The old man, so far as I could understand his *patois*, agreed with the old lady that I was a vivisectionist. The sons protested in garbled English that I was an electrician, and appealed to the dynamos and radiators. They were all nervous against my arrival, although I found subsequently that they had bolted the

countenance: Face.
arrested: Stopped.

elation: Joy.

patois: (Say pat wa) Dialect. Here, a combination of Yiddish and Cockney English.

costermonger: A man who sells such things as fruit, vegetables, and fish in the street from a cart.

front door. The old lady peered into the cupboard and under the bed, and one of the young men pushed up the register and stared up the chimney. One of my fellow lodgers, a costermonger who shared the opposite room with a butcher, appeared on the landing, and he was called in and told incoherent things.

"It occurred to me that the radiators, if they fell into the hands of some acute well-educated person, would give me away too much, and watching my opportunity, I came into the room and tilted one of the little dynamos off its fellow on which it was standing, and smashed both apparatus. Then, while they were trying to explain the smash, I dodged out of the room and went softly downstairs.

"I went into one of the sitting-rooms and waited until they came down, still speculating and argumentative, all a little disappointed at finding no 'horrors,' and all a little puzzled how they stood with regard to me. Then I slipped up again with a box of matches, fired my heap of paper and rubbish, put the chairs and bedding thereby, led the gas to the affair, by means of an india-rubber tube, and waving a farewell to the room left it for the last time."

fired: Set fire to.

"You fired the house!" exclaimed Kemp.

"Fired the house. It was the only way to cover my trail—and no doubt it was insured. I slipped the bolts of the front door quietly and went out into the street. I was invisible, and I was only just beginning to realise the extraordinary advantage my invisibility gave me. My head was already teeming with plans of all the wild and wonderful things I had now impunity to do.

impunity: Freedom from punishment.

200

'See 'em', said one. 'See what?' said the other. 'Why them foot-marks—bare. Like what you makes in mud.

I n going downstairs the first time I found an unexpected difficulty because I could not see my feet; indeed I stumbled twice, and there was an unaccustomed clumsiness in gripping the bolt. By not looking down, however, I managed to walk on the level passably well.

"My mood, I say, was one of exaltation. I felt as a seeing man might do, with padded feet and noiseless clothes, in a city of the blind. I experienced a wild impulse to jest, to startle people, to clap men on the back, fling people's hats astray, and generally revel in my extraordinary advantage.

21
IN OXFORD STREET

Hansom

"But hardly had I emerged upon Great Portland Street, however (my lodging was close to the big draper's shop there), when I heard a clashing concussion and was hit violently behind, and turning saw a man carrying a basket of soda-water syphons, and looking in amazement at his burden. Although the blow had really hurt me, I found something so irresistible in his astonishment that I laughed aloud. 'The devil's in the basket,' I said, and suddenly twisted it out of his hand. He let go incontinently, and I swung the whole weight into the air.

"But a fool of a cabman, standing outside a public house, made a sudden rush for this, and his extending fingers took me with excruciating violence under the ear. I let the whole down with a smash on the cabman, and then, with shouts and the clatter of feet about me, people coming out of shops, vehicles pulling up, I realised what I had done for myself, and cursing my folly, backed against a shop window and prepared to dodge out of the confusion. In a moment I should be wedged into a crowd and inevitably discovered. I pushed by a butcher boy, who luckily did not turn to see the nothingness that shoved him aside, and dodged behind the cabman's four-wheeler. I do not know how they settled the business. I hurried straight across the road, which was happily clear, and hardly heeding which way I went, in the fright of detection the incident had given me, plunged into the afternoon throng of Oxford Street.

"I tried to get into the stream of people, but they were too thick for me, and in a moment my heels were being trodden upon. I took to the gutter, the roughness of which I found painful to my feet, and forthwith the shaft of a crawling hansom dug me forcibly under the shoulder blade, reminding me that I was already bruised severely. I staggered out of the way of the cab, avoided a perambulator by a convulsive movement, and found myself behind the hansom. A happy thought saved me, and as this drove slowly along I followed in its immediate wake, trembling and astonished at the turn of my adventure. And not only trembling, but shivering. It was a bright day in January and I was stark naked and the thin slime of mud that covered the road was freezing. Foolish as it seems to me now, I had not reckoned that, transparent or not, I was still amenable to the weather and all its consequences.

"Then suddenly a bright idea came into my head. I ran round and got into the cab. And so, shivering, scared, and sniffing with

202

the first intimations of a cold, and with the bruises in the small of my back growing upon my attention, I drove slowly along Oxford Street and past Tottenham Court Road. My mood was as different from that in which I had sallied forth ten minutes ago as it is possible to imagine. *This* invisibility indeed! The one thought that possessed me was—how was I to get out of the scrape I was in.

"We crawled past Mudie's, and there a tall woman with five or six yellow-labelled books hailed my cab, and I sprang out just in time to escape her, shaving a railway van narrowly in my flight. I made off up the roadway to Bloomsbury Square, intending to strike north past the Museum and so get into the quiet district. I was now cruelly chilled, and the strangeness of my situation so unnerved me that I whimpered as I ran. At the northward corner of the Square a little white dog ran out of the Pharmaceutical Society's offices, and incontinently made for me, nose down.

"I had never realised it before, but the nose is to the mind of a dog what the eye is to the mind of a seeing man. Dogs perceive the scent of a man moving as men perceive his vision. This brute began barking and leaping, showing, as it seemed to me, only too plainly that he was aware of me. I crossed Great Russell Street, glancing over my shoulder as I did so, and went some way along Montagu Street before I realised what I was running towards.

"Then I became aware of a blare of music, and looking along the street saw a number of people advancing out of Russell Square, red shirts, and the banner of the Salvation Army to the fore. Such a crowd, chanting in the roadway and scoffing on the pavement, I could not hope to penetrate, and dreading to go back and farther from home again, and deciding on the spur of the moment, I ran up the white steps of a house facing the museum railings, and stood there until the crowd should have passed. Happily the dog stopped at the noise of the band too, hesitated, and turned tail, running back to Bloomsbury Square again.

"On came the band, bawling with unconscious irony some hymn about 'When shall we see his Face?' and it seemed an interminable time to me before the tide of the crowd washed along the pavement by me. Thud, thud, thud, came the drum with a vibrating resonance, and for the moment I did not notice

scoffing: Jeering.

irony: Here, a mockery of the fitness, or appropriateness, of the situation.

two urchins stopping at the railings by me. 'See 'em,' said one. 'See what?' said the other. 'Why—them footmarks—*bare*. Like what you makes in mud.'

"I looked down and saw the youngsters had stopped and were gaping at the muddy footmarks I had left behind me up the newly whitened steps. The passing people elbowed and jostled them, but their confounded intelligence was arrested. 'Thud, thud, thud, When, thud, shall we see, thud, his face, thud, thud,' 'There's a barefoot man gone up them steps, or I don't know nothing,' said one. 'And he ain't never come down again. And his foot was a-bleeding.'

"The thick of the crowd had already passed. 'Looky there, Ted,' quoth the younger of the detectives, with the sharpness of surprise in his voice, and pointed straight to my feet. I looked down and saw at once the dim suggestion of their outline sketched in splashes of mud. For a moment I was paralysed.

" 'Why, that's rum,' said the elder. 'Dashed rum! It's just like the ghost of a foot, ain't it?' He hesitated and advanced with outstretched hand. A man pulled up short to see what he was catching, and then a girl. In another moment he would have touched me. Then I saw what to do. I made a step, the boy started back with an exclamation, and with a rapid movement I swung myself over into the portico of the next house. But the smaller boy was sharp-eyed enough to follow the movement, and before I was well down the steps and upon the pavement, he had recovered from his momentary astonishment and was shouting out that the feet had gone over the wall.

"They rushed round and saw my new footmarks flash into being on the lower step and upon the pavement. 'What's up?' asked someone. 'Feet! Look! Feet running!' Everybody in the road, except my three pursuers, was pouring along after the Salvation Army, and this blow not only impeded me but them. There was an eddy of surprise and interrogation. At the cost of bowling over one young fellow I got through, and in another moment I was rushing headlong round the circuit of Russell Square, with six or seven astonished people following my footmarks. There was no time for explanation, or else the whole host would have been after me.

"Twice I doubled round corners, thrice I crossed the road and came back on my tracks, and then, as my feet grew hot and dry, the damp impressions began to fade. At last I had a breathing space and rubbed my feet clean with my hands, and

portico: A porch supported by columns at regular intervals.

impeded: Hindered, stood in the way of.

so got away altogether. The last I saw of the chase was a little group of a dozen people perhaps, studying with infinite perplexity a slowly drying footprint that had resulted from a puddle in Tavistock Square,—a footprint as isolated and incomprehensible to them as Crusoe's solitary discovery.

"This running warmed me to a certain extent, and I went on with a better courage through the maze of less frequented roads that runs hereabouts. My back had now become very stiff and sore, my tonsils were painful from the cabman's fingers, and the skin of my neck had been scratched by his nails; my feet hurt exceedingly and I was lame from a little cut on one foot. I saw in time a blind man approaching me, and fled limping, for I feared his subtle intuitions. Once or twice accidental collisions occurred and I left people amazed, with unaccountable curses ringing in their ears. Then came something silent and quiet against my face, and across the Square fell a thin veil of slowly falling flakes of snow. I had caught a cold, and do as I would I could not avoid an occasional sneeze. And every dog that came in sight, with its pointing nose and curious sniffing, was a terror to me.

"Then came men and boys running, first one and then others, and shouting as they ran. It was a fire. They ran in the direction of my lodging, and looking back down a street I saw a mass of black smoke streaming up above the roofs and telephone wires. It was my lodging burning; my clothes, my apparatus, all my resources indeed, except my cheque-book and the three volumes of memoranda that awaited me in Great Portland Street, were there. Burning! I had burnt my boats—if ever a man did! The place was blazing."

The Invisible Man paused and thought. Kemp glanced nervously out of the window. "Yes?" he said. "Go on."

maze: A confusing network.

intuitions: Direct, immediate insights.

... and then I went to the clothing place and got trousers, a lounge jacket, an overcoat and a slouch hat—

22
IN THE EMPORIUM

accost: Approach and address.

So last January, with the beginnings of a snowstorm in the air about me—and if it settled on me it would betray me!—weary, cold, painful, inexpressibly wretched, and still but half convinced of my invisible quality, I began this new life to which I am committed. I had no refuge, no appliances, no human being in the world in whom I could confide. To have told my secret would have given me away—made a mere show and rarity of me. Nevertheless, I was half minded to accost some passerby and throw myself upon his mercy. But I knew too clearly the terror and brutal cruelty my advances would evoke. I made no plans in the street. My sole object was to get shelter from the snow, to get myself covered and warm; then I might hope to plan. But even to me, an Invisible Man, the rows of London houses stood latched, barred, and bolted impregnably.

"Only one thing could I see clearly before me, the cold exposure and misery of the snowstorm and the night.

"And then I had a brilliant idea. I turned down one of the roads leading from Gower Street to Tottenham Court Road, and found myself outside Omniums, the big establishment where everything is to be bought,—you know the place,—meat, grocery, linen, furniture, clothing, oil paintings even,—a huge meandering collection of shops rather than a shop. I had thought I should find the doors open, but they were closed, and as I stood in the wide entrance a carriage stopped outside, and a man in uniform—you know the kind of personage with 'Omni-um' on his cap—flung open the door. I contrived to enter, and walking down the shop—it was a department where they were selling ribbons and gloves and stockings and that kind of thing—came to a more spacious region devoted to picnic baskets and wicker furniture.

"I did not feel safe there, however; people were going to and fro, and I prowled restlessly about until I came upon a huge section in an upper floor containing multitudes of bedsteads, and this I clambered, and found a resting-place at last among a huge pile of folded flock mattresses. The place was already lit up and agreeably warm, and I decided to remain where I was, keeping a cautious eye on the two or three sets of shopmen and customers who were meandering through the place, until closing time came. Then I should be able, I thought, to rob the place for food and clothing, and disguised, prowl through it and examine its resources, perhaps sleep on some of the bedding. That seemed an acceptable plan. My idea was to procure clothing to make myself a muffled but acceptable figure, to get money, and then to recover my books and parcels where they awaited me, take a lodging somewhere and elaborate plans for the complete realisation of the advantages my invisibility gave me (as I still imagined) over my fellow-men.

"Closing time arrived quickly enough; it could not have been more than an hour after I took up my position on the mattresses before I noticed the blinds of the windows being drawn, and customers being marched doorward. And then a

meandering: Aimless winding.

Omnium: Latin meaning "all," "everything."

contrived: Managed.

number of brisk young men began with remarkable alacrity to tidy up the goods that remained disturbed. I left my lair as the crowds diminished, and prowled cautiously out into the less desolate parts of the shop. I was really surprised to observe how rapidly the young men and women whipped away the goods displayed for sale during the day. All the boxes of goods, the hanging fabrics, the festoons of lace, the boxes of sweets in the grocery section, the displays of this and that, were being whipped down, folded up, slapped into tidy receptacles, and everything that could not be taken down and put away had sheets of some coarse stuff like sacking flung over them. Finally all the chairs were turned up on to the counters, leaving the floor clear. Directly each of these young people had done, he or she made promptly for the door with such an expression of animation as I have rarely observed in a shop assistant before. Then came a lot of youngsters scattering sawdust and carrying pails and brooms. I had to dodge to get out of the way, and as it was, my ankle got stung with the sawdust. For some time, wandering through the swathed and darkened departments, I could hear the brooms at work. And at last a good hour or more after the shop had been closed, came a noise of locking doors. Silence came upon the place, and I found myself wandering through the vast and intricate shops, galleries, showrooms of the place, alone. It was very still; in one place I remember passing near one of the Tottenham Court Road entrances and listening to the tapping of boot-heels of the passers-by.

"My first visit was to the place where I had seen stockings and gloves for sale. It was dark, and I had the devil of a hunt after matches, which I found at last in the drawer of the little cash desk. Then I had to get a candle. I had to tear down wrappings and ransack a number of boxes and drawers, but at last I managed to turn out what I sought; the box label called them lambswool pants, and lambswool vests. Then socks, a thick comforter, and then I went to the clothing place and got trousers, a lounge jacket, an overcoat and a slouch hat,—a clerical sort of hat with the brim turned down. I began to feel a human being again, and my next thought was food.

"Upstairs was a refreshment department, and there I got cold meat. There was coffee still in the urn, and I lit the gas and warmed it up again, and altogether I did not do badly. Afterwards, prowling through the place in search of blankets,—I had to put up at last with a heap of down quilts,—I came upon a grocery section with a lot of chocolate and candied fruits, more than was good for me indeed—and some white burgundy. And near that was a toy department, and I had a brilliant idea. I found some artificial noses—dummy noses, you know, and I thought of dark spectacles. But Omniums had no optical department. My nose had been a difficulty indeed—I had thought of paint. But the discovery set my mind running on wigs and masks and the like. Finally I went to sleep in a heap of down quilts, very warm and comfortable.

"My last thoughts before sleeping were the most agreeable I had had since the change. I was in a state of physical serenity, and that was reflected in my mind. I thought that I should be able to slip out unobserved in the morning with my clothes upon me, muffling my face with a white wrapper I had taken, purchase, with the money I had taken, spectacles and so forth, and so complete my disguise. I lapsed into disorderly dreams of all the fantastic things that had happened during the last few days. I saw the ugly little Jew of a landlord vociferating in his rooms; I saw his two sons marvelling, and the wrinkled old woman's gnarled face as she asked for her cat. I experienced again the strange sensation of seeing the cloth disappear, and so I came round to the windy hillside and the sniffing old clergyman mumbling 'Dust to dust, earth to earth,' and my father's open grave.

" 'You also,' said a voice, and suddenly I was being forced towards the grave. I struggled, shouted, appealed to the mourners, but they continued stonily following the service; the old clergyman, too, never faltered droning and sniffing through the ritual. I realised I was invisible and inaudible, that overwhelming forces had their grip on me. I struggled in vain, I was forced over the brink, the coffin rang hollow as I fell upon it, and the gravel came flying after me in spadefuls. Nobody heeded me, nobody was aware of me. I made convulsive struggles and awoke.

"The pale London dawn had come, the place was full of a chilly grey light that filtered round the edges of the window blinds. I sat up, and for a time I could not think where this ample apartment, with its counters, its piles of rolled stuff, its heap of quilts and cushions, its iron pillars, might be. Then, as recollection came back to me, I heard voices in conversation.

"Then far down the place, in the brighter light of some department which had already raised its blinds, I saw two men

vociferating: Shouting loudly.

gnarled: Twisted and rugged looking, like an old tree.

droning: Speaking in a monotonous, steady tone.

full tilt: Full speed and full force.

approaching. I scrambled to my feet, looking about me for some way of escape, and even as I did so the sound of my movement made them aware of me. I suppose they saw merely a figure moving quietly and quickly away. 'Who's that?' cried one, and 'Stop there!' shouted the other. I dashed round a corner and came full tilt—a faceless figure, mind you!—on a lanky lad of fifteen. He yelled and I bowled him over, rushed past him, turned another corner, and by a happy inspiration threw myself flat behind a counter. In another moment feet went running past and I heard voices shouting, 'All hands to the doors!' asking what was 'up,' and giving one another advice how to catch me.

"Lying on the ground, I felt scared out of my wits. But—odd as it may seem—it did not occur to me at the moment to take off my clothes as I should have done. I had made up my mind, I suppose, to get away in them, and that ruled me. And then down the vista of the counters came a bawling of 'Here he is!'

vista: Long, narrow opening.

"I sprang to my feet, whipped a chair off the counter, and sent it whirling at the fool who had shouted, turned, came into another round a corner, sent him spinning, and rushed up the stairs. He kept his footing, gave a view hallo! and came up the staircase hot after me. Up the staircase were piled a multitude of those bright-coloured pot things—what are they?"

view hallo: The shout given by a huntsman on seeing a fox break cover.

"Art pots," suggested Kemp.

"That's it! Art pots. Well, I turned at the top step and swung round, plucked one out of a pile and smashed it on his silly head as he came at me. The whole pile of pots went headlong, and I heard shouting and footsteps running from all parts. I made a mad rush for the refreshment place, and there was a man in white like a man cook, who took up the chase. I made one last desperate turn and found myself among lamps and ironmongery. I went behind the counter of this, and waited for my cook, and as he bolted in at the head of the chase, I doubled him up with a lamp. Down he went, and I crouched down behind the counter and began whipping off my clothes as fast as I could. Coat, jacket, trousers, shoes were all right, but a lambswool vest fits a man like a skin. I heard more men coming, my cook was lying quiet on the other side of the counter, stunned or scared speechless, and I had to make another dash for it, like a rabbit hunted out of a wood-pile.

ironmongery: Hardware; a general name for all articles made of iron.

" 'This way, policeman!' I heard someone shouting. I found

myself in my bedstead storeroom again, and at the end a wilderness of wardrobes. I rushed among them, went flat, got rid of my vest after infinite wriggling, and stood a free man again, panting and scared, as the policeman and three of the shopmen came round the corner. They made a rush for the vest and pants, and collared the trousers. 'He's dropping his plunder,' said one of the young men. 'He *must* be somewhere here.'

"But they did not find me all the same.

"I stood watching them hunt for me for a time, and cursing my ill-luck in losing the clothes. Then I went into the refreshment-room, drank a little milk I found there, and sat down by the fire to consider my position.

"In a little while two assistants came in and began to talk over the business very excitedly and like the fools they were. I heard a magnified account of my depredations, and other speculations as to my whereabouts. Then I fell to scheming again. The insurmountable difficulty of the place, especially now it was alarmed, was to get any plunder out of it. I went down into the warehouse to see if there was any chance of packing and addressing a parcel, but I could not understand the system of checking. About eleven o'clock, the snow having thawed as it fell, and the day being finer and a little warmer than the previous one, I decided that the Emporium was hopeless, and went out again, exasperated at my want of success, with only the vaguest plans of action in my mind."

IN
THE
EMPORIUM

depredations: Violent robbing and destruction.

"The man who had entered the shop was a short, slight, hunched, beetle-browed man with long arms and very short bandy legs."

23
IN DRURY LANE

ut you begin now to realise," said the Invisible Man, "the full disadvantage of my condition. I had no shelter, no covering,—to get clothing, was to forego all my advantage, to make of myself a strange and terrible thing. I was fasting; for to eat, to fill myself with unassimilated matter, would be to become grotesquely visible again."

"I never thought of that," said Kemp.

"Nor had I. And the snow had warned me of other dangers. I could not go abroad in snow—it would settle on me and expose me. Rain, too, would make me a watery outline, a glistening surface of a man—a bubble. And fog—I should be like a fainter bubble in a fog, a surface, a greasy glimmer of humanity.

Moreover, as I went abroad—in the London air—I gathered dirt about my ankles, floating smuts and dust upon my skin. I did not know how long it would be before I should become visible from that cause also. But I saw clearly it could not be for long.

"Not in London at any rate.

"I went into the slums towards Great Portland Street, and found myself at the end of the street in which I had lodged. I did not go that way, because of the crowd halfway down it opposite to the still smoking ruins of the house I had fired. My most immediate problem was to get clothing. What to do with my face puzzled me. Then I saw in one of those little miscellaneous shops—news, sweets, toys, stationery, belated Christmas tomfoolery, and so forth—an array of masks and noses. I realised that problem was solved. In a flash I saw my course. I turned about, no longer aimless, and went—circuitously in order to avoid the busy ways, towards the back streets north of the Strand; for I remembered, though not very distinctly where, that some theatrical costumiers had shops in that district.

"The day was cold, with a nipping wind down the northward running streets. I walked fast to avoid being overtaken. Every crossing was a danger, every passenger a thing to watch alertly. One man as I was about to pass him at the top of Bedford Street, turned upon me abruptly and came into me, sending me into the road and almost under the wheel of a passing hansom. The verdict of the cab-rank was that he had had some sort of stroke. I was so unnerved by this encounter that I went into Covent Garden Market and sat down for some time in a quiet corner by a stall of violets, panting and trembling. I found I had caught a fresh cold, and had to turn out after a time lest my sneezes should attract attention.

"At last I reached the object of my quest, a dirty fly-blown little shop in a byway near Drury Lane, with a window full of tinsel robes, sham jewels, wigs, slippers, dominoes and theatrical photographs. The shop was old-fashioned and low and dark, and the house rose above it for four storeys, dark and dismal. I peered through the window and, seeing no one within, entered. The opening of the door set a clanking bell ringing. I left it open, and walked round a bare costume stand, into a corner behind a cheval glass. For a minute or so no one came. Then I heard heavy feet striding across a room, and a man appeared down the shop.

tomfoolery: Nonsense.

circuitously: Indirectly; in a round-about way.

Covent Garden Market: A huge fruit and vegetable market in a small, but important area of Central London which also includes the famed opera house, a number of theaters, a beautiful square, and the Bow Street Police Station.

cheval glass: A full-length swinging mirror.

credible: Believable.

bandy: Bowed.

draught: Draft.

"My plans were now perfectly definite. I proposed to make my way into the house, secrete myself upstairs, watch my opportunity, and when everything was quiet, rummage out a wig, mask, spectacles, and costume, and go into the world, perhaps a grotesque but still a credible figure. And incidentally of course I could rob the house of any available money.

"The man who had entered the shop was a short, slight, hunched, beetle-browed man, with long arms and very short bandy legs. Apparently I had interrupted a meal. He stared about the shop with an expression of expectation. This gave way to surprise, and then anger, as he saw the shop empty. 'Damn the boys!' he said. He went to stare up and down the street. He came in again in a minute, kicked the door to with his foot spitefully, and went muttering back to the house door.

"I came forward to follow him, and at the noise of my movement he stopped dead. I did so too, startled by his quickness of ear. He slammed the house door in my face.

"I stood hesitating. Suddenly I heard his quick footsteps returning, and the door reopened. He stood looking about the shop like one who was still not satisfied. Then, murmuring to himself, he examined the back of the counter and peered behind some fixtures. Then he stood doubtful. He had left the house door open and I slipped into the inner room.

"It was a queer little room, poorly furnished and with a number of big masks in the corner. On the table was his belated breakfast, and it was a confoundedly exasperating thing for me, Kemp, to have to sniff his coffee and stand watching while he came in and resumed his meal. And his table manners were irritating. Three doors opened into the little room, one going upstairs and one down, but they were all shut. I could not get out of the room while he was there, I could scarcely move because of his alertness, and there was a draught down my back. Twice I strangled a sneeze just in time.

"The spectacular quality of my sensations was curious and novel, but for all that I was heartily tired and angry long before he had done his eating. But at last he made an end and putting his beggarly crockery on the black tin tray upon which he had had his teapot, and gathering all the crumbs up on the mustard stained cloth, he took the whole lot of things after him. His burden prevented his shutting the door behind him,—as he would have done; I never saw such a man for shutting doors,—

and I followed him into a very dirty underground kitchen and scullery. I had the pleasure of seeing him begin to wash up, and then, finding no good in keeping down there, and the brick floor being cold to my feet, I returned upstairs and sat in his chair by the fire. It was burning low, and scarcely thinking, I put on a little coal. The noise of this brought him up at once, and he stood aglare. He peered about the room and was within an ace of touching me. Even after that examination, he scarcely seemed satisfied. He stopped in the doorway and took a final inspection before he went down.

"I waited in the little parlour for an age, and at last he came up and opened the upstairs door. I just managed to get by him.

"On the staircase he stopped suddenly, so that I very nearly blundered into him. He stood looking back right into my face and listening. 'I could have sworn,' he said. His long hairy hand pulled at his lower lip. His eye went up and down the staircase. Then he grunted and went on up again.

"His hand was on the handle of a door, and then he stopped again with the same puzzled anger on his face. He was becoming aware of the faint sounds of my movements about him. The man must have had diabolically acute hearing. He suddenly flashed into rage. 'If there's anyone in this house,' he cried with an oath, and left the threat unfinished. He put his hand in his pocket, failed to find what he wanted, and rushing past me went blundering noisily and pugnaciously downstairs. But I did not follow him. I sat on the head of the staircase until his return.

"Presently he came up again, still muttering. He opened the door of the room, and before I could enter, slammed it in my face.

"I resolved to explore the house, and spent some time in doing so as noiselessly as possible. The house was very old and tumble-down, damp so that the paper in the attics was peeling from the walls, and rat infested. Some of the door handles were stiff and I was afraid to turn them. Several rooms I did inspect were unfurnished, and others were littered with theatrical lumber, bought second-hand, I judged, from its appearance. In one room next to his I found a lot of old clothes. I began routing among these, and in my eagerness forgot again the evident sharpness of his ears. I heard a stealthy footstep and, looking up just in time, saw him peering in at the tumbled heap

diabolically acute: Inhumanly or supernaturally sharp.

pugnaciously: In a quarrelsome manner.

215

and holding an old-fashioned revolver in his hand. I stood perfectly still while he stared about open-mouthed and suspicious. 'It must have been her,' he said slowly. 'Damn her!'

"He shut the door quietly, and immediately I heard the key turn in the lock. Then his footsteps retreated. I realised abruptly that I was locked in. For a minute I did not know what to do. I walked from door to window and back, and stood perplexed. A gust of anger came upon me. But I decided to inspect the clothes before I did anything further, and my first attempt brought down a pile from an upper shelf. This brought him back, more sinister than ever. That time he actually touched me, jumped back with amazement and stood astonished in the middle of the room.

"Presently he calmed a little. 'Rats,' he said in an undertone, fingers on lip. He was evidently a little scared. I edged quietly out of the room, but a plank creaked. Then the infernal little brute started going all over the house, revolver in hand and locking door after door and pocketing the keys. When I realised what he was up to I had a fit of rage—I could hardly control myself sufficiently to watch my opportunity. By this time I knew he was alone in the house, and so I made no more ado, but knocked him on the head."

"Knocked him on the head!" exclaimed Kemp.

"Yes—stunned him—as he was going downstairs. Hit him from behind with a stool that stood on the landing. He went downstairs like a bag of old boots."

"But—! I say! The common conventions of humanity—"

"Are all very well for common people. But the point was, Kemp, that I had to get out of that house in a disguise without his seeing me. I couldn't think of any other way of doing it. And then I gagged him with a Louis Quatorze vest and tied him up in a sheet."

"Tied him up in a sheet!"

"Made a sort of bag of it. It was rather a good idea to keep the idiot scared and quiet, and a devilish hard thing to get out of—head away from the string. My dear Kemp, it's no good your sitting and glaring as though I was a murderer. It had to be done. He had his revolver. If once he saw me he would be able to describe me—"

"But still," said Kemp, "in England—to-day. And the man was in his own house, and you were—well, robbing."

216

"Robbing! Confound it! You'll call me a thief next! Surely, Kemp, you're not fool enough to dance on the old strings. Can't you see my position?"

"And his too," said Kemp.

The Invisible Man stood up sharply. "What do you mean to say?"

Kemp's face grew a trifle hard. He was about to speak and checked himself. "I suppose, after all," he said with a sudden change of manner, "the thing had to be done. You were in a fix. But still—"

"Of course I was in a fix—an infernal fix. And he made me wild too—hunting me about the house, fooling about with his revolver, locking and unlocking doors. He was simply exasperating. You don't blame me, do you? You don't blame me?"

"I never blame anyone," said Kemp. "It's quite out of fashion. What did you do next?"

"I was hungry. Downstairs I found a loaf and some rank cheese—more than sufficient to satisfy my hunger. I took some brandy and water, and then went up past my impromptu bag—he was lying quite still—to the room containing the old clothes. This looked out upon the street, two lace curtains brown with dirt guarding the window. I went and peered out through their interstices. Outside the day was bright—by contrast with the brown shadows of the dismal house in which I found myself, dazzlingly bright. A brisk traffic was going by, fruit carts, a hansom, a four-wheeler with a pile of boxes, a fishmonger's cart. I turned with spots of colour swimming before my eyes to the shadowy fixtures behind me. My excitement was giving place to a clear apprehension of my position again. The room was full of a faint scent of benzoline, used, I suppose, in cleaning the garments.

"I began a systematic search of the place. I should judge the hunchback had been alone in the house for some time. He was a curious person. Everything that could possibly be of service to me I collected in the clothes store-room, and then I made a deliberate selection. I found a handbag I thought a suitable possession, and some powder, rouge, and sticking-plaster.

"I had thought of painting and powdering my face and all that there was to show of me, in order to render myself visible, but the disadvantage of this lay in the fact that I should require turpentine and other appliances and a considerable amount of

rank: Strong smelling.

impromptu: Thrown together; improvised.

dominoes: Loose, hooded cloaks.

sound: Intact, complete.

time before I could vanish again. Finally I chose a mask of the better type, slightly grotesque but not more so than many human beings, dark glasses, greyish whiskers, and a wig. I could find no underclothing, but that I could buy subsequently, and for the time I swathed myself in calico dominoes and some white cashmere scarfs. I could find no socks, but the hunch-back's boots were rather a loose fit and sufficed. In a desk in the shop were three sovereigns and about thirty shillings' worth of silver, and in a locked cupboard I burst in the inner room were eight pounds in gold. I could go forth into the world again, equipped.

"Then came a curious hesitation. Was my appearance really—credible? I tried myself with a little bedroom looking-glass, inspecting myself from every point of view to discover any forgotten chink, but it all seemed sound. I was grotesque to the theatrical pitch, a stage miser, but I was certainly not a physical impossibility. Gathering confidence, I took my looking-glass down into the shop, pulled down the shop blinds, and surveyed myself from every point of view with the help of the cheval glass in the corner.

"I spent some minutes screwing up my courage and then unlocked the shop door and marched out into the street, leaving the little man to get out of his sheet again when he liked. In five minutes a dozen turnings intervened between me and the costumier's shop. No one appeared to notice me very pointedly. My last difficulty seemed overcome."

He stopped again.

"And you troubled no more about the hunchback?" said Kemp.

"No," said the Invisible Man. "Nor have I heard what became of him. I suppose he untied himself or kicked himself out. The knots were pretty tight."

He became silent and went to the window and stared out.

"What happened when you went out into the Strand?"

"Oh!—disillusionment again. I thought my troubles were over. Practically I thought I had impunity to do whatever I chose, everything—save to give away my secret. So I thought. Whatever I did, whatever the consequences might be, was nothing to me. I had merely to fling aside my garments and vanish. No person could hold me. I could take my money where I found it. I decided to treat myself to a sumptuous feast, and then put up at a good hotel, and accumulate a new outfit of property. I felt amazingly confident,—it's not particularly pleasant recalling that I was an ass. I went into a place and was already ordering a lunch, when it occurred to me that I could not eat unless I exposed my invisible face. I finished ordering the lunch, told the man I should be back in ten minutes, and went out exasperated. I don't know if you have ever been disappointed in your appetite."

"Not quite so badly," said Kemp, "but I can imagine it."

"I could have smashed the silly devils. At last, faint with the desire for tasteful food, I went into another place and demanded a private room. 'I am disfigured,' I said. 'Badly.' They looked at me curiously, but of course it was not their affair—and so at last I got my lunch. It was not particularly well served, but it sufficed; and when I had had it, I sat over a cigar, trying to plan my line of action. And outside a snowstorm was beginning.

"The more I thought it over, Kemp, the more I realised what a helpless absurdity an Invisible Man was,—in a cold and dirty climate and a crowded civilised city. Before I made this mad experiment I had dreamt of a thousand advantages. That afternoon it seemed all disappointment. I went over the heads of the things a man reckons desirable. No doubt invisibility made it possible to get them, but it made it impossible to enjoy them when they are got. Ambition—what is the good of pride of place when you cannot appear there? What is the good of the love of woman when her name must needs be Delilah? I have no taste for politics, for the blackguardisms of fame, for philanthropy, for sport. What was I to do? And for this I had become a wrapped-up mystery, a swathed and bandaged caricature of a man!"

He paused, and his attitude suggested a roving glance at the window.

"But how did you get to Iping?" said Kemp, anxious to keep his guest busy talking.

"I went there to work. I had one hope. It was a half idea! I have it still. It is a full blown idea now. A way of getting back! Of restoring what I have done. When I choose. When I have done all I mean to do invisibly. And that is what I chiefly want to talk to you about now."

"You went straight to Iping?"

Delilah: A treacherous, deceitful woman. In the *Bible* Delilah persuaded Samson to reveal the secret of his great strength, which lay in his long, thick hair. She cut his hair while he slept and then turned him over to his enemies.

caricature: An exaggerated imitation.

"Yes. I had simply to get my three volumes of memoranda and my cheque-book, my luggage and underclothing, order a quantity of chemicals to work out this idea of mine,—I will show you the calculations as soon as I get my books,—and then I started. Jove! I remember the snowstorm now, and the accursed bother it was to keep the snow from damping my pasteboard nose."

"At the end," said Kemp, "the day before yesterday, when they found you out, you rather—to judge by the papers—"

"I did. Rather. Did I kill that fool of a constable?"

"No," said Kemp. "He's expected to recover."

"That's his luck, then. I clean lost my temper, the fools! Why couldn't they leave me alone? And that grocer lout?"

"There are no deaths expected," said Kemp.

"I don't know about that tramp of mine," said the Invisible Man, with an unpleasant laugh.

"By Heaven, Kemp, you don't know what rage *is!* To have worked for years, to have planned and plotted, and then to get some fumbling purblind idiot messing across your course! Every conceivable sort of silly creature that has ever been created has been sent to cross me.

"If I have much more of it, I shall go wild,—I shall start mowing 'em.

"As it is, they've made things a thousand times more difficult."

"No doubt it's exasperating," said Kemp, drily.

lout: Clown, bumpkin, bungler.

purblind: Stupid, dull.

"But now," said Kemp, with a side glance out of the window, "what are we to do?"

ut now," said Kemp, with a side glance out of the window, "what are we to do?"

He moved nearer his guest as he spoke in such a manner as to prevent the possibility of a sudden glimpse of the three men who were advancing up the hill road—with an intolerable slowness, as it seemed to Kemp.

"What were you planning to do when you were heading for Port Burdock? *Had* you any plan?"

"I was going to clear out of the country. But I have altered that plan rather since seeing you. I thought it would be wise, now the weather is hot and invisibility possible, to make for the South. Especially as my secret was known, and everyone would be on the lookout for a masked and muffled man. You have a line of steamers from here to France. My idea was to get aboard one and run the risks of the passage. Thence I could go by train into Spain, or else get to Algiers. It would not be difficult.

221

There a man might always be invisible—and yet live. And do things. I was using that tramp as a money box and luggage carrier, until I decided how to get my books and things sent over to meet me."

"That's clear."

"And then the filthy brute must needs try and rob me! He has hidden my books, Kemp. Hidden my books! If I can lay my hands on him!"

"Best plan to get the books out of him first."

"But where is he? Do you know?"

"He's in the town police station, locked up, by his own request, in the strongest cell in the place."

"Cur!" said the Invisible Man.

"But that hangs up your plans a little."

"We must get those books; those books are vital."

"Certainly," said Kemp, a little nervously, wondering if he heard footsteps outside. "Certainly we must get those books. But that won't be difficult, if he doesn't know they're for you."

"No," said the Invisible Man, and thought.

Kemp tried to think of something to keep the talk going, but the Invisible Man resumed of his own accord.

"Blundering into your house, Kemp," he said, "changes all my plans. For you are a man that can understand. In spite of all that has happened, in spite of this publicity, of the loss of my books, of what I have suffered, there still remain great possibilities, huge possibilities—"

"You have told no one I am here?" he asked abruptly.

Kemp hesitated. "That was implied," he said.

"No one?" insisted Griffin.

"Not a soul."

"Ah! Now—" The Invisible Man stood up, and sticking his arms akimbo began to pace the study.

"I made a mistake, Kemp, a huge mistake, in carrying this thing through alone. I have wasted strength, time, opportunities. Alone—it is wonderful how little a man can do alone! To rob a little, to hurt a little, and there is the end.

"What I want, Kemp, is a goal-keeper, a helper, and a hiding-place, an arrangement whereby I can sleep and eat and rest in peace, and unsuspected. I must have a confederate. With a confederate, with food and rest—a thousand things are possible.

"Hitherto I have gone on vague lines. We have to consider all that invisibility means, all that it does not mean. It means little advantage for eavesdropping and so forth—one makes sounds. It's of little help, a little help perhaps—in housebreaking and so forth. Once you've caught me you could easily imprison me. But on the other hand I am hard to catch. This invisibility, in fact, is only good in two cases: It's useful in getting away, it's useful in approaching. It's particularly useful, therefore, in killing. I can walk round a man, whatever weapon he has, choose my point, strike as I like. Dodge as I like. Escape as I like."

Kemp's hand went to his moustache. Was that a movement downstairs?

"And it is killing we must do, Kemp."

"It is killing we must do," repeated Kemp. "I'm listening to your plan, Griffin, but I'm not agreeing, mind. *Why* killing?"

"Not wanton killing, but a judicious slaying. The point is, they know there is an Invisible Man—as well as we know there is an Invisible Man. And that Invisible Man, Kemp, must now establish a Reign of Terror. Yes—no doubt it's startling. But I mean it. A Reign of Terror. He must take some town like your Burdock and terrify and dominate it. He must issue his orders. He can do that in a thousand ways—scraps of paper thrust under doors would suffice. And all who disobey his orders he must kill, and kill all who would defend them."

"Humph!" said Kemp, no longer listening to Griffin but to the sound of his front door opening and closing.

"It seems to me, Griffin," he said, to cover his wandering attention, "that your confederate would be in a difficult position."

"No one would know he was a confederate," said the Invisible Man, eagerly. And then suddenly, "*Hush!* What's that downstairs?"

"Nothing," said Kemp, and suddenly began to speak loud and fast. "I don't agree to this, Griffin," he said. "Understand me, I don't agree to this. Why dream of playing a game against the race? How can you hope to gain happiness? Don't be a lone wolf. Publish your results; take the world—take the nation at least—into your confidence. Think what you might do with a million helpers—"

The Invisible Man interrupted Kemp—arms extended. "There are footsteps coming upstairs," he said in a low voice.

"Nonsense," said Kemp.

"Let me see," said the Invisible Man, and advanced, arm extended, to the door.

THE
PLAN
THAT FAILED

wanton: Reckless, unrestrained.

lone wolf: A person who shuns the company of others to pursue his interests alone.

223

intercept: Stop him before he could reach the door.

And then things happened very swiftly. Kemp hesitated for a second and then moved to intercept him. The Invisible Man started and stood still. "Traitor!" cried the Voice, and suddenly the dressing-gown opened, and sitting down the Unseen began to disrobe. Kemp made three swift steps to the door, and forthwith the Invisible Man—his legs had vanished—sprang to his feet with a shout. Kemp flung the door open.

As it opened, there came a sound of hurrying feet downstairs and voices.

With a quick movement Kemp thrust the Invisible Man back, sprang aside, and slammed the door. The key was outside and ready. In another moment Griffin would have been alone in the belvedere study, a prisoner. Save for one little thing. The key had been slipped in hastily that morning. As Kemp slammed the door it fell noisily upon the carpet.

Kemp's face became white. He tried to grip the door handle with both hands. For a moment he stood lugging. Then the door gave six inches. But he got it closed again. The second time it was jerked a foot wide, and the dressing-gown came wedging itself into the opening. His throat was gripped by invisible fingers, and he left his hold on the handle to defend himself. He was forced back, tripped and pitched heavily into the corner of the landing. The empty dressing-gown was flung on the top of him.

aghast: Amazed.

Halfway up the staircase was Colonel Adye, the recipient of Kemp's letter, the chief of the Burdock police. He was staring aghast at the sudden appearance of Kemp, followed by the extraordinary sight of clothing tossing empty in the air. He saw Kemp felled, and struggling to his feet. He saw him rush forward, and go down again, felled like an ox.

Then suddenly he was struck violently. By nothing! A vast weight, it seemed, leapt upon him, and he was hurled headlong down the staircase, with the grip at his throat and a knee in his groin. An invisible foot trod on his back, a ghostly patter passed downstairs, he heard the two police officers in the hall shout and run, and the front door of the house slammed violently.

groin: The region around the lower part of the abdomen and the thigh.

He rolled over and sat up staring. He saw, staggering down the staircase, Kemp, dusty and dishevelled, one side of his face white from a blow, his lip bleeding, and a pink dressing-gown and some underclothing held in his arms.

"My God!" cried Kemp, "the game's up! He's gone!"

"He must be caught," said Adye. "That is certain." "But how?" cried Kemp, and suddenly became full of ideas.

For a space Kemp was too inarticulate to make Adye understand the swift things that had just happened. They stood on the landing, Kemp speaking swiftly, the grotesque swathings of Griffin still on his arm. But presently Adye began to grasp something of the situation.

"He is mad," said Kemp; "inhuman. He is pure selfishness. He thinks of nothing but his own advantage, his own safety. I have listened to such a story this morning of brutal self-seeking! He has wounded men. He will kill them unless we can prevent him. He will create a panic. Nothing can stop him. He is going out now—furious!"

25
THE HUNTING OF THE INVISIBLE MAN

"He must be caught," said Adye. "That is certain."

"But how?" cried Kemp, and suddenly became full of ideas. "You must begin at once. You must set every available man to work. You must prevent his leaving this district. Once he gets away, he may go through the countryside as he wills, killing and maiming. He dreams of a reign of terror! A reign of terror, I tell you. You must set a watch on trains and roads and shipping. The garrison must help. You must wire for help. The only thing that may keep him here is the thought of recovering some books of notes he counts of value. I will tell you of that! There is a man in your police station,—Marvel."

"I know," said Adye, "I know. Those books—yes."

"And you must prevent him from eating or sleeping; day and night the country must be astir for him. Food must be locked up and secured, all food, so that he will have to break his way to it. The houses everywhere must be barred against him. Heaven send us cold nights and rain! The whole countryside must begin hunting and keep hunting. I tell you, Adye, he is a danger, a disaster; unless he is pinned and secured, it is frightful to think of the things that may happen."

"What else can we do?" said Adye. "I must go down at once and begin organising. But why not come? Yes—you come too! Come, and we must hold a sort of council of war,—get Hopps to help—and the railway managers. By Jove! it's urgent. Come along—tell me as we go. What else is there we can do? Put that stuff down."

In another moment Adye was leading the way downstairs. They found the front door open and the policemen standing outside staring at empty air. "He's got away, sir," said one.

"We must go to the central station at once," said Adye. "One of you go on down and get a cab to come up and meet us—quickly. And now, Kemp, what else?"

"Dogs," said Kemp. "Get dogs. They don't see him, but they wind him. Get dogs."

"Good," said Adye. "It's not generally known, but the prison officials over at Halstead know a man with bloodhounds. Dogs. What else?"

"Bear in mind," said Kemp, "his food shows. After eating, his food shows until it is assimilated. So that he has to hide after eating. You must keep on beating,—every thicket, every quiet corner. And put all weapons, all implements that might be weapons, away. He can't carry such things for long. And what he can snatch up and strike men with must be hidden away."

"Good again," said Adye. "We shall have him yet!"

"And on the roads," said Kemp, and hesitated.

"Yes?" said Adye.

"Powdered glass," said Kemp. "It's cruel, I know. But think of what he may do!"

Adye drew the air in sharply between his teeth. "It's unsportsmanlike. I don't know. But I'll have powdered glass got ready. If he goes too far—"

"The man's become inhuman, I tell you," said Kemp. "I am as sure he will establish a reign of terror—so soon as he has got over the emotions of this escape—as I am sure I am talking to you. Our only chance is to be ahead. He has cut himself off from his kind. His blood be upon his own head."

He stopped this quiet man, attacked him, beat down his feeble defences, broke his arm, felled him, and smashed his head to a jelly.

26
THE WICKSTEED MURDER

human perceptions: Here, man's senses of sight and sound.

The Invisible Man seems to have rushed out of Kemp's house in a state of blind fury. A little child playing near Kemp's gateway was violently caught up and thrown aside, so that its ankle was broken, and thereafter for some hours the Invisible Man passed out of human perceptions. No one knows where he went nor what he did. But one can imagine him hurrying through the hot June forenoon, up the hill and on to the open downland behind Port Burdock, raging and despairing at his intolerable fate, and sheltering at last, heated and weary, amid

228

the thickets of Hintondean, to piece together again his shattered schemes against his species. That seems the most probable refuge for him, for there it was he re-asserted himself in a grimly tragical manner about two in the afternoon.

One wonders what his state of mind may have been during that time, and what plans he devised. No doubt he was almost ecstatically exasperated by Kemp's treachery, and though we may be able to understand the motives that led to that deceit, we may still imagine and even sympathise a little with the fury the attempted surprise must have occasioned. Perhaps something of the stunned astonishment of his Oxford Street experiences may have returned to him, for he had evidently counted on Kemp's co-operation in his brutal dream of a terrorised world. At any rate he vanished from human ken about midday, and no living witness can tell what he did until about half-past two. It was a fortunate thing, perhaps, for humanity, but for him it was a fatal inaction.

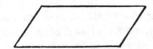

ken: Knowledge and awareness.

During that time a growing multitude of men scattered over the countryside were busy. In the morning he had still been simply a legend, a terror; in the afternoon, by virtue chiefly of Kemp's drily worded proclamation, he was presented as a tangible antagonist, to be wounded, captured, or overcome, and the countryside began organising itself with inconceivable rapidity. By two o'clock even he might still have removed himself out of the district by getting aboard a train, but after two that became impossible. Every passenger train along the lines on a great parallelogram between Southhampton, Manchester, Brighton, and Horsham, travelled with locked doors, and the goods traffic was almost entirely suspended. And in a great circle of twenty miles round Port Burdock, men armed with guns and bludgeons were presently setting out in groups of three and four, with dogs, to beat the roads and fields.

parallelogram: A four-sided rectangular figure whose opposite sides are parallel.

bludgeons: Short sticks or clubs with one end thicker than the other.

Mounted policemen rode along the country lanes, stopping at every cottage and warning the people to lock up their houses, and keep indoors unless they were armed, and all the elementary schools had broken up by three o'clock, and the children, scared and keeping together in groups, were hurrying home. Kemp's proclamation—signed indeed by Adye—was posted over almost the whole district by four or five o'clock in the afternoon. It gave briefly but clearly all the conditions of the struggle, the necessity of keeping the Invisible Man from food and sleep, the necessity for incessant watchfulness and for a prompt attention to any evidence of his movements. And so swift and decided was the action of the authorities, so prompt and universal was the belief in this strange being, that before nightfall an area of several hundred square miles was in a stringent state of siege. And before nightfall, too, a thrill of horror went through the whole watching nervous countryside. Going from whispering mouth to mouth, swift and certain over the length and breadth of the county, passed the story of the murder of Mr. Wicksteed.

If our supposition that the Invisible Man's refuge was the Hintondean thickets, then we must suppose that in the early afternoon he sallied out again bent upon some project that involved the use of a weapon. We cannot know what the project was, but the evidence that he had the iron rod in hand before he met Wicksteed is to me at least overwhelming.

Of course we can know nothing of the details of the encounter. It occurred on the edge of a gravel pit, not two hundred yards from Lord Burdock's Lodge gate. Everything points to a desperate struggle,—the trampled ground, the numerous wounds Mr. Wicksteed received, his splintered walking-stick; but why the attack was made—save in a murderous frenzy—it is impossible to imagine. Indeed the theory of madness is almost unavoidable. Mr. Wicksteed was a man of forty-five or forty-six, steward to Lord Burdock, of inoffensive habits and appearance, the very last person in the world to provoke such a terrible antagonist. Against him it would seem the Invisible Man used an iron rod dragged from a broken piece of fence. He stopped this quiet man, going quietly home to his midday meal, attacked him, beat down his feeble defences, broke his arm, felled him, and smashed his head to a jelly.

Of course he must have dragged this rod out of the fencing before he met his victim; he must have been carrying it ready in his hand. Only two details beyond what has already been stated seem to bear on the matter. One is the circumstance that the gravel pit was not in Mr. Wicksteed's direct path home, but nearly a couple of hundred yards out of his way. The other is the assertion of a little girl to the effect that, going to her afternoon school, she saw the murdered man *"trotting"* in a peculiar manner across a field towards the gravel pit. Her pantomime of his action suggests a man pursuing something on the ground before him and striking at it ever and again with his walking-stick. She was the last person to see him alive. He passed out of her sight to his death, the struggle being hidden from her only by a clump of beech trees and a slight depression in the ground.

Now this, to the present writer's mind at least, lifts the murder out of the realm of the absolutely wanton. We may imagine that Griffin had taken the rod as a weapon indeed, but without any deliberate intention of using it in murder. Wicksteed may then have come by and noticed this rod inexplicably moving through the air. Without any thought of the Invisible Man—for Port Burdock is ten miles away—he may have pursued it. It is quite conceivable that he may not even have heard of the Invisible Man. One can then imagine the Invisible Man making off—quietly in order to avoid discovering his presence in the neighbourhood, and Wicksteed, excited and curious, pursuing this unaccountably locomotive object,—finally striking at it.

No doubt the Invisible Man could easily have distanced his middle-aged pursuer under ordinary circumstances, but the position in which Wicksteed's body was found suggests that he had the ill luck to drive his quarry into a corner between a drift of stinging nettles and the gravel pit. To those who appreciate the extraordinary irascibility of the Invisible Man, the rest of the encounter will be easy to imagine.

But this is pure hypothesis. The only undeniable facts—for stories of children are often unreliable—are the discovery of Wicksteed's body, done to death, and of the blood-stained iron rod flung among the nettles. The abandonment of the rod by Griffin, suggests that in the emotional excitement of the affair, the purpose for which he took it—if he had a purpose—was abandoned. He was certainly an intensely egotistical and unfeeling man, but the sight of his victim, his first victim, bloody and pitiful at his feet, may have released some long pent fountain of remorse which for a time may have flooded whatever scheme of action he had contrived.

After the murder of Mr. Wicksteed, he would seem to have struck across the country towards the downland. There is a story of a voice heard about sunset by a couple of men in a field near Fern Bottom. It was wailing and laughing, sobbing and groaning, and ever and again it shouted. It must have been queer hearing. It drove up across the middle of a clover field and died away towards the hills.

THE WICKSTEED MURDER

locomotive: Full of motion.

quarry: Prey.
nettles: Prickly plants which grow profusely on wastelands.
irascibility: Irritability.

hypothesis: Assumption or guess.

That afternoon the Invisible Man must have learnt something of the rapid use Kemp had made of his confidences. He must have found houses locked and secured; he may have loitered about railway stations and prowled about inns, and no doubt he read the proclamations and realised something of the nature of the campaign against him. And as the evening advanced, the fields became dotted here and there with groups of three or four men, and noisy with the yelping of dogs. These men-hunters had particular instructions in the case of an encounter as to the way they should support one another. He avoided them all. We may understand something of his exasperation, and it could have been none the less because he himself had supplied the information that was being used so remorselessly against him. For that day at least he lost heart; for nearly twenty-four hours, save when he turned on Wicksteed, he was a hunted man. In the night, he must have eaten and slept; for in the morning he was himself again, active, powerful, angry, and

malignant, prepared for his last great struggle against the world.

The voice laughed "I'd kill you now if it wasn't the waste of a bullet," it said.

Kemp read a strange missive, written in pencil on a greasy sheet of paper.

"You have been amazingly energetic and clever," this letter ran, "though what you stand to gain by it I cannot imagine. You are against me. For a whole day you have chased me; you have tried to rob me of a night's rest. But I have had food in spite of you, I have slept in spite of you, and the game is only beginning. The game is only beginning. There is nothing for it, but to start the Terror. This announces the first day of the Terror. Port Burdock is no longer under the Queen, tell your Colonel of Police, and the rest of them; it is under me—the Terror! This is day one of year one of the new epoch,—the Epoch of the Invisible Man. I am Invisible Man the First. To begin with the rule will be easy. The first day there will be one

27
THE SIEGE OF KEMP'S HOUSE

the Queen: Queen Victoria, the longest reigning monarch in English history—63 years, 7 months, and 2 days—from 1838 to 1901.

233

execution for the sake of example,—a man named Kemp. Death starts for him to-day. He may lock himself away, hide himself away, get guards about him, put on armour if he likes; Death, the unseen Death, is coming. Let him take precautions; it will impress my people. Death starts from the pillar box by midday. The letter will fall in as the postman comes along, then off! The game begins. Death starts. Help him not, my people, lest Death fall upon you also. To-day Kemp is to die."

When Kemp read this letter twice, "It's no hoax," he said. "That's his voice! And he means it."

He turned the folded sheet over and saw on the addressed side of it the postmark Hintondean, and the prosaic detail "*2d. to pay.*"

He got up slowly, leaving his lunch unfinished,—the letter had come by the one o'clock post,—and went into his study. He rang for his housekeeper, and told her to go round the house at once, examine all the fastenings of the windows, and close all the shutters. He closed the shutters of his study himself. From a locked drawer in his bedroom he took a little revolver, examined it carefully, and put it into the pocket of his lounge jacket. He wrote a number of brief notes, one to Colonel Adye, gave them to his servant to take, with explicit instructions as to her way of leaving the house. "There is no danger," he said, and added a mental reservation, "to you." He remained meditative for a space after doing this, and then returned to his cooling lunch.

He ate with gaps of thought. Finally he struck the table sharply. "We will have him!" he said; "and I am the bait. He will come too far."

He went up to the belvedere, carefully shutting every door after him. "It's a game," he said, "an odd game—but the chances are all for me, Mr. Griffin, in spite of your invisibility. Griffin *contra mundum*—with a vengeance."

He stood at the window staring at the hot hillside. "He must get food every day—and I don't envy him. Did he really sleep last night? Out in the open somewhere—secure from collisions. I wish we could get some good cold wet weather instead of the heat.

"He may be watching me now."

He went close to the window. Something rapped smartly against the brickwork over the frame, and made him start violently back.

"I'm getting nervous," said Kemp. But it was five minutes before he went to the window again. "It must have been a sparrow," he said.

Presently he heard the front-door bell ringing, and hurried downstairs. He unbolted and unlocked the door, examined the chain, put it up, and opened cautiously without showing himself. A familiar voice hailed him. It was Adye.

"Your servant's been assaulted, Kemp," he said round the door.

"What!" exclaimed Kemp.

"Had that note of yours taken away from her. He's close about here. Let me in."

Kemp released the chain, and Adye entered through as narrow an opening as possible. He stood in the hall, looking with infinite relief at Kemp refastening the door. "Note was snatched out of her hand. Scared her horribly. She's down at the station. Hysterics. He's close here. What was it about?"

Kemp swore.

"What a fool I was," said Kemp. "I might have known. It's not an hour's walk from Hintondean. Already!"

"What's up?" said Adye.

"Look here!" said Kemp, and led the way into his study. He handed Adye the Invisible Man's letter. Adye read it and whistled softly. "And you—?" said Adye.

"Proposed a trap—like a fool," said Kemp, "and sent my proposal out by a maid servant. To him."

Adye followed Kemp's profanity.

"He'll clear out," said Adye.

"Not he," said Kemp.

A resounding smash of glass came from upstairs. Adye had a silvery glimpse of a little revolver half out of Kemp's pocket. "It's a window, upstairs!" said Kemp, and led the way up. There came a second smash while they were still on the staircase. When they reached the study they found two of the three windows smashed, half the room littered with splintered glass, and one big flint lying on the writing table. The two men stopped in the doorway, contemplating the wreckage. Kemp swore again, and as he did so the third window went with a snap like a pistol, hung starred for a moment, and collapsed in jagged, shivering triangles into the room.

"What's this for?" said Adye.

"It's a beginning," said Kemp.

Hysterics: A nervous disturbance characterized by such symptoms as fainting, convulsions, or paralysis.

resounding: Ringing, echoing.

235

bloodhounds: Large dogs with long, smooth, drooping ears and a highly developed sense of smell.

"There's no way of climbing up here?"

"Not for a cat," said Kemp.

"No shutters?"

"Not here. All the downstairs rooms—Hullo!"

Smash, and then whack of boards hit hard came from downstairs. "Confound him!" said Kemp. "That must be—yes—it's one of the bedrooms. He's going to do all the house. But he's a fool. The shutters are up, and the glass will fall outside. He'll cut his feet."

Another window proclaimed its destruction. The two men stood on the landing perplexed. "I have it!" said Adye. "Let me have a stick or something, and I'll go down to the station and get the bloodhounds put on. That ought to settle him! They're hard by—not ten minutes—"

Another window went the way of its fellows.

"You haven't a revolver?" asked Adye.

Kemp's hand went to his pocket. Then he hesitated. "I haven't one—at least to spare."

"I'll bring it back," said Adye, "you'll be safe here."

Kemp, ashamed of his momentary lapse from truthfulness, handed him the weapon.

"Now for the door," said Adye.

As they stood hesitating in the hall, they heard one of the first-floor bedroom windows crack and clash. Kemp went to the door and began to slip the bolts as silently as possible. His face was a little paler than usual. "You must step straight out," said Kemp. In another moment Adye was on the doorstep and the bolts were dropping back into the staples. He hesitated for a moment, feeling more comfortable with his back against the door. Then he marched, upright and square, down the steps. He crossed the lawn and approached the gate. A little breeze seemed to ripple over the grass. Something moved near him. "Stop a bit," said a Voice, and Adye stopped dead and his hand tightened on the revolver.

"Well?" said Adye, white and grim, and every nerve tense.

"Oblige me by going back to the house," said the Voice, as tense and grim as Adye's.

"Sorry," said Adye a little hoarsely, and moistened his lips with his tongue. The Voice was on his left front, he thought. Suppose he were to take his luck with a shot?

"What are you going for?" said the Voice, and there was a quick movement of the two, and a flash of sunlight from the open lip of Adye's pocket.

236

Adye desisted and thought. "Where I go," he said slowly, "is my own business." The words were still on his lips, when an arm came round his neck, his back felt a knee, and he was sprawling backward. He drew clumsily and fired absurdly, and in another moment he was struck in the mouth and the revolver wrested from his grip. He made a vain clutch at a slippery limb, tried to struggle up and fell back. "Damn!" said Adye. The Voice laughed. "I'd kill you now if it wasn't the waste of a bullet," it said. He saw the revolver in mid-air, six feet off, covering him.

"Well?" said Adye, sitting up.

"Get up," said the Voice.

Adye stood up.

"Attention," said the Voice, and then fiercely, "Don't try any games. Remember I can see your face if you can't see mine. You've got to go back to the house."

"He won't let me in," said Adye.

"That's a pity," said the Invisible Man. "I've got no quarrel with you."

Adye moistened his lips again. He glanced away from the barrel of the revolver and saw the sea far off very blue and dark under the midday sun, the smooth green down, the white cliff of the Head, and the multitudinous town, and suddenly he knew that life was very sweet. His eyes came back to this little metal thing hanging between heaven and earth, six yards away. "What am I to do?" he said sullenly.

"What am *I* to do?" asked the Invisible Man. "You will get help. The only thing is for you to go back."

"I will try. If he lets me in will you promise not to rush the door?"

"I've got no quarrel with you," said the Voice.

Kemp had hurried upstairs after letting Adye out, and now crouching among the broken glass and peering cautiously over the edge of the study window sill, he saw Adye stand parleying with the Unseen. "Why doesn't he fire?" whispered Kemp to himself. Then the revolver moved a little and the glint of the sunlight flashed in Kemp's eyes. He shaded his eyes and tried to see the source of the blinding beam.

"Surely!" he said, "Adye has given up the revolver."

"Promise not to rush the door," Adye was saying. "Don't push a winning game too far. Give a man a chance."

"You go back to the house. I tell you flatly I will not promise anything."

wrested: Violently pulled.

multitudinous: Crowded.

parleying: Speaking; discussing terms.

Adye's decision seemed suddenly made. He turned towards the house, walking slowly with his hands behind him. Kemp watched him—puzzled. The revolver vanished, flashed again into sight, vanished again, and became evident on a closer scrutiny as a little dark object following Adye. Then things happened very quickly. Adye leapt backwards, swung round, clutched at this little object, missed it, threw up his hands and fell forward on his face, leaving a little puff of blue in the air. Kemp did not hear the sound of the shot. Adye writhed, raised himself on one arm, fell forward, and lay still.

For a space Kemp remaining staring at the quiet carelessness of Adye's attitude. The afternoon was very hot and still, nothing seemed stirring in all the world save a couple of yellow butterflies chasing each other through the shrubbery between the house and the road gate. Adye lay on the lawn near the gate. The blinds of all the villas down the hill-road were drawn, but in one little green summer-house was a white figure, apparently an old man asleep. Kemp scrutinized the surroundings of the house for a glimpse of the revolver, but it had vanished. His eyes came back to Adye. The game was opening well.

Then came a ringing and knocking at the front door, that grew at last tumultuous, but pursuant to Kemp's instructions the servants had locked themselves into their rooms. This was followed by a silence. Kemp sat listening and then began peering cautiously out of the three windows, one after another. He went to the staircase head and stood listening uneasily. He armed himself with his bedroom poker, and went to examine the interior fastenings of the ground-floor windows again. Everything was safe and quiet. He returned to the belvedere. Adye lay motionless over the edge of the gravel just as he had fallen. Coming along the road by the villas were the housemaid and two policemen.

Everything was deadly still. The three people seemed very slow in approaching. He wondered what his antagonist was doing.

He started. There was a smash from below. He hesitated and went downstairs again. Suddenly the house resounded with heavy blows and the splintering of wood. He heard a smash and the destructive clang of the iron fastenings of the shutters. He turned the key and opened the kitchen door. As he did so, the shutters, split and splintering, came flying inward. He stood

238

aghast. The window frame, save for one cross bar, was still intact, but only little teeth of glass remained in the frame. The shutters had been driven in with an axe, and now the axe was descending in sweeping blows upon the window frame and the iron bars defending it. Then suddenly it leapt aside and vanished. He saw the revolver lying on the path outside, and then the little weapon sprang into the air. He dodged back. The revolver cracked just too late, and a splinter from the edge of the closing door flashed over his head. He slammed and locked the door, and as he stood outside he heard Griffin shouting and laughing. Then the blows of the axe with its splitting and smashing consequences, were resumed.

Kemp stood in the passage trying to think. In a moment the Invisible Man would be in the kitchen. This door would not keep him a moment, and then—

A ringing came at the front door again. It would be the policemen. He ran into the hall, put up the chain, and drew the bolts. He made the girl speak before he dropped the chain, and the three people blundered into the house in a heap, and Kemp slammed the door again.

"The Invisible Man!" said Kemp. "He has a revolver, with two shots—left. He's killed Adye. Shot him anyhow. Didn't you see him on the lawn? He's lying there."

"Who?" said one of the policemen.

"Adye," said Kemp.

"We came in the back way," said the girl.

"What's that smashing?" asked one of the policemen.

"He's in the kitchen—or will be. He has found an axe—"

Suddenly the house was full of the Invisible Man's resounding blows on the kitchen door. The girl stared towards the kitchen, shuddered, and retreated into the dining-room. Kemp tried to explain in broken sentences. They heard the kitchen door give.

"This way," cried Kemp, starting into activity, and bundled the policemen into the dining-room doorway.

"Poker," said Kemp, and rushed to the fender. He handed the poker he had carried to the policeman and the dining-room one to the other. He suddenly flung himself backward.

"Whup!" said one policeman, ducked, and caught the axe on his poker. The pistol snapped its penultimate shot and ripped a valuable Sidney Cooper. The second policeman brought his poker down on the little weapon, as one might knock down a wasp, and sent it rattling to the floor.

THE
SIEGE OF
KEMP'S HOUSE

penultimate: Next to last.
Sidney Cooper: A painting by Thomas Sidney Cooper, English landscape and cattle painter.

At the first clash the girl screamed, stood screaming for a moment by the fireplace, and then ran to open the shutters— possibly with an idea of escaping by the shattered window.

The axe receded into the passage, and fell to a position about two feet from the ground. They could hear the Invisible Man breathing. "Stand away, you two," he said. "I want that man Kemp."

"We want you," said the first policeman, making a quick step forward and wiping with his poker at the Voice. The Invisible Man must have started back, and he blundered into the umbrella stand. Then, as the policeman staggered with the swing of the blow he had aimed, the Invisible Man countered with the axe, the helmet crumpled like paper, and the blow sent the man spinning to the floor at the head of the kitchen stairs. But the second policeman, aiming behind the axe with his poker, hit something soft that snapped. There was a sharp exclamation of pain and then the axe fell to the ground. The policeman wiped again at vacancy and hit nothing; he put his foot on the axe, and struck again. Then he stood, poker clubbed, listening intent for the slightest movement.

He heard the dining-room window open, and a quick rush of feet within. His companion rolled over and sat up, with the blood running down between his eye and ear. "Where is he?" asked the man on the floor.

"Don't know. I've hit him. He's standing somewhere in the hall. Unless he's slipped past you. Doctor Kemp—sir."

Pause.

"Doctor Kemp," cried the policeman again.

The second policeman began struggling to his feet. He stood up. Suddenly the faint pad of bare feet on the kitchen stairs could be heard. "Yap!" cried the first policeman, and incontinently flung his poker. It smashed a little gas bracket.

He made as if he would pursue the Invisible Man downstairs. Then he thought better of it and stepped into the dining-room.

"Doctor Kemp," he began, and stopped short—

"Doctor Kemp's in here," he said, as his companion looked over his shoulder.

The dining-room window was wide open, and neither house-maid nor Kemp was to be seen.

The second policeman's opinion of Kemp was terse and vivid.

240

"The invisible man" he cried, with a vague indicative gesture, and by an inspiration lept the excavation.

Mr. Heelas, Mr. Kemp's nearest neighbour among the villa holders, was asleep in his summer house when the siege of Kemp's house began. Mr. Heelas was one of the sturdy minority who refused to believe "in all this nonsense" about an Invisible Man. His wife, however, as he was subsequently to be reminded, did. He insisted upon walking about his garden just as if nothing was the matter, and he went to sleep in the afternoon in accordance with the custom of years. He slept through the smashing of the windows, and then woke up suddenly with a curious persuasion of something wrong. He looked across at

28
THE HUNTER HUNTED

Kemp's house, rubbed his eyes and looked again. Then he put his feet to the ground, and sat listening. He said he was damned, and still the strange thing was visible. The house looked as though it had been deserted for weeks—after a violent riot. Every window was broken, and every window, save those of the belvedere study, was blinded by the internal shutters.

"I could have sworn it was all right"—he looked at his watch—"twenty minutes ago."

He became aware of a measured concussion and the clash of glass, far away in the distance. And then, as he sat open-mouthed, came a still more wonderful thing. The shutters of the drawing-room window were flung open violently, and the housemaid in her outdoor hat and garments, appeared struggling in a frantic manner to throw up the sash. Suddenly a man appeared beside her, helping her,—Dr. Kemp! In another moment the window was open, and the housemaid was struggling out; she pitched forward and vanished among the shrubs. Mr. Heelas stood up, exclaiming vaguely and vehemently at all these wonderful things. He saw Kemp stand on the sill, spring from the window, and reappear almost instantaneously running along a path in the shrubbery and stooping as he ran, like a man who evades observation. He vanished behind a laburnum, and appeared again clambering a fence that abutted on the open down. In a second he had tumbled over and was running at a tremendous pace down the slope towards Mr. Heelas.

"Lord!" cried Mr. Heelas, struck with an idea; "it's that Invisible Man brute! It's right, after all!"

With Mr. Heelas to think things like that was to act, and his cook watching him from the top window was amazed to see him come pelting towards the house at a good nine miles an hour. "Thought he wasn't afraid," said the cook. "Mary, just come here!" There was a slamming of doors, a ringing of bells, and the voice of Mr. Heelas bellowing like a bull. "Shut the doors, shut the windows, shut everything! the Invisible Man is coming!" Instantly the house was full of screams and directions, and scurrying feet. He ran himself to shut the French windows that opened on the veranda; as he did so Kemp's head and shoulders and knee appeared over the edge of the garden fence. In another moment Kemp had ploughed through the asparagus, and was running across the tennis lawn to the house.

"You can't come in," said Mr. Heelas, shutting the bolts. "I'm very sorry if he's after you, but you can't come in!"

pitched: Fell heavily or with force.

vehemently: Heatedly, strongly, or violently.

laburnum: A small tree which produces pods and bears many bright yellow flowers.

pelting: Full speed, racing.

veranda: An open portico or roofed gallery extending along a building as a protection or shelter from the sun or rain.

242

Kemp appeared with a face of terror close to the glass, rapping and then shaking frantically at the French window. Then, seeing his efforts were useless, he ran along the veranda, vaulted the end, and went to hammer at the side door. Then he ran round by the side gate to the front of the house, and so into the hill-road. And Mr. Heelas staring from his window—a face of horror—had scarcely witnessed Kemp vanish, ere the asparagus was being trampled this way and that by feet unseen. At that Mr. Heelas fled precipitately upstairs, and the rest of the chase is beyond his purview. But as he passed the staircase window, he heard the side gate slam.

Emerging into the hill-road, Kemp naturally took the downward direction, and so it was he came to run in his own person the very race he had watched with such a critical eye from the belvedere study only four days ago. He ran it well, for a man out of training, and though his face was white and wet, his wits were cool to the last. He ran with wide strides, and wherever a patch of rough ground intervened, wherever there came a patch of raw flints, or a bit of broken glass shone dazzling, he crossed it and left the bare invisible feet that followed to take what line they would.

For the first time in his life Kemp discovered that the hill-road was indescribably vast and desolate, and that the beginnings of the town far below at the hill-foot were strangely remote. Never had there been a slower or more painful method of progression than running. All the gaunt villas, sleeping in the afternoon sun, looked locked and barred; no doubt they were locked and barred—by his own orders. But at any rate they might have kept a lookout for an eventuality like this! The town was rising up now, the sea had dropped out of sight behind it, and people down below were stirring. A tram was just arriving at the hill foot. Beyond that was the police station. Was that footsteps he heard behind him? Spurt.

The people below were staring at him, one or two were running, and his breath was beginning to saw in his throat. The tram was quite near now, and the Jolly Cricketers was noisily barring its doors. Beyond the tram were posts and heaps of gravel,—the drainage works. He had a transitory idea of jumping into the tram and slamming the doors, and then he resolved to go for the police station. In another moment he had passed the door of the Jolly Cricketers, and was in the blistering fag end of street, with human beings about him. The tram driver and his

ere: Before.

precipitately: Suddenly, unexpectedly.

gaunt: Grim, abandoned, empty.

Tram

saw: Cut, pain.

transitory: Fleeting, brief.

243

navvies: Construction workers.

greengrocer: Fruit and vegetable seller.

apparition: Unexpected approach.

grasped: Understood.

helper—arrested by the sight of his furious haste—stood staring with the tram horses unhitched. Further on the astonished features of navvies appeared above the mounds of gravel.

His pace broke a little, and then he heard the swift pad of his pursuer, and leapt forward again. "The Invisible Man!" he cried to the navvies, with a vague indicative gesture, and by an inspiration leapt the excavation and placed a burly group between him and the chase. Then abandoning the idea of the police station he turned into a little side street, rushed by a greengrocer's cart, hesitated for the tenth of a second at the door of a sweetstuff shop, and then made for the mouth of an alley that ran back into the main Hill Street again. Two or three little children were playing here, and shrieked and scattered running at his apparition, and forthwith doors and windows opened and excited mothers revealed their hearts. Out he shot into Hill Street again, three hundred yards from the tram-line end, and immediately he became aware of a tumultuous vociferation and running people.

He glanced up the street towards the hill. Hardly a dozen yards off ran a huge navvy, cursing in fragments and slashing viciously with a spade, and hard behind him came the tram conductor with his fists clenched. Up the street others followed these two, striking and shouting. Down towards the town, men and women were running, and he noticed clearly one man coming out of a shop-door with a stick in his hand. "Spread out! Spread out!" cried some one. Kemp suddenly grasped the altered condition of the chase. He stopped, and looked round, panting. "He's close here!" he cried. "Form a line across—"

"Aha!" shouted a voice.

He was hit hard under the ear, and went reeling, trying to face round towards his unseen antagonist. He just managed to keep his feet, and he struck a vain counter in the air. Then he was hit again under the jaw, and sprawled headlong on the ground. In another moment a knee compressed his diaphragm, and a couple of eager hands gripped his throat, but the grip of one was weaker than the other; he grasped the wrists, heard a cry of pain from his assailant, and then the spade of the navvy came whirling through the air above him, and struck something with a dull thud. He felt a drop of moisture on his face. The grip at his throat suddenly relaxed, and with a convulsive effort, Kemp loosed himself, grasped a limp shoulder, and rolled uppermost. He gripped the unseen elbows near the ground.

244

"I've got him!" screamed Kemp. "Help! Help hold! He's down! Hold his feet!"

In another second there was a simultaneous rush upon the struggle, and a stranger coming into the road suddenly might have thought an exceptionally savage game of Rugby football was in progress. And there was no shouting after Kemp's cry,—only a sound of blows and feet and a heavy breathing.

Then came a mighty effort, and the Invisible Man threw off a couple of his antagonists and rose to his knees. Kemp clung to him in front like a hound to a stag, and a dozen hands gripped, clutched, and tore at the Unseen. The tram conductor suddenly got the neck and shoulders and lugged him back.

Down went the heap of struggling men again and rolled over. There was, I am afraid, some savage kicking. Then suddenly a wild scream of "Mercy! Mercy!" that died down swiftly to a sound like choking.

"Get back, you fools!" cried the muffled voice of Kemp, and there was a vigorous shoving back of stalwart forms. "He's hurt, I tell you. Stand back!"

There was a brief struggle to clear a space, and then the circle of eager faces saw the doctor kneeling, as it seemed, fifteen inches in the air, and holding invisible arms to the ground. Behind him a constable gripped invisible ankles.

"Don't you leave go of en," cried the big navvy, holding a bloodstained spade; "he's shamming."

"He's not shamming," said the doctor, cautiously raising his knee; "and I'll hold him." His face was bruised and already going red; he spoke thickly because of a bleeding lip. He released one hand and seemed to be feeling at the face. "The mouth's all wet," he said. And then, "Good God!"

He stood up abruptly and then knelt down on the ground by the side of the thing unseen. There was a pushing and shuffling, a sound of heavy feet as fresh people turned up to increase the pressure of the crowd. People now were coming out of the houses. The doors of the Jolly Cricketers were suddenly wide open. Very little was said.

Kemp felt about, his hand seeming to pass through empty air. "He's not breathing," he said, and then, "I can't feel his heart. His side—ugh!"

Suddenly an old woman, peering under the arm of the big navvy, screamed sharply. "Looky there!" she said, and thrust out a wrinkled finger.

THE HUNTER HUNTED

Rugby football: Forerunner of American football in which the ball may be kicked, carried, or thrown, provided it is not thrown forward, and a player in possession of the ball may be tackled bodily.

stalwart: Strong, sturdy, brave.

shamming: Pretending.

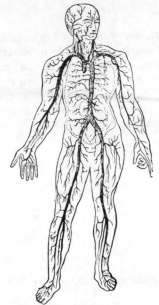

Figure showing veins and arteries

garnets: Precious stones of deep red.

sent packing: Speedily dismissed.

And looking where she pointed, everyone saw, faint and transparent as though it was made of glass, so that veins and arteries and bones and nerves could be distinguished, the outline of a hand, a hand limp and prone. It grew clouded and opaque even as they stared.

"Hullo!" cried the constable. "Here's his feet a-showing!"

And so, slowly, beginning at his hands and feet and creeping along his limbs to the vital centres of his body, that strange change continued. It was like the slow spreading of a poison. First came the little white nerves, a hazy grey sketch of a limb, then the glassy bones and intricate arteries, then the flesh and skin, first a faint fogginess, and then growing rapidly dense and opaque. Presently they could see his crushed chest and his shoulders, and the dim outline of his drawn and battered features.

When at last the crowd made way for Kemp to stand erect, there lay, naked and pitiful on the ground, the bruised and broken body of a young man about thirty. His hair and beard were white,—not grey with age, but white with the whiteness of albinisms, and his eyes were like garnets. His hands were clenched, his eyes wide open, and his expression was one of anger and dismay.

"Cover his face!" said a man. "For Gawd's sake, cover that face!" and three little children, pushing forward through the crowd, were suddenly twisted round and sent packing off again.

Someone brought a sheet from the Jolly Cricketers, and having covered him, they carried him into that house.

...there lay, naked and pitiful on the ground, the bruised and broken body of a young man about thirty.

So ends the story of the strange and evil experiment of the Invisible Man. And if you would learn more of him you must go to a little inn near Port Stowe and talk to the landlord. The sign of the inn is an empty board save for a hat and boots, and the name is the title of this story. The landlord is a short and corpulent little man with a nose of cylindrical protrusion, wiry hair, and a sporadic rosiness of visage. Drink generously, and he will tell you generously of all the things that happened to him after that time, and of how the lawyers tried to do him out of the treasure found upon him.

"When they found they couldn't prove who's money was which, I'm blessed," he says, "if they didn't try to make me out a blooming treasure trove! Do I *look* like a Treasure Trove? And then a gentleman gave me a guinea a night to tell the story at the Empire Music 'all—just tell 'em in my own words—barring one."

And if you want to cut off the flow of his reminiscences abruptly, you can always do so by asking if there weren't three manuscript books in the story. He admits there were and proceeds to explain, with asseverations that everybody thinks *he* has 'em! But bless you! he hasn't. "The Invisible Man it was took 'em off to hide 'em when I cut and ran for Port Stowe. It's that Mr. Kemp put people on with the idea of *my* having 'em."

29

THE EPILOGUE

guinea: An English gold coin worth 21 shillings. The gold supposedly came from Guinea. The guinea has not been coined since 1813.

asseverations: Emphatic declarations or assertions; oaths.

247

pensive: Thoughtful.

And then he subsides into a pensive state, watches you furtively, bustles nervously with glasses, and presently leaves the bar.

He is a bachelor man—his tastes were ever bachelor, and there are no women folk in the house. Outwardly he buttons—it is expected of him—but in his more vital privacies, in the matter of braces for example, he still turns to string. He conducts his house without enterprise, but with eminent decorum. His movements are slow, and he is a great thinker. But he has a reputation for wisdom and for a respectable parsimony in the village, and his knowledge of the roads of the South of England would beat Cobbett.

parsimony: Thriftiness.

And on Sunday mornings, every Sunday morning, all the year round, while he is closed to the outer world, and every night after ten, he goes into his bar parlour, bearing a glass of gin faintly tinged with water, and having placed this down, he locks the door and examines the blinds, and even looks under the table. And then, being satisfied of his solitude, he unlocks the cupboard and a box in the cupboard and a drawer in that box, and produces three volumes bound in brown leather, and places them solemnly in the middle of the table. The covers are weather-worn and tinged with an algal green—for once they sojourned in a ditch and some of the pages have been washed blank by dirty water. The landlord sits down in an armchair, fills a long clay pipe slowly—gloating over the books the while. Then he pulls one towards him and opens it, and begins to study it—turning over the leaves backwards and forwards.

sojourned: Stayed; remained for a time.

His brows are knit and his lips move painfully. "Hex, little two up in the air, cross and a fiddle-de-dee. Lord! what a one he was for intellect!"

Presently he relaxes and leans back, and blinks through his smoke across the room at things invisible to other eyes. "Full of secrets," he says. "Wonderful secrets!

"Once I get the haul of them— *Lord!*

"I wouldn't do what *he* did; I'd just—well!" He pulls at his pipe.

So he lapses into a dream, the undying wonderful dream of his life. And though Kemp has fished unceasingly, and Adye has questioned closely, no human being save the landlord knows those books are there, with the subtle secret of invisibility and a dozen other strange secrets written therein. And none other will know of them until he dies.

fished: Here, hinted; tried to trick or draw out information.

Backword

H. G. WELLS
ADVENTURER INTO THE FUTURE

The High Street in the English town, Bromley, Kent, was as shabby a street as one could find anywhere. In one of the dingy, badly built houses bordering High Street, Herbert George Wells was born in 1866.

His father, Joseph Wells, had been a gardener on a country estate called Up Park. His passion in life was the game of cricket, somewhat resembling American baseball, which he had played professionally for two seasons. His mother, Sarah, had been a housemaid at Up Park where she and Joseph had met. Soon after they were married, a cousin of Joseph offered to sell them, on very easy terms, a little china and crockery shop in Bromley.

Wishing to rise from the domestic servant class, Joseph arranged to buy the shop, called "Atlas House" because of a figure of Atlas in the shop window. Neither Joseph nor Sarah had sufficient business sense to realize that the obliging cousin wanted to sell the shop because it was losing money. Neither had they the ability to improve trade in the shop. Joseph had put all the money he had into the shop and also pledged the small inheritance he expected. He and his wife were caught in a miserable trap of hard work and failure. They

stayed twenty-four years in the shop where their children, "Frankie," "Freddie," and "Bertie" were brought up.

Bertie's first memories were of the dingy shop, the "parlor"—elegant name for a threadbare room furnished with battered odds and ends—and the small back yard, half brick-paved and half bare earth.

The Wonderful World of Books

Bertie learned the alphabet from his mother, and then, holding fast to Freddie's hand, he went to what was called a "dame" school. In one room of a private house, the small school was taught by an elderly woman who actually knew little more than her pupils. When Bertie began to read, a new world opened to him through the town library. He learned, as book-loving children always do, to travel over strange continents and seas and to meet heroes of history along with jungle beasts and naked savages. He had no story books of his own, but he never needed them for he could make up his own stories.

His first real school was Mr. Thomas Morley's Academy in Bromley. It was an old-fashioned school. The curriculum was laid out in Mr. Morley's first prospectus in 1849: "Writing in both plain and ornamental style, Arithmetic logically, and History with special reference to Ancient Egypt." By the 1870's, when Bertie was one of his pupils, there had been no great advance in the curriculum. Most of the boys expected to grow up to be clerks and the bookkeeping they learned fulfilled their educational needs. Bertie left the school when he was fourteen, the usual age for the poor in England of that day. He had indeed learned all that Mr. Morley had to teach. Most of his real education had been through the books he had read.

A Start in Life

Thinking that his school days were over, Bert's mother arranged for him to be apprenticed to a draper's establishment, the English equivalent of an American dry goods store. His duties, aside from sweeping and dusting, were to handle the cash and make an accounting of it at the end of each day. He was an incredibly poor bookkeeper. Never once, he said later, did the money and the accounts balance. It was not surprising, therefore, that he remained with the firm of drapers for only a few months.

His next venture in life was with a relative, called by the courtesy title, Uncle Williams. He had started a little school in a Somerset town with the improbable name of Wookey. He offered to make Bert an assistant teacher. This seems an unlikely position for a four-teen-year-old boy with a very sketchy education, but Bert accepted with pleasure. The truth soon came out. Uncle Williams had no certification for teaching, and after a few brief months, the school had to be abandoned. The experience had some real value for Bert. He had really tried, however poorly, to do something he wanted to do instead of being an unwilling cog in a business machine.

By this time his parents had given up the struggle at Atlas House. His mother had returned to Up Park, this time as housekeeper. His father, crippled by an accident, lived in a cottage nearby. Bert went to stay with his mother until he could make another start. The owner of Up Park had a good private library, and in the months Bert spent there he eagerly read books he had never before even heard of. He read Tom Paine and Voltaire, and discovered Plato's *Republic*, the picture of an ideal society which was to influence his later philosophy.

Another Start

Somehow, Bert's mother conceived the idea of his becoming a pharmaceutical chemist, the English term for druggist. Bert entered upon his second apprenticeship, but it, too, was very short-lived. However, his employer sent him to the local Midhurst Grammar School to study Latin, which was considered basic to pharmacy. He learned something of Latin, but more of science.

The fees for qualifying as a chemist were more than his mother could afford, and of necessity, he gave up this prospective career. His mother tried once more to make him a draper's assistant. His two brothers were draper's assistants and this perhaps seemed to her an inevitable way of life. Bert hated the idea, but he yielded to her pleas to "be a good boy" and return to a draper's shop. From the beginning he hated the work. He hated it so much that, as he later recorded, he thought he must burn down the shop, drown himself, or break his apprentice's agreement. Fortunately, he chose the latter course.

His old teacher from the Midhurst Grammar School offered him a place as school usher, that is, a teaching assistant. This was his first opportunity for intensive reading and congenial study. He used it to such good purpose that, at eighteen, he won a scholarship to study biology at the Normal School of Science in London.

Here he had the great good fortune to have as an instructor, Thomas Henry Huxley, the great English biologist. Huxley conveyed to him a conviction of the biological theory of the evolution of the human species. Wells never became a scientist, but his education in science formed the basis for his later fantasy stories.

After college, teaching seemed the logical career. His first position was at the Holt Academy in Holt, a small town in Wales. His work there was interrupted by serious illness, which was diagnosed as tuberculosis—"consumption" was the usual name for it then. He stayed with friends while he made a slow recovery from the acute phase of his disease. In this period of enforced inaction, he wrote the original draft of the story that eventually became *The Time Machine*.

When he was well enough to work again, he became assistant House Manager at the Henley House School. It was a small private school for boys and was poorly equipped for teaching Wells' subject, chemistry. He tried to write in his leisure time, but the results were discouraging. His teaching was again interrupted by a bout with illness.

Resolved to leave the schoolroom and to try some other line of work, he turned to journalism. He and a former classmate produced a small handbook for students, *Honours Physiography*. The twenty pounds the publisher paid them (at that time a little less than one hundred dollars), divided equally, was hardly an incentive toward a writing career.

After reading an article·on writing by J. M. Barrie Wells concluded that in writing intellectual articles he had been aiming too high—he would "aim lower—and hit." He began to write essays, sketches, and dialogues in a light, humorous style which were readily accepted by magazines. He had made several false starts in life, but now he had found his direction.

In 1895 he published his first novel, *The Time Machine*, which he had started earlier, but left unfinished. It was immediately successful. With almost breathless speed he produced a succession of scientific romances: *The Wonderful Visit, The Island of Doctor Moreau, The Invisible Man, The War of the Worlds, The First Men in the Moon, The Food of the Gods*, and *In the Days of the Comet*. All of these books were characterized by fertile imagination coupled with technical skill in handling biological and astronomical fancy.

Wells' deepest interest was in his passionate concern for human beings and for society as a whole. He had seen his parents beaten down by poverty and his two older brothers caught on a dull treadmill—of the family, only he had escaped. This concern led him to abandon fantasy for depicting the realism of lower middle-class life. In his novels, *Love and Mr. Lewisham, Kipps, Tono Bungay*, and *The History of Mr. Polly*, he held up a gently humorous mirror to the toils, frustrations, muddled hopes, and rare gleams of beauty in the common people among whom he had lived. This was his period of greatest achievement as a novelist.

This same concern led him to become an active socialist and to join the Fabian Society.

The Fabians believed that socialism would be reached by gradual steps rather than by cataclysmic social change. Wells' vision of a utopian society led him to write such books as *Mankind in the Making, New Worlds for Old, A Modern Utopia, First and Last Things*. Later he found much to criticize in the methods of the Fabian Society, and eventually he resigned from it. In this period of his life, he and Amy Catherine Wells, also a writer, were married.

The first World War shook Wells' faith in some of his utopian theories of the progress of man. Considering now that human society could progress only if man could adapt himself to his changing environment, Wells began his great work of social education, *The Outline of History*, published in 1920 and revised in 1931. *The Science of Life*, written with his oldest son, G. P. Wells and Julian Huxley, and a later book, *The Work, Health and Happiness of Mankind*, contained some of the same ideas.

He continued to write fiction, but he had almost lost his magic touch. Only in his reminiscences, *Experiment in Autobiography*, did he regain his old sprightliness. He was ill and growing old. The outbreak of the Second World War destroyed his last belief in the ability of man to save himself from holocaust. His final books, *The Outlook for Homo Sapiens* and *Mind at the End of its Tether*, reflect his bitter disillusionment. He died in 1946.

In spite of the pessimism to which age and world circumstance brought him, the tone of the great body of Wells' writing is of genial optimism and eager adventurousness. The humorous novels of his middle period are among the finest contributions to the realistic novel. His scientific romances have a poetic quality which lifts them into high fantasy.

Wells has been called the father of modern science fiction, yet he was more concerned with humanity than with revolutionary inventions—more concerned with what a new idea would do to people and the way they lived, than with the idea itself.

At some time, probably all of us have had the desire to see and not be seen or to move about where other people are while they remain quite unaware of our presence. In a crude way, this is sometimes almost accomplished. Hunters and soldiers dress in clothes with a camouflage pattern that matches their surroundings so well that they are very difficult to see. At night or in a fog a device called a "snooperscope" can be used to see by invisible rays of heat called "infra-red rays." In the gaming casinos of Nevada, mirror-like "one-way glass" is used in the ceilings so that security guards, invisible to the visitors, may keep a sharp watch for pickpockets, cheaters or anything else that might interfere with the players.

Everyday Invisibility

Many things in our world are invisible and very commonplace. We can feel, but cannot see the air around us. A polished block or sheet of glass submerged in water may be almost invisible even though it is as real and solid as our own body. The waves radiating

Only a very small part of the radiant energy around us can be seen by our eyes. Perhaps the real miracle is that things are visible at all!

The Atom's Structure

All matter is made up of very small particles called atoms. It is generally believed that atoms consist of a fairly heavy nucleus with various numbers of very small and very light electrical charges orbiting in space around the nucleus. A nucleus resembles an extremely small sun with even smaller planets rotating in rings around it in the black, empty void we call "space." Some scientists believe the "electrons" surrounding the nucleus are shells of energy vibrating in a fairly constant location in relation to the nucleus, but all agree that the atom is mostly just empty space.

The Length of Light Waves

With so much empty space, it would seem that all light would go merrily through everything just like the waves from a radio station. One of the currently popular theories about light is that it is made up of very short waves or pulses moving through space much like waves moving across a pond when a pebble is tossed into it. The wave lengths (the distance

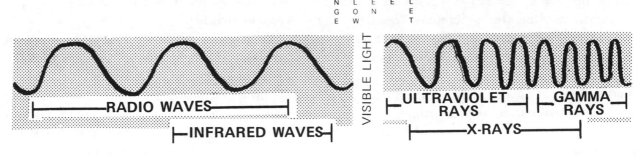

THE ELECTROMAGNETIC SPECTRUM

RED ORANGE YELLOW GREEN BLUE VIOLET

VISIBLE LIGHT

RADIO WAVES

INFRARED WAVES

ULTRAVIOLET RAYS

GAMMA RAYS

X-RAYS

from a radio transmitter are invisible and travel easily through our bodies. "Infra-red" heat rays, mentioned above, are invisible, as are the ultra-violet rays that cause sunburn and X-rays and cosmic rays which penetrate many things. We feel the effect of gravity holding us against the earth; yet it is invisible.

between pulses) of visible light are very, very short—almost as small as the atoms. Visible light waves are from 700 nanometers long for the deepest red color to the shorter 400 nanometer waves for the lightest violet. A nanometer is one billionth of a meter long. A meter is 39.37 inches long.

The Wide "Invisible" Spectrum

The "visible spectrum" is actually only a very narrow band of the waves of radiant energy surrounding us. It contains the colors we see in a rainbow. Other waves vary in length from several miles, for very low frequency radio waves, through waves of about the length of three inches used for radar. The "infra-red" heat rays are just below the red end of the visible colors. Much shorter in length than the violet end of the color spectrum are the ultra-violet rays, X-rays, and the shortest we have been able to detect, the cosmic rays from outer space which penetrate even the thickest lead and also go deeply into the earth.

Most substances do not pass the pulses of visible light through them. They absorb most of them and reflect only a few colors back in the general direction they came from. A simple way to understand what may happen when one of these tiny waves or pulses of light energy strikes an atom would be to imagine a small boy pushing a swing or hitting a big rubber ball. The swing moves away and then back, and if the boy does not move out of the way, it will push him. If a number of swings are lined up so one will hit the next when it swings, the push will be transmitted down the line to the last swing. So the pulses of light make the atoms vibrate or "oscillate" to a higher energy state and then back to their normal energy state, first receiving a pulse of light and then sending one back out. If the material is a clear, transparent crystal or liquid, all colors are moved from the outer layer of atoms on through the other layers of atoms until it is radiated from the far side almost identical to the wave or pulse that struck it on the first side. Some materials do not re-radiate the light in the same wave length as the one that hit it, instead they "fluoresce" in a different color. The invisible ultra-violet rays inside a fluorescent lamp are converted to visible white light in that way by the chemical coating on the inside of the tube. Most black substances convert the visible colors into infra-red (heat rays).

Red paint absorbs most of the wave lengths of visible light except the red ones, which it reflects. The same applies to yellow and blue paint. If we mix red and yellow paint, we will get orange because the red does not, as a rule, absorb all of the yellow rays, and the yellow does not quite absorb all of the red rays. If you look at a rainbow, you will see that the red and yellow colors are fairly close together. However, if we mix blue with the red and yellow, we get gray or black because the red paint will absorb *all* of the blue rays, and the blue will absorb all of the red as well as the yellow rays that the red did not absorb. Black is not really a color, but the lack of color. White is a mixture of all of the visible wave lengths (colors) of light.

If we could change the atoms of a material so they did not reflect any of the visible rays of light and, at the same time, the atoms would send all of the colors unchanged through to the opposite side, then that material would be invisible to our eyes! Or, if we were to enclose an object or person in a shell that could convert visible light waves into radio waves as they passed through the shell and convert the radio waves back to light waves on the other side of the shell, the shell and its contents would be perfectly transparent and invisible.

Perhaps we are lucky that none of us are invisible. The light shining through the back of an invisible person's head and into the back of his eyes might give him a real "bright outlook," but he probably could not see anything else unless he used wave lengths of light outside the visible spectrum for seeing.

However, we cannot say that a "Cloak of Invisibility" is impossible. Many of the things in old science fiction stories that seemed strange and impossible then are just common everyday things today. Things like space travel, radar, computers, television and even sub-miniature radio transmitters inside olives!

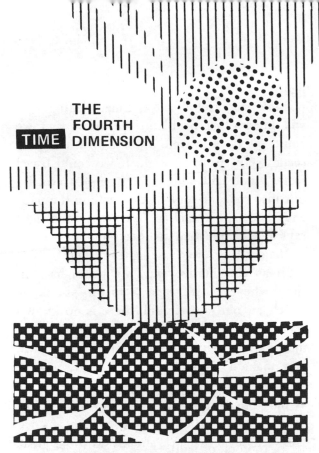

THE FOURTH TIME DIMENSION

We all think we know what it is, but can any of us really describe it? Does it go forever onward like the steady tick of a clock? Or does it move in a curve? Can it be turned back? Will it ever be possible to travel into the future or look back into the past? We may have some of the answers sooner than we think. Many of the things that were "impossible" imaginings of science fiction writers a few years ago are just ordinary things today, and our exotic, space-age technology turns more and more of the "impossible" into reality almost every day.

Some mathematicians believe that to properly describe any object, you must state its length, width, height . . . and the time when it exists: the *Fourth* Dimension.

Measuring Time

Primitive men were probably only aware of time as night and day, the full moon and the new moon, and the seasons. Then, as their intelligence and civilization became more advanced, the calendar was invented. Of the various ways which followed to tell the time of day, the sundial was one of the earliest and most common. A sundial uses the moving shadow cast by the sun to tell the time of

day. This is not a very accurate method, however; because the sun's arc in the sky gradually shifts as the seasons change.

For use indoors, a "water clock" was invented. A steady stream of water runs through a small hole into a container. Numbers on the side of the container mark the time it takes for the water to fill the container. Numbers or notches on the side of candles were also used, to mark the time as well as the still-popular "hourglass" with sand falling through a small tube between two containers. Today, the hourglass is generally used only as a decoration or to time soft-cooked eggs or telephone calls. Then came the pendulum clock, powered by weights on the end of a chain, that is

wound on a drum geared to the "escapement" works that swing the pendulum. Now, we have our watches and clocks with precision balance wheels that keep fairly accurate time for months on end, electric clocks kept in accurate synchronism by the power company's generators, and even electric wristwatches with tiny tuning forks vibrating at one steady tone to keep accurate time. The most accurate clocks of all are the "atomic clocks" of the National Bureau of Standards that will run several million years before registering an error of even one second!

We have reached an era when we can keep very good track of time, but we cannot change its pace one tiny bit. There is an abundance of precise mathematical equations, formulae and theories in our reference books, on the blackboards of research laboratories and on television shows; yet Physics, Chemistry, and Astronomy, all involved with time in one way or another, are only partly understood by our best scientists. Much turbulent and sometimes angry discussion takes place when students and experts of various and often conflicting theories get together. Some believe that space is "curved" in such a way that if you were to look out into the night sky with a telescope, provided you could see far enough, you would be looking at the back of your own head—or, rather, where that place was several billion years ago.

We do look back in time when we look at the moon, sun, or any other remote object. We do not see the moon where it is now or as it is now, but where it was a bit over one second ago. It takes light almost one second, traveling at 186,000 miles per second, to travel the 200,000 miles from the moon to the earth. We see the sun as it was about nine minutes ago and the nearest star, Alpha Centauri, as it was about four and a half years ago. The light from some of the very remote stars and galaxies travels millions of years before it reaches our telescopes. Therefore, we are really looking millions of years into the past when we observe them.

Some scientists believe that time slows down as we go faster and that it stops at the speed of light. An astronaut traveling at the speed of light to a star a million light-years away (a "light-year" is the distance that light travels in one year) and then returning to earth, would find our planet two million years older than when he left, but he would have aged only the time he was moving slower than light. If that is true, some day it may be possible to travel ahead in time. Getting back will be another problem! We know that we could *see* back in time if the light leaving the scene were strong enough. If we could travel faster than light, an observer could travel far out into space to look at the earth in the past, and then, still traveling faster than the light rays at which he had just been looking, return to the earth before those light rays left!

In an imaginative way, we travel back in time whenever we read a history book or watch an old movie. Still, there is no known way really to "be" there . . . except in our imagination. What about the future? Will we ever make a "crystal ball" that really works? Or find some way to actually observe events as they might take place at some time yet to come? Perhaps—but not by any means we know about now. We already know a great deal about some of the things that will take place in the future: the position of the sun, the phases of the moon, the times of high and low tides, the weather, and many other things that occur in regular cycles.

On the entrance to the National Archives in Washington, D.C. are the words, "THE PAST IS PROLOGUE, STUDY THE PAST." It means that the past is a good indication of the future. Even the rise and fall of great nations seems to happen in some kind of cycle. Over a century ago, Lord Macaulay predicted that the United States would become the most powerful nation on earth and then, like the Roman Empire centuries earlier, fall to barbarians. The United States, however, is supposed to breed its *own* "barbarians" within its *own* boundaries! Lord Macaulay may have been doing some imaginary time traveling. Someday—and that day may not be very far in the future—a very complex computer, programmed to deal accurately with all of the various things in the past that affect the future, may create a three-dimensional motion picture of our coming steps across the sands of time.